"Will y...

"What will I see if I do?"

Vulnerability and hope shone in her eyes, and he lifted a hand to her hair, brushing a curl off her cheek before he answered. "We'll descend through time, through the history of this continent. We'll touch an earth no man ever walked upon."

She couldn't pull her eyes from his. "And find opals fit for the queen?"

His fingers lingered on her cheek. "Fire and all the colors of the spectrum, eternally doomed to darkness if we don't bring them to the light. Will you trust me enough to go down with me?"

She nodded.

His hand dropped to his side, but his smile continued to warm her. "Then I'll show you a world you haven't seen before."

Just before caution intruded once more, Kelsey let herself wonder if the world Dillon was going to show her extended beyond the perimeters of the Rainbow Fire mine.

Dear Reader,

When two people fall in love, the world is suddenly new and exciting, and it's that same excitement we bring to you in Silhouette Intimate Moments. These are stories with scope and grandeur. The characters lead lives we all dream of, and everything they do reflects the wonder of being in love.

Longer and more sensuous than most romances, Silhouette Intimate Moments novels take you away from everyday life and let you share the magic of love. Adventure, glamour, drama, even suspense— these are the passwords that let you into a world where love has a power beyond the ordinary, where the best authors in the field today create stories of love and commitment that will stay with you always.

In coming months look for novels by your favorite authors: Kathleen Eagle, Heather Graham Pozzessere, Nora Roberts and Marilyn Pappano, to name just a few. And whenever you buy books, look for all the Silhouette Intimate Moments, love stories *for* today's woman *by* today's woman.

Leslie J. Wainger
Senior Editor
Silhouette Books

Emilie Richards
Rainbow Fire

Silhouette Intimate Moments

Published by Silhouette Books New York

America's Publisher of Contemporary Romance

SILHOUETTE BOOKS
300 East 42nd St., New York, N.Y. 10017

ISBN: 0-373-07273-2

First Silhouette Books printing February 1989

Printed in the U.S.A.

Books by Emilie Richards

Silhouette Romance

Brendan's Song #372
Sweet Georgia Gal #393
Gilding the Lily #401
Sweet Sea Spirit #413
Angel and the Saint #429
Sweet Mockingbird's Call #441
Good Time Man #453
Sweet Mountain Magic #466
Sweet Homecoming #489
Aloha Always #520
Outback Nights #536

Silhouette Intimate Moments

Lady of the Night #152
Bayou Midnight #188
*From Glowing Embers #249
*Smoke Screen #261
*Rainbow Fire #273

Silhouette Special Edition

All the Right Reasons #433
A Classic Encounter #456

* Tales of the Pacific series

EMILIE RICHARDS

believes that opposites attract, and her marriage is vivid proof. "When we met," the author says, "the *only* thing my husband and I could agree on was that we were very much in love. Fortunately, we haven't changed our minds about that in all the years we've been together."

The couple lives in Ohio with their four children, who span from toddler to teenager. Emilie has put her master's degree in family development to good use—raising her own brood, working for Head Start, counseling in a mental health clinic and serving in VISTA.

Though her first book was written in snatches with an infant on her lap, Emilie now writes five hours a day and "rejoices in the opportunity to create, to grow and to have such a good time."

This country has an opal heart
A heart of heat and thirst and drought
A heart that beats with rainbow dreams
That keep the unbeliever out.

And if I take my own heart there
To mine the dream that never dies
What dreams will I have left behind?
What promises exchanged for lies?

Yet still my brothers, sisters, come
The starry-eyed, the fool, the liar
To mine a dream, to touch the past
To search the earth for rainbow fire.

Chapter 1

She had landed on the moon. Without benefit of rocket, space suit or NASA's famed countdown, she had landed on the moon, and the trip had only taken three hours, ninety-one dollars and the wind-tossed flight of a Cessna 421.

Kelsey Donovan squinted at the dusty landscape that spread in front of her like a Jules Verne fantasy. She half expected to see astronaut litter: abandoned space buggies, useless rocket modules, or, at the very least, competitively waving flags proclaiming a race for control of the heavens.

Instead the sun beat down on her bare head, reminding her that this was Coober Pedy, South Australia. If she didn't find shade quickly, her legs were going to crumple, and she was going to litter this remote corner of Planet Earth with her slender body and small, battered suitcase.

Kelsey picked up the suitcase once more and began to trudge down the track that had been pointed out to her by the airport taxi driver who had grudgingly dropped her off half a mile back. Half a mile was nothing. In her quest for mastery of her body and emotions, she had once run miles every day as a prelude to more difficult training. Her small-boned frame and delicate milkmaid skin said nothing about the strength of the woman underneath.

But even a strong woman could be defeated by a blazing midafternoon sun that reflected off coarse red earth like a raging bonfire.

She wouldn't think about it. She would put one foot in front of the other and keep walking. She would not curse herself for turning down liquids on the flight from Adelaide; she would not curse herself for wearing her best forest green dress and matching heels. She would not curse the faith that had brought her to this strange place.

This place. This strange, sterile, desolate place. Why would a man like Jake Donovan choose to live among barren red hills in a country that wasn't his own? He would be sixty now, a time when even rugged men begin to think about reaping the rewards of years of hard work. Kelsey had been told often enough that Jake was a dreamer, a man with no common sense and no sense of responsibility. She had been told that he chased the pot of gold at the end of the rainbow and found his pleasure in the chase. But there was no rainbow here, and no pleasure that she could see. Just an endless vista of dust and earth and shimmering heat.

And one slowly melting woman with a dream she had nurtured since she was three years old.

She stopped again, pulling a tissue from her pocket to wipe her forehead. Surely she should have reached the house by now. But there wasn't a house in sight; in fact, she had seen nothing resembling one since she had left the airfield. Perhaps if she had gone into town, as the taxi driver had insisted, she wouldn't be so disoriented now. Certainly there had been houses in town. She could have checked into the motel, along with the other three passengers and the rest of her luggage, then found a ride to Jake's front doorstep. But she had been stubborn—a trait that some people claimed was synonymous with the Donovan name. She had waited twenty-one years for this moment, and she hadn't wanted to wait even one more hour.

So the disgruntled driver had dropped her at a fork in the road and pointed, muttering something with a heavy accent that she hadn't taken the time to decipher. Half a mile later, she wished she had made more of an effort.

Kelsey trudged along the dusty track again, lifting one foot, then the other. The track curved, skirting a clump of naked hills to her right, but she had almost passed the first before she noticed a door in its side.

A door in a hill.

"Curious and curiouser," she mumbled with a tongue that felt swollen and heavy. She wondered if the door led to a mine. This was opal mining country. If she opened the door, would it lead to riches beyond imagining? Or would there be nothing except darkness and mildew and disappointment?

She wished she could find out. Instead she hiked on to the next hill, past another door, and then to the next.

There was a door in this hill, too, but unlike the others, it wasn't constructed of ill-fitted planks leaning haphazardly against a narrow hole. The door was sturdy and green, a door meant for a brick ranch house in some suburban subdivision. And in front of the door was a flat stone porch crowded with plants and shaded by a grass roof like a South Sea island hut.

On the porch, in a straight back chair, was a man. Kelsey felt a voluminous surge of relief. Only then did she allow herself to recognize the fear that she had struggled so hard to suppress. She had learned something about the Australian outback today. She would never underestimate it again.

"Excuse me." She cleared her throat, then tried again, moving off the track toward the man. "Excuse me," she said a little louder.

The man had one hand buried deep in the fur of a dust-drenched cat at his feet. At her words, he lifted his head and stared at her as if she were a mirage.

Kelsey noted brown hair not yet touched by gray and the bronzed skin of a man in his early thirties. This man was certainly not her father, but maybe he could lead her to him. "I'm looking for Jake Donovan's house." She swallowed painfully. "Would you mind pointing me in the right direction?" She watched surprise spread across his features as she swayed in the blazing sunlight. His face blurred as sweat dripped into her eyes, and she blinked twice. "Please?" she added when he didn't say anything.

"Jake Donovan?" he asked finally, his voice resonant with the music of Australia. He stood, stretching to a height that towered over her five foot four. "Who's looking for him?"

She shut her eyes and swayed again, half expecting to feel the earth rise to meet her. "Kelsey Donovan," she said through thirst-parched lips. "His daughter."

* * *

The apparition was real. The wraithlike female was flesh and bones and pale red-gold hair, a curling mane of it that reached past her shoulder blades in a fiercely glorious profusion. Her skin was cream, scorching to an unhealthy rose as Dillon watched. And if his first impression had been correct, her eyes, now squeezed tightly shut, were the pale brown of outback desert before the spring rains.

Dillon took two huge strides to the collapsing woman and circled her with arms that were turning black and blue from the battering of another rescue mission that day. "Here, let's get you into the shade."

Kelsey let him take her weight for a moment. Gratefully she leaned against his chest, barely aware of anything except strong arms and the rasp of a cotton shirt against her face. "I'm sorry," she murmured. "I guess I'm just not used to the sun. I feel like a fool."

Dillon realized he was just about to stroke her hair. His right hand hovered over the gold-red mass like a falcon with no place to roost. "Let's get you into the shade," he repeated awkwardly. He was suddenly very much aware that he was holding a beautiful stranger in his arms and that the smell of his own filthy clothing had been replaced by the fragrance of lavender.

Half-assisting, half-dragging, he helped her to the porch and seated her in the chair he had just vacated. He gave the cat a helpful nudge with the toe of his boot and watched him slink a yard or two to rest between potted plants. "Are you going to pass out?" he asked, turning his attention back to the young woman.

Kelsey shook her head, and Dillon nodded in satisfaction. "I'll get you a drink." Without waiting for her answer, he disappeared inside, coming back out a moment later with a glass of water. "Take it slow, a sip at a time."

Kelsey gripped the glass with trembling hands. Every bit of coordination she still possessed went into guiding it to her mouth. The first sip tasted like salvation. Three sips later she cleared her throat. "Thanks."

Dillon went back inside and returned with a wet washcloth. Kelsey flashed him a wan, grateful smile and bathed her face and hands, appreciating the moist coolness against her heated skin. "I don't even know your name."

"My name's Dillon. Dillon Ward." Dillon satisfied himself that she was recovering before he took the chair next to her. He watched her smooth the cloth over her cheeks until the worst of the flush disappeared. Only then did he let himself think about her announcement. "So you're looking for Jake."

"Am I looking in the right part of the universe?"

Dillon didn't know how to answer. He made a steeple of his hands, resting his unshaven chin on his fingertips. "You say you're his daughter."

Kelsey drained the glass and wished for another. She turned to examine the man she had only viewed through sweat-tainted eyes. He wasn't just tall, he was broad, although she would stake her life on the fact that there wasn't an ounce of fat on him anywhere. His shoulders were wide enough to create problems in doorways, and his chest strained against the buttons of a remarkably grimy shirt. His curly hair was shaggy and rumpled, and what might otherwise be an intriguing face was dirt-streaked and unshaven. He was an unlikely savior, but her savior nonetheless. "I *am* his daughter." She set the glass beside the washcloth on a wooden table. "Can you tell me where to find him, or shall I push on?"

"You won't find him if you push on," Dillon said grimly.

"I was told his house was nearby."

"This is his dugout." Dillon gestured behind him. "Rather, it's my dugout. He's been living with me recently. Jake and I are partners."

"Partners?" She savored the sweet thrill of being so close to the end of a search that had begun a lifetime ago. In strange ways she had been searching for Jake Donovan since he had walked out of her life with nothing more than a kiss on her chubby, baby cheek.

"Mining partners."

Kelsey wet her lips and tried to figure out how anyone could live inside a hill. "Is he inside?"

"He's not."

She ignored her frustration. "Then where is he?"

Dillon wondered how he had worked beside Jake for years and never once heard him mention a daughter. He wanted to dispute her claim, at the least tell her she was mistaken, that this was not the Jake Donovan she was looking for. But there was something about the anticipation in her brown eyes that forced him to be silent about his qualms. And if she were indeed Jake's daughter, he sensed how devastating it would be if he told Kelsey Donovan that in all the years Dillon had known him Jake had never mentioned a daughter, never mentioned a marriage, never mentioned anyone name Kelsey. The news would be almost as devastating as what he had to tell her instead.

"Where is he?" she repeated.

"Jake's been hurt," he said, watching to see if he was going to have to pick her up off the ground after all. "There was an accident at the mine. Jake's in the hospital."

Kelsey heard the words, but she couldn't absorb them. They skittered somewhere in the sunshine, just out of reach. "Hurt?"

He passed a hand over his hair, belatedly giving a thought to his appearance. If he and Kelsey had met on a dark city street, he would probably have struck terror in her heart. But then, no one looked like a prince after crawling through mine drives dragging rescue equipment and lights and....

"There's no pretty way to tell you," Dillon said. He stared at the horizon, wishing for the first time that there was a tree to focus on. But there was nothing, just red-brown dirt and conical hills, a numbing sameness that was broken only by patches of scruffy saltbush. There might still be the occasional wildflower—pink hops and even Sturts desert pea—hiding in the shade. But from his porch he couldn't see them.

Kelsey felt herself deflate, like a balloon slowly losing helium. She had come so far. So far. "What happened?"

"He fell down a fifty-foot shaft."

She nodded blankly, as if she understood. "He's been hurt."

Dillon was exhausted. He hadn't slept for sixty hours; he hadn't eaten for twelve, and then he had only wolfed down someone's idea of a sandwich so he could keep searching for the man who now lay unconscious in a hospital bed. Dillon was a man of both warmth and wit—or so he had been told by the occasional women in his life. Now his insides were frozen, and each word he spoke was a death knell.

"I'll take you to him," he said wearily.

Jake was hurt, maybe dying. Kelsey mentally repeated the words, trying them out like a half-memorized poem. Jake was hurt. Her *father* was hurt. She felt nothing except the first sting of sunburn on her cheeks. Giving up, she looked down at her sweat-stained, dust-covered dress. "I should change."

Dillon wondered if Kelsey even knew what she had said. She was in shock; the response had been rote. Someone, somewhere, had taught her that a clean dress could solve any of life's problems. "Have you got something else?"

Kelsey gestured to the small suitcase she had brought with her. "Only photographs," she said softly. "Photographs of me with my father. And my birth certificate. I didn't want to leave them in the taxi." She sighed. When she looked up, Dillon saw that her eyes were still dry. "I've come too far to be stopped by a dirty dress." She stood and inclined her head toward him, jutting her strong, pointed chin in a movement that made his heart drop to his stomach. "Will you please take me to see him now?"

And because Dillon had seen Jake's own pointed chin assume the same angle more times than he could begin to count, he rose to his feet. There was nothing else about Kelsey Donovan that was like Jake, but at that moment there was no one in the world who could have persuaded him that she wasn't Jake's child. And Jake was Dillon's partner, his mate.

He grasped her elbow, although for whose support he wasn't sure. "We'll be there in ten minutes."

If the Coober Pedy landscape resembled the moon's surface the Coober Pedy hospital resembled Star Trek's *Enterprise*. Contemporary and low-lying, with a corrugated roof that overlapped and intermittently swept to the ground in bold architectural statements, the building had been perfectly designed for its outback environment. With her sense of reality suspended, Kelsey followed Dillon through its corridors. She knew she had suffered too much sun, too much disappointment. But the sense of being trapped in a bubble wasn't vanishing quickly enough.

Her father had been hurt. The man she hadn't seen in more than two decades had fallen fifty feet down a mine shaft. Yet she could feel nothing.

The waiting area was sparkling clean and freshly painted, with nothing except a tiny, brightly trimmed Christmas tree to mar its antiseptic perfection. Kelsey watched as Dillon murmured something to a young woman behind a counter marked "Enquiries." The woman didn't seem surprised to see a man as disheveled as Dillon in the immaculate hallway. She only nod-

ded and pointed to two chairs. Dillon came back to Kelsey and
led her to them.

He waited until she was seated. "The doctor is still with Jake.
The nursing sister says she'll tell him you're here."

Kelsey closed her eyes. "I'm surprised there are a doctor and
a hospital in this town."

"I'll bet you're surprised there's anything here."

"Or anyone."

"There's opal here."

Kelsey heard the unspoken coda. "And that's enough of a
reason to live in the middle of nowhere?"

Dillon tipped up the wide brim of the rust-colored felt hat he
had jammed on his head before guiding Kelsey into the truck
he called a "ute." "We call it the never-never when we're not
calling it home."

"Does my father call it home?" She heard her own longing
and knew the protective bubble had burst.

Dillon heard the longing, too, and he didn't know what to do
about it. Jake's daughter was as much of a mystery as Jake's
accident. "Jake's not much of a talker," he said, closing his
eyes. "He doesn't call it anything."

"I've heard he *was* quite a talker." She couldn't remember,
herself. Sometimes she thought she could glimpse the past. She
could almost hear a man's laughter or a rough, gravelly voice,
almost feel strong arms lifting her into the air, tossing her high
and catching her as she squealed in delight. Strong arms catching her.

Always catching her.

Dillon didn't ask Kelsey what she had meant. He had spent
years in the States, but he had never gotten used to the ease with
which people there delved into each other's souls. For all their
hearty, matey-good-cheer, Australians were more reticent when
it came to talking about their pasts. It wasn't a difficult attitude to understand in a nation that had once been a convict
colony.

He wasn't sure which was better or worse; he was only sure
that though he was curious, asking Kelsey Donovan to tell him
about her relationship with her father would be as foreign as
lying on a bed of nails.

Kelsey saved him the trouble. Now that reality was beginning to intrude again, she felt the first tingling of fear. She

rarely chattered, but now she couldn't avoid it. She had to talk or explode. "I haven't seen my father for twenty-one years."

His answer was safely innocuous. "A long time."

"What's he like?"

What was Jake Donovan like? Or rather, what could Dillon tell the brown-eyed, butterscotch-blond beauty sitting beside him? Jake was a dinkum partner and mate, a man who would stand up for you in a pub brawl and suffer the consequences. But he was also a boozer, a storyteller who often didn't know the truth from a lie, and a hopelessly restless dreamer. He would be the worst kind of father. Dillon had to shove down the desire to tell Kelsey to run for her life. There was nothing waiting for her down the hall except sorrow and disappointment. "I don't know how to answer that," he said at last. "Exactly what did you want to know?"

Everything. She wanted to know everything. How Jake looked, how he dressed. What he ate for breakfast and drank with his dinner. Did he have a new wife? Were there other children bearing the Donovan name, sisters and brothers with Australian accents?

Kelsey stifled the barrage of questions, recognizing a thread of hysteria among them. This was no time to be crushed by emotions she had carefully suppressed most of her life. She forced herself to go slowly. "Tell me how long you've known my father."

"Four years."

She nodded as if the answer were a pearl of great price. "And have you been partners that long?"

"I'd say we have."

"Here?"

"On and off."

Kelsey controlled her frustration. "What does that mean?"

"Mining opals takes money. If you're not on opal, you've got to make money somewhere else. At one time or another Jake or I have had to go off and make enough to continue here."

"What does . . . Jake—" she momentarily pondered how strange the name sounded sliding off her tongue "—do when he goes off?"

"Anything he can. He's tried his hand at shearing sheep on some properties east of here, fishing up near Darwin."

She nodded, her brow wrinkling as she began to slowly picture the Jake Donovan in her photographs doing those things. "And then he comes back here?"

"When he has the cash."

Kelsey turned to get a better look at Dillon. Under a deep, dirt-streaked tan, he was pale with exhaustion—if such a thing were possible. "None of that matters, though, does it? He's lying in there hurt, maybe dying."

"It won't help Jake any for you to be thinking like that," he warned her.

"Tell me what happened."

Dillon had been waiting for this question, but he still wasn't prepared to answer it. How could he explain what he didn't understand? "Jake's as sure-footed as a goat. I've seen him walk a rail fence when he was a stubbie away from being embalmed. Then two nights ago he fell down a fifty-foot mine shaft that he'd dug himself."

"Were you with him?"

"Not blooming likely. He was supposed to be with me. We were going to drive up to Mintabie in my ute to see an old mate of his. When Jake didn't show, I went looking for him. Found him this morning."

Kelsey felt her head spin. Her father had lain helpless and alone for more than a day in the bottom of an opal mine. "Why did it take so long?"

Dillon had asked himself the same question repeatedly since he had come across Jake's chilled body wedged in the dead-end mine drive. "Because we looked in the wrong places," he said, tipping his hat back, then thinking better of it. He grabbed it by the brim and slammed it to the floor. "We looked in the wrong places like a mob of bloody drongos!"

"Nobody thought to look in the mine?" Kelsey's head no longer spun. It buzzed with the beginnings of anger. "He's a miner. Wouldn't that make sense?"

Dillon heard steel replacing the soft music of her voice. He admired the sound at the same time that he felt a jolt of irritation at the words. "Make sense? What sense was there for Jake to be at the mine, down a shaft and wedged in a drive we abandoned six months ago?"

"How do you know he fell?"

"From his injuries. It looks like he fell, then started to crawl in a daze. Maybe he thought he could get out."

"Why shouldn't he have been at the mine?"

"We'd knocked off work an hour before. I took him into town in my ute. He was going to nip in for something to eat and then meet me at the Opal Showcase to have some stones looked at. Nothing more than potch with a little color, but Jake was hopeful they'd bring a few dollars. He was running low."

She ignored the unfamiliar terms. "And when he didn't show?"

He heard the steel harden into a razor-edged weapon. "I didn't think much about it. I waited at the pub to give him a ride to Mintabie, another town up the road. Going there was his idea, so I knew he'd come. But he didn't."

"And that's when you started to look for him."

"That's right. Only we wasted time looking everywhere we shouldn't have. We even searched the mine at dawn the next morning, but we didn't search the parts that were closed off. There wasn't any reason for Jake to be there."

Kelsey was too upset to probe Dillon's voice for emotion. Other than one display of temper, he sounded like a dead man. And he probably was dead on his feet, if he had been searching for her father since Friday night. "Who's the 'we' you keep referring to? Were the police looking for him, too?"

He exhaled forcefully, blowing a brown curl off his forehead. "This is Coober Pedy, not Sydney. We settle most of our problems ourselves. I found a couple of miners to help me search." He paused, then decided to tell her the truth. "Everyone else thought Jake was sleeping off a bender somewhere. It's happened before."

"But he'd only been missing an hour or two when you began to worry. How could he have drunk enough?"

"It doesn't take Jake that long to tie one on when he's trying hard. Especially on a Friday night."

Kelsey had been prepared to meet a hard-drinking, hard-living man. That description and many less flattering ones had been thrown up to her for twenty-one years. Apparently the assorted relatives who had tried to convince her that her father was worse than no good had been right about his drinking. And apparently he hadn't changed.

But lots of people drank. Lots of working men tied one on after a hard week. She would have been more surprised if Jake had been different.

Carefully she assembled the details of Dillon's story in a brain still numb from near heatstroke and shock. Her father had failed to show up for an appointment. She wondered what most men would have done if they'd been waiting for Jake Donovan to appear and he hadn't. Obviously Dillon and her father had a special relationship. Although he wasn't blowing his own horn, Dillon's explanation made it clear that he had saved her father's life. Through her shock and sadness she felt a surge of warmth for the man beside her.

"It sounds like my father was lucky you cared enough about him to worry." Kelsey hesitantly leaned over and reached out to touch Dillon's arm. His bare flesh was as hard as the gem he mined.

Dillon felt the delicate brush of her fingertips and smelled the enticing scent of lavender. He didn't want to respond to Kelsey Donovan. He was too weary to respond. He responded anyway. "Your father's my mate. He would have done the same for me." He shifted his head so that their eyes were level. "Now we just have to help him pull through his stay in the hospital."

Kelsey noted the deep sea-green of Dillon's eyes. They were absolutely sincere, but there was a spark igniting in them that had nothing to do with sincerity. She lifted her hand, then dropped it back in her lap. Dillon was a stranger, and she was a long way from home.

"Dillon?" A short, round man in a white coat approached. Kelsey noted the universal symbols of silver chart and stethoscope. She stood as Dillon did.

"Is my father going to be all right?" she asked before either man could speak.

Dillon exchanged looks with the physician, who was an old friend. He knew immediately that the news wasn't going to be good. He moved closer to Kelsey, and his arm brushed her side for support. "This is Dr. Munvelt," he said in introduction. "He's been with your father since we brought him in."

"We'll be transferring Jake to the hospital in Adelaide as soon as a plane arrives." Dr. Munvelt looked at his shoe, as if he might catch something from meeting the eyes of a healthy person. "He regained consciousness briefly, but he wasn't alert. We'll know more after tests."

"Is he going to be all right?" Kelsey had to restrain the urge to cradle Dr. Munvelt's chin in the palm of her hand to align his eyes with hers.

"Is he going to live? I think so. Yes, I think so. But he's going to be crook for some time yet. The brain is a funny thing." He continued to examine his shoe. "A funny, funny thing."

She was horrified by all the things he didn't say. She knew Dillon sensed her feelings, because he moved closer. "Will he make a complete recovery?" she asked.

"I'm not certain what you mean, but if you want to know if he'll be able to walk and talk and—"

"Of course that's what I mean."

"I truly don't know. Time will tell."

Dillon felt Kelsey's slight body crumple. His arm moved to her shoulder to steady her. "Miss Donovan is understandably concerned," he told the doctor. "She hasn't seen her father in years, and she's traveled a long way."

"How long?"

For a moment Kelsey wondered if he was asking for a mileage count. Then she realized he wanted to know how long since she had seen Jake. "Twenty-one years." She watched his head snap up. "May I see him now?"

"Did he know you were coming?" the doctor asked.

Kelsey realized she had both men's rapt attention. "No. I haven't heard from him during those years, either." She was surprised that it still hurt to admit her father's abandonment. There had been times as a child when she had written long, tearful letters to her absent father, then written her own replies in the most masculine script she could manage. She had needed to pretend that his reasons for leaving her had been good ones. But those days were long gone. She was an adult now, with an adult's understanding of human frailties. She straightened her shoulders and cast the hurt away.

"You must be very disappointed to find things in such a state," Dr. Munvelt murmured.

"I'll be going to Adelaide with him," Kelsey said, taking charge of the conversation and her feelings again. "I'll stay with him while he recovers. But I'd like to see him now, if you don't mind."

"I'm afraid I do." Dr. Munvelt's eyes were troubled. "How old are you, Miss Donovan?"

She couldn't imagine why it mattered, but she humored him. "Twenty-four."

"Then you haven't seen or heard from Jake since you were a child of three?"

She shook her head, stiffening at the sympathy she saw. "He had his reasons."

"I'm sure you're right. But can you guess the impact seeing you now might have on him?"

"I don't know what you mean. He'll be glad—"

"The brain is a funny thing," he said, repeating his earlier statement. "After a trauma like the one your father has suffered, more trauma, emotional trauma, is frightfully unwise. If your father regains consciousness to be told that the young lady sitting beside the bed is his daughter, a daughter who was a baby the last time he saw her, I don't know what might happen."

She stiffened more, drawing away from Dillon's supportive hand. "What are you saying?"

"Simply that if you're going to wait for your father to recover, it will have to be somewhere other than at his side. He'll be monitored and told about you when it's appropriate."

"But I'm his daughter."

"Precisely."

Dillon wanted two things. The first was twenty-four hours of sleep, the second, a good hot meal, preferably fed to him intravenously. He did not want anything to do with the confrontation before him. But even though he was exhausted and famished, he couldn't ignore Kelsey's plight any more than he'd been able to ignore the softness of her breasts pressed against his side. He was discovering that even under the worst of circumstances, Kelsey was hard to ignore, period.

He spoke before the argument could continue. "Look, Ed, Jake's not conscious now, is he?"

Dr. Munvelt shook his head sadly.

"Then let her go in and see him while he's still unconscious. She can't traumatize him if he doesn't know she's there. She's come a few miles for the privilege, wouldn't you say?"

The doctor looked relieved. "Would that be satisfactory?" he asked Kelsey.

She would puzzle out the doctor's logic later. Now she grasped at the chance to realize the dream that had fueled her childhood. "For now."

Dr. Munvelt started down the hall. Kelsey realized she was supposed to follow him, but after several steps she turned back to look at Dillon. His eyes were heavy-lidded, as if he were about to fall asleep standing up. "Thanks," she said, just loudly enough for her voice to carry. "Go home and get some sleep. I'll handle it from here."

As tired as he was, he was strangely reluctant to do that. Who would be there for Kelsey when she emerged from Jake's room, heartsick and wounded? The answer was inescapable. "I'll wait and drive you to the motel."

Kelsey didn't trust easily. She didn't allow herself to be drawn to people, because from experience she knew how disappointing it could be. But despite the training of a lifetime she was filled with warmth for the man who had come to her aid and her father's. Dillon Ward. A most unusual man. "You don't have to," she said.

"I'll be here."

Kelsey took in the weary lines of his face, the pale hue of exhaustion beneath his tan, the tired slope of his shoulders. Dillon was offering support to a stranger when he was drained himself. If a man could be judged by the friends he chose, then her father was the man she believed him to be. She tried to smile, unaware of the effect on Dillon. "I don't know how long they'll let me stay."

"I'll be here."

She nodded and turned back to follow the doctor.

When they were out of sight Dillon turned, too, but it wasn't his comfortable chair he found behind him. "Sergeant Newberry," he said without surprise, nodding at the Coober Pedy police officer. "Spreading the usual cheer?"

Sergeant Newberry's expression didn't change. "I've got some questions for you, Ward."

"I thought we'd already strained your resources."

The man didn't blink. "I've come up with something new to think about."

Dillon was too exhausted to stand a moment longer. He pushed past the policeman and draped his body across the chair. "Thinking at all's unique for you, wouldn't you say?"

"Tired, Ward?"

"A bit," Dillon said, closing his eyes.

"Don't let me keep you awake." Sergeant Newberry paused. "Just tell me why you tried to kill Jake Donovan, then I'll let you sleep as long as you'd like."

Chapter 2

The man in the hospital bed was her father. Kelsey said the words over and over to herself while another part of her screamed that it had all been a mistake. This could not be Jake Donovan, the man she had dreamed about for twenty-one years.

Dr. Munvelt eyed her cautiously, as if he were afraid that in a moment he might have two patients. "I know he looks bad," he began.

"Bad?" Kelsey turned wild eyes on him. "He looks dead."

"Most of us would if we'd been through what he has."

Kelsey stepped a little closer. If Jake had been lying in an urban hospital he would be hooked up to every high-tech machine that would fit beside his bed. Here he was receiving oxygen, fluids and the ministrations of one nurse. "Isn't there anything else you can do for him?"

"We can fly him to Adelaide, which we'll be doing shortly. He's stable for now, Miss Donovan. The equipment in Adelaide might be more sophisticated, but the care's no better."

"Tell me the truth. What are his chances of recovery?"

He twisted his fingers together and kept his eyes on them. "I'm not a fortune-teller. I can't make a guess that would mean anything. Jake's a fighter, I know that. He'll give it what he's got, and so will we. With the good Lord's help, maybe it will be enough.''

Kelsey stepped closer. The man in the bed looked nothing like the pictures she had always treasured. The man had been auburn-haired and laughing, with a clean-shaven face and a twinkle in his eyes. This man's head was covered with bandages. Most of the hair she could see was on his chin in a long, grizzled beard, and what little peeked from beneath the gauze wrappings was no longer auburn but the color of bones bleached by the sun. His skin was tanned in patches, but it hadn't taken years in the Coober Pedy sun without a fight. His face was a mass of wrinkles; his nose had the fine network of prominent veins that testified to countless hours at the pub.

Kelsey wished she could see him standing up. She wished she could see him with his eyes open, fondly gazing at the daughter he had wondered about for twenty-one years. "He was sixty in March," she said, taking the final steps to his bedside. "On St. Patrick's day."

She had spent that evening alone, toasting the man she had never expected to see again. And then the phone had rung, and her life had changed, along with Jake's. "I've been looking for him since I was old enough to write letters. On his birthday I found out he was in Australia. I found out he was here two weeks ago."

"And you didn't ring him?"

"What could I say in a phone call?"

The doctor cleared his throat, as if that much sentiment was too awkward to handle. "I should think that if Jake recovers steadily, it won't be too long before he can be told about you."

"How long is too long?"

"Two weeks. Three?"

She pushed down the beginnings of panic. Later she would deal with how to manage such a long stay. "I'll take a room near the hospital."

"Perhaps someone there can help you settle in."

Kelsey continued to stare at Jake. Finally she turned to the doctor. She saw that the nurse had already stepped out of the room. "Could I be alone with him for just a moment?"

Dr. Munvelt looked uneasy. "I don't know...."

"I'll call you if there's a change, and I won't stay long."

He still seemed uncertain. "I'll be waiting just outside."

"Thank you." Kelsey waited until she heard the door close. Then she leaned over Jake's bed, tentatively reaching down to smooth her fingers across one grizzled cheek.

"Well, Jake, so here we are." He lay completely still under the ministrations of her fingertips. "Twenty-one years later."

She was filled with memories that were probably no more than wishful thinking. The sound of a voice, a squeal of laughter, warm, strong arms lifting her. And an Irish lullaby. She hummed a little, wondering if it had really been Jake who had sung the song to her. She had known the melody for as long as she could remember, had been punished once for singing a verse in front of the first aunt she had gone to live with after her mother's death. She no longer knew any of the words, but the melody still lived inside her.

"When you're better," she crooned, "maybe you can teach me the lyrics. Then I can sing it to your grandchildren someday."

Jake didn't stir. Kelsey drew back and stared at him. Jake Donovan had led a hard life. The signs were unmistakable. If there was anything left of the man her mother had married, it was locked deep inside him. For the first time since she had heard about the accident, her eyes glistened with tears. She might never know any more, never *have* any more, than this one moment with her father.

"Jake...Daddy," she whispered. "I'm here now. I'll take care of you. All you have to do is get better."

He continued to lie still and silent. Kelsey took one more long look at Jake Donovan, then turned and left the room.

Sergeant Eugene Newberry was a man in exile. No one was sure just why, but rumors—a favored form of outback communication—abounded. Some said that he had made an enemy of the South Australian governor. Some said it was the prime minister. Some with more imagination had placed him in any number of compromising positions with any number of compromised Australian women.

Whatever the reason, it was clear that Sergeant Newberry was an unhappy man. It was also clear that he didn't want to be in Coober Pedy; he didn't like Coober Pedy or anyone in it. And most of all, he didn't like Dillon Ward.

Dillon Ward didn't like Sergeant Newberry, either. Now, with the man standing over him, breathing accusations of murder, Dillon merely shrugged. "Why would I want to murder Jake? We're mates."

"There's a small matter of some stones he was supposed to take into the Showcase today."

Dillon forced his eyelids apart. Sergeant Newberry hovered over him with all the subtlety of a wedgetail eagle circling to swoop down on dinner. "Those stones were worthless."

"You were taking worthless stones to the Showcase?"

"I wasn't taking anything," Dillon explained wearily. "Jake was taking them. I was to meet him there."

"But of course he never showed."

"As it turns out, he was a bit tied up in a mine shaft."

"When you found him, did you find the stones, too?"

"I wasn't looking for opal, Sergeant. I was looking for Jake."

"Opal?" the police officer asked with interest. "I thought you said the stones were worthless."

Dillon's laugh was humorless. "You've been in Coober Pedy what, two months? Three? It appears you still need to learn a few terms." He pretended to lecture. "Opal's a form of silica, similar to quartz, but with water in its structure. If the silica spheres are arranged in an even pattern, the stone is precious opal, the reason most of us came here to the back of beyond. If the spheres are absent or irregularly arranged, the stone doesn't produce color, and we call it potch opal or just potch." He tipped his chair back against the wall. "Have we cleared that up?"

"Don't patronize me, Ward."

Dillon ignored him, continuing in the same tone. "The opal Jake was taking to the Showcase was potch with a little color. Sometimes Gary buys it and sells it cheaply to tourists who don't want to spend money on the real thing. Jake was hoping to make enough to tide himself over until he got paid for some good stones he had taken to Sydney."

He watched Sergeant Newberry's eyes light up. The sergeant was tall, with the translucent pallor of Australia's famed witchety grub and the physique of a man trying to survive in a country stalked by famine. The only compelling thing about him was the fanatic glitter of his blue eyes.

"Good stones?" the sergeant murmured, caressing each word. "Did you say anything about good stones before?"

"I didn't. Those stones have nothing to do with Jake's accident."

"Don't they? Who knew about the stones besides you?"

"I reckon whoever Jake told about them."

"And whom might that be?"

"Half of Coober Pedy, if he'd had enough to drink."

"And if he hadn't?"

"Nobody."

"Were the stones worth killing a man for?" Sergeant Newberry asked in a casual voice that didn't deceive Dillon one iota.

"There are some who'd say there's nothing worth killing a man for," Dillon answered. "Unless he's trying to kill you."

"Dillon?"

Dillon set the front legs of his chair down and stood. Kelsey walked toward him, her eyes glistening with unshed tears but her chin still tilted proudly. He didn't know what to say. He only knew that he had rarely wanted so badly to offer comfort.

"I could only stay a few minutes." Kelsey stopped just in front of him. "Dr. Munvelt said they should be transferring him soon."

"You'll be leaving then yourself?"

"Dr. Munvelt said there won't be room for me in the plane. I'll have to follow tomorrow."

Dillon gently touched her shoulder, his fingers brushing one silky strand of hair. "That will be best, anyway. You're done in. You can rest tonight."

Kelsey's eyes signaled her gratitude.

"Are you talking about Jake Donovan, miss?"

For the first time Kelsey became fully aware of the man standing just behind Dillon. She took in his uniform and the grim set of his mouth. "That's right. You're from the police?"

"Sergeant Newberry at your disposal."

Kelsey extended her hand. "Kelsey Donovan, Jake Donovan's daughter."

Sergeant Newberry held her hand a little too long. "I wasn't aware Jake had a daughter. That wasn't in the information Mr. Ward gave me."

Kelsey switched her gaze back to Dillon. The question she hadn't been able to ask had been answered. "My father never told you about me, did he?"

Dillon wanted to wrap his big hands around Sergeant Newberry's skinny throat. "We didn't talk much about the past."

She smiled wanly. "You must not have talked about it at all."

"He wouldn't have been proud of leaving you, Kelsey."

Sergeant Newberry stepped between them. "How did you hear of your father's accident, Miss Donovan? You got here quickly."

"I'm afraid it's a coincidence. My father and I haven't been…in touch. I just discovered where he was, and I came to see him."

"A terrible shock, then, to find him in the hospital." Before Kelsey could acknowledge it, he went on. "A terrible shock to find that he had been the victim of a murder attempt."

Kelsey stared blankly at him.

"You did know we suspect attempted murder?"

She shook her head. "I don't know what you mean? Why would anyone want to murder my father?"

"That's what I'm trying to find out." Sergeant Newberry turned to include Dillon. "Mr. Ward here is trying to help me. You see, he knows everything about your father." He hesitated, pinching the tip of his chin as if in deepest thought. "Especially how much old Jake is worth. Mr. Ward stands to gain the most from knowing, after all. Or *stood* to gain the most," he added after a short pause. "Of course, now that there's a next of kin…." His voice trailed off.

Kelsey felt a chill go through her despite the warm temperature in the hospital corridor. She turned her eyes to Dillon and saw that he had seen her shiver. "You didn't tell me anyone suspected a murder attempt."

Dillon read the dismay, the denial, and finally, the beginning of suspicion in her eyes. He tried to reassure her. "Sergeant Newberry's been watching too much telly. I saw no point in worrying you until he has something concrete to go on."

"Somebody pushed your father down that shaft, then left him for dead. Somebody who knew the last place anyone would look was an abandoned mine." Sergeant Newberry smiled. "Someone who may even have been leading the rescue party."

Through the gray fog of his fatigue, Dillon saw red. He stepped forward and gripped the police officer's lapels. "I'll thank you to keep your thoughts to yourself until you've got some kind of proof."

"You could be charged for threatening me."

Dillon tightened his grip. "Try it," he said, lingering over each word. "See how far you get, Sergeant." He shoved the smirking man a full foot, then dropped his hands. "Now take your two-bob accusations somewhere else so I can escort Miss Donovan to the hotel."

Sergeant Newberry pretended to ignore Dillon's orders, but he stepped backward another pace. "Have you thought about what you'll be doing with your father's mine, Miss Donovan?"

Kelsey looked from man to man. The gratitude she had felt evaporated, to be replaced with wariness. Wariness was more familiar, anyway, and from long experience, she knew it was safer. If she suddenly felt alone and surrounded by hostile strangers, at least it was a feeling she knew well.

She tried to compose herself. "What do you mean?"

"The Mining Act says your father's claim has to be worked for not less than twenty hours a week or he loses it."

"I'll be working it," Dillon told Kelsey, his tone controlled and his words clipped. "Until I can find someone to help, I can work the necessary hours."

"A bit like a dingo minding the sheep, wouldn't you say?" Sergeant Newberry asked.

Dillon stepped toward him, but the police officer made a smooth retreat. "Miss Donovan, your father's claim may be consolidated with Ward's here," Sergeant Newberry continued, "but the law says that the opal that's found in your father's claim belongs to him, no matter who works it."

Dillon dismissed his words with an abrupt wave. "Jake and I split everything we find fifty-fifty, no matter where we find it."

"You didn't take his share of the fall," Kelsey said softly. "He's the one lying in that bed down the hall."

Sergeant Newberry's suspicions were to be expected. But Kelsey's affected Dillon like a jolt to an exposed nerve. "Do you think I don't know? I spent nearly forty hours looking for him.''

"In all the wrong places." Kelsey didn't want to believe that Dillon was responsible for her father's fall. She didn't want to believe he wanted Jake Donovan dead. But neither did she want to believe that Jake was injured and unconscious, yet that was irrefutable.

Dillon had never had to defend himself to anyone, and he wasn't about to start. He took a moment to swallow his anger. "I'll take you to the hotel now. Then I'm going home to get some sleep. You'd better do the same if you're going to catch a plane out of here tomorrow."

"We'll be looking after things here for Jake," Sergeant Newberry assured her, though his next words diluted the pledge. "As well as we can."

"Do you mean the mine?" Kelsey asked.

"The mine. The investigation. It's just too bad there won't be someone right on the scene to look after your father's interests. You don't have a brother, do you?"

Kelsey straightened a little. "I've never needed a brother. I fight my own battles." She saw the incredulous looks on both men's faces and straightened a little more. "Always," she added for emphasis. "And quite well."

"I'll take you to your hotel," Dillon repeated, reaching for her arm.

"I don't think so," she said, shaking off his hand. "I'll find my own way."

Dillon's hand dropped to his side. He took in the smug look on Sergeant Newberry's face and the way Kelsey was trying to dust the ceiling with her butterscotch curls. Suddenly he was more tired, if that was possible. "Have it your own way," he said, bending down to retrieve his hat. "Good day, Sergeant." He nodded to Kelsey. In a moment he was gone.

"I'd watch that one," Sergeant Newberry said, his gaze following Dillon down the hall.

"I won't be here to watch him," Kelsey said wearily.

"A pity, that." The sergeant's gaze floated over Kelsey. "I'll do what I can, but there's really little anyone can do unless they're on the spot all the time. Just don't be surprised if your father recovers and there's not an opal left in the Rainbow Fire mine."

* * *

The motel room was quiet, if not plush. Kelsey sat cross-legged on her bed, counting her money once more, as if by doing so the amount might double. Unfortunately the count was less this time by one dollar.

She had appallingly little to see her through the weeks of Jake's recovery. She hadn't expected to stay in Australia for more than two weeks. She had her ticket home and five hundred Australian dollars. She had counted on a slightly better exchange rate; she had counted on prices in the land down under being cheaper.

And, if she were honest, she had counted on being able to stay with Jake once she found him.

Kelsey knew better than to count on anything or anyone, but this time her good judgment had been suspended. She had wanted to see Jake so badly that, one week before Christmas break, she had taken leave from her job as a teacher's aide, taken the money she had been saving for her final semester at the University of North Carolina and bought her ticket.

She had been low on funds before. Too often, in fact. The night she had graduated from high school, her grandmother had handed her a new suitcase, a fifty-dollar bill and wished her well, spoiling the unexpected generosity by asking for her house key with the next breath. Kelsey had moved into a mobile home with a girlfriend until she had found a job—not an easy task in the small North Carolina town where she had been branded a rebel and a troublemaker. But after two weeks of peanut butter sandwiches she had found work at the local laundry, and while her schoolmates had gone off to college, she had washed, dried and folded towels until she had enough money for a one-way ticket to Raleigh.

Life had been better where no one knew her past. She had graduated from laundry to day-care center, and finally, to teacher's aide in an exclusive private school. Along the way she had picked up college credits every time she saved enough money to pay for them until she was within only a few credits of receiving her degree.

Not one of the last six years had been easy. What she had accomplished, she had accomplished alone, but then, that had been the pattern of her life from the day her mother died and left her a quasi-orphan at age five. She had been fed and clothed by relatives who didn't want her, shunted back and forth between houses like unwelcome cargo. She had learned not to respond to comments about her parents, learned not to listen to the fights about whose turn it was to take her in next. And somewhere along the way, she had learned to stop expecting Jake to rescue her.

But she had never learned to stop caring that somewhere in the world she had a father who once had hugged her and played with her and sung her an Irish lullaby.

She still cared.

"Five hundred dollars." Kelsey looked down at the foreign bills spread over her bed. She knew just how quickly five hundred dollars would slip away. And once it was gone, there would be nothing to replace it. Her visa was very specific. She could not work while she was in Australia.

She would have to be careful to make the money last. Once she got to Adelaide she would have to find an inexpensive room where she could cook her own meals. And she would have to pray not only that Jake recovered, but that he recovered quickly.

Kelsey still couldn't believe her father was going to have to recover without her by his side for the first weeks. Hours had passed since her conversation with Dr. Munvelt, and right now Jake was probably in a bed in the Adelaide hospital. She'd had time to nap a little, to snack on some crackers she had bought at the airport, and to think about the doctor's words. Reluctantly she had accepted his decree, at least temporarily. Once in Adelaide, however, things could change.

She was still staring at the piles of bills when the ringing of the phone beside her bed split the silence. The sound was a link with civilization, and Kelsey answered it with enthusiasm.

Her enthusiasm had diminished severely by the time she hung up the telephone. The caller had been Dr. Munvelt, who had graciously reassured her that Jake had made the flight with no particular difficulties. The physician in charge of his case in Adelaide felt that Jake's chances of a recovery were good, although he cautioned that it might take some time. Additionally, however, the Adelaide physician concurred with Dr. Munvelt. Kelsey's presence would be a new blow that could slow recovery. They would stay in touch with her, but they didn't want her at the hospital just yet. His suggestion was that Kelsey see a bit of Australia while she was waiting.

"A bit of Australia!" Kelsey angrily threw her pillow against the wall, scattering cash in the resulting draft. Which bit of Australia could she afford to see? How far would five hundred dollars take her? How many nights at a hotel? How many meals? If she was penny-pinching cautious, she might be able to stay two weeks. But the truth was inescapable. Her money was probably going to run out before Jake was ready to see her.

She shouldn't have come.

Kelsey slid off the bed and knelt to pick up the scattered bills. She had learned years before just how far self-pity would get her. Five thousand towels, not self-pity, had gotten her out of the town of her birth. Years of inquiries, letters, phone calls and just plain snooping, had gotten her the information about Jake's whereabouts. She had come all the way across the world for a reunion with her father. Somehow, some way, she would still manage it.

Once the money was back in her wallet, Kelsey felt better. There was little she could do about Jake right now. There was little she could do about her dwindling funds. The only thing she could do anything about was the empty feeling in her stomach. Earlier she had showered and washed her hair, obeying all the cautionary signs about water shortages. Now she slipped on wheat-colored jeans and a soft peach-colored shirt and ran a brush through her long tangled curls.

Outside the air was cooler. At home in December, the ground was sometimes touched with snow. Here, December was the beginning of summer, and red dust caressed everything she saw. Even without the dust, the town was anything but scenic. Coober Pedy consisted of starkly simple block and pre-fab buildings placed along a narrow blacktop road. There were a few cultivated trees softening the harsh view, and the silver gleam of water tanks with thirsty mouths that yawned at the cloudless night sky.

Kelsey had come thousands of miles to a place not unlike the old American West. For a moment the idea caught her fancy. The happiest home she had known after her mother's death had been with a classmate's parents who had invited Kelsey to spend the weekend when she was seven and kept her for six months. Eventually Kelsey's relatives had been shamed into bringing her back to live with them when her friend's family moved to Colorado. But Kelsey had been left with warm memories of a cowgirl costume made just for her and rides on a pony at the park. For months afterward she had secretly vowed to escape to Deadman's Gulch or Tombstone, where cowgirl costumes and pony rides were the status quo and little girls could whoop and holler without being punished.

Kelsey wondered if Jake had escaped to Coober Pedy for any of the same reasons. There were few frontiers left in the world, but this was certainly one of them. With the moon reflecting off corrugated iron roofs and the ghostly outlines of desert hills against the horizon, she could be in nineteenth-century Nevada or California.

She felt a brief surge of excitement. Jake's blood certainly ran through her veins. She wondered if he would be proud or appalled to find that his daughter was a dreamer, too.

She had wandered both sides of the street, sidestepping for the occasional truck that flashed by, when she noticed the hotel at the rise of the hill. The parking lot was crowded with cars and pickups, and rock music drifted through the closed door. A hotel promised food and the clatter of other people, both of which she needed.

Kelsey was through the door and four steps into the room before she realized her error. If she'd been thinking clearly she would have realized that rock music and sedate dining didn't go hand in hand. Rock music and hard-drinking men did, however. She was standing in a pub, and except for one lone female behind the bar, she was the only woman in the spacious room.

She was outside again when she felt strong arms catch her. Flustered, she realized she had walked right into a man coming in the door. She lifted her head, stepping backward away from him. The man was familiar and unfamiliar at the same time. "Dillon." She stepped back again, taking a good long look.

"You're looking better. Did you get some rest?" Dillon's tone was polite, but only just.

"Apparently *you* did." Kelsey marveled at the difference a shower, a shave and some rest had made in the man in front of her. She hadn't realized just how attractive he was, but now the truth was unmistakable. Dillon was a man any woman would be proud to claim. His features were rugged—she would bet anything his nose had been broken at least once—but they added up to strength and unashamed masculinity. With his mane of brown curls and deep green eyes, he radiated a healthy yet disturbingly sensual vitality, a vitality that had been hidden earlier by his exhaustion.

"I slept," he said. He didn't say that he had slept restlessly, tossing and turning while the image of Jake wedged in a mine drive tormented him. He didn't say that he had thought of Kelsey more than once, too, and cursed the suspicion he had seen in her eyes. "I decided I needed to eat more than I needed to sleep."

Kelsey noticed the way the sleeves of his white shirt were rolled back to expose tanned, muscle-roped forearms. Before she lifted her eyes she quelled the desire to notice more. He might look like a different man, but he was still the same man a cop had as much as accused of trying to murder her father.

Dillon knew what her silence said, but he ignored the message. "Have you eaten, then?"

"I...no, I came in here but...." She stopped, not willing to admit that the crowd of men had scared her away. "I wasn't sure they served food."

"Counter meals. It's a little late, but I can sweet talk Melly into two if you're game." He listened to his own offer and wondered why he had made it. Kelsey Donovan had fallen hook, line and sinker for Eugene Newberry's slander. Dillon was no longer under any obligation to help her.

There were few women in the world who wouldn't treat this situation with the greatest caution. There were few women in the world with the resources to feel safe, even when threatened. Kelsey was one of them. She lifted her chin, thrusting it outward in a movement bigger men than this one had learned to respect. "Fine. Thank you."

Kelsey climbed one notch in Dillon's estimation. She was no longer the wilting flower of the afternoon, but a woman willing to take a chance. She was also a female who could make a man grovel at her feet. Earlier she had tugged at all the right places inside him, even through his exhaustion. Now he felt her fragile beauty wrap around his guts like the scent of lavender.

"Let's go see," he said gruffly, not happy about his own response.

"And while we're at it, maybe you can tell me why you or someone else wants to murder my father."

One more notch. Kelsey was already through the door, but Dillon stopped her with a hand on her shoulder. "What gives you the courage to say something like that?"

"Faith in my ability to protect myself," she said, shrugging off his hand. "And remember that, Dillon." She flashed him a smile that could chill a heart so it froze mid-beat. "Because I only give one warning."

Chapter 3

"What'll it be? Pork or rump steak?"

Kelsey stared at the woman across the bar, not only because the accent had been American, but because the woman was one of the most flamboyant Kelsey had seen. She recovered quickly. "Steak."

"Another Yank, huh?" The woman extended her hand over the counter. "Melanie Morel. Melly to my friends, and you and I are destined to be friends. There's nothing else to do here."

"Kelsey Donovan." Kelsey felt the rasp of jewelry against her skin. She lowered her eyes and saw that Melly wore a huge opal on each finger, two on her pinky. "That's an impressive collection of rings."

"My boyfriend, Gary, owns the Opal Showcase. I advertise." She waved her hand in demonstration.

Melly advertised more than opals. Everything about her was a neon sign. Her black hair was clipped Marine Corps short on the sides and back, but the top was longer and spiked into a riotous thatch. She augmented the look with one chin-length earring and a red and gold metallic tank top. No makeup marred her perfect magnolia petal skin except for a dusting of powder that glittered like tiny stars under the fluorescent lights.

"Where are you from?" Kelsey asked, fascinated by this gaudy cockatoo in a land too desolate for sparrows.

"Nebraska." Melanie struck an exaggerated pose. "Can't you see the farm girl in me?"

Kelsey just smiled, and it was answer enough.

"What about you, Dillon?" Melly asked, turning to flutter her eyelashes. "What would you like?"

"The steak and a schooner."

"Don't you love his voice?" Melly almost purred the words. "Dillon has the deepest voice in Coober Pedy."

"I'm starving, Melly, me love." Dillon reached over the counter and affectionately touched her nose with the tip of his finger. "Feed me."

"I'm at your command," she said with good-natured flirtatiousness. "Always." She turned and filled two large glasses with beer, setting them in front of Kelsey and Dillon. "My shout," she explained to Kelsey. She laughed at Kelsey's blank look. "That's Australian for 'my treat.' They're words you'll never need to say yourself. There's not a man in this bastion of chauvinism who'll let you shout him a drink, but *you'll* be shouted plenty."

Kelsey tasted the beer. It was dark and rich and absolutely to her liking. It also went straight to her head. "Thanks," she said, toasting Melly with her glass. "I think I'll have to sit to drink this."

Dillon motioned toward a table, and Kelsey wound her way in that direction. The pub was large and modern, with wooden tables on one side and pool tables on the other. One area with a small stage and sound equipment was obviously set aside for dancing.

"The town social center?" Kelsey asked as she set her glass on the table. She wasn't oblivious to the approving male looks aimed in her direction, just uninterested.

"One of them. We also have churches, a school with a community swimming pool, sports fields, a golf course—" Dillon stopped, noting the surprise on her face. "Did you think we holed up like bats in a cave? This is a town of five thousand, give or take away a thousand at any one time. We have a newspaper, a hospital—"

"I know about your hospital."

Dillon was momentarily silent. When he spoke, there was no emotion in his voice. "Have you heard anything more about Jake?"

"He made it to Adelaide."

"Jake's a tough old bird. He'll walk out of there on his own two feet."

"And come back to what? Another murder attempt?"

Dillon sprawled in his chair, slowly sipping his beer. "Why don't you ask me why I tried to kill him?"

Kelsey choked in the middle of a swallow.

"Don't you want to know?" he prompted.

Kelsey recovered after a fit of coughing into a napkin thoughtfully provided by Dillon. "Why did you?" she asked at last. "I would be interested."

"First you have to understand the way our claims work." He observed her reaction. "For the grand total of fifteen dollars, each person who applies for a Precious Stones Prospecting Permit—a Miner's Right—gets to peg a claim fifty meters by fifty meters. After he registers it, the claim is his to work, and if he wants, he renews it a year later. The law allows up to four permit holders to peg adjoining claims and consolidate them."

"So why did you try to kill Jake?"

"Obviously because we found opal on his claim and not on mine."

Kelsey had finished half her beer before she spoke again. "Is that your story, or the sergeant's?"

"Will it matter if I tell you?"

She couldn't tell a lie. "I don't know."

"Fair enough."

The conversation was interrupted by Melly, who arrived with two plates covered with steak, salad and fries. "I forgot to ask you how you liked it, so it's medium," she said, setting the plate in front of Kelsey. "And I know how you like yours," she said, smiling provocatively at Dillon.

Kelsey glimpsed the longest, most elegant legs she had ever seen beneath the shortest black skirt. "As good as a Nebraska sirloin?"

"I'll never tell." Melly winked. "Don't leave before we talk. I should get a break sometime."

The steak was good, although Kelsey was so hungry she could hardly judge. Neither she nor Dillon said a word until both had finished their meal.

"Well, we had starvation in common," Dillon said finally.

Kelsey observed the way his casual posture pulled his shirt tight against his broad chest and shoulders. She glimpsed a heavy gold chain that she hadn't noticed before and wondered what lay hidden under the top button of his shirt.

"If nothing else," he added.

Kelsey was torn between sympathy for the meals he had missed while he searched for her father and suspicion that it might have been his own doing. She kept both out of her voice. "Tell me why the sergeant believes you tried to kill Jake."

"He wants to suspect me of something. He's got a personal grudge."

She raised one eyebrow.

"A month ago I caught the good sergeant out on another miner's claim. Fossicking."

"Fossicking?"

"Looking for opal someone else has missed. Sifting through mullock...." Dillon saw that she didn't understand and back-tracked. "When you dig a shaft or a drive, the dirt and rock you remove is called mullock. Somehow or other, depending on the method you use, it ends up on the ground above in heaps. Sometimes people noodle through the dirt for fun, trying to find pretty potch or opal chips the miner missed. That's all right on abandoned claims, but to do it on an active one, you need the miner's permission. Newberry wasn't doing it for fun, and he didn't have permission."

"What do you mean, he wasn't doing it for fun?"

"There was a rumor he was spending more time digging through other people's claims than doing his job. Looking for early retirement, I guess. We handle things ourselves here. We're not a bunch of sniveling dobbers who run around and tell tales. When I found out what Newberry was doing, I told him to stop."

"You told him to stop?"

"Let's just say I told him in such a way as to make him listen."

"And that's why he's accusing you of murdering my father?"

"You decide."

The story seemed straightforward enough. Kelsey imagined it wouldn't be difficult to check it out. Coober Pedy was probably a town where everyone knew everyone's business. "The sergeant intimated that you had something to gain from Jake's death. Something like opals?''

Dillon was tired of explanations, but he figured he'd better finish what he'd started. "Coober Pedy is a town of instant rich men. One morning you go down into your mine, just like you've gone down into it every day for a year. You tap a little, pry out a little stone, and the next thing you know you're holding a miracle in the palm of your hand. That's one story. Then there's the other one. One morning you go down into your mine, just like you've done every day for years. You tap a little, pry out some more potch, and suddenly it hits you. The mine's a duffer and you're a failure. You've always been a failure, and you always will be. You put a gun to your head, and a week later, somebody finds you at the bottom of your mine.''

Kelsey shuddered at the graphic picture.

Dillon saw the shudder, but he wasn't sorry. She had to know how it was. "Jake and I have always fallen somewhere in the middle. We find opal, but nothing to add to the crown jewels. Triplet opal. It's worth something, but nothing like the opal that makes an instant rich man. The opal we've dug has kept us going and kept us hoping. Nothing more.''

"Then you're saying there's nothing to Sergeant Newberry's accusations except revenge?''

Dillon tried to decide whether to finish the story. He doubted that anything he could tell Kelsey would change her opinion, but he owed her the truth solely because she was Jake's daughter. "About three months ago,'' he said finally, "Jake started a new drive on his claim. I helped him, but after a while, it looked like a duffer. Jake wouldn't give up on it, so I let him work on it alone while I worked on a more promising drive. I wasn't getting much, but I thought I might be getting close. Jake got lucky before I did.''

Kelsey sipped the last of her beer, her brown eyes dissecting each expression that crossed Dillon's face. "Go on.''

"Jake found a small pocket of precious opal. As far as we could tell, it wasn't part of a bigger vein, but the few stones that were there promised to be good ones. Jake has a mate in Sydney, a jeweler who's asked him to bring him his best finds. This bloke cuts and polishes the stones, then sells them, giving Jake a commission. It's a slightly riskier way of doing business, because he could ruin the stones. But Jake trusts him, so he took the stones there, knowing he would make more money if everything went as planned. We should make a bit when they sell."

"We?"

"Jake and I split everything fifty-fifty. We're mates."

"What is this 'mate' bit?"

Dillon knew there was no easy way to explain it. The vast interior of Australia might never have been settled by Europeans if they hadn't adopted the concept of mateship. "We stand by each other. You might say it's an outback tradition."

"Just like you stood by and pushed him down a mine shaft so you'd get the money from the stones my father found?"

Dillon knew that he had seen Kelsey at her most vulnerable. Now her emotions were out of reach. Or almost. He had seen the slight flicker of doubt in her desert-brown eyes. She didn't know what to think, but she didn't want to believe he had been the one to harm Jake.

He leaned forward. As he had expected, she didn't back away.

"I came to Coober Pedy with a diploma in engineering and a chip on my shoulder. Your father laughed at the diploma and knocked the chip all the way to Darwin the first night we met. Six months later he saved my life. He shoveled me out of a shaft he'd warned me not to go into alone and poured a bottle of Foster's over my head. I still owe him for that."

Kelsey struggled against believing Dillon. She was in a strange country, in a frontier town much like her childhood fantasies of Deadman's Gulch. If life had taught her one thing, it was that she could trust herself.

"You two look much too serious." Melly draped herself over a chair beside Kelsey, arranging her long legs to their best advantage. "I'd better shout you both another schooner."

"I'll pass." Kelsey realized she and Dillon were still staring at each other. The impact of his unflinching green eyes was almost physical. Reluctantly she turned her gaze to Melly. "Thanks anyway."

"So tell me where you're from."

"North Carolina. Raleigh."

"Kelsey Donovan," Melly said, reflecting. "Related to Jake?"

Kelsey nodded. "His daughter."

"I didn't know old Jake had a family. Nobody but Dillon here, that is." Melly shot Dillon a flirtatious smile; then she sobered. "Lord, I forgot. He's been hurt, hasn't he?" She turned back to Kelsey. "That's why you're in town. How is he?"

"He's in Adelaide now. They say he made the trip well."

"He'll be fine. Old Jake's too ornery to stay in a hospital."

"So I've been told."

"You'll be going down to be with him?" Melly asked.

Kelsey started to say yes, but without good reason she switched her gaze back to Dillon. He was nodding, as if answering for her. He wanted her to go to Adelaide and wait until Jake recovered enough to see her. She could see it in his eyes, read it in the impatient nods. Dillon Ward wanted her out of Coober Pedy.

"I haven't decided yet," she said, still watching Dillon. "I might just stay here."

"Gonna do a little mining?" Melly asked, scraping a fleck of paint off the table with a long, blood-red fingernail.

Kelsey had only made her comment to see Dillon's reaction. Now Melly's question stopped her cold, and she forgot about Dillon entirely. Kelsey faced the other woman. "What did you say?"

"Are you gonna do a little mining? You know, find a few opals down in Jake's mine while you're here?"

Kelsey couldn't believe she hadn't thought of that possibility. Sergeant Newberry had as much as suggested it, but she had been too immersed in grief. Now she considered the idea. There was nothing she could do for Jake in Adelaide. She couldn't even see him. But there was something she could do for him in Coober Pedy. She could keep an eye on the Rainbow Fire mine and Dillon Ward at the same time. Maybe she could even find some opal.

"Yeah, I think that's exactly what I'm going to do," Kelsey said, warming to the idea. "As his only living relative, I'm sure I must have the legal right, especially if I don't intend to sell anything I find."

Dillon broke her train of thought. "You're not going down into the mine."

Kelsey hadn't expected enthusiasm from Dillon, but neither had she expected him to forbid her. "You don't think so?" she said casually. "How do you plan to stop me? I'm not as easy to sneak up on as my father.'' She heard Melly draw a sharp breath, but Kelsey didn't take her eyes from Dillon's. ''I have all Jake's good reflexes, and *I* know how to guard my back.''

Dillon's eyes crystallized into emerald ice. ''There's nothing you can do here that would help matters.''

''No? Whose matters wouldn't I help?''

Melly stood, obviously uncomfortable. ''Well, I'll leave you two lovebirds to settle this by yourselves.''

Kelsey stood, too. ''I think I'll take that beer after all.''

''Kelsey.''

She turned her head over one shoulder and raked Dillon with a haughty gaze. He had said her name with all the finesse of a drill sergeant. ''What?''

''How do you plan to mine the Rainbow Fire without my help?''

''I imagine Sergeant Newberry will help me think of a way.''

''Newberry's a toad, but even he wouldn't want a woman down in that mine.''

She tossed her hair behind her shoulders. ''We'll see.''

Kelsey was halfway across the room before trouble came looking for her. A young dark-haired man who was shooting pool backed in her direction. With some fancy footwork, Kelsey just managed to avoid cushioning the wrong end of his cue in her thigh. She frowned briefly before she started toward the bar again.

She stopped when strong fingers bit into her shoulders. Kelsey allowed herself to be turned.

''Y'almost lost the game for me, doll.''

The words were as ridiculous as the accent. The man wasn't a native Australian. Wherever he was from, he had learned to speak English by watching old Hollywood gangster movies. Kelsey knew a Jimmy Cagney imitation when she heard one.

''If you almost lost the game,'' she said politely, ''it's because you weren't paying attention.'' She lifted her shoulders to dislodge his hands, but the young man gripped them harder.

''I'd rather lose the game than you.''

Kelsey put all body systems on alert. ''I don't like being manhandled.''

''Maybe y'haven't been handled by a real man.''

The macho pretense was so overblown it was laughable. But Kelsey knew better than to smile. ''Please let go of me,'' she said as pleasantly as she could.

"Let her go, Serge. We've got a game to finish," said the man standing beside the table.

"Let go of me, Serge," Kelsey echoed, her eyes locked with his faintly bloodshot ones.

"A kiss to make up for causing trouble."

Kelsey had never been the kind of woman who could flirt her way out of situations. She knew that Serge was slightly drunk and showing off, but he was really no more than a boy just coming into manhood. Melly would have wrapped her arms around him and kissed him until he was embarrassed enough to push her away. Kelsey's response was different.

"Let go of me now," she said quietly, "and we can both forget this happened."

"Forget?" Serge laughed loudly. "How'm I gonna forget you, doll?"

Kelsey sighed as he pulled her closer. "I'm afraid you're not," she said just before she twisted and brought her elbow sharply against his ribs. His howl of pain accompanied the release of her shoulders. He bent over momentarily, hugging his midsection.

Kelsey backed away a step. "Are you all right?" she asked solicitously.

He straightened, snarling in a language she didn't understand. When he lunged at her in an excess of ruined manly pride, she simply danced aside and watched him sprawl to the floor.

The room was suddenly silent. Even the taped music had come to an end. Before anyone could reach them, Kelsey squatted beside Serge. "Are you all right?" she asked loudly enough for the men nearest her to hear. "I'm afraid you slipped on something. The floor's pretty slick."

"Leave me alone."

"I'm so sorry. I guess you just had some bad luck." She stood, almost colliding with Dillon. Since the entire episode had taken only seconds, she knew he must have left his chair at the first sign of trouble.

He took her arm with all the courtesy of a grappling hook and guided her away from the other men. "You're Jake's brat all right. Nothing he likes better than a barroom brawl."

Her eyes narrowed. "That's me. Born to fight."

Dillon pulled her toward the bar. Serge's pool partner was already helping him to his feet. "Only difference is that Jake outweighs you by about ten stone. When he goes after someone, the odds are even.''

"Weight's what does it, then?''

Dillon dropped her arm and sprawled against the counter. He clenched his hands on the counter edge to keep from holding her to his side. In the moment right before her skirmish with Serge, he had recognized an extraordinary need to protect her. He was a man who would always come to a woman's rescue, but this time he'd felt as if something global was at stake. He told himself it was just that he owed it to Jake.

"You've got courage," he said. "It took courage to come here, courage to hear about your father, courage to accuse me of trying to murder him.''

"And?''

"I reckon it'll take courage to realize you'll be better off leaving Coober Pedy. Serge gave you a taste of what it'll be like if you stay. Most of the women in town are under a man's protection. The ones that aren't are like flypaper to the Serges here.''

"Serge won't bother me again.''

Dillon shook his head. "You're wrong. You've hurt his pride. He'll try to prove something now, and his friends will, too.''

Melly set a beer in front of Kelsey and another for Dillon. "A neat trick," she said, wiping the counter. "You must have had a few lessons in self-defense.''

"A few." Kelsey lifted the glass to her lips.

"A few lessons won't do you any good if he comes after you sober." Dillon played with his glass, making designs on the frosted side with his index finger.

"You don't think so?''

"He's a cheeky kid. I know him. His mine's next to the Rainbow Fire.''

"Good, at least I've met a neighbor.''

"Don't stay, Kelsey." Dillon stopped beating around the bush. "You won't be safe in Coober Pedy.''

Kelsey watched Melly move away. She waited until she was out of earshot. "I can handle what comes my way, Dillon." As soon as she had said his name, she wondered why. It established an intimacy that she wanted no part of. This was the man who might have injured Jake.

"Can you handle mining? Climbing fifty feet or more into a bloody dark hole every day, swinging a pick, operating dangerous equipment, setting charges?"

"I can."

Dillon fought the urge to touch her, but even as he fought, he was lifting her wrist in his hand. "You were made to wear opals, not to mine them. I'll have no part of you down there."

"No?"

He didn't tell her the real reason he was afraid for her. Sergeant Newberry wasn't the only person in Coober Pedy who believed someone had tried to kill Jake. Dillon believed the same. Kelsey's life could be in danger from more than amorous miners and tunneling machines. She could be in danger from Jake's attacker. And until Dillon was sure just who that was, he wanted Kelsey safely away.

"I didn't hurt your father." Dillon dropped her wrist, then reached behind him and picked up his glass. "I owe Jake my life. I'll take care of the Rainbow Fire. You take care of yourself and get out of here."

"I'm staying." She hadn't been sure until the words were said. Then she knew they were true. This was where she belonged, at least until she was allowed to see Jake. She owed Jake that much for the memory of an Irish lullaby. "And just so you won't worry...."

Kelsey knew she was tired and light-headed from the beer. Even as she approached the nearest table to pull a broken ladder-back chair from under it, she told herself she was showing off, breaking one of the most important rules she had been taught. She ignored the voice inside her head that was trying to reason with her.

She lifted the chair and carried it back to the bar, setting it between two stools so that it lay over them like a helpless sacrifice. She took two deep breaths, flexing her hand once as she got into position. Then, all internal voices silenced, she brought the side of her hand down across one of the rungs on the chair's back and watched it split cleanly in two. Another breath held, another rung, until the chair back lay in pieces.

She noticed the quiet in the room when she was finished. It was the same quiet that had followed her skirmish with Serge. Then there was a hearty round of applause. Kelsey ignored it. "I can do it with my feet, too. I'm hoping you'll just take my word for that, though. The chair's had it."

Dillon saw Kelsey's flush of triumph, but he also saw the embarrassment in her eyes. She was pleased at what she could do, and embarrassed at her pleasure. "Black belt?" he asked, raising one brow.

"Second degree."

He reached for her hand and ran his fingers over the calluses that had so recently shattered wood. In all other ways, the hand was deceptively fragile—for a murder weapon. "Well, you told me you fought your own battles, didn't you?"

"I did."

"Serge was luckier than he knew."

Kelsey pulled her hand from his. Dillon's hand stroking hers was strangely sensual. It healed the stinging flesh and soothed her embarrassment at the same time that it kindled a certain restlessness inside her. "I shouldn't have hit him at all. I should have thought of a way to get away from him."

"You should have let *me* hit him." Dillon listened as the room began to buzz with normal speech. "You know what you've done, don't you?"

"I hope I've shown you and everyone here that I won't be messed with."

"Not my intention."

"I'd shout the chair if I could, but the boss says that'll be three dollars fifty," Melly said, coming back to peer over the counter at the broken chair. "He says he's giving it to you cheap."

"Tell him it was worth it." Kelsey rummaged in her pocket, coming up with the correct amount for both the chair and the dinner. "I'll be seeing you around, Melly. I'm going to stay a while."

Melly's smile was like warm honey. "Where are you staying?"

"The motel."

"Lucky thing. Gary owns it. I'll stop by sometime."

"Do that." Kelsey nodded to Melly, but it was Dillon she addressed her next words to. "I'll be at the mine tomorrow. It would be easier if you told me how to get there."

He was tempted to let her walk. Dillon knew how poorly Kelsey had tolerated the afternoon's heat. On the other hand, if someone had tried to murder Jake, they would have a good go at Kelsey if they offered her a ride and took her somewhere even the roos avoided. A black belt wouldn't be worth a drop of water if someone got her lost in the back of beyond.

He was trapped by a woman who made Jake look cooperative in comparison.

"You're grinning," Kelsey observed.

Dillon sobered immediately. There was nothing to grin about. The situation was as volatile as a crate of gelignite in the Coober Pedy sun. Despite himself, however, he couldn't help but admire her stubborn courage. Jake might never recognize it, but Kelsey was a daughter to be proud of.

"If you're determined to come, I'll take you myself."

Kelsey considered his offer. "How do I know you won't leave me somewhere in the middle of the desert?"

He gave her credit for a healthy survival instinct. "You'll have to trust me, won't you?"

"Like my father did?"

"That would be too much to ask." Dillon casually touched her arm. "But you can start by trusting me enough to take you to the mine in the morning."

She realized she had little choice. "What time?"

"Eight. It's cooler then, though once we're down, it doesn't matter."

"I'll be waiting."

"I don't doubt it." Dillon watched her walk away. "Kelsey?"

Kelsey turned. "What?"

"Lock your door tonight."

She smiled at the advice and considered its sources. "Oh, I should be safe. Whoever tried to kill my father took him by surprise. I don't like surprises." She turned back to the door, carefully skirting the pool tables. In a moment she was gone.

"And some people think living here is dull," Melly said from behind Dillon.

At that moment Dillon would gladly have settled for dull. "Time to call it a night."

"I could check on her on the way home."

"Just don't take her by surprise, she might sever your head from your body." Dillon put his money on the counter to the sound of Melly's laughter and followed Kelsey's path.

From his station by the pub door, he watched her walk down the street and turn into the motel lot before he got in his ute and started home.

Chapter 4

At 7:15 the next morning Kelsey's sleep-fogged brain was between her knees, her curls sweeping the floor as she did stretching exercises to try to wake up. A knock on the door brought her upright. "Who's there?" she called.

"Melly."

She never would have expected Melanie Morel to be an early riser. "I'm coming." Kelsey padded sleepily across the floor and unlocked the door. Melanie stood on the other side dressed in more—and brighter—flowers than a botanical garden.

"I brought you a present." Melanie held out a steaming coffee cup and a plate covered with a napkin.

"Come on in." Kelsey took the dishes and ushered the other woman into the room.

"Is it safe?" Melanie eyed Kelsey's white *gi*, the traditional karate uniform. "Or will I be target practice?"

"I was just doing warm-ups. There's not enough room in here for anything lethal."

"You were pretty lethal last night."

Kelsey had awakened early that morning with a stinging sense of guilt. She had studied karate since she was eighteen, not as a passing fancy, but as a life-style. It had taught her more than self-defense skills, and one of the most important lessons she had learned was to be humble about her accomplishments. "I was pretty upset last night," she said, putting the dishes on the dresser and motioning toward the bed. "Have a seat."

"Go ahead and eat," Melanie told her, sprawling against the pillows. "While it's still hot."

Kelsey took the napkin off the plate and inhaled, her mouth watering. "Biscuits." Her eyes widened. "And grits and ham? Do they eat grits in Australia?"

"Not hardly. Believe it or not, we always ate them at home in Nebraska. My mother's from Georgia, so she keeps me supplied."

Kelsey sat in a vinyl wing chair and set the plate on her lap. "It was so nice of you to think of me."

"I wanted you to feel at home."

Kelsey looked up and smiled. Melanie was a psychedelic portrait against the sheets. Her off-the-shoulder peasant blouse was covered with blue and orange cabbage roses. Her skirt was a pattern of black and white stripes with giant sprigs of violets sprinkled over it. She wore purple rubber thongs on her delicate feet and opals on every finger. "Thank you."

"So how do you like town?"

Kelsey munched on a biscuit and contemplated the question. "Well, it's different," she said finally.

"Different as in awful." Melanie put her arms behind her head and leaned farther back. "Actually, it's not. There's a lot of spirit in Coober Pedy."

"How'd you end up here?" Kelsey started on the grits. She didn't have the heart to tell Melanie that she was one of the few people in North Carolina who thought they tasted like glue.

"I took a year off after college to travel. I met Gary in Perth just before I was supposed to go back home to take a job in my father's insurance company." She laughed good-naturedly. "Can you imagine me selling insurance? Anyway, Gary brought me back to Coober Pedy with him, and I've been here ever since."

Kelsey guessed that "ever since" had been a year or two. Melanie was about her own age. Gamely she swallowed the last of the grits. "You must like it if you've stayed."

Melanie rolled her eyes. "I like Gary. And when we get tired of the heat and the flies, we pack up and go down to Adelaide or over to Sydney for a holiday. But I'm always glad to come back."

Kelsey didn't ask why. If it weren't for people who enjoyed living on the frontier, the United States would sit squarely on Plymouth Rock, and Australia would be a few settlements rimming Botany Bay. "If you've been here that long," she said instead, "you must know my father fairly well."

"He's been a regular customer."

Kelsey didn't want to reveal much of her past, but neither did she want to lose this opportunity to find out a little more about Jake and Dillon. "I haven't seen him for some time," she said in a classic understatement. "He's always been a wanderer."

"He hasn't wandered much since he came to Coober Pedy. Some men come, stay a month or two, then leave, and we never see them again. I guess they get sick of going underground and chipping away at nothing. Not your father, though. You can say what you want about old Jake, but he sticks to it."

Kelsey guessed that was supposed to be a point in Jake's favor, although she wasn't sure why. Sticking to a marriage, sticking to a family, those were virtues. But chipping away at nothing? She set down the empty plate and picked up the coffee mug. The coffee was strong, the first good cup she'd had since crossing the International Date Line. "What else could you say about old Jake?" She smiled to show that she hadn't taken offense at the name.

"Oh, he's kind of quiet. Not shy, exactly, just quiet. He scowls a lot, like he's always got something on his mind. He doesn't make friends—except Dillon, of course—and he doesn't make enemies. Sometimes when he's had too much to drink he gets all loosened up, and he entertains us with Irish ditties. He's an honest-to-God barroom tenor."

Irish ditties. Kelsey swallowed more than her coffee. "And Dillon's his only friend?"

"Don't get me wrong, everybody likes Jake, it's just that he doesn't encourage friendships. You know?"

He hadn't encouraged family, either. As always, Kelsey was filled with a mixture of emotions. Love for the father she didn't know and sadness that he was who he was. "Tell me about Dillon."

"Oh, now there's a different story. Dillon encourages everybody to be his friend. He's every man's mate and every woman's fantasy."

"Not every woman's."

"Well, I did notice you two weren't exactly hitting it off."

Melanie didn't have to be too astute to figure that out. Kelsey continued probing. "You said he and my father were friends."

"Better than friends. Mates. I'll never believe Dillon had anything to do with Jake's fall."

Kelsey filed away the fact that Sergeant Newberry's suspicions were now common knowledge. "Why not?"

"Jake was like a father to Dillon, if you can imagine Jake being a father to anyone...." Melanie's voice trailed off. "I'm sorry," she said, obviously embarrassed. "I didn't mean that the way it sounded."

Kelsey waved aside her apology. "So they were close, but doesn't greed have strange effects on people? What if my father found opal in his share of the mine and Dillon wanted it?"

Melanie shrugged. "I guess stranger things have happened. I know Dillon and Jake have been fighting lately."

Kelsey suppressed a chill, but before she could follow up on Melanie's words, Melanie went on.

"But I like Dillon. No one with eyes that green could be a murderer. Not even for opal." Melanie pushed herself off the bed. "I'd better scat. I'm supposed to help Gary at the Showcase today, and I've still got some chores to do around here. The maid went walkabout."

"'Walkabout'?" Kelsey asked, only half following the conversation.

"Nell's an Aborigine. She works hard when she's here, but every once in a while she just takes off with her family. They go up into the Territory to be with their tribe and do whatever it is that Aborigines do. Drives Gary crazy, but me, well, I guess I understand. Someday Gary may wake up and find a note on my pillow, 'Gone walkabout.'"

Kelsey heard a note of seriousness behind Melanie's flip humor. "I'm sure he'd be sorry."

"For a second or to." Melanie grinned and the moment vanished. "I'll take the plate and cup back now and save myself a trip."

"Thanks for the breakfast." Kelsey smiled at the woman who had so easily become a friend. "Let's do lunch sometime."

Melanie laughed. "The Ritz or the Carlton, my dear?"

"One for soup and one for salad."

Melanie opened the door. "I'd settle for a hot dog stand. American hot dogs are one thing good old Mom can't ship." With another goodbye, she was gone.

Kelsey was still smiling when she stripped off her *gi* and stepped into the shower. Halfway through soaping her body clean, Melanie's words came back to her. Jake and Dillon had been fighting. The smile was immediately stored away with her initial trust in the man she was going to spend the day with.

Dillon knocked once, then twice. On the second knock Kelsey's door swung open. He frowned and stepped over the threshold. The light was off, and the shade on the small window was drawn shut. Kelsey's suitcase was nowhere to be seen.

Dillon snapped on the light and walked toward the center of the room. She was gone; there was no doubt about it. Even the bed was neatly made, as if the room had already been cleaned for another guest.

He was about to find someone to ask what was going on when the door to the bathroom creaked open. As Dillon watched a pair of well-filled blue jeans led the way, followed by a torso, naked except for the towel strung over a pair of delicate female shoulders. Topping the ensemble was a face with wide brown eyes and a head of glorious gold-red hair escaping another towel.

"How did you get in?" In little more than a second, Kelsey had wrapped the towel around her breasts like a Tahitian *pareau*. She tucked it tightly under her arms.

"I knocked, and the door opened. It wasn't locked." Dillon tried to remind himself that the offense had been serious, but all he could think about was the momentary glimpse of her lovely young breasts, breasts he could have cupped perfectly in his hands. He forced himself to speak without clearing his throat. "You were supposed to keep it locked."

"You can be sure I'll double-check next time." Kelsey knew her skin was tinged the hue of ripe apricots. "You don't mind if I get dressed, do you?" she asked.

The irony in her voice didn't escape Dillon. He called on his sense of humor to get him through the next charged moment. "I'd probably mind more if you didn't. We have a hard day ahead of us. I don't need a distraction."

"Far be it for me to be a distraction." She walked to the bed, careful not to get too close to him. She bent to pull her suitcase from under it, holding the towel firmly in place as she did. "I'll be out in a moment."

"Take your time." Dillon tried to divert his thoughts by surveying the room again once she was safely out of sight. There was absolutely no sign that anyone had spent the night here. No wrinkle on the bedspread, no visible item of clothing or toiletries. Even the ashtray was set exactly in the middle of the nightstand, as if the distance had been measured on all sides. He stooped to examine the suitcase. Lifting the top he let his gaze roam over Kelsey's possessions. Every item of clothing was folded neatly and separated by immaculate layers of tissue paper. Smaller items were out of sight in labeled fabric pouches. He replaced the top and stood, wondering what such extreme neatness said about Kelsey's personality. He wondered if she ever felt at home enough anywhere to make a mess. What had happened to her? Where had she lived after Jake's desertion?

The door creaked again, and Kelsey came back into the room. "I'm almost ready."

She had plaited her hair into a long braid, but the shorter top and sides were a riot of curls around her face. As he watched she sat on the bed to pull on tennis shoes.

Although she was now dressed, Dillon couldn't get the image of Kelsey's half-naked body and startled brown eyes out of his mind. He had never seen skin so lovely, never felt such an urgent desire to run his hands along a woman's slender curves to see if they felt as soft as they looked. He'd had his share of lovers, but he couldn't remember this fierce need. He was an action awaiting a conclusion, and the strength of the feeling disturbed him.

Kelsey felt Dillon's eyes on her. She wasn't oblivious to the tension in the room. She felt it, too. In fact she had felt it ever since some childish, willful, foolish part of her had been pleased by Dillon's expression when he'd seen her half-undressed. "You're staring."

Dillon realized she was right. "You'll need sturdier shoes."

"This is all I have with me."

His eyes flickered up to the peach blouse she had worn the night before. He forced himself to ignore what it covered. "And that shirt won't last a day."

"Then I'll have to buy another, won't I?" Kelsey knew better than to argue with Dillon's prediction. The blouse was lightweight cotton, perfect for a North Carolina summer of lemonade drinking and fly swatting. The shoes were thin and cheap, pulled from a discount store sale bin. Nothing she owned had been made for the punishment of opal mining.

"You'll find our stores expensive. Merchandise is brought in from the south. It's hauled a fair distance."

She had tried to put her financial worries out of her mind, but Dillon's words brought them back. "I guess I don't have much choice."

"Not if you're really going to spend some time in the Rainbow Fire. Of course, if this is just a whim, you could save yourself a good bit of cash."

She stood. "I don't have whims."

He tried not to smile. "I believe you."

"I'm ready."

"I'm not," he said, giving up the battle and liberating a grin. "But I guess my choices are between zero and nothing."

"That about sums it up," she said, trying to ignore the grin *and* the man.

Outside the sun was already baking the earth. If there had been a dewfall, it was only a memory. Every breath Kelsey took seemed to crackle in her lungs. She would have given some of her tightly guarded cash for ten percent humidity.

Silently she followed Dillon to his truck. Green and silver, it was a dusty, battered vehicle with a long metal grid across the front. Dillon turned the key and it roared to life like Frankenstein's monster. He pulled out to the road with a screech and squeal of tires, caused more by loose gravel in the lot than adolescent theatrics.

"I forgot to tell you to bring something to eat. Not a single tea room or deli out in the field."

Kelsey didn't tell him that she was going to be skipping lunch until she was safely back in Raleigh. She just nodded. "I'll be fine."

"You won't be fine. You'll be hungry. The work's hard, and there's nothing much to think about except the next meal. I'll share with you today. Tomorrow you bring your own."

"I'll be fine."

He shot her another grin. "You're a hard case."

The town was already behind them. Kelsey looked out over the monotonous landscape and tried to forget the man beside her. After only twenty-four hours in the outback she was starved for the sight of a tree. Grass would have been nice, and the blue shimmer of a lake even better.

"Doesn't the harshness of this country get to you?" she asked, glancing at Dillon. "It's so desolate."

"There's a certain beauty if you let yourself see it."

"Children born here wouldn't know about woods and meadows."

"Children born in cities don't always know about woods and meadows, either. And children born in woods and meadows don't know about deserts or skyscrapers."

"Why were you and my father fighting?"

Dillon swerved off the blacktop onto a dirt road. The truck rattled and jarred them with each bump. "You'll have to get used to these roads."

Kelsey hung tightly to the seat's edge, trying not to crack her head on the windshield. "You could slow down."

"The bumps get worse that way. This way we fly over the top."

If there was a spark of sense in his answer, Kelsey couldn't see it.

"Do you always bash people with nasty questions in the middle of a pleasant conversation?" Dillon continued once they had reached a slightly smoother stretch of road.

"If I need to."

"Where did you hear that Jake and I had been fighting?"

"Not your concern."

"I could say the same."

She laughed humorlessly. "Your fights with my father are my concern. They might be Sergeant Newberry's, too."

"There weren't any fights."

Kelsey hung on tighter as Dillon swerved to miss a huge hole in the middle of the road. If rain ever fell and filled the hole with water, Kelsey knew she would have the lake she yearned for.

When the ride was only normally jolting again, she continued. "I've heard there were fights. Did my father want to keep all the money from the sale of his opals?"

"Keeping all the money never entered his mind."

"That's hard to believe."

"Not if you know Jake. Money's not important to your father. The fun stopped the minute the opals were out of the dirt." Dillon volleyed friendly honks with an approaching truck. Kelsey lifted a hand to wave back at the smiling driver and ended up in a heap against Dillon's thigh. She had an instant impression of heat and strength before he spoke. "Comfortable?"

"As comfortable as being staked out on an ant hill." Kelsey slid back to the other side of the truck. "About the fights...."

He risked a quick glance. She was staring straight ahead and nothing could have pried her fingers off the dashboard. "You know, Kelsey, I don't want you here. But if you're going to stay, we can make the best or the worst of it. Yammering at each other is the worst of it."

"I want to know why you were fighting with my father."

Dillon knew that a piece of truth was the only thing that was going to silence her questions. "We weren't fighting, but I've been trying to get him to cut down on boozing. After he found the stones Jake was a different man—for a while. Then when he kept looking and found nothing else, he started hitting the bottle so hard I was having to drag him out of bed every morning and the pub every night."

Dillon's story made a certain kind of sense, considering what Kelsey knew about Jake. "And that was all?"

Dillon regretted having to lie, but he didn't want Kelsey to know everything about her father. She should have some illusions. He didn't want to be the one to tell her that Jake might have brought his misfortune on himself. "That was all."

Kelsey stared straight ahead at the unchanging scenery. She fought her inclination to believe him. Although she was trying hard to be wary of Dillon and to take Sergeant Newberry's accusations seriously, she knew she wasn't succeeding. Dillon was a charmer, one minute the rugged outback miner, the next an engaging rogue with a heart-stopping grin. But even more important, there was an honesty and warmth that flowed from him. Even with all her reasons to be suspicious, it was becoming increasingly difficult to confront him.

Dillon read her silence correctly. "You know, Kelsey, when we're fifty feet under the earth, you're going to have to trust me. There's no room for karate down there. I outweigh you by a good five stone, and I can sit on you if I'm forced to. Once we're down that shaft, we're mates. No room for suspicions, no room for fears."

"But enough room for murder." Kelsey let herself scrutinize his profile. There was nothing there to frighten any woman—at least, nothing to make her fear for her life. There was only strength and hard masculinity. Sensitivity and humor. And honor. She hadn't found honor in Sergeant Newberry's face. And she was trained—well-trained—to look for it. She could trust her training and her intuition, or she could trust a policeman with an ax to grind.

Or, more typically, she could avoid trusting anyone. At least for now.

"If you're really afraid I'll murder you," Dillon said, "I'd advise you to stay above ground and boil the billy when I go below."

"That doesn't sound very savory."

Dillon detected her lighter tone. He guessed a decision had been made. "We won't stay down long today. Just long enough to show you the ropes."

"And who's going to boil poor Billy?"

Dillon glanced at Kelsey. There was almost a smile on her face. He realized how much he wanted to see one. "I'll boil the billy and show you how. We'll make an Aussie of you."

"Like you made one of Jake?"

"Jake made one of himself."

"I suppose that makes me half-Aussie, doesn't it?"

"Which half?"

She couldn't help smiling. "Does it matter?"

He heard the smile in her voice, but it was gone by the time he turned his head again. "It might if I ever take a notion to trespass on foreign territory."

"Take no notions, Dillon. One hundred percent of me is foreign territory and strictly off-limits."

"There's a man, then?"

"No man."

He wondered why. Kelsey was one of the most striking women he had ever seen. Her strong features, butterscotch hair and peaches-and-cream complexion radiated vitality, while her soft brown eyes exposed a certain unconscious vulnerability that stirred him deeply. And he knew other men had been stirred, too. They must have been.

"There *was* someone, you fought, and now you're put off by men," he guessed out loud.

"Wrong, wrong and right. Are we almost there?"

"Another mile." Dillon pulled over to let the vehicle coming toward him have a wider berth.

"What on earth is that?" Kelsey stared at the huge machine flagged with fluorescent banners and a Wide Load sign. It resembled a semi with a giant's trash can hanging upside down from a diagonal scaffold.

"A blower. A sort of vacuum cleaner for miners. The fan draws mullock out of the shaft, and it collects in that bin at the top until it's emptied."

"Do you have one?"

"Jake and I are part of a cooperative. We share equipment. A bit slower that way, but less dear." Dillon stretched his arm across the back of Kelsey's seat, but he was careful not to touch her. "So there's no man, hasn't been a man, but you're off men anyway?"

Kelsey eased herself forward, turning as she did. "Why does it matter?"

"I suppose it doesn't. Yet."

"Sometimes three letter words can be as obscene as four."

His smile was slow and easy. "You've been asking all the questions, Kelsey. I thought it was my turn."

"I've been asking about my father, not about you."

"What would you like to know?"

"Not a thing."

"I'd like to know about you."

"There's nothing to tell."

Without conscious permission his fingers slipped forward to weave into the strands of her braid. "Where did the red hair come from?"

"My father." She shook her head, and reluctantly he let his hand slide back to the seat. "Has Jake's hair been white since you've known him?"

"Always. And there's no red in his beard."

"The blower is gone," she observed.

Dillon forced both hands to the steering wheel and pulled back onto the road. He was curiously reluctant to let the intimacy of the moment pass. "Tell me about your mother."

"There's not much to tell."

"I'll wager there's something."

Kelsey remembered little about Mary Donovan, but, surprisingly, she found herself sharing it with Dillon. "She laughed a lot, and she was always sure Jake was coming back. When I was five she was killed trying to stop a neighbor's child from chasing a cat into the street. I had relatives who were sure she'd done it just to spite them."

He hated to think what that said about the rest of Kelsey's childhood. "And you never saw Jake again?"

"He stopped writing after my mother died. Before that I remember we'd get letters from places I'd never heard of, but my mother would pull out my little globe and show me where he was. She took in children to make enough money to feed us, and she waited for Jake. She never gave up hope." Kelsey didn't add that it was only years later that she had lost hope, too. Jake's return was a dream that had died hard.

Dillon was sure that once Kelsey was alone again, she would chide herself for telling him so much. He didn't want to make her regrets worse, so he changed the subject. "When we get to the mine, have a look around while I unload our equipment. Just watch where you set every foot. Jake and I are right good about marking our shafts, but not everyone is. You can be on solid ground one moment and at the bottom of a hole in the next."

"I'll be careful. What would it do to your reputation if two Donovans ended up unconscious in the Rainbow Fire?"

Dillon swung the ute around and turned off the engine. His grin was a warm caress. "I can't say about my reputation, but the Donovans wouldn't be able to hold their heads up, would they?"

Trying to ignore the grin that was doing funny things to her stomach, Kelsey opened her door and stepped down, checking the ground at her feet first. Since they had entered the mining field, the vista had changed. There were conical heaps of dirt as tall or taller than a man scattered over the flat plain. Machinery of all sizes lay in various stages of repair, although some particularly abused pieces looked as if they would never be used again.

Proceeding with caution, Kelsey wove her way in and out of the accumulated junk that littered the area between machines and hills. Crumpled sheets of corrugated iron, metal barrels, two-by-fours and the sadly rusted shell of a jeep were a maze of man-made eyesores. Something pink caught her eyes, and

she bent over to see one lovely pale flower growing in the shade
thrown by the jeep's running board.

"Ready?"

Kelsey was startled. For a moment she had forgotten all
about Dillon. Now he was standing right beside her, and she
could feel the brush of his leg against hers as he stooped. She
gestured to the flower. "How can anything grow out here?"

His voice held the same note of wonder as hers. "It's hard to
imagine, I know, but millennia ago, when water flowed freely,
this was a fertile plain. Before that it was a vast cretaceous sea."
Dillon's eyes took on a faraway gleam. "Come swim with me,
Kelsey."

Kelsey straightened and tried to break the spell he was casting. "You haven't been out in the sun long enough to get
crazy."

He straightened, too, and moved closer. His words were
spoken softly. "Come swim with me, Kelsey. Come see the
ocean's treasures."

And this was the man who was supposed to have pushed Jake
down a mine shaft? Kelsey searched Dillon's face. For that
moment he was a dreamy-eyed visionary. "Swim under the
earth?"

"Treasures no man has ever seen."

"I don't know what you mean."

"You've no imagination?" He shrugged. "Then come dig in
the dirt with me, and help me gather some specimens of silica."

For a moment Kelsey had seen a glimpse of the real man under the veneer of casual good humor. She doubted many people glimpsed that man. An outback dreamer clad in worn
denim and rainbow-fire hope.

She was a dreamer, too, although no one knew it. She had
lived her life dreaming of the things she would have one day.
Love, the warmth of laughter, acceptance. Now the lure of his
dreams was impossible to ignore. For just a moment she abandoned the caution that had long ago taken the place of visions
and stepped closer. "What will I see if I come?"

He saw her lower the steel shield that protected her from
everything and everyone. Vulnerability and hope shone in her
desert-brown eyes. His gaze melted into hers, and he lifted a
hand to her hair, brushing a curl off her cheek before he answered. "We'll descend through time, through the history of

this continent. We'll touch an earth no man ever walked upon and swim through seas no whale ever knew.''

She couldn't pull her eyes from his. "And find opals fit for the queen?''

His fingers lingered on her cheek. "Fire and all the colors of the spectrum, eternally doomed to darkness if we don't bring them to the light.''

She wanted to cover his hand and hold the rough tips of his fingers against her skin. Instead she thrust her own hands into her pockets. But she couldn't stop her words. "I'll swim with you.''

"You'll trust me enough to go down with me?''

She nodded.

His hand dropped to his side, but his smile warmed her instead. "Then I'll show you a world you haven't seen before.''

Just before caution intruded once more, Kelsey let herself wonder if the world Dillon was going to show her extended far beyond the perimeters of the Rainbow Fire.

Chapter 5

Access to the Rainbow Fire was by a series of vertical steel ladders. Each nine-foot section was hooked to the section above it and secured to the side of the meter-wide shaft. Kelsey had never seen a narrower ladder. She listened with little enthusiasm to the whine of the generator that would power the lights for her descent.

"I'll carry a torch, too, just in case something goes wrong with the lights. We've been having problems with a short in the line somewhere. I'll go first." Dillon replaced his battered felt hat with a bright yellow hard hat. He threw one just like it to a doubtful-looking Kelsey. "This is Jake's. I reckon he won't mind you wearing it. You shouldn't go down without one, though nearly everybody does."

Kelsey set the hat on her head. It was too large, but when she removed the hat to adjust it, she saw she was doomed. It couldn't be made any smaller. On her curls again, it tilted toward her nose, and she pushed it back, aware that that was how she was destined to spend the day.

Dillon ignored her difficulty. After their moments of intimacy, Kelsey had given him a wide berth every time he had gotten within feet of her. He suspected it was just as well. This was no time for intimacy. Not with a murderer on the loose.

Not with a police sergeant who wanted badly to convict him of causing Jake's accident. And not with Kelsey herself suspecting the worst. If Kelsey wanted a return to their former distance, perhaps she was the smarter of the two.

"Tell me now if you're afraid of heights or closed-in places," he shouted over the noise of the generator.

Kelsey had a more than healthy respect for both, but she wasn't going to tell Dillon. She knew fear well. It was the taste of copper when you fought an opponent with better speed and coordination than your own. It was watching the edge of a foot coming toward you and knowing you could do nothing but absorb the blow. Fear was something you lived with, and, in the end, you performed better because of it. She made a megaphone of her hands. "I'll be fine."

"I take it that's your motto. Just promise me I won't have to carry you back up the ladder."

"No one's ever had to carry me anywhere."

Dillon thought that was a shame, but he didn't say so. Independence was a virtue, but pushed to an extreme it could be a handicap. He had known his share of old-timers, swagmen who had wandered their whole lives through the outback, living off the land and an occasional station job. Sadly, once, years before, he had also discovered the bones of one, picked clean by dingoes and crows, off on a trail where no one had been for months. Bones and a swag rolled around a fresh change of clothes that protected the tattered photograph of a woman. The man had lived an independent life. But Dillon knew he had died lonely.

"There's not much I can tell you that will help," he said, pushing the thought away. "Put one foot under the other and hold on tight. I promise the bottom is there."

She opened her mouth, but Dillon interrupted. "And yes, I know. You'll be fine." Without another word he stepped over the collar of corrugated iron surrounding the shaft and onto the ladder. In a moment he had disappeared.

Kelsey didn't know how long it took to climb down a fifty-foot ladder, but she did know she was going to wait until Dillon signaled her. The last thing she wanted to do was put a foot on his head. She inhaled deeply, aware that this would be the last fresh air to fill her lungs until she came back out of the meter-wide hole in the earth. A noise from the road running into the field made her raise her head. A red truck, decidedly more battered than Dillon's, was arriving in a cloud of dust. She watched as the truck skirted the field, then pulled up to park near the mine.

Through the dust-coated windshield Kelsey could see that the driver was Serge.

Serge of the drunken groping and Jimmy Cagney accent. Serge, who she had felled with one well-aimed blow. Kelsey knew it was too late to start down the ladder. As she waited for him to get out of the truck, she planned her strategy.

"H'lo, doll."

"Good morning, Serge." He was still far away, but even from a distance she could see that his eyes were narrowed slits.

"Whatcha doing here?"

"Half this mine belongs to my father." Kelsey watched Serge come closer until he was standing only a few yards away. "I'm going down to see it with Dillon Ward. You know Dillon?"

"Yeah. You laid me out good last night, doll."

"You were pretty drunk."

His eyes narrowed further until they were hardly open. "You wanna try it again?"

She shook her head. Kelsey knew she was on the line. If he thought she was afraid, he would probably come after her. If he thought she was cocky, he would probably come after her even faster. "I don't want to try anything," she said pleasantly. "You're a big, strong man, Serge. I got lucky last night. Of course, I could get lucky again, but I'd rather not take the chance. Neither one of us needs to get hurt over this, do we?"

"I didn't get that kiss."

"I'll just bet this town's full of women waiting to kiss you," she said soothingly.

"Yeah." He watched her for a moment, then turned to walk back toward his truck. Kelsey saw more dust on the horizon, and in a minute Serge had been joined by another man, a beefy blonde wearing shorts and no shirt. Serge gestured toward her, but neither man moved.

A voice from below interrupted her speculations. Over the noise of the generator she wasn't sure what Dillon had yelled, but she guessed it was the equivalent of "come on down."

Holding tightly to the shaft rim, she levered herself onto the ladder. She had been up and down ladders before, but never one that was absolutely vertical and narrower than she was. She felt for the next rung. It was lower than she had expected it to be, and she felt her first pang of uncertainty. Still holding tight, she felt for the next rung. Then the next.

There was no light below, and the light above was only about a yard-wide patch of blue sky. Kelsey kept her eyes focused on the spot of blue as she descended, watching it get smaller and smaller until it was nothing more than an iridescent halo.

Why weren't the lights on? Kelsey knew if she were descending into light she wouldn't be as frightened. But now her palms were damp, sliding along the dust-slicked aluminum frame as if they were oiled. She didn't dare dry her hands on her jeans for fear she would slip. Nothing stood between her and a quick descent except forty feet of steps.

From somewhere far below her she heard a curse. She wanted to call down to Dillon for reassurance, but her pride stopped her. Moments ago in the sunlight she had let her emotions rule. Now darkness and fear pulled her back to reality. Dillon was the man accused of trying to murder her father. His charm was worth nothing, and her vulnerability had been inexcusable.

Her foot slipped on the next rung, and for a moment she hung suspended with nothing but her hands to break her fall. Her wet palms slid down the frame and she slipped several feet before her toe caught another rung. With her whole body trembling, she clung to the ladder, biting her lip. The circle of sky overhead was no larger than a silver dollar, the void below a bottomless pit.

There was nothing to do but continue down. She could not give in to her fear, could not let Dillon win this round. She had only her courage to see her through. And it was only courage that might help her father.

Still trembling, she found another rung, then another. She began to count, visualizing the hypnotic series of kicks and punches that began each training session in her karate *dojo*. Clearing her mind of anything else, she put one foot below the other and descended into nothingness.

The last step was the longest, and the most difficult. She gasped when her foot dangled in mid-air, finally touching earth. In a split second she felt the press of Dillon's body.

"Kelsey?" For a moment Dillon's arms closed around her as if to make sure it was her.

"You were expecting someone else?" She didn't like the sound of her voice. Her struggle for courage was in it.

He uttered a string of words that taught her Australian cursing was very close to American. "I wasn't expecting anyone," he finished up. "I yelled up to you to stay above."

"I'm sorry." And she was. Desperately sorry that for no good reason she had just undergone an experience destined to live in her memory forever.

"The bloody lights went out when I'd gotten about halfway. That short in the cord, I reckon."

"You've got a flashlight, don't you?"

Her answer was a thin stream of light playing along mottled rust-colored walls that closed along the narrow passageway. "Turns out the battery's a bit weak. I'm trying to conserve it. I've got candles to light in another chamber." He flicked off the light and returned the mine to darkness.

Kelsey's reaction was to grab his arm. "Can't you keep it on?"

"Not while we're standing here. If I do, it won't get me to the chamber where the candles are." Unerringly he touched her cheek in reassurance. "I'm sorry. No one knows what black is until they're at the bottom of a mine."

She was unwilling to lose that bit of human warmth. She gripped his arm tighter. "No."

Dillon felt the fine tremors in her hand, the clamminess of her skin. And he remembered the first time he had descended into an unending void. It took little effort or thought to pull her close. His hand hovered over her hair, then dove into it, loosening her braid and spreading the thick wealth over her shoulders.

Kelsey's token resistance lasted only a moment. Then, gratefully, she leaned against him and absorbed his warmth. For that instant she was just a woman who needed comfort. And Dillon was the man she wanted to give it to her. He was strong, yet he held her as if she were as precious as his beloved opal. She felt the rough caress of cotton against her cheek and smelled the fragrance of sunshine. She shut her eyes so she could pretend that when she opened them she would be standing on the good earth instead of inside it. "I'll be all right in a minute."

"I know." Dillon thought about strength and decided that the greatest strength was to know when you needed help. He knew few women—few men, either—who would have climbed down a fifty-foot ladder into nothingness, knowing that danger might wait for them at the bottom. Kelsey was the most courageous woman he knew, and that, added to this momentary vulnerability, made her unbelievably attractive.

It was only a matter of seconds before he felt her body change from pure acquiescence to resistance. The process fascinated him. One moment she was curled against him like the cat who lived on his front porch, the next she was rigidity itself. "Kelsey Donovan," he murmured. "One part warm woman, one part warrior."

She tried to pull away, but there was no place to go. She had felt comfort change to something else, and she wasn't even sure if the change had radiated from her or from Dillon. All she knew was that his strong, warm arms could easily become habit-forming. And he was a habit that might be as insidiously dangerous as the most addictive drug. "Let's find those candles."

"Is there anyone you'd trust enough to hold you when you're scared?"

"You've held me more than any man." Kelsey put her hands against Dillon's chest as a warning. "And I trust you less."

If her words were true, she'd never had a lover. Dillon felt desire explode through his body at the thought. Desire was quickly followed by chagrin. Innocence had tantalized the nineteenth-century man. Dillon lived in a nineteenth-century town, but he was all twentieth century. What throwback part of him was even interested? Under the circumstances, Kelsey was as off-limits as his neighbor's mine.

And if that was true, why hadn't he let go of her? "You have reason not to trust me," he said quietly. "I'm not sure I trust myself."

Kelsey felt the ladder pressing into her back. "Dillon," she warned.

He told himself he was going to let her go. He wondered if she was sophisticated enough to note the changes in his body.

"Dillon," she repeated.

He forced himself to release her. He stepped back, wishing he could put even more room between them. But there was a small matter of claystone walls keeping them in touching distance. "I'm going to turn on the torch. You can follow me to get the candles or stay here. Because of the shaft it's not as dark here as in the rest of the mine. I can't guarantee the torch will last the whole way."

She was nerves waiting to jangle. And not just from the darkness and frightening climb. "Why didn't you put in fresh batteries?"

He smiled a little at her tone. "Because I can find my way around the Rainbow Fire in the dark, and it doesn't frighten me."

She worked hard to put emotional distance between them, since physical distance was out of the question. "Maybe you wanted to frighten me."

"If I wanted to frighten you, Kelsey, there would be better ways to do it." He flicked on the light and started along the main drive. "Come on, if you're coming."

Kelsey watched the weak beam of light bob along the mottled walls. Indecision ripped at her. Then she was following close behind him.

Dillon decided to act as if nothing had happened. "We keep our equipment stored over this way, in a drive that duffered out. We'll get the candles, then maybe I can find out what's wrong with the lights."

"That would be nice."

He chuckled at the understatement. Several feet ahead something caught his eye, and he bent to examine it. Kelsey plowed into him, and he had all he could do to keep from sprawling forward.

Kelsey was immediately contrite. "I'm sorry." She listened to the hollow sound of her voice bouncing off the walls. "I'm too close, I guess."

"I'll warn you next time I stop." Dillon straightened and held the object in his hand. It was a comb, and he had never seen it before in his life. He pocketed it to consider later. The beam from his torch wavered sadly. "We'd better get going," he advised, "before we're in the dark."

"There aren't any beams holding this mine up."

"The rock holds it up. We don't need timbers. Do you see how cool it is down here? This is why we live underground."

Somewhere between the ladder and the supply area, Kelsey realized just how defenseless she would be if the flashlight went out, Dillon disappeared into the resulting void, and she was left with nothing and no one to guide her back to the ladder. Even the mine shaft could be blocked to smother all traces of sunlight.

"I saw Serge before I came down," she said, forcing herself to speak nonchalantly.

"Serge is a good bloke to stay away from."

"The town seems filled with people like that."

He hooted in delight. "You don't want to stay away from me. I stand between you and total darkness."

"You could leave me down here in the dark, I suppose, but Melly knows I came here with you today, and Serge saw me climbing down."

"And I had such plans," he teased.

"I guess you'll have to put them on hold."

"Abso-bloody-lutely. I'll just have to come up with something else. Maybe I'll pull out my old Agatha Christies to get a fresh idea."

Unwillingly, Kelsey felt herself smile. "Where on earth are we going?"

"Right here." Dillon came to an abrupt halt. This time he was prepared for Kelsey to plow into him, and he wasn't disappointed. "A bit spooked, are we?"

"I'm looking forward to candlelight," she admitted.

"I like my candlelight with a thick Porterhouse and a beautiful woman." He turned and gave her an appreciative smile. "All I need is the Porterhouse."

"The candles."

"The candles." Ducking, Dillon crawled into a space no more than three feet high. "It'll be dark for a moment. Just close your eyes and count to fifty. I'll be out by then."

Kelsey was reminded of a birthday party she had once attended where she had been blindfolded while the other children hid. When she had finally removed the blindfold, it was to find that the children had all gone next door to play.

"I'm coming after you on fifty-one," she warned.

"You'll seal me in if you do."

"How do I know that hole in the wall doesn't lead right back to the shaft?"

Dillon backed out and turned to face her. "You don't. You'll have to trust me. You know the word, don't you, Kelsey?"

"Five letter words can be as obscene as four."

Her expression was as nonchalant as her tone, but Dillon could see signs of inner turmoil. He bit back harsh words and touched her cheek instead. "Fifty, Kelsey. I'll try to be back in forty."

She had no choice but to watch him crawl back into the tunnel. Her eyes were tightly shut, and she had just reached thirty-seven, when she felt a hand touch her shoulder. "You can open your eyes," Dillon said. "And see a truly lovely sight."

The passage was bathed in the glow of candles. Dillon had lit three, setting two at the mouth of the supply area. He handed the other to her.

Kelsey took the candle and watched its flickering patterns against the rust and cream dappled walls. "Lovely," she murmured, "but not as lovely as sunshine."

"You'll get used to being down here."

"What happens next?"

Dillon was mesmerized by the glow of Kelsey's skin in candlelight. The flame warmed and deepened the peach blush of her complexion and set her hair on fire. What happened next? Next he gave himself a lecture about the young woman who half-believed he had tried to murder her father. Next he reminded himself that he was here to mine opals, not to start something that couldn't be finished.

"Next I fix the lights," he said, turning his back on her to pick up the other candles. "Then I'll give you a tour of the mine. That should be enough exposure for today."

Kelsey watched Dillon amble back the way they had come. She had no reason to follow him so closely this time. Her candle shone brightly, and there were no drafts to extinguish it. She kept Dillon in sight, but she stayed well behind him. Kelsey had seen the softening of his gaze as he stared at her. She had seen enough desire to recognize it, if not to understand it.

She had never really cared what men saw in her, and, until now, she had hardly paid attention to it. When Dillon looked at her that way, however, it was hard not to pay attention.

Dillon Ward. He had seen her at her most defenseless, and she could almost blame the warmth in his eyes on his mistaken belief that he needed to protect her. She knew from experience that men were most comfortable when they felt superior. She also knew how angry they could be if they discovered they weren't.

No one had made the mistake of underestimating her for a long time. She had learned the hard way never to show signs of weakness, and the word had gotten out that Kelsey Donovan was nobody's easy mark. But how did that image reconcile with the woman Dillon had seen in the last twenty-four hours? She had almost fainted in his arms from heatstroke. She had leaned against him at the hospital, letting him absorb some of the impact of the bad news about Jake. She had flagrantly violated her own ethics by demonstrating her defense skills in front of him, and just today she had let him comfort her when the dark of the mine overwhelmed her.

Dillon had seen a Kelsey Donovan no one else had seen in a very long time. She had acted like a wimp.

"Wimp?" Dillon stopped, waiting for Kelsey to catch up.

She couldn't believe she had spoken her thoughts out loud. "Do you know the term?"

"It's one of those tidbits of American slang that sounds like what it is."

"I'm not a wimp, Dillon. It's too bad I've been acting like one."

He wanted to tell her that she was one of the bravest women he'd ever known. He wanted to tell her to go easier on herself, that accepting her weaknesses was as important as nurturing her strengths. Instead he just shrugged. "No worries."

She was at a loss for anything else to say. "So what can I do while you fix the lights?"

"Why don't you explore? You can't really get lost, everything converges on the main passage eventually. If you do get turned around, just give me a yell, and I'll come looking for you." He reached into his pocket and handed her a pack of matches and another candle. "Just in case."

Half an hour later Kelsey was wandering through one of the tunnels that honeycombed the mine when Dillon found her. She had wandered through the low-ceilinged tunnels, smoothing her fingertips along claystone ridges that swirled in muted color. She had picked at protruding pebbles with her fingernails and pretended they were opals. She had begun—just a little—to understand why Jake Donovan had stayed in Coober Pedy. The Rainbow Fire hummed a siren's song.

"The lights are beyond fixing," Dillon said with no preliminary greeting. "I'm going to have to replace them."

"I'm sorry."

"Found any opals?"

The corners of her mouth turned up in a reluctant smile. "Not a one. But then, a chunk could fall on my head, and I might not recognize it."

He smiled at the rueful note in her voice. "We'll make a gouger out of you next time we come down."

"Not likely, but we can give it a shot."

Dillon took note of her sadly shortened candle. He had planned to show Kelsey more, but today wasn't going to be the day. Strangely enough, he was reluctant to leave. There was an intimacy about being under the earth together that he would be sorry to lose. "Ready to see the sky again?"

She was more than ready, although she wasn't going to tell him. "I suspect climbing up will be easier than climbing down."

"I'll be right behind you." By dwindling candlelight Dillon led her through the passageway to the ladder. With one foot on the bottom rung, he peered up at the shaft, his face creased by a frown. "There's a bloody joker loose, it seems."

Kelsey looked up, too. Instead of a blue dot of sky, there was nothing. She hadn't realized how much she had counted on seeing that small slice of heaven. "What happened?"

"Somebody's idea of fun. The shaft's sealed up tight as a miser's wallet."

Chapter 6

W hat do you mean, it's sealed up?" Kelsey forced herself to remain calm.

"Somebody's covered the shaft with something."

"How hard will it be to remove it?"

Dillon shrugged. "Depends on what it is. I'll have to go up first and see."

"That means leaving me here alone."

Sympathy shone in his eyes. "I'm sorry. There's nothing for it."

Suspicions gathered like clouds before a rainstorm. "You were here all that time trying to fix the lights. Didn't you notice it was covered then?"

"It wasn't covered then."

Kelsey didn't want to believe it, but she knew that Dillon would have had the time to climb the ladder, pull something over the shaft, then climb back down. Her mind was racing along the worst possible path when Dillon stopped her with a frustrated wave of his hand.

"Look, Kelsey, I'm not going to climb up the ladder un-block the shaft, climb out, then cover it again. If I wanted to leave you in the mine alone, I'd have done all that while you were off wandering. I'd never have come to find you and lead you back here."

She wasn't sure she was thinking clearly, but what he said made sense, even when she tried to poke holes through it.

Frustrated when she didn't respond, Dillon put his hands on Kelsey's shoulders and forcibly moved her to one side. "I'm getting tired of your suspicions," he said. "I ought to leave you down here just to shut you up." He started up the ladder with the ease of a man who did it every day.

She bristled. "That wouldn't shut me up. I'd scream."

"And who'd hear you? Your good mate, Serge? It was probably Serge who threw iron over the shaft."

Kelsey hadn't had time to point the finger at anyone but Dillon. Now, as she paused to think, his words made sense. "Do you really think so?" she asked finally.

Dillon was already halfway up. "*I* think it was Serge. *You* think it was me. Who's to say?"

"I don't think it was you," she yelled up at him. "You're right. You would have left me wandering around."

His voice sounded far away. "Too blooming bad I missed my chance."

Kelsey felt suddenly very alone. Dillon had disappeared into the darkness. She looked at the candle in her hand and saw that she had little more than an inch to go. The candleholder was a pool of sickly white wax. What would Dillon do if he couldn't move what blocked the shaft? "Come on, Dillon," she muttered. She wondered how he would find enough purchase on the ladder to thrust anything off the top. He would have to hold on with one hand while he pushed. She wondered how he would do it. She wondered if he could do it.

Her thoughts were interrupted by a shouted command.

"Set the candle on the floor right before you start up. If you're lucky it won't burn out and leave you in the dark. About halfway you'll have some sky to help."

Kelsey looked up and saw the silver dollar patch of blue. Then her candle was on the floor and she was ten feet in the air before she even had time to think about what she was doing. The trip up the ladder was just as precarious as the trip down had been, but she was ascending into sunshine and fresh air. She almost flew.

At the top she grasped the timbers supporting the metal collar and lifted herself out to the unbelievably sweet earth. She was still rejoicing silently when she realized that Dillon was nowhere to be seen.

"Dillon?" Her jubilation began to fade. She spun and noted that his truck was still where he had parked it. He hadn't driven off and left her, but neither was he anywhere in sight. "Dillon?" she called a little louder.

She saw a movement behind a scrub-covered ridge to one side. Determined to catch up with him, she headed in that direction, carefully watching her step. When she had just crossed the first ridge she saw him coming back over a second. He looked up, and she got the distinct impression that his smile was a cover-up for some darker emotion.

"So you made it, did you?" he asked.

"What are you doing over here?"

He appeared to be thinking of an answer. "Checking some tracks," he said finally. "They didn't lead to anything."

Kelsey knew he was lying. And she knew something more. Dillon didn't often lie, or he would be better at it. "What were you really doing?"

She had her hands on her hips, and her clothes and skin were covered with a fine haze of dust a shade darker than her hair. Dillon would have admired the effect if he hadn't been so enraged. "Leave it, Kelsey. You don't really want to know."

"You'd be surprised." Kelsey stepped around him and started over the second ridge, but Dillon caught her easily.

"Don't. It's not a pretty sight."

She shook off his hands only to have them settle on her shoulders again with more force. "What isn't?"

He regretted having to tell her almost as much as he regretted not finding Serge in the act of blocking the shaft. He would accuse, and Serge would deny. In the end, Dillon would be left with no satisfaction.

"There was a piece of iron blocking the shaft," he said slowly. "But I didn't reckon on what would be weighing it down."

Kelsey frowned, no longer fighting him. "What was?"

"A dead roo. A female. Someone shot her straight through the heart."

"That'll be thirty-four dollars fifty." The friendly man at the Miner's Store wrapped Kelsey's new hard hat and khaki work shirt in brown paper, tying the package with a length of string. "You're certain I can't sell you the boots?"

Kelsey counted out each dollar with a sinking feeling in the pit of her stomach. "Afraid not."

"I'd hate to see your foot bashed if a rock falls on it."

"So would I." Kelsey handed him the money. "But limping's cheaper than your boots."

He laughed. "They'll be here if you change your mind. Don't get much call for a size four. No, we don't."

Kelsey took her package with a forced smile and headed back out into the Coober Pedy sunshine. It was late afternoon, and the temperature was high enough that she was glad she hadn't learned to convert from Celsius to Fahrenheit so that she could compare it to home. She needed a hat to wear outside as well as one for under the ground, but the latter was essential while the former was merely comfortable. She had brought plenty of sunblock with her, and, since her experience yesterday, she had drenched herself in it before going outside.

She couldn't have made it without the hard hat, though. Because of its size, her father's was no protection. And she couldn't have made it without an appropriate shirt to wear. Her peach blouse was already ripped along one sleeve from scraping against narrow mine walls. Now she was thirty-four fifty poorer and thirty-four times more worried about how she was going to manage until Jake could see her.

At least Jake was holding his own. She had placed a call to Adelaide when she returned from the mine, and she had been able to speak directly to Jake's doctor. He and his staff were optimistic. Jake had regained consciousness twice since arriving, and his vital signs were stable. The doctor had promised to call her daily to give her information and immediately if there was a change she should know about.

In the meantime she was going to stay in Coober Pedy despite blocked mine shafts and slaughtered kangaroos.

The luscious smells from a narrow storefront almost pulled Kelsey inside. Dillon had shared his lunch with her on the way back to town, and, after a minimum of protests, she had eaten a sandwich and banana. But now her stomach told her she should be thinking about dinner. Unfortunately, her wallet said otherwise.

She had already eaten two full meals that day, and she was going to have to continue that pattern is she wanted to save money. She would look forward to a good breakfast and ignore the dinner she was missing. With an iron will, she continued down the street toward the motel that was eating up her cash.

Eating.

"Where was I on the evening of December first?" Dillon stretched his long legs in front of him in a deceptively casual pose. "Haven't you been watching too much television, Sergeant?"

"I'll thank you to answer the question."

Dillon lifted his eyelids just enough to regard the man pacing in front of him. He had ignored the police sergeant's orders to come in for questioning as long as he was able. Now he hoped that the impending dinner hour would make this session painlessly short. "You'll wear yourself out for nothing," he said. "Pacing won't threaten me into confessing something I didn't do."

Sergeant Newberry raised his voice. "Where were you?"

"Half the town can tell you. I was at the pub waiting for Jake to show up."

"Not between seven and seven-forty. You left, supposedly to see if you could find him."

"And I didn't."

Sergeant Newberry scribbled something on a notepad. "The trip from the pub to the Rainbow Fire takes fifteen minutes if the road is clear. Four minutes on the bitumen, eleven through the mine field."

"Apparently addition's your subject."

"By my calculations, you could have driven there, pushed Jake down the shaft and come back, all in forty minutes."

"Einstein couldn't have estimated it more closely." Dillon leaned back in his chair. "Except for one thing."

"Don't keep me in suspense," Sergeant Newberry mocked.

"I'm afraid I can give you a list of people who saw me looking for Jake here in town during that time."

The sergeant's pencil paused.

"Starting with a deacon of the Catacomb Church."

There was a snapping sound as pencil lead succumbed to pressure. Dillon reached inside his shirt pocket and held out a pen.

Sergeant Newberry ignored the offer, dropping his pencil on the desk behind him. "You got to the pub at six. That doesn't explain what you were doing before that."

"I was digging a fifty-foot grave for Jake. You only think it was a mine shaft."

"Why you should think this is funny is beyond my comprehension."

"I'll tell you what's beyond your comprehension." Dillon set all four legs of his chair on the floor. "Friendship and loyalty." He stood. "I assume we're finished?"

"What were you doing before six?" The sergeant's voice was a decibel louder.

Dillon was tempted to walk out of the police station without answering any more questions. Inbred respect for the law, not fear, made him stay. He repeated the story he had already given right after Jake's rescue.

"Jake and I quit work a little past four. We went back to the dugout, showered and changed our clothes. Then I dropped Jake off in town so he could get some tucker. I was going to eat with him, but I remembered that I had two stones I wanted to ask Gary to set for me, so I told Jake I'd meet him at the Showcase at half past five and went back to the dugout."

"Stones?"

Dillon kept impatience out of his voice. "Pieces of boulder opal I got from a friend in Queensland."

"What did you do then?"

"I picked up the stones and drove to the Showcase. When Jake didn't show up there by six, I went over to the pub."

"What time did you get to the Showcase?"

Dillon shrugged. "Half past five or so."

"We have no one who remembers seeing Jake in town that afternoon." Sergeant Newberry's smile was thin-lipped and self-congratulatory. "No one."

"And you've questioned everyone in Coober Pedy?"

The smile altered a fraction. "Of course not."

"I'd say your work's cut out for you." Dillon tipped his hat. Then, before the sergeant could respond, he opened the door and strode out to the street.

Evening had come suddenly, as it so often did in outback Australia. The sky was still an artist's palette of scarlet and gold, but in minutes the only light illuminating the streets would be man-made. Crows perched on power lines, cawing their goodbye to the day, and three pink and gray galahs circled overhead, flashes of color to rival the sunset.

With little to block the magnificent panorama, sunset was Coober Pedy's consolation prize, the one time of day when even the most skeptical couldn't believe God had forgotten this remote corner of the world.

Tonight Dillon hardly noticed the sky. He felt an odd restlessness that had nothing to do with fiery sunsets or even his conversation with the police sergeant. A lame attempt to blame it on Jake's misfortune didn't work, either. He was forced to admit that his restlessness had more to do with Jake's daughter.

Kelsey Donovan, whose hair rivaled the sunset's gold, and whose gut-twisting mixture of flash, innocence and temper were like the opal he'd given his life to. Kelsey Donovan who at this moment was probably sitting in her motel room, hungry and too proud to admit it.

Dillon never would have realized Kelsey's predicament if he hadn't happened in to the Miner's Store. One short conversation with the clerk there had educated him quickly. As the man had humorously repeated Kelsey's joke about a limp being cheaper than boots, Dillon had recalled the expression on her face at the pub as she had counted out money for her meal and the chair she had broken. Mix one joke, one pained expression and one denial that she needed to bring lunch to the mine, and you ended up with one young woman who was trying desperately to hang on to what money she had until her father could see her. One hungry young woman.

None of that was his concern. Dillon tipped the brim of his hat a little higher and started down the street. If Kelsey got too hungry, she would go back to the States, where she belonged. She would be spared whatever was brewing around the Rainbow Fire, spared facing a father who would probably hurt her again, spared the fever that seemed to infect every person who had ever mined for opal.

And Dillon himself would be spared the onslaught of desert-brown eyes and sunset hair.

He needed a woman, any woman. He needed the feel of a woman's body under his, a woman's grace and laughter, a woman's soft fingertips soothing away the turmoil of the day. His growing fascination with Kelsey Donovan was nothing more than a man's need for solace and sex. He muttered the two words as he strode down the street, knowing as he did that he no more believed them than he believed that Jake had thrown himself down an abandoned mine shaft.

He was in front of the motel before he realized where he had been heading. His ute was parked at the pub, where he had intended to grab a meal and a cold Foster's, so why was he standing in the motel parking lot like a bloody drongo? And why, now that he realized where he was, wasn't he moving off up to the hill?

Muttering expletives against men who made fools of themselves over opals and women, he started across the lot.

There were twenty-one piles of bills laid carefully in rows up and down Kelsey's bed. Some part of her had demanded visible proof that she could stay in Australia for three weeks. She had the proof in front of her now. She could stay in Australia if she either quit eating or quit sleeping in a bed. There was no way she could do both.

The news wasn't good, but then she had known that before she had methodically built twenty-one piles. Now it was indisputable and her choices clear. Either she limited her stay to two weeks, or she found cheaper accommodations.

The problem was that the only cheaper accommodation in Coober Pedy was a cave cut into the side of a hill where tourists camped. She wasn't too proud to stay there, but she had no sleeping bag, no pillow, no mattress to cushion the hard rock floor. She had priced those items at the Miners' Store, and, as Dillon would have said, they were dear—a peculiar word for something that didn't seem dear at all but absolutely "undear" to her way of thinking. If she bought what she needed, paid the camping fee, paid for the use of the showers behind the cave and paid for all her meals, she would still be short the money she needed.

And there it was again. Self-pity. The ugly emotion that seemed to have sprung to life in the Australian sunshine.

Sweeping the piles into one neat stack, Kelsey deposited the bills back in her wallet. There were two empty places inside her that were fast merging into a boundless hole. One was the result of hunger, the other of discouragement. There was nothing to be done about the first, but the second might respond to some positive action.

She was still sitting on the bed racking her brain for one positive idea when someone began to pound on her door.

Kelsey realized there was no one she didn't want to see. Even Serge's presence would have taken her mind off her stomach and her problems. In a moment she had thrown the door open.

Dillon stood on the threshold, his arm still raised.

Kelsey hadn't expected Dillon. More, she hadn't expected this rush of excitement.

She hid it well. "Checking to see if I'd gotten scared and left?"

"Gotten smart and left," he corrected. "I knew better."

She didn't move out of the doorway. "What can I do for you then?"

The answers that burst into his mind were absolutely not repeatable. He cleared his throat. "I thought maybe you'd let me take you to dinner."

Kelsey's stomach rumbled in anticipation even as her brain made a different decision. "Thank you, but I don't think so."

Dillon had anticipated her refusal. He admired her pride as he worked his way around it. "Do you like Greek food? Italian?" He ignored the way her head bobbed from side to side. "Barbecue? Continental?"

"You're shattering my fantasies of the wild, wild west."

"We're quite a civilized lot."

"Too bad the man who pushed my father down the shaft didn't know that."

"Seafood?"

Kelsey shook her head again, sorry she hadn't gotten a rise out of him. He was impossible to put on the defensive. "Nothing."

"Then come with me while I eat. I want to talk to you about the accident."

She had been steeling herself to close the door. Instead she frowned and stepped a little closer to the threshold. "What about the accident?"

"I haven't been completely honest."

"Tell me now."

Dillon shook his head. "Over dinner. Where we can talk comfortably."

Kelsey tilted her chin a notch. "I've eaten."

He knew she was lying. He had heard exhibit A—a voracious rumble that rivaled a Northern Territory road train. "Then come watch me and have a drink. My shout."

She wasn't sure she could sit across a table from Dillon, nursing a drink while he ate. There was no guarantee she wouldn't snatch the food off his plate. Still, she owed it to her father to find out everything she could. "Where shall I meet you? I have to change."

"There's a little place up near the hotel that makes a pizza smothered with everything." He tried not to smile as he tormented her. "Anchovies, capsicum, pineapple, ham, pepperoni, mushrooms," he paused, then drew out the next word. "Prawns."

Kelsey schooled herself to nonchalance. "The name of this place?"

"Gero's Pizza Palace."

"I'll meet you there in a few minutes."

He nodded, retreating a few steps before he turned back to her. Kelsey was just closing the door. "Italian sausage," he added. "Did I forget to mention the Italian sausage?"

The door banged shut. Dillon whistled all the way to Gero's.

Kelsey didn't know why she had bothered with dressing up. Maybe it was because her wheat jeans were dirty and her blue jeans too disreputable. Maybe it was because even with air conditioning, the night was stultifyingly hot and not made for pants at all. Whatever the reason, she was fully conscious of the admiring stares that followed her as she walked down Hutchinson Street to meet Dillon. She found the restaurant with her nose before she located it with her eyes. One good sniff told her that he hadn't exaggerated about the quality of the pizza. The second sniff almost made her turn around.

Dillon was at the counter chatting with the dark-haired woman behind it when Kelsey opened the door. She listened to the tinkle of a cowbell and watched as he turned to investigate. His eyes swept up her slender figure, resting seconds too long on the bare expanse of leg exposed by her short skirt, then continued up to the narrow span of her waist and the soft swell of her breasts covered by cotton jersey the color of goldenrod.

"Come meet Anna." Dillon turned back to the woman at the counter. His mouth was suddenly dry, and he took a large swallow of his beer to moisten it.

Kelsey joined him at the counter. "Hello, Anna. I'm Kelsey Donovan."

"I know who you are," Anna said, a grin distorting the well-cushioned contours of her face. "You're the girl who breaks chairs with her hand. Could you teach me to do that? I've got a chair or two I'd like to break."

"Over Gero's head?" Dillon asked.

Anna poked him playfully. "How did you know?"

"A lucky guess." Dillon turned to Kelsey. "What will you have?"

"A Coke."

Anna went to the refrigerator case behind the counter and pulled out a familiar-looking bottle, setting it in front of Kelsey. "The pizza, it'll be out in a minute." She touched Kelsey's arms before she could follow Dillon to a nearby table. "Dillon and you, you're friends?"

"I wouldn't say that exactly." Kelsey watched Anna nod anyway.

Anna lowered her voice. "I watch over him, you know, like a mama. There's no woman in his life. There should be." Her eyes narrowed as she assessed Kelsey. "Yes."

Kelsey had the sinking feeling that "yes" meant trouble. "Maybe you know my father. Jake Donovan?"

"Jake, he's your father?" Anna's eyes narrowed a fraction more. "No, you're nothing like him. You look like your mother?"

"I'm told I do." Kelsey didn't want this opportunity to pass without pumping Anna for a little information. "Dillon says that he and my father were very close."

"Mates."

Since she had never heard the word said with an Italian accent before, Kelsey had to smile. "Then they seemed like friends to you?"

"Come for dinner tomorrow. By yourself. I'll make you lasagna, and we'll talk. No one's lasagna is better or cheaper." Anna winked.

Kelsey's mouth watered. "I'll come."

Dillon watched the women's exchange from a table near the dust-streaked window. Or rather, he watched Kelsey's bare legs and the graceful way her skirt brushed her thighs as she shifted her weight. He had seen Melly in skirts shorter than Kelsey's— Melly of the long, thoroughbred legs and the flawlessly trim ankles. But he had never been as entranced as he was now. Kelsey's legs were slender, too, but their perfect curves had been enhanced by superb physical conditioning. They had the subtle strength of a dancer's legs, and he admired that strength almost as much as he admired the sweep of her calves.

He watched her skirt flare as she turned to join him. The movement tightened the jersey shirt against her breasts. There were other things to admire about Kelsey Donovan. Entirely too many, in fact. And he was spending too much time indulging himself.

Kelsey came to the table and slid her Coke to the spot farthest from Dillon before she took a seat. She hoped the pizza would arrive after he had finished telling her about Jake's accident. Then she could make a quick exit before the torture began. "So, what did you want to tell me?"

"No chatting first? No, 'well, how was your afternoon? Weather's awfully hot, wouldn't you say?'"

"I chat with my friends." Kelsey took a sip of her soda and relished the effect of the jolt of sugar and caffeine on her empty stomach. "By no stretch of the imagination are we friends, Dillon."

"No worries. We can fix that. Tell me about *your* afternoon."

Kelsey tried to stifle her frustration. Dillon would reveal his thoughts when he was ready and not a bite of pizza before. "There's nothing to tell." She waited, but he just smiled. She took another sip, then another. "Oh, all right," she said, wishing she could wipe away his smile and the one shallow dimple that accented a freshly shaved cheek. "How was the rest of your day?"

"Just fine."

"Now will you tell me what you dragged me here to tell me?"

That entirely masculine dimple deepened. "Dragged you here?"

Her angry retort was smothered by the spicy aroma of pizza just out of the oven. Anna set it on the table between them. "I'll be back with your plates. You might need a bigger table." She winked and left.

Kelsey had never seen a pizza like the one that was inches from sliding into her lap. It was gigantic, and there wasn't a spot on it that wasn't loaded with toppings. "I told you I wasn't eating," she said, trying not to inhale as she talked.

"Too right. I'll just take the leftovers home for tomorrow's dinner." He waited until Anna had set plates and forks in front of each of them before he spoke. "Sure you won't have a slice?"

Kelsey could cheerfully have strangled him. "I couldn't eat one bite." And she couldn't. One bite would lead to another, and another, and....

"Then you don't mind if I dig in?"

"Mind? Why should I mind?" She finished half her drink in one gulp.

Dillon shook her head. "There's just one thing wrong with this pizza."

Kelsey couldn't imagine what it could be. The pizza looked perfect to her.

"I forgot to tell Anna to leave off the prawns. I can't say they're my favorite." He pried a large prawn from under the mozzarella and Parmesan layering the surface. Dangling it in front of Kelsey, he wrinkled his brow. "You wouldn't mind if I put them on your plate, would you? No other place I can see."

"Help yourself." Kelsey watched as the succulent-looking prawn was joined on her plate by six equally as succulent specimens.

"Shame I don't like them." Dillon shook his head regretfully. "Shame I don't like mushrooms, either." He heaped the offending mushrooms on top of the prawns. "I shouldn't think you've ever had a pizza with pineapple on it, have you? Never can find one when I'm in the States. Yanks don't know what they're missing." He speared a pineapple chunk and held it to her lips. "Can't have you going home without trying this."

Obediently, Kelsey opened her mouth like a baby bird and let Dillon feed her the pineapple. She chewed slowly, savoring every bite. "Dillon, what were you going to tell me about my father's accident?"

With infinite patience, he coaxed a slice of pizza off the pan, lifting it high so that the mozzarella stretched into finely spun strands. "A beautiful sight, isn't it?" With a sigh, he took his first bite. "No one makes pizza like Anna. I've been to Italy, and it's no better there. Different, but not better. But then, Australian pizza's the best in the world."

She opened her mouth to disagree only to find Dillon's fork at her lips again.

"Try this sausage and tell me what you think. Anna'll want to know your opinion. She told me she's purchasing this from a new supplier."

The sausage was in Kelsey's mouth before she could refuse. As she chewed she watched with annoyance as Dillon took the remaining slices of sausage off the pizza and transferred it to the growing mound on her plate, shaking his head.

"About Jake's accident," he said while she was still chewing.

Kelsey swallowed the sausage along with her protest. "It's about time."

"I haven't been all-up straight with you."

"Is this where you tell me you really did try to kill my father?"

"You wouldn't be saying that so much if you really believed it was true. You'd like to believe it, because it's an easy answer. If I didn't do it, there are no other leads as to who might have." Dillon wiped his mouth and reached for another slice. "No other leads *you* know of, anyway."

Kelsey wondered if he were right. Dillon was a convenient target for her frustration. But did she really believe he was capable of trying to murder Jake? Everything she had been taught about real character denied it. "What do you mean, no leads I know of?"

"I've a theory I haven't told anyone else." Dillon watched with satisfaction as Kelsey fingered a slice of sausage. She was so absorbed in their conversation that she didn't even realize what she was doing. He forced himself not to smile when she popped it into her mouth.

"What's your theory?" Kelsey reached for another slice of sausage and came up with a prawn instead. She chewed it with reverence.

"You've got to promise me that this stays between us," Dillon warned as another prawn followed the path of the first down Kelsey's throat.

"I promise."

Between his own bites of pizza, he watched her start on the mushrooms. "There's no easy way of telling you this, so I'm

going to be blunt. Your father is a bit of a boozer and storyteller."

She waved aside his apology with her third prawn. "I've figured that out. I didn't expect a saint. A saint would have
dropped me an occasional postcard."

"Jake's a good man in his own way." Dillon momentarily
wished that Jake's own way had included his daughter. "But
when he drinks, the yarns get bigger...."

"And more outrageous?"

He nodded. There was something colorful and almost ad-
mirable about a flamboyant storyteller. There was nothing ad-
mirable about the other term for the same thing. *Liar.* He
would spare Kelsey that much. He had a feeling it was one of
the few times anyone had spared her anything.

"This isn't the best place for a storyteller," he went on.
"Especially if the story revolves around opal."

As she finished the prawns Kelsey tried to understand. "In
other words, you think my father might have told someone he'd
found opal when he hadn't?"

He admired her perception. "It's not that he hadn't found
opal. It's that what he found wasn't the beginning of something bigger and better. I heard him shooting off his mouth a
time or two, and we fought about it. He'd had too much to
drink at the time, and we fought about that, too. If Jake exaggerated and told someone that he had made a big hit, then it's
not hard to believe this bloke might have wanted him dead so
he could help himself to the Rainbow Fire's opal."

"Why? You're alive. Wouldn't they know that you'd continue mining?"

"Right-o. They would." He watched her finish the last of the
mushrooms. The sausage was long gone. He lifted a slice of
pizza onto her plate and let his next words still her protest.
"But, you see, I think someone's tried to kill me, too."

Chapter 7

All Kelsey's thoughts of pride and pizza were forgotten. "Tried to kill you?"

"It's a distinct possibility."

"Why haven't you mentioned that before?"

Dillon leaned back in his chair and toyed with his beer. "To be honest, it didn't occur to me."

"Occur to you to mention it."

"Occur to me that someone was trying to kill me."

"Sort of a relaxed attitude, wouldn't you say?"

He shrugged. "I was on my way home from the Rainbow Fire four days ago. Jake was feeling crook, so he'd taken my ute home earlier. The engine on his was missing badly, so I'd told him I would drive it back. I'm a better mechanic than he is."

Kelsey hadn't thought that her father might have transportation of his own. "Where is it now?"

"Jake's ute's as old as this continent, and with more problems. I drove it to the mechanic this morning before I came to get you. He'll need it when he comes back."

If he comes back, she amended silently. "Go on."

"We'd had some rain." He stopped, a glimmer of a smile in his eyes at the disbelief in hers. "We do have rain here. In an average year we get five inches or so. That day we got a full half inch.''

"An honest-to-God flood," she marveled.

His smile reached his lips. "Ever dribble water on a dried-out sponge?" He watched her reluctant nod. "It doesn't soak in, does it? Well, three weeks ago the ground didn't know what to do with water, just like an old sponge. Do you remember the large hole in the road on the way to the mine?"

"The dry lake?"

"It wasn't dry that day. I stopped on the edge of it and got out to check and see how deep the water was. The sky was getting dark, and I remember thinking that I was going to be late for a meal at the pub if I didn't hurry. When I bent down to measure the water with a rod I found in the back of the ute, a bullet sailed over my head."

Kelsey picked up her slice of pizza and took a large bite, although she was too absorbed in Dillon's story to realize it. "What did you do?"

"What any good ex-Digger would. I flattened myself to the ground and swore. There were two more shots, then nothing."

"And you never thought that someone might be trying to kill you?"

"What I thought was that someone was behind some nearby hills, shooting roos, or that some kid was using anything that moved for target practice. I shouted, and the shots stopped, but I never saw anyone. When I got back into town, I asked around, but no one had any answers. I didn't think much about it until yesterday."

"And what changed your mind?"

Dillon reached into his pocket and held out two lumps of metal for Kelsey to investigate. "These. I dug one of them out of the ground beside my truck the day I was shot at."

"And the other?"

"I went back to the mine this afternoon after I dropped you off. This one came out of the dead roo. They're both plain-based lead bullets. Somebody hand cast them."

Kelsey knew little about weapons, but she knew enough to know how unusual that was. If Dillon was telling the truth, this was no coincidence. "Why would someone go to the trouble of making their own ammunition in this day and age?"

"A labor of love...or hate."

"Then you think the roo was a warning?"

"I shouldn't like to say."

"*If* there was a roo." Kelsey finished her pizza and wished she hadn't let Dillon stop her from viewing the evidence herself. This could be a trick to turn suspicion away from him. "And *if* you were shot at."

"You're a hard case, Kelsey." Dillon set another slice of pizza on her plate.

"You've said that before."

"I'll probably say it a time or two more before we're done. There's something else I'll be saying, too."

"What's that?"

"If you continue to waste all your energy being suspicious of me, you'll be no help finding who really injured your father."

She wondered why it pleased her that he wanted her help. "Then you're admitting, loud and clear, that you think someone injured my father?"

He nodded. "The same person who tried to shoot me. Someone who thinks there's more to the Rainbow Fire then the few stones Jake found. Someone who listened to one too many of his stories. Someone who wanted us both out of the way so he could rat the opal."

"I assume that means steal it?"

"Precisely." He watched with satisfaction as she picked up her second slice of pizza. "Opal ratters are the lowest form of life."

"Similar to men who force pizza on starving women?"

He grinned and wondered when she had noticed. "Similar."

"Did you really think I didn't know I was eating?"

"Did you really think I didn't know how hungry you were?"

She let a bite melt on her tongue before she answered. "Just why should you care, Dillon?"

He liked the way she said his name almost as much as he liked the way her eyes showed just a touch of gratitude. "You're Jake's daughter."

"That's never gotten me any mileage. Being Jake's daughter was always a little like being a leper, only there wasn't any cure for it."

"Jake would expect me to take care of you."

"Jake has always expected someone to take care of me," she said philosophically. "But I take care of myself."

"If you don't need anyone, Kelsey, why did you come?"

She tried to ignore the warmth in his green eyes, the empathy in his voice. "I came to put an end to a chapter in my life."

She was lying, but he wasn't sure she realized it. All her yearnings for love and acceptance had surfaced yesterday when she had found out about Jake's injuries. She was trying to bury those yearnings now, but it was too late. He had seen them, and he wouldn't soon forget.

"You should leave," he told her, reaching out to touch her arm. "If someone tried to murder Jake and me, you're not immune to the same fate. If you want a reunion with your father, you're going to have to stay alive."

She couldn't find a trace of deceitfulness in anything he had done. He had brought her here, tricked her into eating dinner, told her his theories about Jake's accident, and now he was trying to protect her again. She couldn't find one thing to fault him for.

"You know, you'd be easier to distrust if you'd just stop being so nice," she said. She licked her fingers before she reached for another slice of pizza. "And if you just weren't so sincere."

"I sincerely wish you'd leave Coober Pedy."

"I sincerely intend to stay." She shook her head as he started to speak. "I'm going to stay, Dillon, I owe it to Jake for fathering me, if not for any other reason. You're right, I was hungry. I don't have much money, and that's dwindling fast. But I'm going to find a way to stay here until I'm not needed anymore. I can camp at the Opal Cave, if I have to, and eat peanut butter sandwiches three times a day. I've lived that way before, and I'm still alive to tell about it."

"Someone may try to kill you."

"I'll be ready."

And she would be. Dillon could see it in the way she held herself. But what good were karate skills against a plain-based lead bullet?

"The pizza's getting cold," she warned him.

He was so deep in thought, he didn't even hear her. Anyone could come and go at the Opal Cave without raising suspicion. Living there, Kelsey would be an easy target for violence. And no one, no one, would notice if she didn't come home one night.

"If you don't eat your share," Kelsey warned again, "I won't be responsible for the consequences."

Could he be responsible for the consequences if Kelsey were killed? Beyond being the one to have to tell Jake, could he live with it if anything happened to her?

"Dillon?"

He grimaced and brought his fist down on the table. "There's nothing for it, then," he said.

Kelsey looked up from her pizza. "Nothing for what?"

"You're going to have to move in with me."

She took her time finishing her slice. "Are you subject to these attacks on a regular basis?" she asked at last.

"I'm not any happier about it than you are." Which was a lie, because some substantial part of him was as happy as a flagman waltzing his Matilda. He concentrated on the more realistic part, the part warning him that Kelsey was going to be nothing but trouble.

"Then why the offer?"

"You're determined to stay. I'm not going to let you starve, and you can't stay at the Opal Cave just to save money. You'll be too exposed there. How could I tell Jake I let you come to harm?"

"Let somebody else tell him."

His hand covered hers as she reached for another slice. "Look, Kelsey, there's room enough for you at my place. You can use the room Jake's been staying in. It's in a separate wing from mine. You'll have your privacy, I'll have mine. More important, you'll be safe."

"Safe from whom?" She pulled her hand from under his, sliding a pizza slice with it.

He sat back. "Where does such a little woman put all that pizza?"

"This was your idea, remember?" She took a bite and chewed blissfully. "Besides, I'm storing up calories."

"You won't have to store up anything if you move in with me. Your father paid me rent until the end of the month, so in a way, the room belongs to you already. You can save your money for a place in Adelaide when the doctor advises you to go down."

"How much does a room underground cost, anyway?" she asked curiously. She had investigated the Opal Cave earlier. It was little more than a man-made cavern, cool and dry, but with none of the luxuries of the motel room. Camping there would be comfortable, but not exactly like home. She wondered how the Coober Pedy residents who lived underground year round survived the austerity and claustrophobia.

Dillon wasn't about to tell her the whole truth. Jake had moved in with him when he couldn't pay the rent on his own dugout. He had paid Dillon for the favor with a smile and a promise—Jake's usual form of reimbursement. "You don't need to worry about what it cost. I gave Jake a bargain."

She tried to imagine being in a cave with Dillon stalking her. Caves usually didn't come with back doors. She shook her head. "I've learned a lot from karate. One of the most important things was never to get my back against a wall. Another was never to put myself at an opponent's mercy."

"I'm sure you also learned to trust your own judgment and count on allies when you need them."

Despite her arguments, Kelsey could see the wisdom in Dillon's offer. She knew she had come to a crossroad. Either she trusted Dillon or she trusted all the other residents of Coober Pedy, including the one who might have tried to harm her father. She was no longer in the position of being able to trust herself alone. Dillon was right. If someone had tried to kill Jake, and if someone had really tried to kill Dillon, then she could be in danger, too. And she would need an ally.

She didn't even know she had sighed until Dillon touched her arm. "Trust me, Kelsey. Your father's trusted me all these years, and now it's your turn to carry on the tradition."

"I can't imagine living underground."

"Then come see what you've been missing." Dillon had heard the remnants of doubt in Kelsey's voice, but he had also heard the beginning of acceptance. "We can finish the pizza there."

"There's not much of it left."

He laughed. "Next time I'll order two."

Kelsey knew little more about Coober Pedy housing than she had the day she had walked down Dillon's road searching for her father. But at least now she knew that all those peculiar doors built into hills were houses—or rather dugouts—where the citizens of Coober Pedy holed up like prairie dogs in a burrow to keep cool.

In Raleigh she lived in the upstairs of an old house where North Carolina sunshine spilled through leaded glass windowpanes and sent rainbows dancing along gleaming wooden floors. Her apartment was crowded with plants and noticeably short on curtains. And on days when thunderstorms split the sky, she turned on every light to remind herself the sun would shine again.

She wasn't a great candidate for underground living.

Dillon turned off the ute's engine but stayed behind the steering wheel. "This is what we call a semi-dugout because it's got a sunroom in the front. Lots of dugouts just have a door in a hill."

"I thought those were mines when I first saw them."

"A dugout can be as luxurious as a castle or as nasty as a rat's hole. And you can't always tell from the outside which it's going to be. Ready to see mine?"

Kelsey wasn't sure she was ready, but she had already come this far. She opened her door in answer.

The day she had met Dillon here, she'd had neither the strength nor the inclination to examine the porch closely. Now she took in the artfully arranged garden at the end away from the door. Potted plants of all sizes and varieties accented natural rock sculptures, uniquely shaped stones that Dillon had obviously collected from the surrounding hills with painstaking care. Sandwiched between two large slabs of nearly transparent gypsum was the cat she had seen the first day.

"Who's your friend?" she asked as Dillon unlocked the door.

He turned to see where she was pointing. "That's Jumbuck."

At the name the cat rose and arched his back in a time-consuming stretch. Then he limped over to see Dillon. Dillon squatted and fondled the cat's ears, as if Kelsey weren't standing there watching him. "How was your day, old boy?" he murmured. The cat rubbed against his leg in answer.

Kelsey had known plenty of large, strong men. Not one of them would have squatted on the ground to ask a cat about its day. "What's Jumbuck mean?"

"It's the Aborigine word for sheep." Dillon stood, and the cat limped back to his home among the rocks. "You know 'waltzing Matilda', don't you?"

"Can't say it's in my repertoire."

"Most Yanks think it's a love song about some sheila named Matilda. Actually it's the story of a swagman, a drifter, who steals a jumbuck and stuffs it in the sack where he stores his food. Unfortunately he gets caught and escapes into a water-hole, a billabong. His ghost haunts it forever after.''

She never would have guessed. ''So where'd the cat get his name?''

''I found some kids in town stuffing him into a bag. I doubt they were going to eat him, but I doubt they had anything good in mind, either. His leg was broken, that's why he limps.''

''And now he's yours?''

''As much as he'll ever be anyone's. He's a proud old bloke. Won't come inside. He scours the hills for food, but he doesn't mind taking a bite of fish from me every once in a while. When it gets really hot, he takes a bath in that saucer behind the rocks over there. I keep it filled for him.'' Dillon swung the door open and stood back. ''After you, Kelsey.''

What could you say about a man who rescued a moth-eaten tabby cat and kept a clay saucer of water for him to bathe in? She shook her head as she preceded him into the dugout. The hardest thing about watching her back would be remembering she had to.

The dugout was a complete surprise. The room she stepped into was flooded with light from the tall windows that faced the porch. There were plants here, too, plants hanging from hooks, plants sitting on the floor, plants decorating shelves.

''This doesn't look like a cave,'' she said, feeling immediately at home.

''I added the sun porch to get some extra light after the rest of the dugout was completed. In the hottest part of summer I draw my draperies, but only when I must.''

''I like it.''

''So do I.'' He gestured to the room in front of them. ''Welcome to my parlor, said the spider to the fly.''

Kelsey ignored him. She walked farther into a room that was like none she had ever seen before. There was nothing re-motely cavelike about it except that the walls were the same rust and cream colored swirls as the Rainbow Fire. In every other way it resembled a normal living room.

''Not what you expected?'' Dillon asked, amused.

''Not at all.'' She ran her fingertips along one wall, which was smooth and shining. ''It's lovely.'' And it was. The room was medium size, but not an ordinary rectangle. There was a cove built off to the left, a cove with an arched ceiling, surrounded by bookshelves carved right into the rock walls. In the center of it were a comfortable easy chair and a small table. "Your library?" she asked, strolling over to admire the selection of books. She saw he favored British mysteries and the classics, with a smattering of science fiction thrown in for good measure.

"One of the advantages of a dugout. If you need something, you just carve it out of the stone. I added this last summer with a pick and shovel."

"Innovative. Most people have to haul building material in, you just have to haul it out."

"By the time I finished, I'd gladly have traded, although I actually made money off this room."

"Made money?"

"When I dug it out, I found enough opal to pay for it one and a half times over."

He moved her along to the next room, but not before she'd had a chance to admire his selection of furniture. It was sturdy and comfortable, pine mostly, with casual blue-plaid upholstery. "Step down," he warned.

Kelsey took the three steps and realized she was in a family room. "Look at this. Dillon, this is delightful."

He smiled at her tone. Every once in a while she forgot to be cautious, and he got to admire the real Kelsey Donovan. There was a lot to admire. "You like my lounge room?"

"I do. But you should have children to enjoy this. It's a child's dream."

Dillon watched her circle the room.

"Pool table, television, stereo. Wet bar."

He shrugged. "Adult toys, I'm afraid."

She wondered suddenly about his past. Had there been a woman he had wanted to share this with? A woman he'd wanted to have his children? "There's room for a toddler to ride a tricycle," she observed. "Room for enormous cities of blocks, room for an easel and a sand-and-water table."

"It sounds like you know children."

"I assist in a first grade. I only have one more semester of college to go, then my internship, and I'll be able to teach."

"The kitchen's next." He led her through a carved archway into an efficient kitchen with a dining area off to the left. "I built it here so that the playroom would be right off it."

She wondered if he had imagined a wife watching out for children as she cooked the family meals. Her curiosity increased. As he led her back through a wide hallway, she noted the shafts in each room, narrow pipes that led to blue sky. "Are the shafts for ventilation?"

"Ventilation and light. I've added more than most people. I experimented with mirrors for a while, too, trying to get the most light possible, but I wasn't successful. I reckon a dugout's a dugout for all that."

"Hardly. This is lovely and unique. You should be proud."

His grin lit the hallway. "First nice thing you've said to me, Kelsey."

She realized he was probably right, and, despite herself, she felt ashamed. She wasn't going to let him know it, though. "I guess I'm going to have to be more careful."

"Or you're going to have to admit you know I didn't push your father down a mine shaft."

She was silent, but she knew she was only one step away from admitting just that. And out loud, too.

"This would be your room." He made an abrupt left turn.

The room was a delight. Round, like a castle turret, with a domed ceiling, the room was different from everything else in the house.

"I'm afraid I had an attack of whimsy when I designed this," Dillon apologized.

Kelsey knew it hadn't been an attack of whimsy. Whether he was aware of it or not, the room had been designed for a child, or children. It was large enough for two little people, and with its grass-green carpeting and walls painted the warm yellow of sunshine, it would have been perfect for them. "This was my father's room?" She couldn't imagine a grown man sleeping here.

"He wasn't here long. He had a place on the other side of town before he came to stay with me."

Kelsey wondered how it would feel to sleep in a bed Jake Donovan had slept in before her. She smiled a little.

Dillon saw her defenses weakening. "So, shall we get your things from the motel?"

Kelsey came back to earth. "Where's your room?"

"On the other side, down the hall from the kitchen."

"I'd like to see it."

That misplaced dimple marred his cheek. "Come on, Kelsey, do you think I intend to sleep in here with you?"

She shook back her mane of hair. "I *have* seen only one bedroom."

"If you're so anxious to see where I sleep," he said with a grin, "follow me."

Back in the hallway she followed him at a discreet distance. "This is the bathroom," he said, pointing before he turned. "We'll have to share. And this is my room." He stopped in front of a closed door. When he didn't move, Kelsey moved around him to turn the knob herself.

Dillon's hand clamped down on her wrist. "Don't."

She was hurt by his curt tone. She answered with sarcasm. "What's wrong? Is this where you store the skeletons of people you push down mine shafts?"

"This wasn't closed when I left this evening."

Kelsey frowned. Her wrist was beginning to throb. "You're hurting me."

With no apology he loosened his grip. "I'm certain I didn't close it."

"How can you remember something like that?"

"I had my hands full of books I was taking back into the living room. And I don't close doors, anyway. There's no need, with just me living here."

"Then who closed it?"

"An excellent question. Stand back, would you?" Dillon dropped her wrist. When she didn't move, he turned his head to stare at her. "Way back."

There was no humor in his eyes now. There was deadly intent, and anger. Kelsey was glad she wasn't on the other side of the door. "What are you going to do?" she asked, without moving an inch.

"I'm going to kick the bloody door open. And you're going to stand back. Understand?"

She had never seen him this way before. She didn't even give his words a second thought. She moved back. Way back. Dillon nodded. "Thank you." Without another word he gave the door one shark kick, flattening himself against the opposite wall in a single, explosive movement.

The door hit the wall behind it with a bang, then creaked as it swung back toward the threshold. It stopped short of closing.

"Well, you showed that door," Kelsey said. "That'll teach it for shutting without your permission."

"I'll take your sarcasm in small doses and not at all right now, thanks." Dillon nudged the door with his toe until it was open once more. "Stay where you are. I'm going to turn on the light." He reached around the door frame and clicked a switch, leaping back immediately afterward.

Nothing happened. "Could the bulb be burned out?" Kelsey asked, beginning to feel the first prickles of fear.

"Quite a coincidence if it were, wouldn't you say?" Dillon peered into the room, but the soft light from the hallway barely penetrated. He joined Kelsey, taking her arm to restrain her from entering the room. "I've got a torch in my workroom. I'll get it. You go back to the living room while I explore."

"Not on your life."

"An apt sentiment." His grip tightened, and he steered her toward the workroom. "By any chance were you a cheeky kid? Was your desk in the corner in primary school?"

She tossed her head. "Just in grades one through three. In fourth grade I got a teacher who asked me to do things instead of telling me."

"Will you go into the living room and wait, please?"

"No." Kelsey felt Dillon's fingers tighten in frustration. She felt a surge of sympathy for him. "I'm not trying to be difficult."

"You're difficult without trying."

"Dillon, I'm worried, too. I don't want you going in there without backup." When he dropped her arm she leaned against the doorjamb as he went into a well-stocked workroom and pulled a large flashlight off a pegboard hook. "What do you think you're going to find?"

"I have no way of knowing."

"Shouldn't you call the police?"

He laughed humorlessly. "Sergeant Newberry would love that, wouldn't he now?"

"Then let me help you."

There was nothing he could do, and he knew it. "Stay in the hall, then."

Kelsey knew compromise when she heard it. "At first," she agreed.

"Don't even come with me if you're not willing to do what I tell you to. This is my house," he reminded her as she started to protest.

She suddenly realized what they were arguing about. She was offering to risk her safety for him, and he was denying her the chance. She frowned. "You keep trying to protect me."

"Just do as I say."

She was so busy trying to figure how this side of Dillon fit with Sergeant Newberry's accusations that she forgot to protest. "Fine," she murmured.

Dillon started back down the hall. At his door he stopped. "I'll let you know if there's any reason to be concerned."

"This could all be your imagination. Breezes blow doors closed and lights burn out."

"I changed those bulbs last week. And we're underground. Breezes are one problem we don't have."

She ignored the last. "Maybe there's a short in the wiring."

Dillon flicked the flashlight switch and flooded the hallway with more light. "I don't plan to be long."

Kelsey watched him step over the threshold. She could see nothing except the wavering beam of his light. She stifled the impulse to ask him if he had seen anything yet. She was sure he would tell her. There was a burst of light from the bedroom, and she stepped closer to the doorway.

"The bulbs in both lamps were loose," Dillon called.

Kelsey stepped closer until she was on the threshold.

"Couldn't stay back," he said, peering at her over his shoulder.

"An insatiable curiosity." Kelsey scanned Dillon's bedroom. It was large and attractive, with walnut furniture, including a huge rolltop desk. The center of the room was taken up by a king-size bed covered with an orange and gold striped comforter. Framed prints of the outback decorated the walls.

"Nothing looks out of place so far," Dillon observed.

"Maybe nothing is."

"I'd be just as glad if it weren't."

Kelsey watched him examine each piece of furniture. Then he carefully opened the closet door. From the gingerly way he handled everything, she knew he was worried about explosives. When he was satisfied the closet hadn't been tampered with, he knelt beside the bed and peered beneath it.

"That about does it, don't you think?" Kelsey asked.

"There's nothing different that I can see."

Kelsey wondered if he had staged this entire scene for her. Was she supposed to believe that he had risked his life to be certain the room was safe? Somehow she couldn't believe it, but the possibility still lingered. "Apparently you were imagining things."

"I don't mind imagining things if just once it keeps me from making a costly mistake." He stood, brushing the knees of his trousers. "But I didn't make a mistake this time. The door wasn't closed when I left."

"My, my. We hate to admit when we're wrong." Kelsey stood her ground as he approached.

Dillon put his hands on each side of the door frame, his face inches from hers. "Have you ever wondered, Kelsey Donovan, why you're trying so hard to mistrust me?"

"Self-preservation."

He moved a little closer. "Exactly what part of yourself are you trying to preserve, woman? Haven't you figured out by now that I'm not going to hurt you? I'm on the same side you are."

"What are you trying to get at?"

"There's more to your flippant little remarks and your chin two inches in the air than mistrust. You're trying to keep me at arm's length because you feel the attraction between us."

Her eyes widened, but no other part of her moved. "I'm a very bad person to make a pass at, Dillon."

"I'll agree, but not for the reason you think. I care this much about your damned black belt." He snapped his finger. "But I am beginning to care about you. And that's the best reason I know not to make a pass at you."

Confusion seeped through her defenses. "What's that supposed to mean?" Even to her own ears her voice sounded breathy and very feminine.

"It means that a pass is out of the question." One of Dillon's hands settled in the curls framing her cheek, then threaded through them to rest at the back of her head. "A demonstration of affection is not."

Kelsey watched his mouth descending. In the brief second before his lips touched hers, she told herself that he was kissing her from relief, or from a calculated plan to throw her off guard, or just to get even with her for one too many caustic remarks. The moment his lips touched hers, all those voices were silenced.

He had been right. Their mutual attraction was undeniable, but if she had known it, she had only known it on some subliminal level. And now, one kiss exposed the attraction and named it something else.

Desire.

She tried to pull back, but his hand cupped the back of her head with the comforting touch of a man who knows that eventually he'll get what he wants. He brushed his lips over hers once, again, before he murmured, "Kelsey, why fight everything that happens to you? Just kiss me back. It's so easy."

Easy for everyone else in the world, perhaps, but giving herself was the most difficult thing Kelsey would ever be asked to do. Even a kiss was giving up too much. "Let go of me," she said, taking a deep breath to draw more air into her lungs.

His hand fell away, but his lips settled on hers again in a gentle caress. Strangely she could not pull away now that he no longer held her. He was taking nothing, and although she was giving nothing, this in-between, this place where they weren't quite friends, weren't quite lovers, was a place she felt safe to explore.

Dillon sensed her assent and deepened the kiss a little, stroking his tongue over her bottom lip. She was unbelievably sweet, even though she was denying herself a response. Her eyelids had drifted shut, more like a child who doesn't want to see a hypodermic than a woman who wants to absorb all sensation without the distraction of sight. He stepped closer to her, sheltering her in his arms without actually holding her. With the smallest pressure, she could have broken away.

Kelsey let the warmth of Dillon's body seep into hers. She hadn't even known she was chilled. She felt his eyelashes brush across her cheek, felt the warm brush of his lips as they trailed slowly to her forehead. Felt a surge of desire force never would have provoked. Her hands hung limply by her sides, but as he moved closer still, she resisted, pressing her palms against his shoulders.

The resistance was the signal Dillon needed to stop kissing her. He opened his eyes and moved no closer. But his hands settled at her waist. "You've a way of getting to me," he said softly. He inhaled the scent of lavender, and his hands smoothed down to her hips. "Whether I want you to or not."

"And what about what I want or don't want?"

"I'm not at all certain you know."

She stiffened suddenly, so suddenly that his first reaction was to hold her tighter. His eyes searched hers. He could see her pupils dilating in surprise and the beginnings of fear. "What is it?" he demanded.

"Something just brushed across my ankles," she whispered.

In the split second before he answered, Dillon called himself every name imaginable. "Stand very still."

"Very still," she repeated.

Moving with agonizing slowness Dillon peered over her shoulder. A snake whose orange and brown stripes were the color of his comforter peered back at him from a deadly coil at Kelsey's feet.

Chapter 8

The next few seconds would never be clear in Dillon's mind. Perhaps if he had been given time to think, he would have responded differently. As it was, there was no time. His hands slid back to Kelsey's waist, and he lifted her high in the air, turning ninety degrees as he did to thrust her to safety. In the same second that she hit the ground, he lifted one booted foot and smashed it squarely on the snake's head.

Kelsey's scream unnerved him almost more than the squirming under his boot heel. Both stopped at the same moment.

Satisfied that the snake would never threaten anyone again, Dillon lifted his foot and moved to Kelsey's side. His arms closed around her as she collapsed.

"It's all right, Kelsey," he repeated over and over, stroking her hair. "The snake is dead."

She was battling tears and could do nothing more than nod against his chest. Her arms crept around his waist, and she supported herself by holding him tight. Her knees were embarrassingly weak. "I don't like snakes," she admitted unnecessarily, her voice sounding strangely like her knees felt.

"A healthy attitude here."

She almost didn't want to know why. Almost. "Why?"

"Most of our snakes are poisonous. Not all are deadly, of course...." His voice trailed off as he thought about the one he had just killed.

She lashed out at him, although her arms remained around his waist. "How can you live like this, then? Never knowing when a snake is going to find its way in here?"

She hadn't yet made the connection. Dillon wished Kelsey had realized the truth on her own. Then he would have been spared the decision of whether to tell her or not. As he stroked her hair he seriously considered lying, but in the end he opted not to, simply because he knew the truth would occur to her later. "Kelsey, think hard about what's happened in the last few minutes."

She was still too agitated to think at all. She raised her head and met his eyes. "What do you mean?"

He knew he was going to have to spell it out. "Someone put the snake in my room. That's why the light was off and the door was closed. I didn't find it because we left the door open and it came out into the hall when we went for the torch. But someone had assumed I wouldn't notice the door and my little welcome home party would greet me unawares."

She didn't want to believe him. "You're just guessing!"

"This place is as tight as a drum. Even the air vents are covered with wire mesh. Snakes don't find their way inside."

Add that up with a door that had been closed and light bulbs that had been unscrewed. Kelsey knew he had to be right.

Or he had to be lying about the whole episode.

Perhaps the snake was harmless. She ventured a glance at it. It looked like a close relative of a garter snake. She knew garter snakes intimately because she'd had a cousin who had repeatedly teased her with one. Perhaps Dillon had staged this entire little show to convince her that he could be trusted.

Kelsey's arms dropped to her sides, and she made herself step back. Dillon read the beginnings of distrust in her eyes; he could almost see her thoughts. He could have pointed out that she had insisted on seeing his bedroom. He could have pointed out that he had asked her to wait in the living room when he had first suspected danger. He could even have pointed out that the snake had represented as much danger to him as to her. To his knowledge, snakes couldn't be trained to selectively gnaw on trim little ankles.

He pointed out nothing. "I'll take you back to the motel," he said coldly.

"Please."

He nodded, turning to start down the hallway.

"Dillon?"

He stopped but didn't face her.

"I'd like to take the snake into town for identification."

Dillon could have identified it for her, but he didn't bother. Kelsey would have to find out for herself. And this time, at least, he was the man who was going to let her.

"I'll get you a sack. Just remember, dead snakes have been known to kill people who come in contact with their venom. Be careful how you handle it."

"Then you're saying this snake could kill?"

"I'm saying that, yes."

Kelsey followed him, giving the snake the widest berth possible. She didn't know how she was going to stand carrying it, bag or not, but she knew she must.

"I'd cut off the head for you, but I suspect you'll want to be sure its fangs weren't tampered with." His voice was filled with irony. "Can't have you waking up tomorrow wondering if I'd rendered a deadly snake harmless just to impress you."

Kelsey was caught in the web of her own suspicions. Either Dillon had just saved her life, or he had perpetrated the worst of hoaxes. She couldn't thank him for one while she half believed the other.

Dillon turned the corner into the kitchen and came back with a burlap sack. "Yours." He handed it to her. "I'll be waiting in the ute."

Kelsey took the bag, refusing to let him see how revolted she was at the thought of touching the snake. But she had brought this on herself, and there was nothing to do but go through with it. "Thank you." He was almost through the door of the playroom before her next words stopped him. "I wish things were different." It was the best she could do.

A shake of his head said he didn't believe her. "I doubt you really do, Kelsey. This way you've got a built-in reason to stay clear of me. What would you do if that changed?"

Sergeant Newberry lifted the snake from Kelsey's bag and lovingly ran his thin fingers against its scales. "Quite a nice specimen," he said. "A meter and a half, at least. Even longer, perhaps. I can measure it for you."

"I don't really care how long it is," she said, suppressing a shudder. She wasn't sure which was slimier, the snake or the man. "I'd just like to know what it was, and if it was deadly."

He smiled a smile the snake would have smiled if it could have. "You don't know what it is?"

"I don't."

"First tell me how you came by it."

"Dillon killed it." She saw little reason to go into the whole story, but she thought he ought to know some of it. He was, after all, the law in Coober Pedy. "In his dugout."

"Peculiar place for a death adder."

Kelsey was sure her face had blanched as white as the papers littering the sergeant's desk. "Death adder?"

"Desert death adder. Not quite as deadly as our taipan, but then, our taipan's one of the top two in the world." He sounded pleased, as if Australia had just placed in the reptile olympics. "See this tidy little tail?" He shook it playfully back and forth. "The adder wriggles this when it's hungry, and other smaller reptiles and mammals mistake it for an insect. They become *his* meal instead."

Kelsey's shudder wouldn't be repressed this time. "Please." She took a deep breath. "Do me a big favor. Will you check its fangs? Are they intact? Could he have bitten someone? Killed someone?"

Obligingly the sergeant spread the snake's jaw. "Nothing amiss here. He could have done some damage, that's for certain. Ward smashed his head beaut, didn't he? Use a shovel?"

"A foot."

The sergeant frowned. "He stepped on it?"

Kelsey felt much as she had the day she had trudged through the Coober Pedy sun. "He was wearing boots."

Sergeant Newberry turned the snake's mouth toward Kelsey for her to view. "See the length of those fangs?" he asked gleefully. "Longer than boot leather is thick, I'll wager. Ward could easily have ended up beside your father. Or dead."

She shut her eyes and wished the snake would come back to life and swallow the police officer's finger. "You really don't like Dillon Ward, do you?"

The sergeant tried to pull a cloak of professionalism around him. "Whether I like him or not has nothing to do with my suspicions."

Kelsey wondered if he believed his own words. She knew she didn't. "Will you dispose of the snake for me, please?"

"Right-o."

She nodded and said a perfunctory thank-you. Only when she was outside in the sunshine did she let shame replace her revulsion.

Shame stayed with her through a long, restless night. Shame stayed with her at breakfast and through the remainder of the morning. Dillon didn't come to pick her up to go to the Rainbow Fire, but then, Kelsey hadn't expected him to. What had he gotten from his relationship with her that would make him want to continue it?

Kelsey could have gotten out to the mine on her own, but when Dillon didn't appear, she decided to wait a day. Trust had followed closely on the heels of shame, and now she knew she didn't have to stand over Dillon every moment. The man had risked his life for her; he had saved her father's life. What other proof did she need that she could depend on him to be honest?

She skipped lunch, still uncertain about finances. By one, she was so tired of the motel walls that she braved the midday sunshine.

Drawn to the Opal Showcase in hopes of seeing Melanie, she headed to the other end of town. The hottest sun she ever remembered had made a joke of her sunscreen by the time she arrived. Kelsey realized she was going to have to purchase a hat just to keep the sun from frying her brain. Mentally she subtracted the amount from her ready cash and crossed one more day off her stay in Australia.

One more day unless she took Dillon up on his offer. If the offer still existed.

"Melly?" Kelsey ducked through the door of the Showcase and descended several steps. The shop was built halfway into a hill, with the lavender light of fluorescent bulbs the only adornment on the natural stone walls. But then, the shop didn't need adornment. It had Melanie.

She stood behind a glass showcase filled with Coober Pedy's
raison d'être. "Welcome." Melanie playfully threw Kelsey a
kiss. "To the final stages of greed fever."

"Greed fever?" Today Melanie was dressed in a denim
prairie skirt and a white camisole spangled with silver sequins.
Her hair was covered with a showy blond wig. Kelsey admired
the effect.

"A virtual epidemic. Here and Wall Street. No difference."

"Wall Street is cooler."

"And oh so much more boring."

Kelsey thought of yesterday's encounter of the serpent kind.
"There's nothing boring about Coober Pedy," she agreed.

"So what are you doing here? Shopping for opals? I can give
you the best deal in town."

"I'd love some. But I'm on a budget. I just came to look."

Melanie gestured to the showcase. "Look your fill."

"They're all so beautiful."

"You've been down in Dillon's mine, haven't you?"

Kelsey nodded.

"Hard to believe these beautiful stones come from a place
like that, isn't it?"

"Impossible," Kelsey murmured, admiring one particularly
large opal that had been set as a brooch in gold filigree.

"We've got something else you'd find fascinating." Melanie lifted a hinged section of the counter and invited Kelsey
back. "You've met Gary at the motel, haven't you?"

Kelsey tried to remember. "I don't know. I don't think so.
An older woman has always been at the desk when I've needed
something."

"Then you've got a treat in store for you." Melanie lifted her
eyes toward the heavens, as if seeking strength.

Kelsey followed Melanie through what looked like a storage
area into a workroom. Sitting at a small table was a man wearing a dark canvas apron and what looked like motorcycle goggles. The machine he was bending over whined with the nerve-
tightening cadence of a dentist's drill.

Melanie waited until he straightened and turned off his machine. "Gary? I wanted you to meet Kelsey Donovan, Jake's
daughter. She's a guest at the motel."

Gary removed his goggles, and Kelsey saw immediately why
Melanie had stayed in Coober Pedy. Gary had the good looks
of a young Steve McQueen and a smile that could turn a

woman inside out. The face and smile were crowned by prematurely silver hair that was thick and beautifully cut.

"Hello, Kelsey." He stood, stretching kinks from a long, lean body as he did. "A pleasure to meet you."

Kelsey extended her hand and murmured her own greeting.

"I wanted to show Kelsey the latest addition to your fossil collection. Would you mind?" Melanie asked.

Gary's smile was polite. "Not at all." He stretched again, then made his way to a locked cabinet, pulling a sizeable ring of keys from his pocket to unlock it. He slid a tray off a shelf and brought it over for Kelsey to admire.

Kelsey had expected almost anything except what she saw. "An opal shell?"

Gary nodded. "A bivalve mollusk, ancient relative of a mussel. We call this a solid shell because the opal's made an internal mold of the specimen. Sometimes we find skin shells, opal that's filled space left when shells dissolved out in the bleaching process."

"How old is this?" Kelsey marveled at the flashes of color from the material lapping over the shell from its secret home inside.

"The age of opal is considered to be Late Tertiary, Miocene or Pliocene."

Kelsey looked up and smiled. "That means?"

"Roughly? Anywhere from fourteen to twenty-six million years ago."

"That sort of puts us in perspective, doesn't it?"

"I've told Gary to bury me in an opal mine somewhere when I die. My fondest wish is to have my bones preserved in opal," Melanie said, moving to Gary's side to take his arm.

Kelsey just caught the flicker of annoyance that crossed Gary's face before he covered it with a smile. "Did Melly tell you about my collection?"

"I didn't," Melanie answered before Kelsey could.

"That's a surprise, Melly, love. I've never known you, to keep silent about anything before."

If Melanie felt chastised, she didn't show it. "Gary collects opalized fossils, among other things. He's a regular museum."

"Then this isn't a rarity?" Kelsey asked.

Gary lifted the tray. "Rare enough, but the miners here bring me specimens when they find them, so I've got a rather nice assortment."

"Gary, maybe Kelsey would like to see what you're doing, since she's new here. Then we'll leave you alone." Melanie squeezed Gary's arm, then released him.

"Have you learned much about opal, Kelsey?" Gary asked as he returned the tray and locked the cabinet door.

"I've been down in my father's mine, but that's all."

"I'll be glad to show you what I'm doing." He turned to Melanie, and his voice changed subtly. "Shouldn't you be out front, Melly, love? I'd like to have some opals left to sell."

Melanie laughed. "The way you have the cases wired, Gary, *love*, there's no way anyone is going to break into them without all of Coober Pedy knowing." She held up her hands to ward off his answer. "But I'm going, I'm going."

Gary waited until Melanie was gone. "When I woke up this morning, her hair was black," he said, almost to himself.

Kelsey felt a peculiar urge to stand up for her new friend. Patriotism, she supposed, mixed with the sisters-all cry of feminism. "Melly's made me feel at home here."

"She has that ability, doesn't she?" He shrugged. "Come see what I was doing."

For the next half hour Gary lectured as he cut and ground opal while Kelsey watched. He showed her how large stones were cut to more manageable size, since no one wanted to wear a heavy rock, even a beautiful heavy rock, around their necks. Then he demonstrated the use of the grinding machine, gluing a small piece of opal to a dob stick with sealing wax, then grinding it down until it was a perfect oval.

"The trick is to take out the impurities, sand and such," Gary explained, "without losing much of the stone." He held up the nearly finished product, removing his goggles with the other hand. "When this is just the way I want it, it goes to the polishing wheel, where we use chemicals to help take out the grinding marks. Then I'll assess it."

"You assess by weight?"

"Weight, color, clarity." Gary held the stone to the light as he talked. "The most valuable opal is black. We don't mine that here, although Mintabie, not far away, has some. Good black opal from Lightening Ridge in New South Wales sell for five thousand to eleven thousand dollars a carat."

Kelsey whistled softly. Gary had artist's fingers, and he caressed the stone as he turned it so that color flashed in radiant hues.

"Here in Coober Pedy, most of our opal's lesser quality but more plentiful. The clearer the opal, the more valuable, but we look at other factors, too. Red-fire opal is more valuable than green, which is more valuable than blue. Harlequin opal, opal where the color shows up in patches, is more valuable than pin-fire opal where the color shows up in tiny specks."

Gary's voice was prayerful in its intensity. Kelsey suspected he was a man fascinated with his work. Possibly obsessed. "I saw a lot of black opal in the showcase outside, and it didn't seem terribly expensive."

"That's not black opal, not really. Those pieces are what we call triplets. We glue thin opal slices to a dark base. That way the colors of the opal are captured and controlled. They don't diffuse. Then we cap off the stone with a crystal quartz cabochon, and we have a lovely piece of jewelry at a fraction of the price of a black opal cabochon. Depending on the quality of the opal, the triplet can be fairly inexpensive or worth a great deal."

Kelsey remembered Dillon saying that most of the Rainbow Fire's opal had gone for triplets. Now she understood. "There's not much money for the miners in that, is there?"

Gary's voice lost its dreamlike quality. "Don't let this place fool you, Kelsey. Everyone here lives on a dream. Coober Pedy gets two, maybe three good hits a year. No more than that."

"What's a good hit?"

"Something over the three hundred thousand dollar mark. Maybe three percent of the rest of our miners make a good income, another three make reasonable wages. And then there's the rest...."

Kelsey remembered dilapidated doors shoved against holes in hillsides. She imagined she knew what group those miners belonged in. Suddenly she wanted Gary to confirm what Dillon had told her about the Rainbow Fire's productivity.

"My father," she began. "Where did he fit in that breakdown?"

Gary rubbed the opal against the sleeve of his shirt as he talked. "Your father's luck has never really been steady. Sometimes he's successful, sometimes he's not. He's struggled, but Jake's a fighter. He's always hung in until things got better."

Kelsey hoped that Jake was going to carry that fight into his hospital room. Her phone call with his doctor that morning had revealed that Jake had made little progress. Sensing Gary's impatience to get back to work, she held out her hand. "I won't take up any more of your time. You've given me a good introduction. I'm beginning to understand what this is all about."

His handshake was warm and strong. "Let me know when you understand it all. I'm not certain I understand it myself."

Back in the showroom Kelsey waited for Melanie to release the lock on the counter. After Melanie's remark about security alarms, she wasn't taking any chances by doing it herself.

"What do you think?" Melanie reached into the case and brought out a tiny opal triplet on a silver stickpin. "You can't live here and not own an opal. This will start your own collection."

Kelsey was touched. "It's lovely."

"I thought the green in the stone would go nicely with your skin and hair. Put it on."

Kelsey slid the pin through the lapel of her blouse. "How does it look?"

"Wonderful. Now you're official."

"Officially what?"

"A victim of greed fever." Melanie reached over the counter and straightened the pin. "Did you like Gary?"

Kelsey was reserving judgment, as she always did, but she wasn't going to tell Melanie that. "He's very nice."

"I'm not sure that's the word I'd use." Melanie stepped back. "Charming, though, isn't he? I can't seem to do without him."

For a moment Kelsey could think of no man but Dillon. There had never been a man in her life she couldn't do without. In fact, there had been very few men in her life at all. And not one of them had affected her like the man who had kissed her last night. Right before he had saved her life.

"Kelsey?"

Kelsey's head snapped up. "Do you understand men, Melly?"

"Better than I'd like to."

"What would you do if you had treated one badly and wanted to make amends?"

Melanie considered the question. "I'd take him to bed."

Kelsey considered her answer. "Short of that?"

"You could always say you were sorry. Are we talking about Dillon?"

Kelsey realized she was asking for advice. She never asked for advice because it was just one more way of putting yourself in another person's debt. And it was one more way of sacrificing privacy. Now she had done both, and she didn't even care. "Suspicion is a destructive thing, isn't it?"

"A little can be healthy."

"Only if it's not misplaced."

"Invite him out to dinner, tell him you're sorry, and let nature take its course."

Kelsey thought the first two ideas had merit, although the thought of humbling herself and spending money at the same time filled her with horror. "Good advice," she said, wishing she didn't have to take it.

"Glad I could help."

They chatted for a few moments until a small busload of tourists flooded the showroom with enthusiasm and cash. After another thank-you Kelsey went back into the sunshine and wished her next encounter with Dillon was already over. She ignored the small voice inside her that insisted her encounters with Dillon were just beginning.

That night Anna served Kelsey lasagna that surpassed her pizza—if such a thing were possible. Then she sat across the table from her, leaning on her elbows and watching intently as Kelsey chewed her first bite. "Well?"

Kelsey rolled her eyes blissfully. "Why on earth are you in the middle of the outback cooking your heart out?"

"You like it?"

"I like it."

Anna slapped the table. "I knew you would. I make the best lasagna in Coober Pedy. You come and eat my lasagna every Wednesday, and you'll grow fat and happy here. Like me."

Kelsey stopped chewing. Three Wednesdays of Anna's lasagna probably wouldn't deposit more than an ounce or two on her slender body. She suspected Anna had something more long range in mind. "I'm only going to be here a few weeks."

Anna pulled a mimeographed menu out of her apron pocket. "I made a list of reasons why you should stay." She shoved it under Kelsey's plate. On the back of today's specials was a list, painstakingly copied in the most beautiful script Kelsey had ever seen. "The first reason, that's a selfish one. That thing you do..."

"Karate?"

Anna nodded. "It's a good thing. My little boy, Giorgio, he wants to learn it. He watches that movie all the time."

Kelsey was beginning to understand. "*The Karate Kid?*"

Anna nodded. "Giorgio, he watches it every chance he gets on our video recorder. He goes around the house scrubbing the air with one hand, wiping with the other, but the other kids, they still pick on him at school."

Kelsey hid a smile. "You know, Anna, karate's not really like that. You have to study hard, and it's a lot of work."

"You don't live in the outback if you don't like work. If you don't like work you go live by the beach somewhere and let coconuts fall on your head. Finish your lasagna." Anna reached across to Kelsey's plate and broke a breadstick in half, buttering it lavishly and handing it to Kelsey to eat.

Obligingly Kelsey took a bite. "Anna, I owe Dillon a dinner. If I bring him here tomorrow, will you make us some of this lasagna?"

"Ravioli. Dillon is a good man. He needs a good woman." Anna seemed to think that was the more important issue. She put her finger on the list. "Number two."

Kelsey leaned back in her chair, suppressing a smile. "Now how do you know I'm a good woman?"

"You gave Serge what he's been asking for since he came to this town. I'd like to shake your hand."

Kelsey was more interested in Dillon and Jake than Serge, but she couldn't resist one question. "Do you think Serge will try to get revenge for what I did? Dillon seems worried."

"You made him lose face. He won't like you for that. Yes, Serge, he could try to hurt you." Anna frowned. "Maybe I'd better make a different list, huh?"

"Do you know him well?"

"He eats in here sometimes, but he never finishes his pizza. Nobody leaves without finishing my pizza." Anna sniffed disdainfully. "You're not finished with the list."

Kelsey had already seen the last item. It was so much like number two that she had hoped to ignore it. "How can you possibly know that Dillon and I are right for each other? We hardly even know each other. And you've only seen us together once."

"Dillon, he's like my son." Anna ignored the fact that she was only a little older than Dillon. "I've been trying to find him a woman for years. He don't like any of the women I find for him. Good-looking, smart women, too. But I see the way he looks at you. He looks at you like he looks at my pizza."

Kelsey managed to swallow the last bit of her breadstick without choking. "Anchovy or pepperoni?" she asked when she was sure it was safe.

"My special pizza," Anna said proudly as she stood to serve a new customer. "The one with everything on it."

The dinner had been wonderful, but later, after Kelsey paid Anna and left, she decided the boost to her self-esteem had been priceless. She had been favorably compared to Anna's pizza. She had a whole new sense of feminine allure.

Out on the street she admired the mauve-streaked golden sky, which was casting an ethereal glow over the little mining town and softening everything it touched. As the sun sank behind distant hills, the twilight air grew cooler and more humid. Filled with the herb-laden wealth of Anna's lasagna and the power of her own resolve, Kelsey started toward the pub.

She would see Dillon tonight. He would be at the pub, she would see him, and they would talk. They would talk, she would try to explain that she'd had to be careful, and he would understand. He would understand and they could go back to being... Being what? Kelsey tried to imagine what they could go back to being.

A man materialized from the shadows to stop just in front of her. "Hey, doll, whatya doing out by yourself?"

Mentally Kelsey demoted herself to white belt for not paying attention to her surroundings. She distributed her weight evenly on both feet, levering herself forward so that she could be ready to dodge and run. "Were you waiting for me, Serge?"

"I was waiting."

Kelsey scanned the area to see if he had brought backup. They were alone. "I don't know why," she said quietly. "We have nothing to talk about."

"I don't wanna talk, doll."

She wished his source of B movie dialogue would dry up. "We have that much in common. I don't want to talk, either. I just want to wish you a pleasant evening and walk on by."

He snorted, and she shifted forward a little more. She knew she could beat him in a race, but first she had to get away.

"Where's your boyfriend?" Serge inched a little closer, but Kelsey stood her ground, meeting his eyes in an unflinching gaze.

"Do you really want trouble?" Kelsey asked, ignoring his question.

"I don't like what you did to me, doll."

"And I didn't like what you did to me. I'd say we're dead even."

Serge lifted his hand, as if to reach for her. Kelsey spun away from him as another figure stepped out of the shadows.

"I'd say Miss Donovan was dead right," Dillon told Serge, moving closer as he talked. "And I'd say it's a dead cert you'd better be out of here in three seconds."

"I wasn't doin' nuthin to your lady friend, Ward."

"One...." Dillon stepped closer.

Serge seemed to be weighing the situation.

"Two...."

Serge shoved his hands into the pockets of his ragged jeans. "Your bodyguard won't always be here," he told Kelsey, although he didn't take his eyes from Dillon's. Then, spinning on one heel, he turned and started down the street.

Dillon took a step in his direction, but Kelsey held him back, her fingers resting against his bare arm. "Don't. Let him go. He's all talk."

Dillon looked down at the long, delicate fingers that lay so naturally against his skin. He had told himself he wouldn't react to Kelsey Donovan again, but the lecture hadn't stuck. "I've heard rumors about Serge and women. Stay away from him."

Kelsey bristled. "What do you think was going on here? Did you think I encouraged him?" She held up her hand to ward off his answer and forced herself to speak more gently. "I'm trying to stay away from Serge. But apparently he's been following me. Were you following me, too?"

"In a manner of speaking."

"Which manner of speaking? The one that says you were?"

Dillon folded his arms in front of him. "I was looking for more death adders to put under my bed, actually."

Kelsey scuffed her toe in the road and watched the dust billow. "I've got something to say to you, and it isn't easy for me."

"Get on with it, Sunset. I've been looking forward to it all day."

She lifted her eyes to his. "Sunset?"

"The color of your hair. Sunset's gold."

The nickname unnerved her more than the encounter with Serge had. This would be easier if Dillon were just any man she had misjudged. But he wasn't. He was Dillon Ward. And Dillon Ward was a force to reckon with. She wet her lips, wishing she could clear her throat. "Look, I can't make a real apology. I wish I'd never had to suspect that you hurt my father. But put yourself in my place. How could I trust you?"

"Could? That has a certain implication."

His eyes were the green of summer grass. Clear and green and absolutely impossible to read. She would have appreciated a spark of sympathy. "All right. I know I was wrong."

"Do you?"

"I do."

"And?"

She thrust out her chin. "I can't say I'm sorry. I had to be sure about you." She hesitated. "And now that I am, I'd like to thank you for saving my life." She hesitated again. "And my father's."

"I won't say don't mention it."

The small measure of defiance that had gotten Kelsey this far drained away. Tentatively she smiled, hoping to kindle the same in him. "I'd like to be friends."

"That would be unique."

The smile died. "Look, I don't blame you if you don't want to be friends. But I do plan to stay here, and I would like to continue going out to the mine with you."

"You're asking?"

"I'm asking."

"You're asking, not telling? Not demanding? Not insisting?"

"I'm asking."

He nodded. "Then let's go get your things."

It took Kelsey a moment to make the adjustment from the mine to her living situation. "My things?"

"If you're serious about staying, I want you where I can keep an eye on you. I don't have time to sleuth around in the shadows waiting for you to come to harm. I want you right beside me."

Kelsey knew she should protest. She knew she should assert herself and point out, once again, that she was perfectly well-equipped to care for herself. But the truth was that, for what-ever reason—financial, safety, comfort, or something that was a combination of all those and more—she wanted to move into Dillon's dugout.

"I'll come." But she couldn't let him think he had won. As Dillon started down the road, she touched his arm to stop him. "After all," she added, "you're the one they've been trying to kill. Someday soon, you might need my help."

Chapter 9

The next morning there was no sunshine streaming through leaded glass windowpanes. There was only the soft glow of incandescent bulbs seeping under the doorway to caress sunshine-yellow walls. Kelsey stretched, reaching for the lamp beside her bed as she did.

Squinting, she peered at her watch, forcing her sleepy eyes to focus. Six o'clock. Some internal time clock had alerted her that it was morning; there were certainly no other signs, no bird song, no sunrise glow, no dew-freshened air.

Morning in a cave, and a cave it was, even if the walls were sunshine-yellow. A cave with a resident caveman who would be up soon if he wasn't already, a caveman who had politely installed her in this room the night before and then disappeared into his own room without so much as a "sleep well."

But then, Kelsey couldn't really blame Dillon for last night's aloofness. He was a man who was naturally warm and considerate, but he was nobody's puppy dog, to come running with tail wagging after a vicious kick. He had saved her life at the risk of his own, and she had repaid him with suspicion. He was wary now of being insulted again. And maybe a little wariness would be best. Wariness could prevent complications for them both.

Kelsey forced herself to sit up and swing her legs over the side of her bed, digging her toes into the green carpeting. She always woke slowly. It routinely took her eyes fifteen minutes to focus and her brain another fifteen to send decodable messages to the rest of her body. At the end of an hour she was herself again, ready to take on the world. Before that she was anyone's easy mark.

So obviously the first hour of her morning was not a good time to encounter Dillon. She needed her wits about her with him. That thought sent her to her feet. She drew her knee high and executed a clumsy roundhouse kick, feinting with a right jab as she did. She barely stayed erect.

"Shower," she mumbled sleepily. "Coffee."

She smoothed her turquoise nightshirt over her bottom before she wove her way to the door. There was silence in the hallway and no visible sign of Dillon. Satisfied that she could make it into the bathroom without encountering him, she gathered the clean clothes that she had laid out in a neat pile the night before and started down the hall.

Padding barefoot past his room she listened for signs of waking. There were none, nor were there signs of life from the kitchen. Dillon was probably still asleep, and she would be wide awake, showered and ready for anything when he finally woke up.

Except that as she pushed the bathroom door open she discovered she had miscalculated. Billows of soap-scented steam greeted her, as did the sight of a muscular giant wrapped from the waist down in a white bathtowel. She cursed her brain for being as foggy as the bathroom mirror.

Dillon watched the steam turn Kelsey's sleep-ruffled waves into ringlets. Not for the first time he wondered what it would feel like to lose his hands in the shining wealth of her hair. So much hair for such a small woman.

So much woman.

Her skin was flushed and her eyes heavy-lidded. He could see surprise war with befuddlement. Without a doubt she was not a morning person. Dillon tried to suppress a smile and failed. His eyes drifted down to skim over the turquoise shirt that stopped mid-thigh to expose a vast expanse of leg. So much leg for such a small woman.

So much woman.

"You're supposed to be in bed," she mumbled.

He lifted one eyebrow and wondered if it was pulling his smile wider, higher. He waited for her next inanity.

She rubbed one fist over an eyelid, as if to insist it open farther. "I was sure you were."

"Disappointed?"

On some barely conscious level Kelsey knew she really shouldn't be standing in the bathroom with a man who was wearing nothing more than a towel, an uncut opal on a gold chain and a dimple-adorned grin. Especially if that man was Dillon. She blinked and wondered why her eyes were taking a complete census without asking her brain for permission. She wondered how she was going to feel after the census was completed and tabulated. As warm and tingly as she did now?

Disappointed? What was there to be disappointed about? The man was perfection. Trim and firm and muscular. Broad-shouldered and narrow-hipped, with none of the beer-belly slackness of some of his counterparts. And she should know, because except for what the small rectangle of terrycloth covered, every part of him was exposed. She cleared her throat. "Disappointed?" Her voice squeaked.

"Disappointed that I'm not in bed." Dillon watched the flush on her cheeks deepen. When she didn't speak, he lifted his hand and caressed her jaw. "Sunset, are you awake?"

The touch did what the visual census had not. She was jolted into consciousness. She felt her cheeks burn. "I'm sorry." She backed up a step. "I'll leave you to finish in here. I really must be half-asleep."

"I believe I prefer you all soft around the edges like this."

She couldn't dispute that. But soft in the head was more like it. She turned to head back down the hall.

"Don't hurry off. You can have the bathroom. I'll dress in my room." Dillon's hand settled on her shoulder.

Kelsey wondered if the imprint of his hand would be etched in her skin when she took off her nightshirt. *Soft in the head and getting softer all the time.* "I don't want to rush you." She tried hard to sound normal while she tried to rebuild her decaying defenses. But so far she was only conscious, not strong. Strength took more than two open eyes and a nervous system that was tuned for takeoff.

Dillon let himself touch her hair. One long curl twined around his fingers. "I'm not rushing. I can dress in my room as easily as in here."

She didn't turn. "You must be in a hurry to get to the Rainbow Fire."

"I reckon I've got some work to do around here before I go anywhere."

He sounded as if he thought she would understand, but her brain wasn't working well enough yet to think past the warm, strong hand on her shoulder. "Work?"

He laughed softly. Her voice was as unfocused as her eyes. Somehow it pleased him to see a chink in her armor, even if the chink was only a metabolism that worked at snail speed in the mornings. "Work. I've got to make certain no more little pets are dropped off in my bedroom." He paused. "Or yours." He felt the faint tremor that shook her body just before he dropped his hand. "I took care of things temporarily yesterday morning, but today I've got to make certain we stay safe."

Starless velvet darkness had closed around them when they had come back to the dugout last night. Kelsey knew only that Dillon had asked her to stand back as he had unlocked the door. "What did you do?"

"I trip-wired my front door."

She was awake now. Fully awake. She turned, hands on hips. "You did what?"

"Wired the front door. For explosives. A temporary measure until we get to the bottom of this."

"And what if I'd decided to go for a walk last night?"

He grinned as he outlined an unmistakable mushroom cloud with his hands. "Boom."

Kelsey took a menacing step forward. "You bastard."

"Ah, the lady comes awake with a vengeance."

"Just what do you mean, boom?"

His eyes danced with humor. "I suppose if you'd gone through the front door there wouldn't have been enough left of you to feed to a kookaburra."

She didn't know if his grin was because that thought pleased him or because he just enjoyed seeing her angry. Whichever it was, she wanted to wipe it off his face. "Apparently that's what you hoped. Maybe I was right about you before. Maybe you have it in for the Donovans, after all."

The grin disappeared. "You lack a sense of humor. But you make up for it with an overdose of paranoia."

"I've never thought dying was funny."

"I wired the door, but the wires aren't hooked to a thing. They're there for the effect. It's an old trick your father taught me. Used to wire Rainbow Fire for real until he nearly blew a finger off. Then he started pretending he was wiring it, and it worked just as well."

"Then why did you have me stand back last night when you unlocked the door?"

"To fool anyone who might have been watching."

It was all too much for her: the sight of Dillon's magnificently perfect and nearly unclothed body; the early morning hour; his Aussie sense of humor; and the fact that she had, once again, thought the worst of him. She sagged against the sink, all signs of life gone. "Then why didn't you say so?"

"I thought you'd realize I was having fun with you. I forgot that nothing's funny to you."

"That's not really true." She met his eyes. "It's just that there's been nothing to laugh at here, Dillon. These haven't been the funniest few days of my life."

He felt her words cut right through both of them. Without thinking, he stepped closer and put his arms around her to help heal the wound. "I'm sorry, Sunset. I should have realized this isn't the time for jokes."

Kelsey rested her cheek beside the opal on his chest. His skin was still faintly damp and cushioned by a liberal mat of hair. Warning bells rang even as she relaxed against him. "I guess I'm not used to your sense of humor."

Since humor was now the farthest things from his mind, Dillon's arms tightened a little. "What is it about you Donovans, anyway? You're a right difficult lot to get along with, yet I don't seem to be able to stay away from you."

"Maybe you like trouble." And maybe she did, too. Why else would she still be resting in his arms? Why else would she have her cheek nestled against his chest like a woman who'd just been well loved?

"I never thought I liked trouble." Dillon gave in to the overwhelming desire to lose his hands in Kelsey's hair. It flowed over his fingers with a life of its own. "And I shouldn't like you. You're suspicious and cynical and as prickly as an echidna."

"Echidna?"

"A bit like your porcupine. It relies on its strength and its prickly spines to stay alive. You've got that much in common."

She laughed a little, her warm breath ruffling the soft hairs of his chest. "But you can't hug an echidna."

"Even an echidna has its soft spot, its vulnerable area."

And this echidna, at least, was just beginning to comprehend how vulnerable she was. Kelsey could feel Dillon's body react to the feel of hers. There was nothing between them except a towel and her nightshirt, and if she didn't move quickly, the towel was going to be history.

Dillon seemed to realize the same thing, because he moved before she could, dropping his hands to the scrap of terrycloth at his waist. "Take your shower," he said gruffly. "I'll see you at breakfast."

"Yes." She felt dizzied at the sudden loss of his warmth, and even dizzier when she realized how much of herself she had just given him. She tried to sound businesslike. "I'll help you with whatever precautions you're planning to take."

"No you won't." Dillon watched her eyes narrow, and his voice grew heavy with irony. "My apologies. You're an expert on gelignite, then?"

"You said the wires were for show."

"Yesterday they were. After today they won't be."

"Wouldn't it be simpler and safer just to change the locks?"

"Whoever broke in here didn't leave as much as a scratch on the keyhole. We're working against a professional. Not a lock in the world would keep him out. Fear of blowing off a hand might, though. And I'm not going to trust a decoy for another night."

"What can I do?"

"Cook us some tucker. You do cook?"

"I have to eat, just like anyone else." Kelsey flattened herself against the sink and made room for Dillon to pass. She kept her gaze high, and he kept his hands on his towel. When he had gone, she stepped under the warm shower spray, but her sense of purpose was destroyed. She had never been more fully awake.

There was no coffee anywhere in Dillon's house, so Kelsey cheerlessly drank steaming tea that was as black as an outback night. There was no jam for the toast, so she ate hers plain and tried not to watch Dillon spoon stewed tomatoes over his. Tolerance faded at coddled eggs, however. After she had cooked them to specification, his looked as if he should drink it in orange juice. She continued boiling hers until it was as resilient as a tennis ball.

Sitting across the table from Dillon was strangely intimate. His hair was still damp, curling around a face that was strong enough to endure its softening influence. He had left the top three buttons of his shirt undone, more like a man who'd lost his concentration in the midst of dressing than a man with something to prove. She surmised that much because the fourth button looked as if it were only half done. Kelsey's gaze drifted to it time and time again in fascination, waiting for it to pop open.

They conversed politely, although seconds later she had no idea what had been said. But she was acutely aware every time his gaze skimmed over her, every time he abruptly looked away, as if he were trying to train himself to ignore her.

She hadn't often sat in such casual intimacy with a man. In the past, when she'd thought about it, she had decided that she had the instincts of a nun. She, too, had devoted her life to other pursuits, eschewing the pleasures a man could bring. Now she wondered why. Had it been fear that a man might leave her as her father had? Had she grown so strong that she didn't need anyone else in her life? Or was she still frightened that she wasn't strong enough?

"Pass the salt, please."

Kelsey handed Dillon the salt shaker, and their hands collided. There was no jolt of electricity, only the feeling that the touch should have lasted longer and an awareness of loss when his hand was back at his plate.

She watched him salt his egg and eat it with the last bits of toast. He ate the way he did everything else, politely, but with a sense of purpose. She suspected that anyone who had ever been fooled by Dillon's good manners and gentle ways had learned quickly about the steel beneath them.

He finished quickly and stood. "If you'll take care of the dishes, I can get started on wiring the lock."

She nodded, still wrapped up in her thoughts.

"When I'm done, I'll take you into town. The mechanic rang while you were showering. Your father's ute should be ready this afternoon. I'd like to bring it back here if you think you can drive it.''

"I've had some experience with trucks.'' She lifted her eyes and saw that he was watching her. His eyes flicked away and he turned to take his dishes to the sink. "With my father's truck available, I'll be able to get myself around. You won't have to worry about me.''

"I don't want you out of my sight.''

And she knew that if she wasn't out of his sight at least occasionally, they were going to end up somewhere neither of them belonged. "I can take care of myself.'' She softened her voice. "I'll be careful. And I'll let you know where I'm going.''

He grunted, although not in assent. "I've got work to do.''

Kelsey watched as he strode from the room. She had work to do, too. And the hardest work of all was going to be remembering that, in his own way, Dillon was as dangerous to her health as the man who might be stalking her.

To keep busy she spent the morning cleaning, her ear cocked for a telltale boom from the front porch. Dillon passed through the house several times, muttering to himself, but by lunchtime he seemed satisfied with the results of his labor. He took Kelsey outside for a lesson on opening the front door without losing her hand, a procedure that was surprisingly simple once she knew what she was doing. A neatly lettered sign beside the doorknob informed the unwary that entering the Ward dugout without permission could be fatal.

"And all your friends read English?'' Kelsey asked. In the last few days she had learned that Coober Pedy was populated by the representatives of forty-eight countries. The town was a mini United Nations, without protocol or diplomatic immunity.

"My friends don't pick the lock on my door. That's the only way to trigger this.''

Relieved that some friendly Ukrainian neighbor with a yen for a few minutes of gossip wouldn't be blown to bits, Kelsey followed Dillon back inside. They stopped in the kitchen. "I made soup,'' she told him. "And cheese sandwiches. I hope that's all right.''

Dillon was struck by the domesticity of the moment. When had a woman last anticipated his needs and fixed him a meal? There had been a growing emptiness inside him for years, an emptiness that couldn't be filled with one thoughtfully pre-

PLAY
SILHOUETTE'S

LUCKY HEARTS

GAME

AND YOU COULD GET

- ★ FREE BOOKS
- ★ A FREE CLOCK/CALENDAR
- ★ A FREE SURPRISE GIFT
- ★ AND MUCH MORE

TURN THE PAGE AND
DEAL YOURSELF IN →

PLAY "LUCKY HEARTS" AND YOU COULD GET...

★ Exciting Silhouette Intimate Moments® novels—FREE
★ A Lucite Clock/Calendar—FREE
★ A surprise mystery gift that will delight you—FREE

THEN CONTINUE YOUR LUCKY STREAK WITH A SWEETHEART OF A DEAL

When you return the postcard on the opposite page, we'll send you the books and gifts you qualify for, absolutely free! Then, you'll get 4 new Silhouette Intimate Moments® novels every month, delivered right to your door months before they're available in stores. If you decide to keep them, you'll pay only $2.49* per month, a savings of 26 cents off the cover price, and there is <u>no</u> charge for postage and handling! You can cancel at any time by marking "cancel" on your statement or returning a shipment to us at our cost.

★ Free Newsletter!

You'll get a free newsletter—an insider's look at our most popular authors and their upcoming novels.

★ Special Extras—Free!

When you subscribe to Silhouette Books, you'll also get additional free gifts from time to time as a token of our appreciation for being a home subscriber.

*Terms and prices subject to change.

pared lunch. It was the emptiness of a man too long alone, the emptiness of a man who has lived on dreams and found that dreams alone can't nourish body or soul.

Sometimes he had dreamed of a woman who would share his life. But what woman would come willingly to Coober Pedy to make her home? A starry-eyed romantic who was so much in love that she believed she could surmount the heat and flies, the dust and plodding sameness of the days? How long would the romance last? One year? Two?

"You don't like cheese?" Kelsey was surprised at the far-away expression on Dillon's face. Apparently she had triggered more than his appetite.

"I might like it too much." He didn't add that he might like *her* too much. It was fine to dream of an anonymous woman sharing his life. It wasn't fine to pretend that the woman could be Kelsey. Kelsey whose purity of purpose and spirit was like a harlequin opal, simmering with flashes of brilliance and color, and lit by enough fire to keep a man warm for the rest of his days.

"That doesn't make sense," she said with a frown. "Did you want me to make something you didn't like?"

He smiled to reassure her. "Thank you for lunch. I didn't expect it."

His gratitude was a surprise. And something more. It touched a place inside her that was only just beginning to make itself known. She felt absurdly shy, as if she wanted to retreat somewhere and examine this new sensitivity to see if it needed protection or the healing sunshine of more exposure.

"It's just lunch." She turned away from his smile. "I owe you that much."

"You don't owe me a thing."

"I feel like I do. And I always pay my debts."

He looked around the kitchen, noting the changes she had made. It was now as neat and orderly as her suitcase. "And do you keep track of them in a book somewhere to be sure you're always paid up and free?"

Put that way, it did sound ridiculous. "I suppose in a way I do," she said, half to herself. "But I was raised to. Every relative I lived with kept track of what I owed, not so much because they expected payment, but more just to keep me in line. I grew up thinking debts and credits were the only way people related to each other." She realized Dillon might misunderstand and think she was complaining. "It wasn't necessarily a bad thing," she added. "I learned not to lean on anyone."

"You could do with learning to lean a little."

She laughed humorlessly. "I've leaned on you repeatedly."

"And that embarrasses you?"

"Humiliates me."

"What if I told you I liked it?"

The husky sound of his voice made her turn to stare at him. "Then I'd say you were like men everywhere, Dillon. You want a woman in your debt. And that's just what I guard myself against."

"And if you're in my debt, just what am I going to demand for payment?" He moved up behind her back, pinning her against the cabinets. His breath whispered through her hair. "Your soft, sweet body? Your hand in marriage? Your love?"

For one ridiculous moment none of those demands sounded half bad. Then she came to her senses. "I wouldn't put it past you or any man."

"And if you didn't want any of those things, you could just say no. What man would be fool enough to try and force a black belt into his bed?"

He had a way of taking apart her defenses and exposing their flaws. But there were things he didn't know. "Why do you think I *am* a black belt?"

Dillon put his hands on her shoulders and gently turned her to face him. "Do you want to tell me?"

She injected carelessness into her voice. "It's simple, really. I'm a black belt because I haven't always understood the way men think. You see, I grew up understanding debts and credits, I just didn't understand that when a man buys you a few dinners and says he loves you, he thinks that's his ticket to do anything he wants. He thinks you *owe* him your soft, sweet body." She watched his eyes begin to smolder. She wasn't sure who his anger was directed at, but she went on anyway.

"When I was eighteen, I learned that lesson the hard way. The man was big and strong. Innocent that I was, I believed him when he said we were stopping by his apartment to pick up something he'd forgotten. I might still be there if a neighbor hadn't heard my screams and called the police."

Dillon clenched his fists, but he kept his lips welded firmly together. There was nothing he could say that could help Kelsey. He only wished he could get his hands around the neck of the bloody bastard who had abused her.

Kelsey cleared her throat. Funny, but after all these years, she still had to clear her throat when she told the story. "It took me a while to recover. Emotionally, that is. Luckily the police got there quickly enough that I didn't have more than a few bruises to show for the experience. But what spirit he left me was black and blue for months. Then one day I realized I had to do something. I was scared of my own shadow, and I'd turned into a recluse. I heard about a self-defense class at the Y, so I enrolled. It was a start, but not nearly enough to make me feel safe. The instructor had her own *dojo*, and I started regular karate classes a few weeks later. I lived and breathed it for years. I'd go straight to the *dojo* every day after work, and I'd work out and train until they shut the doors. I was quick and flexible, but strength came slowly. I moved up the ranks inch by inch until one day I realized I wasn't afraid anymore."

Dillon could have told Kelsey that wasn't true. She was afraid of men, perhaps not physically, but afraid to trust them. He knew, without being told outright, that Kelsey hadn't let a man get close to her since she had nearly been raped. And why would she? From what he knew of her life, every man in it had let her down.

"Not all men want to hurt you, Sunset." He refrained from touching her. Instead he tried to let his voice breach the inches between them. "Some men are healers."

She lifted her chin. "Are they? Where do they hide?"

"You can't see them if you wear blinders."

Blinders of fear and anger. She knew what he meant. What he didn't know was how comforting those blinders could be, because with them she didn't have to take chances. "The soup is getting cold," she said pointedly.

As cold as the empty lives of a man and a woman who badly needed the warmth of love? "I'll get the bowls." Dillon leaned toward her, reaching above her head. His chest brushed the softness of her breasts, and his reaction was instantaneous. He heard the quick intake of Kelsey's breath, but she didn't move. He stretched closer until the bowls were in his hand. He wanted to stay that way forever, on the verge of something incredible without the realities of rejection and mutual pain. But no one could live forever on the edge. His eyes locked with hers, and he saw defiance veiling the very real needs of a passionate woman.

He stepped back. "Why don't you sit down? I'll get the soup."

Disappointment fought relief. Neither won. "I'll get the sandwiches." Kelsey moved to the counter and gathered the platter and napkins.

Lunch was much like breakfast: polite conversation she couldn't remember seconds later and a constant simmering awareness of the man sitting across from her. Kelsey was relieved when the last sandwich had disappeared.

"If we leave now, we can fetch your father's ute and still have time to go down in the mine for a while. Does that suit you?" Dillon leaned back in his chair and finished the tea he had brewed himself.

"Suits me fine. I'll change my clothes and be back in a minute." Kelsey stood, relieved to leave the room. Dillon watched her go and told himself, that he'd better get used to her retreats. Their relationship would be made of them.

The trip into town was made in silence. The garage was little more than a tin shack with dusty cars in laughably straight rows waiting for servicing. Dimitri, the mechanic, was a bearded Greek who regaled them with pleasantly accented tales of the town until Kelsey had almost forgotten why she and Dillon were there.

Jake's pickup—a term that Dillon informed her meant something much more suggestive than a truck in Australia—was as ageless as the outback and rustier and dustier than anything Kelsey had seen in Coober Pedy. A sane man would have sold it as scrap metal years before, but then, from everything Kelsey knew of her father, he was not a particularly sane man. Surprisingly the truck started immediately when she got behind the wheel. Whether it was a last gasp or a new lease on life, she wasn't sure. But it sounded good enough to get her out to the Rainbow Fire. There was no window to roll down—she wasn't even sure windows had been invented when the pickup rolled off the assembly line—so Kelsey stuck her head out the opening and told Dillon she would follow him to the mine.

Halfway out of the rock and car strewn lot, the pickup stalled. Kelsey started it again and drove several feet before it stalled once more.

Dillon stopped and went around to the front. Without a word, he threw up the hood and disappeared behind it. In a moment the story-telling Greek was at his side. Kelsey waited in the dubious shade of the cab until the hood closed with a grinding shriek. Dimitri motioned to the space she had just left. "Pull in and we'll have another go at it."

"It just needs a quick adjustment," Dillon told her, coming around to the side. "Shouldn't take more than a few minutes."

"You go ahead, then." Kelsey watched refusal spread over his features. "Go on, Dillon," she insisted. "I'm safe enough in plain sight of Dimitri. I know my way out to the mine from here, but I'll listen patiently while you quiz me anyway."

Dillon debated. He had wanted to explore the Rainbow Fire thoroughly for booby traps before Kelsey followed him down the shaft. This way he would have time to take precautions without making her a vulnerable target on the ground above him. He calculated the risks and decided she should wait while he went ahead. "I'll warn Dimitri about what's been going on. He can be trusted."

"I'll be along just as soon as I'm sure the truck will get me there."

Dillon nodded. Then, on an impulse, he reached through the window opening and brushed his thumb along her cheekbone. "You'll be careful, Sunset?"

Every time he called her by that absurd nickname, she got the most peculiar sensation. "I'm always careful," she said brusquely to cover her feelings. "I was careful before I met you, Dillon, and I'll be careful after I'm back in the States."

He wasn't hurt, because he saw the way her brown eyes had changed at his question. Outback desert after the first spring rains. Soft and full of promise. "When you get to the mine honk twice, and I'll be up in a flash. Don't leave the ute until you see me."

"Go on and stop worrying."

He smiled, and though he doubted she was aware of it, Kelsey smiled, too. He was gone in a moment.

Fifteen minutes later Kelsey stood under the slight protection the hood offered from the rising wind, which was sweeping fine particles of dust through the yard. She listened to Dimitri's explanation of what was still wrong with the carburetor. She didn't understand trucks, but she did understand that another half hour would be needed to finish repairing this one. She didn't mind the wait, but she resigned herself to the probability that Dillon would come back to look for her.

"I think I'll wait at the Pizza Palace," Kelsey told Dimitri, shading her eyes against the wind. "If Dillon comes back, would you tell him where I am?"

Dimitri waved her on, his head under the hood once again.

By the time Kelsey emerged from the Pizza Palace after finalizing that night's dinner plans with Anna, the wind was stronger. There was a powder-fine haze of dust in the air that tinted everything with a rosy glow. This rosy glow wasn't synonymous with well-being, however. The dust coated her skin, seeping into her very pores as she made her way back to Dimitri's.

Dimitri was inside, flat on his back under a Holden station wagon when Kelsey found him.

"Everything's all fixed?" she questioned him.

He answered in Greek, following the long unintelligible explanation with an affirmative grunt. Kelsey thanked him, but just as she was climbing into the truck out in the lot, a goo-coated Dimitri caught up with her. "You'd best wait here or go home." He pulled a rag from his back pocket and wiped unsuccessfully at his oil-stained hands. "Dillon won't want you driving out to the Fifteen Mile Field in this." He gestured to the air around them. "Dust storm's sweeping in. Don't like the looks of it."

On cue, a strong gust of wind swept across the bare lot, spinning debris in its wake. The dust seemed to grow thicker as they talked. "We have dust storms in my country, too," Kelsey said nonchalantly. After all, she had read The Grapes of Wrath.

"Then you know to go home."

Kelsey shook her head. "Home" was Dillon's dugout with a lock on the door that might blow her hand off. Despite Dillon's assurances to the contrary, she wasn't taking any chances. "I'll be fine. I'll just go a little way, and then if it looks bad, I'll come back here. But if I don't show up, Dillon's going to worry."

Dimitri pulled at his beard, greasing it liberally as he did. "Dillon won't like it if I let you go."

Kelsey pulled herself up to her full height. "*Let* me go? You can't stop me from going, Dimitri."

He seemed surprised, as if her logic were beyond him. "You'll just go a little ways? You'll turn back?"

"Yes, Dimitri," she singsonged.

He squinted at his watch, rubbed it against a clean place on his shirt pocket, then checked it again. "Three o'clock. I'll remember."

She smiled. "You do that." Turning back to the truck, she stepped up, slamming the door behind her.

Chapter 10

Kelsey swore softly at the potholes and ruts that jolted every part of her body until there was no longer a guarantee that her kneebone was connected to her thighbone. She had expected the poor condition of the roads, however. What she hadn't expected was that she might lose her sense of direction. She hadn't realized that the worst problem with outback roads was that there were no landmarks. One patch of scrubby mulga trees or clump of saltbush looked exactly like every other. Especially now that they were covered with a thickening cloud of dust.

The cracked windshield of Jake's truck was coated with a layer of dirt that blocked the finer details Kelsey might have used for identification. And, not surprisingly, the windshield wipers didn't work. She supposed that wasn't a problem Jake would have worried about in country that received five inches of rain in a good year. But it was a problem she had to worry about now.

The wind picked up as she drove, rattling the side panels of the truck and forcing her to grip the steering wheel with all her strength. When the dirt on the windshield built to unmanageable levels, she pulled to the side of the road and got out to wipe it with her hands, grimacing as the wind coated her with a new layer to add to the dust that had blown in through the truck windows.

She was back in the truck and out on the road again before she realized that she had only streaked the dirt, not removed it. She slowed her pace, leaning forward to peer through the deepening haze for the turnoff to the mine field where the Rainbow Fire was located.

Something large blew past her on a swirling gust of wind. She slammed on the brakes and swerved. The object stopped, turned in her direction to give her a soulful, nonverbal lecture, then hopped on.

"A kangaroo." Now why should that surprise her? She was in Australia, after all. In the middle of the outback. In a dust storm. "Terrific, Kelsey," she muttered. She shifted gears and revved the motor, fully intending to pull back onto the road. The motor revved and the gears ground, but the truck didn't move. She made her second exit from the cab, going around to the back to see what kind of trouble she had gotten herself into.

One wheel was firmly on the road, the other was in a hole, a natural depression that had grown deeper from the spinning tire. By the time she had scoured the area for rocks to fill the hole, her skin felt as if it were an inch deep in dust, and her hair was as stiff as a wire brush. The wind continued to grow stronger, whirling in cyclone-like gusts that picked up dust and debris and sent it spinning through the air. Visibility decreased as the wind increased, and even though Kelsey was able to get the pickup back on the road, she questioned the wisdom of trying to find the Rainbow Fire.

The problem was that she wasn't absolutely certain how to find her way back to Coober Pedy, either. She had made several turns, turns that had been uncomplicated and obvious when she had made them with Dillon. Now, with visibility decreasing, she wasn't sure she could find them again.

Stubborn pride had gotten her into this. She only hoped she had some redeeming quality to get her out of it.

Sensing that she was closer to the mine than to town, she decided to push on. She traveled in low gear, hitting every bump and rut in the road and stopping often to hand wipe the windshield. Her misgivings grew with the shrieking of the wind, until both were at the highest pitch.

Perhaps it was the wind, or perhaps her own fears, that masked the rumbling on the road behind her. Whichever it was, the rumbling had become a loud roar before Kelsey recognized the sound of danger. The road beneath her shook in warning, and the clouds of dust behind her parted like the Red Sea to reveal the largest semi she had ever seen bearing down on the pickup.

She wrenched the wheel sharply to the left and braced herself for impact. The flopping tailgate of the pickup caught the blow, sending it careening out of control over the side of the road into a wide ditch that culminated at the base of a hill. The semi roared on, hidden once more by thick, red clouds.

Kelsey rested her forehead against the steering wheel and forced herself not to cry. Her hands shook as she lifted them to rub her eyes. She waited for the jolt of pain that would tell her that she was injured, but it didn't come. Somehow, miraculously, she was alive and unharmed.

When she could manage, she sat straighter and peered through the dense, dry fog. She could see the outline of the hill that had halted the pickup's mad rush to safety. She had stopped just short of of the face, and the antique front fender of the pickup was lodged against a soft plateau of dirt leading up to the side of the hill. Shuddering, she tried not to imagine what would have happened if the truck had plowed full speed into the hillside. She had been saved, both by the slow speed she had been traveling and the dirt that had absorbed the impact. Too, although she couldn't thank the semi driver for much, he had obviously swerved as soon as he had seen her. And although he hadn't stopped to hear words of gratitude, his quick reflexes, along with hers, had probably saved her life.

Dust blew in the windows until there was no benefit to being inside the cab. Kelsey recovered most of her self-control before she opened the door and got out to inspect the damage to the pickup. Surprisingly, there didn't seem to be too much. The fender was bent beyond recognition, and the right front tire was quickly going flat, but nothing else seemed to be damaged except that the tailgate was gone, probably riding the wind to Timbuktu, or the Australian equivalent. With a tow chain, she and Dillon could pull the pickup back a few feet to where the ground was flat enough to change the tire, and, if she were lucky, she could probably be on her way again.

Except that Dillon wasn't there. In fact, he might never be there, because he might never find her. There was still no guarantee she had been traveling on the right road.

New fear replaced the residue left from the accident. Dust coated Kelsey's throat and plugged her nostrils. Each breath tickled her lungs with talcum-fine particles. How long did a dust storm last? Minutes? Hours? The wind swirling past her threatened to lift her off her feet and deposit her in the land of Oz. Except that the Aussies claimed this *was* the land of Oz. Which left her little hope for respite.

Forcing herself to be calm, she stood beside the dubious shelter of the cab and considered her options. She could get back inside the pickup and wait for the end of the storm, an end that might take hours or, worse, days. Or she could go back out to the road and wait for a rescue that might happen momentarily. Or next week sometime.

Her choice seemed clear, although she wasn't sure just how long she would last by the roadside. The wind might be whirling, but it did little to subdue the fierce heat of the outback summer afternoon. The sun was a brilliant spot in the haze above her. She wouldn't want to make bets on which force of nature was going to defeat her first: heat, dehydration, or dust cutting off the very air she was struggling to breathe.

There was little she could do about the first two problems, but with what ingenuity she could summon, she fished out a rag that had been stuffed in a gaping hole in the front seat and dipped it in the rust-tinged water of the radiator, tying it across her face, bandit-style, to help block the dust from her mouth and lungs. Then she made her way to the roadside, clinging to the dead branches of a mulga tree to anchor herself against the wind.

She had lost track of time in her struggle to find the Rainbow Fire, but as the sky slowly darkened, she knew the day wasn't ending. Instead, as if in answer to her unspoken prayer, dust was slowly blocking the sun. She couldn't even guess how far above her the storm reached, but the encroaching darkness began to dull the sun's fury. At least she had one less problem to contend with.

Unfortunately the darkness brought its own problems. Visibility decreased even farther, until she wasn't able to scan more than a few yards in any direction. If someone else was insane enough to be out on the road, there was a good chance they might not see her.

Kelsey concentrated on every sound. She hadn't paid close enough attention when she was driving, and she had suffered the consequences. Now she listened for every changing nuance. The shifting cadences of the wind became the focus of all her considerable energy. She held herself rigid against its force, straining to hear beyond it for the rumble of an engine, the honk of a horn, the blessed sound of a human shout. Dillon's shout.

She had no idea how long she had braced herself in the branches of the mulga when she heard the first whimper of an engine over the wind's screams. At first she wasn't sure it was real. She wanted so badly for the sound to be a car or truck that she wondered if she were imagining it. The wind picked up in fierce gusts that threatened to lift both her and the mulga tree, and for a moment all she could do was fight to maintain her hold.

Seconds later, a faint lull reassured her. The hum of the engine was unmistakable, although the changing wind made it impossible to tell which direction it was coming from. But it was coming. With luck she would be on her way soon, protected from the dust and the wind by some Australian good Samaritan.

At the next lull, she shouted, lifting the rag that protected most of her face. The wind picked up again, tossing her words to the four corners of the earth, but the engine was louder now, moving closer. She shouted again and was confident that this time her shout could have been heard. The purr grew louder, and she felt the first real stirrings of gratitude. She hadn't let herself dwell on the full ramifications of her predicament, but now she did. She was lucky to have survived the brush with the semi; she was doubly lucky to be rescued from the dust storm. Perhaps the next time she was about to encounter danger, she might think twice about ignoring good advice.

She shouted again, waving one arm, although she couldn't see anything through the haze in either direction. "Hello! Can you hear me? It's Kelsey Donovan!"

The sound of the engine died. At first she couldn't believe it. Perhaps the wind had picked up, masking the rumble momentarily. She strained to hear over the wind's roar, but there was nothing.

"Hello! Is anybody out there?" she shouted. There was no sound except the wind. She shouted again, and then a third time.

She couldn't believe it. Apparently the truck had turned off, perhaps taking a side road to a mine, or a house in the middle of nowhere. She hadn't been heard; she hadn't been seen. She was alone again, with dust driving into every pore of her body.

She shouted once more, expecting no response.

A faint click, almost masked by the wind's fury, was the answer she hadn't expected.

She strained to hear more, but nothing followed the click. She struggled to think what it could have been. The sound was familiar, yet out of place in the storm. Protecting her eyes, she struggled to peer through the rust-colored haze as she shouted one last time.

"Is anybody out there?"

There was no answering shout. No repeated click. No engine's hum. Only the unmistakable whine of a bullet as it passed over her head to cleanly pierce the rust-colored haze and split the wood of the mulga tree.

Dillon thoroughly examined the Rainbow Fire for booby traps. Nothing was evident, but he couldn't shake the feeling that someone else had been in the mine today, just as he couldn't shake his growing feeling that something was wrong with Kelsey.

They had known each other only days, yet he felt a bond with her that surpassed any he had ever known with a woman. He understood her in a way that had nothing to do with days or years, but everything to do with soul and spirit. He understood her well enough to know that the strong, courageous woman she had become still nurtured the tiny seed of a girl, frightened and alone. Her extreme neatness stemmed from a child's need to make sense and order out of a life controlled by uncaring adults. Her displays of strength and courage were a way of striking a blow for that girl, and she was capable of acting without considering all the consequences.

He hoped he was wrong. He hoped that Kelsey was back in Coober Pedy, waiting for him to return. He knew Dimitri well enough to realize that Jake's ute probably hadn't been ready on time. He also knew Dimitri well enough to believe that he would watch out for Kelsey, if Kelsey let him.

Dillon finished up his examination and started back to the main shaft. He was anxious to head back to town just to be certain things were all right. At the shaft, his fears were enhanced. Fine red particles floated down from the air above. The particles danced in the generator-powered light like fairy dust.

Dillon had seen the wind pick up and the dust blow as he had driven toward the Rainbow Fire. But wind and dust weren't unusual in outback South Australia. He had been too preoccupied to consider the worst case scenario. Now he did. Coober Pedy was in the throes of a dust storm, and Kelsey was out in the middle of it.

All other possibilities fled from his mind. He held his watch to the light. It was almost quarter past three. If Kelsey had set out for the mine, she would be here by now. Perhaps Dimitri had coaxed her to stay in town and not try the trip, but with painful perception, he knew the truth. No words of caution would have kept Kelsey from starting toward the mine.

But something or someone had kept her from getting here.

The ladder was slick with dust, but Dillon held on grimly, taking the steps two at a time. At the top his mouth went dry at the scene before him. Everything in his limited field of vision was covered with bull dust—the fine red particles that Jake had once laughingly called outback snow. The landscape had been transformed into a caricature of itself. Blowers and tunneling machines were grim, twisted sculptures against a rust-shaded horizon. His ute was a red-velvet throne.

He held tightly to the top rung of the ladder and listened to the wind howl. He had seen storms like this last for hours. Once he had watched dust blanket Coober Pedy for days. He had spent those days inside, alone, wondering why he lived in such a place. Now he wished that loneliness was all he had to worry about. It was much worse knowing that Kelsey was out in the storm somewhere.

And he knew she was. He could feel the certainty growing as the gusts of wind did.

Fighting to maintain his balance, he hoisted himself over the top of the shaft to the ground. In seconds he had fastened a sheet of iron to the shaft with a set of new locks he had brought with him. Not that he expected the locks to keep anyone out. But they would be visible proof to the intruder that Dillon knew someone had been in the mine. He was involved in a war of nerves, and he didn't intend to ignore either his offense or his defense.

He had made the trip to and from the Rainbow Fire so many times that he could drive it blindfolded, but today he drove cautiously, his narrowed gaze sweeping back and forth across the limited field of vision for signs of Jake's antiquated ute. He sensed rather than heard the rumble of a road train coming toward him, and he pulled to the edge of the road to let it pass, cursing softly as it did. He was all too familiar with the huge truck tractors pulling two and sometimes three, fifty-meter trailers behind them. Outback towns existed because the road trains transported goods to and from them, but that didn't make it easier to swallow the bushranger tactics of the drivers who stopped for no one and nothing in their race to their next destination. He hoped Kelsey hadn't encountered this one.

Back on the road, he continued his search until he reached Coober Pedy. The town was newly awash in dust, and its residents had gone home to hole up, lowering vent caps and sealing doorways until their dugouts were cozy fortresses against the storm. Dillon didn't even try the garage. He drove straight to Dimitri's dugout. In a moment he was banging on the door.

Just out of the shower, Dimitri came to the door still toweling his hair dry. He took one look at Dillon and shook his head slowly, sending droplets of water bouncing across his foyer floor. "She's right stubborn, that one. Left here at three o'clock to go out to the mine."

Dillon looked at his watch. That had been forty-five minutes before. "You're sure about the time?"

"Abso-bloody-lutely."

Dillon didn't even ask why Dimitri hadn't stopped Kelsey. He knew. "She didn't make it there. And I didn't see her on the way back."

"I'll ring your dugout."

Dillon waited in the foyer while Dimitri made the call. Dust caked every inch of his body and coated every hair. Dimitri's dugout was spotlessly clean.

Dimitri returned and shook his head. "Let me get my oil-skin."

Dillon wasn't too proud to accept help when Kelsey's life might depend on it. "I'll start on ahead."

"I'll crisscross the back roads."

"Right-o. Just don't get yourself lost."

Dimitri snorted. "And don't you do anything foolish, my friend. The little one's as much trouble as her father."

"More trouble." Dillon took the time to spare one brief smile. "More fun, too."

Back in his ute, Dillon followed the road out of Coober Pedy. The dust was so thick that he couldn't see Dimitri behind him, but he knew he was there by the sound of his ute's engine, just as he knew when Dimitri diverged on a side road that led to a small community of dugouts. Dillon didn't think that Kelsey would have mistaken the turnoff for the correct one, even if the dust was blanketing all landmarks. But this was no time to second guess her. In a storm like this one, anything was possible.

Where was she? Dillon wished he would climb into Kelsey's head and hear the thoughts that had brought her out into the middle of a howling outback storm. Was it a case of a fool rushing in? Was she once again testing herself to see if she had grown strong enough to withstand anything and anyone? Or had it been a simple error in judgment?

No matter. Kelsey was out here somewhere, and he had to find her. He slowed his pace, peering into the almost impenetrable veil of dust for any signs, no matter how small, that someone had recently passed this way.

Kelsey's only hope was that the storm wouldn't ease.

She had no time to dwell on the irony of that thought. Flattening herself against the sandstone hill that had demolished Jake's fender, she sidestepped slowly, peering through dust-reddened eyes into the fury of the storm. There was no sign of life in the swirling dust clouds, just as there had been no sign earlier. But there was a bullet lodged in the dead wood of a roadside mulga to prove that she was not alone.

Someone was stalking her with deadly intent, and her only defense lay in the thickness of the dust and her own silence. She moved slowly, with the lithe, spare movements that had taken her years to perfect. Not so much as a rock moved beneath her feet, and not so much as a breath was audible. Her body was under strict control, even if her mind was racing with fear.

She had gotten from the tree to Jake's truck in a matter of seconds. Now she was moving carefully along the hill, intending to follow it to another in the long chain of hills and gullies that rimmed this section of road. Her hunter had the same problems and possibilities that she did. If she were lucky, he would search for her in the wrong places. If she weren't lucky, he would find her with unerring instinct.

She took another step around the hill, then another, listening over the roar of the wind for any sound that might give her clues. There was a distance of twenty yards separating this hill from the next, and she calculated the odds of making it that far. Out in the open she would be a clear target, if it weren't for the dust. With the dust it was hard to say if she was a target at all. It depended on the wind. If she ran in the midst of a heavy gust, she would certainly be camouflaged. If she ran between gusts— and there would be no way to tell when she started which would be the case—she could be seen if the stalker were close enough.

Either way, if she ran or if she didn't, she was taking a chance. She balanced the possibilities and decided to run. At the beginning of the next strong gust of wind, she took off, speeding across the empty distance as she prayed that the gust would last. It didn't, but no shot rang out to tell her that she had been exposed. She rested between rocks at the base of the hill and planned her next move.

Minutes merged with minutes, hills with hills, as she made her way farther from the road. She rested at last in a cavelike projection of twin boulders and let the dust settle over her until she was indistinguishable from the rest of the landscape.

Kelsey was nowhere to be found. Dillon arrived at the Rainbow Fire hoping to see Jake's ute parked beside the locked mine shaft. But the mine field was abandoned. Everyone with any sense had gone home to wait out the storm. Everyone except Kelsey.

Without bothering to get out, he turned and started back toward town, stopping only when he saw Dimitri's ute sloughing its way through the dust at the entrance to the Fifteen Mile Field.

"No sign of her?"

Dimitri stuck his head through his window and grimaced as dust filtered into his clean hair and beard. "No worries, we'll find her."

"Did you search the old road leading off to the Break-aways?"

"No. Do you want me to?"

Dillon waved his hand in refusal. "You go back the usual way. Maybe you'll see something I haven't. I'll take some of the side roads."

"What'll I do if I find her?"

Dillon shifted gears. "Turn her over your knee."

The old road leading out to the Breakaways, a reserve at the foot of the Stuart Ranges, had been abandoned years ago in favor of a better, straighter route. But Dillon knew that the beginning of the road provided a shortcut for some road train drivers who saw it as a way of cutting off extra miles and avoiding mining equipment that was being hauled to any of the nearby fields. Because of that fairly frequent usage, the road wouldn't have looked abandoned to Kelsey, especially in the midst of a storm. Conceivably she might have confused the turn onto it for the correct one several miles up the Stuart Highway. Although Dillon knew that possibility was a long shot, he wanted to give it a try.

He wove in and out of roads, some barely more than paths, until the road widened perceptibly. Then he slowed his pace, searching both sides of the road as his ute fought against the shrieking, driving wind.

Less than a mile from the highway he stopped. There were no telltale tire tracks; the wind had taken care to smooth the ground to satin perfection. There was only a glimpse of metal caught between rocks a short distance from the road. Dillon reached for the full-length brown oilskin that he kept in his ute for emergencies. Snapping it as protection against the wind, he stepped out and went to investigate.

The large slab of metal rattled against the rocks that held it, like a prisoner rattling prison bars. Dillon drew closer, shading his eyes against the stinging dust. The metal was so misshapen and dust covered that for a moment he didn't recognize it. Then, his heart beat faster, he bent to run a finger down the distorted edge.

The metal had once been the tailgate of a ute. Jake's ute.

He straightened and looked for signs of the ute itself. Dust greeted him, coating every particle of exposed skin and blurring his vision. He cupped his hands around his mouth and shouted. "Kelsey? Are you out there?"

The wind screamed back at him.

He turned toward the road, following its barely perceptible edge on foot. He wasn't even sure which way to go; he only knew that he was finally on the right track. Kelsey had been here, and there had been an accident.

A hundred yards from the tailgate, he saw the dim, dust-coated outline of Jake's ute. He started to run, covering the short distance like a man possessed. At the ute, he threw open the door and stared inside. Kelsey was gone.

Dillon wasn't certain whether to be relieved or distressed. She had been here, and there had been an accident, but now she was gone. He didn't know how, and he didn't know where. He only knew he had to find her.

But where? Along the road? Or had she wandered through the hills, dazed and disoriented? He considered his choices, then decided that if she were walking along the road, he could find her quickly in his ute. But if she were wandering alone through the open country, he could only find her on foot. His immediate choice seemed clear.

He cupped his hands around his mouth again. "Kelsey! Are you out there?"

When there was no answer, he started along the chain of low hills leading into the desert.

Every muscle in Kelsey's body was tied in knots, but with the self-discipline she had spent her adult years achieving, she made no attempt to change position. The dust had settled over her, just as it had settled over the rocks that sheltered her. So long as she didn't move, she was indistinguishable from them.

Where was her hunter? Was he even now following the trail she had tried so hard not to leave? Did her footprints stand as testimony in the soft ground? Or had they been covered by the dust, a wind-driven gift from some guardian angel?

And when the wind died, what was she to do?

A strong gust sent debris spinning through the air. With it came the trace of a human voice. She resisted the temptation to lift her head in panicked surprise. Listening intently, she concentrated on the silences between howling gusts. There was nothing to hear.

If her hunter were near, would she be able to hide, or would she have to defend herself? And what defense did she, cramped and aching, have against even a single bullet?

"Kelsey!"

This time the voice was clear and close. This time her head snapped up of its own volition. "Dillon." She whispered the word. For one awful moment she agonized over whether she had mistaken the voice. Would anyone care enough about another person to search for them in a storm like this one? Or was her hunter hoping she would believe the impossible?

No! With a burst of faith, she clawed her way between the rocks. "Dillon!"

She couldn't see anyone, only dust and spinning debris, but she heard his answer. "Kelsey, thank God."

"Here, Dillon. By the rocks."

When he finally materialized out of the storm, the expression on his face destroyed any doubts she had about how much he cared. With a sob, she threw herself into his arms and wondered if she would ever find the strength to leave them again.

Chapter 11

Dillon wove his fingers through Kelsey's hair and tugged to bring her face to his. He had meant to demand an explanation, but one look at the joy in her eyes was his undoing. With a groan, he covered her dirt-streaked face with kisses, finally claiming her mouth. He tasted dust and desire as she wrapped her arms around his back and pressed her body against his.

He finally tore his lips from hers, pulling her head to rest against his shoulder. "What are you doing out in the middle of the bloody desert?" he demanded.

Kelsey came back to her senses slowly. When she did, she realized they were standing in the open, targets for anyone who wanted to track them through the storm. "Someone tried to kill me." She grabbed his hand and pulled him toward the shelter of the hill where she had huddled in fear. "He may still be out there somewhere," she said softly.

Dillon wasn't sure if the red haze he saw was dust or fury. "Tell me."

Kelsey suppressed a shiver at his tone. This man was not the man who had kissed her moments ago. This man was as singleminded and deadly as her hunter. "I was run off the road by a gigantic truck," she said, moving close to him so her words wouldn't carry. His response was to the point and profane.

Somehow Kelsey couldn't keep herself from touching him. Her hands slid between his, begging to be clasped. He didn't deny her. "I found my way back to the road and braced myself against a tree, hoping someone would come along." She stopped, wondering if she should tell the truth. "Hoping *you* would find me," she said at last. "Dillon, I was such a fool."

He agreed, but his hands tightened around hers. "Go on."

"After a while I heard the rumble of an engine, and I thought I was going to be rescued. Then the rumble stopped. I heard a click, and then nothing. I shouted, giving my name. A bullet split the tree over my head."

"And you didn't see anything?"

"No."

"What did you do then?"

"I made my way out here, hoping I'd be impossible to find."

"You bloody well were. I was about to go back out to the road."

She made a small sound of dismay, and Dillon pulled her close again, wrapping his arms around her back. He meant to reassure her, but at the first touch of her body against his, he kissed her again, a hard, bruising kiss that had nothing to do with reassurance.

Kelsey parted her lips for the assault of his. She was alive, but now she *felt* alive. Alive and overjoyed to be. She had always fought this intimate intrusion of a man into her solitude. Now she welcomed it and wondered if she would ever want to be alone again.

His hands slid slowly to her waist, molding her flesh as his mouth molded hers. She was pliant in his arms, no trace of the woman who had once demanded that he not hold her. She wanted to be held. She wanted him to hold her. She wanted *him*.

Finally, Dillon was the one to break away. For moments he had forgotten dust and danger. He had forgotten everything except the way she felt in his arms. "I've got to get you back to the dugout," he said, forcing speech through a throat constricted with desire.

Her arms tightened around his waist for support. For a moment she could think of nothing except the kiss. Then reality filtered in. "What if the man with the gun is out there somewhere?"

"I didn't see a vehicle, Sunset. I think he left. It's probably safe, but we'll go slowly. I won't let anything happen to you."

She had just a trace of her old spirit in her voice. "And I won't let anything happen to you."

Dillon smiled unevenly, ruffling her hair. Clouds of dust swirled into the air to meet the clouds still swirling about them. "You're a sight. A real dust bunny."

"You're no Beau Brummell yourself."

"Let's go home."

And somehow, the way he said the last word was all she needed to gather her waning strength to make the trip.

Kelsey doubted that she would ever be able to rid herself of all traces of the dust storm unless she took a week-long shower. Coober Pedy had a new, reliable water plant, but water was still neither plentiful nor cheap. She used what was available as judiciously as possible until she was hopeful she had scrubbed away everything except the invisible residue that still seemed to clog each pore.

Dillon approached with his own towel when he heard the bathroom door open. Kelsey stepped out, her hair a tangle of wet ringlets, her complexion a shining apricot and rose. When she saw him, her eyes lit up in a way that made him forget he was still covered with dust.

He cleared his throat, telling himself not to step closer. "You look a sight better."

"Do I? I feel like a sprig of saltbush." She lifted one hand self-consciously to her hair. "My hair still feels stiff."

He told himself not to touch her even as his hand stretched out to stroke her curls. "Not to me."

Unconsciously she stretched toward his hand, like a cat having her ears scratched. "Dillon, I'm sorry. I should have listened to Dimitri."

They had encountered Dimitri on the way back to Coober Pedy. The dust-coated mechanic had let Kelsey know his feelings about liberated women.

Dillon tried not to notice the way she rubbed her cheek against the back of his fingers. "No worries about him. He likes to stay busy. Now you've given him something to do."

Kelsey winced at his humor. At that moment Dimitri was probably towing Jake's ute back to the garage. Both he and

Dillon had assured her it was a job that couldn't wait for the storm's end. Cars and trucks left by the side of the road were certain to be immediately stripped and torched, a local form of revenue and recreation.

"I didn't know that a dust storm could be that fierce." Kelsey was sorry when Dillon dropped his hand, but she didn't want to examine that feeling, or the others that were making themselves known. She just wanted to enjoy them for a while before the world intruded.

"We don't usually have murderers skulking around, hiding behind dust clouds."

"That's the first time I've been threatened directly."

"You're forgetting Serge."

She *had* forgotten him. She hadn't once suspected Serge as she had huddled between those dust-layered rocks. "Do you think it was him?"

Dillon shrugged. Kelsey had never seen a shrug with more deadly intent. She felt a pang of sympathy for Serge. "You're going to find out, aren't you?"

Dillon didn't answer, but she knew he was going to confront Serge just by the way he ignored her question and asked one himself. "Do you know what a miracle it was that I found you?"

For a moment neither of them could mask their feelings. Gratitude and something indefinable shone from Kelsey's eyes. Dillon suspected that his heart was in his. Time seemed to stop.

"I'd like to make some of this up to you," Kelsey said at last, looking away.

Dillon tried not to let his imagination run wild. He waited.

Kelsey felt suddenly shy, a feeling that she thought had died as she'd perfected her karate. "I'd like to take you to dinner. My shout."

He shook his head. "You've hardly enough cash to see you through your stay here, Sunset."

She banished her shyness as unworthy of a grown woman. "Tonight. At the Pizza Palace. Anna's promised us her best dinners," she said firmly.

Dillon saw the subtle lift of her chin, and he wanted to kiss away her stubbornness. But somehow this afternoon he had passed the point where casual kisses were possible. If he kissed Kelsey again, they would end up in bed. And he knew she wasn't ready for that. His hands dug into his towel to keep from reaching for her, and he made his tone matter-of-fact. "You get some rest. If the Palace opens after the storm, I'll be happy to be your guest." He brushed past her and closed the bathroom door behind him.

Kelsey stood in isolation in the hallway and looked at the closed door. Her experience with men was limited, but she knew what she and Dillon had just narrowly avoided. What she didn't know was how she felt about it.

As furtively as it had rolled into town, the dust storm rolled back out again by late afternoon, moving its devastation farther east. Coober Pedy's residents came out of hiding, swapping tales of this storm and worse that had long since passed. Among others, one story flew through town that Sergeant Newberry had been found at an unidentified miner's dugout when the miner returned from work early because of the storm's approach. The rumors varied. Some said that the Sergeant had been caught with the miner's wife; others said that he had been caught poking around the dugout with no good explanation why. Whatever the reason, Sergeant Newberry seemed to be sporting a black eye.

The Pizza Palace was open but nearly empty when Kelsey and Dillon arrived for dinner. Kelsey had made arrangements with Anna earlier in the day as she had waited for Jake's ute to be fixed. Anna had promised to save a bottle of red wine and make ravioli, which she had assured Kelsey was Dillon's favorite.

Now Anna greeted them at the door harboring a chubby, serious boy about ten years old under the ample curve of her arm. "Meet my son, Giorgio. He'll take care of you this evening. Say hello to Kelsey and Dillon, Giorgio."

"How's it going, mate?" Dillon asked, extending his hand.

Giorgio blushed as he shook Dillon's hand. Kelsey wondered what Anna had threatened her son with to get him to wait on them tonight.

"Giorgio, take Dillon and Miss Kelsey to their table."

"Follow me," Giorgio said, clearing his throat immediately.

Kelsey and Dillon followed him through the small restaurant to a door leading to what Kelsey had assumed was a storage room. She caught Dillon's expression. He was trying not to smile. "You arranged this?" he asked just loudly enough for her to hear.

"Not this," she assured him. "I think Anna wants us out of sight."

Giorgio opened the door and stood back so they could enter.

Kelsey had guessed correctly that the room was used for storage. She had guessed incorrectly about Anna's intentions. Anna had transformed what was really no more than a walk-in closet into an intimate, private dining room. Just large enough for a tiny table, the room was lit by candlelight, and the table was draped with ivory linen. Storage shelves lining one wall were curtained off with flowered cotton, and a single fragrant white blossom adorned the table, which was set with delicate china and polished sterling.

"You like it?" Anna stood in the doorway behind them, her arms folded across her breasts.

"It's beautiful," Kelsey assured her, avoiding Dillon's eyes as she turned to Anna.

Anna crossed the room, reaching behind the cotton hiding the shelves and flicked a switch. In a second the room was filled with the sentimental sound of an opera overture. "Puccini," Anna said. "You will digest better to Puccini. Come, Giorgio, we'll start with the wine."

Kelsey waited until the door had closed before she turned to Dillon. "I did not plan this," she said, stumbling over the words. "I simply told Anna I wanted to treat you to dinner. I didn't ask for any of this, this. . . ." Words failed her.

"Romance?" he supplied helpfully. "I'm disappointed. I thought you were trying to seduce me."

Something rumbled in her throat. Before she could push it down, it erupted into laughter. "I wouldn't know how! Is this how it's done?"

Dillon laughed, too, more to keep from grabbing her and showing her than for any other reason. "This is a start, Sunset."

"Apparently Anna thinks so. She told me you need a woman." Kelsey moved to the table to seat herself, but Dillon was behind her immediately, pulling out her chair. His arm brushed her cheek, and his hand lingered on her shoulder before he took his own seat. Kelsey savored a small volley of sensations.

Dillon seated himself. "Well, now that my needs are clear, tell me, do you need a man?"

Just days ago the answer would have been an unequivocal no. Now Kelsey wasn't sure of much of anything. "I've never thought so," she hedged.

"And you've changed your mind?"

"I didn't say that."

"You didn't say anything worth saying, actually."

She lifted her eyes in as flirtatious a movement as he had ever seen from her. "Some things aren't to be talked about."

His heart threatened to quit beating. "But then, you're not a woman a man would want to take by surprise."

"I doubt anything you'd do would surprise me." Her lips curved into a seductive smile. "Coober Pedy's taught me to expect the unexpected. Or maybe you've taught me that."

He could think of other things he wanted to teach her. He shifted in his seat to accommodate the part of him that was volunteering. "Interesting town, Coober Pedy," he said, hoping he wouldn't have to stand very soon.

"It's a funny name. Where did it come from?"

Dillon was glad they were on a safer topic. "It's from an Aborigine phrase, *kupa piti*. It means white man in a hole."

Her laughter echoed off the walls. "How silly the first miners must have looked to the Aborigines."

"How silly we still look. All this fuss for nothing more than sparkling rock."

She shook her head. "More than a rock. Rainbow Fire."

He saw that she really did understand. Already. There were few women who would have—few men, for that matter. A life spent underground searching for the elusive opal was a life wasted, by most standards. "Do you understand how I can live in this place?" he asked, wondering just how far her tolerance stretched.

"I think I like this place." Kelsey saw disbelief in Dillon's eyes, and she struggled to explain. "God knows, it's not beautiful or easy to live in. But there's a spirit here." She realized she was echoing Melanie, and she paused, unable to think of a better way to explain. "The place is crawling with characters."

"One or more of whom is trying to scare—or kill—you."

"I don't like that part."

"And you like getting run off the road by a road train? Getting lost in a dust storm? Death adders curling around your slim little ankles?"

She smiled again, and he shifted in his seat. "I haven't been bored."

"We're not boring." He wanted to tell her to go easy on the smile, that he'd left his self-control somewhere off the old road to the Breakaways, but another part of him refused. Somewhere deep inside he knew he would die for that sensuous curve of her lips, even if the death were slow torture.

The door opened, and Giorgio entered with a bottle of South Australian burgundy. He swallowed audibly. "Mama said to tell you this is almost as good as Italian."

To the boy's obvious relief, Dillon took the wine and corkscrew. "Thank you, Giorgio. I believe I'll pour it myself. Tell Mama we're grateful."

Kelsey watched Dillon go through the time-honored ritual of uncorking the wine bottle. He moved with clean, masculine grace, wasting no energy on flourishes. The sleeve of his navy blazer slid up and down to reveal glimpses of a wide wrist, adorned with nothing more than sprinkles of crisply curling hair. The blazer parted over a white shirt that strained tightly over his chest as he leaned away from the table to remove the cork. She caught the flash of the gold chain he always wore tucked into his shirt, and she imagined the huge opal nestled in the thicket of light brown hair.

She lowered her eyes, suddenly flustered as she remembered what he had looked like wearing nothing more than the opal and a towel.

"You do want some, don't you?"

Kelsey held out her glass. "Yes, please." She kept her eyes on it as he filled it.

Dillon filled his own, then held it up as a toast. "To..." He didn't know what to say.

Neither did Kelsey. Her gaze locked with his. Slowly they clinked glasses, all the unsaid phrases still between them.

In the background, a tenor began to sing.

"This is a scene from *Lady and the Tramp*," she said at last.

He had seen the Walt Disney cartoon. "Tramp takes lady out for a bone dinner, and Tony, the restaurant owner, makes them spaghetti."

"And they share each piece to beautiful music." Kelsey lifted the glass to her lips.

"A truly romantic scene."

"And afterward, Lady ends up at the dog pound."

There were other places where Dillon would prefer to have this lady end up tonight. He wondered why even a child's cartoon led back to that thought. He quickly changed the subject. "You haven't told me if you've heard any more about Jake."

"I spoke to his doctor just before we left." Kelsey rolled her glass between her hands. "He says my father is a fighter. Apparently he's coming along as well as they can expect. He's still not speaking, but he is responding to voices. The doctor expects to be able to tell him about me in a week or two."

Dillon was torn between satisfaction that Jake was improving and disappointment that Kelsey would be leaving. But she needed to leave. Coober Pedy was no place for her to be now. Or ever. "I'm sure you're glad."

On the contrary, she wasn't sure what she felt. She was sorry her father's recovery was going to be slow, but now that she was staying at the dugout, money wasn't a problem. She was in no danger of losing her job unless she didn't return by the end of the holidays. She wanted her father to get well, but she was also aware of a new reluctance to leave Coober Pedy, bullets, snakes and all. That would be difficult to explain to anyone, especially Dillon.

"How do you think Jake will feel when he sees me?" Kelsey didn't miss the way Dillon lowered his eyes. "Tell me the truth, Dillon. I think it would help to know."

"I can't say. He's a man who avoids roots. He doesn't own anything except his ute, and he doesn't have any real mates, except me, I suppose."

"He's had a daughter all these years, though, even if he hasn't talked about me. Maybe he doesn't think of me often, but he must remember I exist."

"But from everything you've told me, it seems he's worked hard to make you forget him."

"I don't remember much." She had never shared her memories with anyone before. Now she took the chance. "Strong arms throwing me into the air. Laughter. And snatches of a song." Over Puccini, she hummed what she remembered. "Someone told me it was an Irish lullaby. Maybe it was Jake."

She watched something indefinable flicker over Dillon's features. "Do you know it?"

Dillon struggled to think of a way to avoid answering. "It's familiar," he said at last, hoping he had been vague enough to stop more questions.

But Kelsey was too astute and too attuned to him not to have seen his struggle. "What is it?"

He didn't want to destroy the fantasies her childhood had been built around. "Just an Irish ditty."

She set her glass on the table. "Define ditty."

"Song."

"Tell me about this one." Steel crept into her voice.

He was trapped. "I've heard Jake sing it, that's all."

"Where and when."

"At the pub."

"A lullaby at the pub?"

"It's not exactly a lullaby, Sunset."

"Then what is it?"

"A drinking song. A naughty drinking song." He took a large swallow of his wine. "A terrible naughty drinking song," he finished.

Kelsey just stared at him. Then her shoulders began to shake, and her chin began to quiver. Dillon watched, appalled at what he had done. "It's a lovely melody," he said, trying to stem the flood. "I'm sure he just hummed it to you."

Kelsey took a deep breath and then exploded. "Damn the man," she said between bursts of laughter that threatened to leave her breathless.

"Me or your father?"

"Both of you!" She grabbed her napkin to wipe her eyes. A fresh burst of laughter left her choking for air.

Dillon wasn't sure if she were hysterical or truly tickled. He waited apprehensively to find out.

"Damn him," she said at last. "The man had no shame, did he? No wonder my aunt paddled my behind. I couldn't sit down for a whole day after I sang that song for her."

"No one should hit a child," he said, narrowing his eyes. "No one should ever have hit you."

This was a man she could love. Kelsey met Dillon's gaze, and suddenly all the laughter was gone, leaving the pain of a little girl in its wake. She tried to make light of it. "I'm sure I wasn't a very nice child. No one could manage me."

"All they had to do was love you."

"I think I must be hard to love."

"I think you're very wrong."

She saw in his eyes what she knew was in hers. She reached for his hand just as the door opened.

"Ravioli and my special salad," Anna announced from the doorway. "Come on, Giorgio. Bring it in."

They ate the first part of their meal in silence, wary of moving closer than they had, afraid they might move apart. The silence wasn't comfortable or comforting, but neither was it a barrier. Instead it was another gateway, one that terrified them both.

Finally, unable to stand it any longer, Kelsey searched for a topic. Her eyes fell on the centerpiece. She gestured toward it. "This flower is beautiful. Do you know what it is?"

"It's a right bit of a surprise in the middle of the outback. But then, Anna's got a green thumb and a tremendous water bill to prove it." Dillon fingered the fragile white petals. "Frangipani. Plumeria, they call it in Hawaii."

She was afraid the conversation was going to end again, so she grasped for his last word. "I came through Hawaii on my way to Australia. It's so lush, so forgiving. I got the feeling that if I dropped litter in the airport courtyard, something fabulous would grow right up to cover it."

"It's not always forgiving. I was there for Hurricane Eve."

She made a small sound of sympathy. "How did you cope?"

"With the help of friends." He knew he didn't need to elaborate, but he wanted to tell her about his experience. He had never shared it with anyone. "They weren't friends at first. They were strangers. And none of us was happy about being thrown together to wait out the storm."

"But that changed?"

"It changed." He didn't know how to explain the way two men, two women and a child had become so important to each other. "Maybe it's a bit like you and me. Adversity can make strange bedfellows."

Her smile was slow, lighting her face by degrees. She wondered if the phrase was a Freudian slip. "In other words, if you hadn't been trapped in a hurricane, you never would have gotten close to these people. Just like you might never have given me a second look if I weren't Jake's daughter and we weren't in danger."

"I'd have looked more than twice." On an impulse Dillon lifted the flower and reached across the table, brushing Kelsey's hair over her ear as he anchored the flower in her butterscotch curls. "I wouldn't have stopped looking."

She held his gaze. "And these people, are they still friends? Or have you forgotten them and drifted apart?"

He knew what she was really asking. Would he forget her? Was their attraction for each other based on the intimacy of their situation or on something more important? "I haven't forgotten them," he said, caressing her cheek before he reluctantly dropped his hand. "Nor will I ever."

Kelsey wasn't even sure why she felt so relieved. "Do you correspond?"

"We drop in and out of each other's lives. The hurricane changed us all. I think we seek each other out to renew that." He could see she didn't understand, but she wanted to. He continued. "There were five of us, all of us about the same age, except for a little girl who was traveling to meet her mother."

"Tell me about them."

He was pleased she wanted to know more. He understood that the questions were a way to know him better. "Julianna and Gray were married, but they had been separated for years. Strangely enough, the hurricane brought them together again. They're living together now, and Julianna is pregnant." He thought of his last phone call from Julianna. "She lost their first baby a long time ago. She's understandably frightened. We speak often."

Kelsey heard the warmth in his voice and knew that Julianna must be special indeed. "And her husband? Gray?"

He smiled. "Gray is the man she needs and loves. They'll make it."

"What about the others?"

"Paige went to New Zealand after Hawaii and met her husband, Adam. I went to their wedding last month, a big Maori affair."

"Romance is all around you."

He crossed a smile and a grimace, creating something lopsided and totally endearing. "Then there was Jody."

"Don't tell me she got married, too?"

"She's eight. Maybe nine by now. Beaut brown eyes and pigtails."

"And what happened to her?"

"She and her mother are traveling, although I don't know just where. There's been some sort of trouble in her past. I only hope she's free from it now."

"And then there's Dillon Ward."

He sipped his wine and tried not to read more into her expression than what was really there. "Then there's me."

"And what's changed for you since the hurricane?"

He couldn't explain. He knew he had grown lonelier, more dissatisfied with his life. He knew he had been touched by the warmth of the love of friends, and that somehow it had opened a place inside him that needed more warmth, more love than friends could ever give him. But he didn't know how to explain that to Kelsey. Or how to explain that he didn't believe that place would ever be filled.

"Dillon?" she coaxed when he had been silent for a time.

"I suppose it's made me curse the miner's life a time or two," he said finally. "But I'm a miner, and a miner I'll stay."

"It's not a prison sentence," she said gently. "Last I heard, Australia wasn't a penal colony anymore."

"But opal is a prison warden, and once you've gone underground, there's no escape."

She didn't understand what he was really saying, but she suspected he had said as much as he would. "Tell me about the opal you wear around your neck."

He reached inside his shirt and pulled out the heavy gold chain so that the uncut chunk of opal could glisten and wink in the candlelight. "It's the first good nobby I ever found. I don't know what it would be worth if it was cut and polished, but it's worth more to me this way. My first piece of rainbow fire."

Kelsey reached across the table to finger the large stone. She still knew little about the worth of opals, but she suspected Dillon was wearing a small fortune around his neck. The stone was alive with color. "You must keep it in a safe when you're not wearing it."

"I wear it all the time." He grinned. "Superstition."

"I thought the superstition was that opal was unlucky unless it was your birthstone."

"In ancient times opal was a gem of good luck. Worn on a man's chest it was thought to strengthen his heart and endow his body with vitality. At one time or another it was thought to shield the wearer from harm and intrigue."

She shook her head regretfully. "I don't think that part's working, Dillon."

"Perhaps not, but there's always my favorite superstition."

She lifted a brow in question.

"A man who wears opal, uncut opal particularly, will be lucky in love. The woman he desires will fall into his arms."

Kelsey dropped her head. "You made that up."

"Did I?" Dillon toasted her with the last of his wine. "You might have to do some research to find out."

She was sure she knew just what kind of research he had in mind. Strangely enough, the idea warmed her blood a degree and sent her heart racing. Kelsey picked up her glass and silently toasted him back.

Dessert was amaretto cheesecake served with espresso. The meal ended right along with the last Puccini aria, and Dillon and Kelsey heaped praise on a blushing Giorgio and a proud Anna before they left.

Outside, the starlit sky held no traces of clouds. The air was clear, the wind nothing more than a cooling breeze. Only the dust still blanketing cars and streaking windows was a reminder of the storm.

Dillon walked Kelsey to the ute, his hand at the small of her back in a seemingly innocent gesture. Kelsey felt his tension, however, and knew that he was alert to every sound, every shadow. She felt his protection not as an insult, but as the support it was meant to be. Dillon protected her because he cared about her, not because he didn't feel she could take care of herself.

"It would help, wouldn't it, if we just understood why someone was trying to kill us," she said.

"I'm not sure someone is," Dillon said, his eyes scanning the far corners of the street. "But if he keeps it up, he might succeed without half trying."

"You mean you think someone is just trying to scare us?"

"I think he's either ambivalent or a right poor shot. He aims high, stops after a shot or two and disappears."

"What about the snake?"

"There was an excellent chance I'd find the snake before he found me. I think our town terrorist is a gambling man."

"He pushed my father down the shaft."

"I think he meant to kill Jake." Dillon opened the ute door and waited until Kelsey was safely in before he went around to his own side. "And I think he's killed before."

For a moment she wasn't sure she'd understood. "Killed before?"

"Jake's not the first victim of violence here. We've had two unsolved murders in the last year. One was an old prospector name of Fred Haskell. Everyone here called him Fizzle Fred, because every lead he ever got on a new field was a fizzle. Old Fizzle Fred never went underground to find his fortune, he just wandered the countryside boring an occasional hole but mostly looking for a place where the opals lay on top of the ground, just for pocketing. He had an old brumby, a wild horse he'd saved from dingoes once up in the Territory, and he'd load that brumby down with supplies and wander miles out into the never-never until he had to come back for more. Sometimes it would be three months or four before anyone saw him. One day eight months ago or so, about a week after he'd loaded up with supplies in town, somebody saw his brumby running loose, pack still tied to his back. We found old Fizzle Fred a few days later."

Kelsey shuddered. "Dead?"

Dillon nodded. "A miner came back from holiday and found Fred's body down his main shaft. Some said he'd gotten desperate and was trying to rat opal, but I know Fizzle Fred had never been down a shaft in his life. Told me once that he couldn't stand a closed-in place. Too much like a crypt."

Kelsey looked straight ahead. "What was the other murder?"

"Some poor soul, we'll never know who, was found on the edge of one of the mine fields. No identification, and...." He paused and tried to think of how to phrase this delicately. "No possibility of a description," he said at last. "Just a pick and shovel and a book on opal mining. We guessed he was just drifting through. We get a lot of strangers here. Somebody between jobs or with no hope of a job comes here to make a quick fortune. The blooming funny thing about it is that sometimes they do. This one didn't, or if he did, he died for it."

"You're sure he was murdered?"

"The police announced it was a case of death by dehydration, a case of the man not being prepared for outback conditions. But an Aborigine tracker who helps the police told me it was no accident. There were unmistakable signs of a struggle, even though there were attempts to cover up the signs. And he says there were still drops of water in the man's water bag. A man crazed with thirst would have drained it dry.''

"How can the police be so apathetic?"

"How much attention does the murder of a skid row bum get in New York City?" Dillon countered.

Kelsey fell silent as the ute wove through the South Australian roads back to Dillon's dugout. She combed through both stories, looking for the connection to Jake's accident and the attempts on her life and Dillon's. "I don't get it," she admitted at last. "Why do you think those murders had anything to do with us?"

He liked the way she said "us." It was a word he would like to hear her say again. "There may be connections, there may not be. But the two men and your father were all victims who were made to look as if they'd suffered from an accident. Jake and Fizzle Fred were both found down mine shafts. All the men were mining, and, with the exception of Jake, they were men with no one to worry about them."

Kelsey knew Dillon was being tactful. Dillon had worried about Jake, it was true. But she suspected no one else in town would have noticed his absence. Jake had been almost as alone as the other men.

"How does this fit with your theory that someone believes one of my father's exaggerations about the opal he'd found?"

Dillon shrugged. "I don't know, but I have a feeling it's all connected. I just wish I knew the key." He pulled off the road in front of his house and turned off the engine. "But you've worried enough for tonight. Now you need a good sleep." He opened his door and stepped out.

Kelsey opened her door before Dillon could come around. She walked with him to the dugout and watched as he manipulated wires. Jumbuck came forward out of the shadows and rubbed against Kelsey's bare legs, purring as he did. She squatted and rubbed his head, surprised he had volunteered such affection.

Dillon opened the door, then turned to watch. "Trying to steal my cat?"

"He's lonely for a woman's touch."

Dillon could empathize. He watched as Kelsey rose, a quick motion that showed just how well-trained her body was. He caught glimpses of the black-belt Kelsey at the oddest times. The spareness of a sudden movement, the fluid grace of a gesture, the effortless swing of her hips or shoulders. There was nothing masculine about the way her body had responded to its conditioning. Rather she was totally feminine, her sensuality enhanced because her body, and her control of it, bordered on perfection.

She preceded him through the door, and Dillon had to remind himself not to touch her, not to put his hands on the swaying hips to still her. Not to pull her back against him.

Inside, Kelsey turned. In subtle ways the entire evening had led up to this moment. Dillon stood back from her, his eyes giving nothing away. She was a mixture of emotions. "I guess it's time to say good-night."

"It is getting late."

"What are our plans for tomorrow?"

"We'll go to the mine."

Kelsey waited, though for what she had no clear idea. She couldn't take the lead, because she didn't know where she wanted to go. When she saw that Dillon wasn't going to move toward her, she turned away. "Then I'll see you in the morning."

Dillon wished it were that easy. But he knew he had one more hurdle to overcome before they said their final good-night and he could retire with his regrets. "I have to check your room," he said gruffly.

She turned back, puzzled. "My room?"

"I have to be sure everything is all right."

She was hurt by his tone. "I can check."

"I won't sleep if I can't see for myself that you're going to be all right."

She thought she heard concern mixed with something else. For a moment she wasn't certain, but then his eyes gave away his secret. They were hungry, the proverbial starving man peering in at a banquet. He wanted her, and not having her was torture. She felt suddenly humbled. And proud. "Fine," she said softly, not certain yet what she was agreeing to, but just as certain that in a few minutes she would know. "I'll come with you."

He stopped pretending. "I'm not sure that's a good idea."

"Neither am I." Kelsey tossed her head and started down the hall. Dillon, with no choices left, followed in silence.

Chapter 12

Are you going to get down on your hands and knees and look under the bed?"

"I plan to, yes." Dillon didn't look at Kelsey as he answered. He'd had one glimpse of her leaning gracefully against the doorjamb, and one glimpse had been enough. He had memorized the sleek curve of her legs, covered well above her knees by a blue denim skirt, the way her breasts pushed against her soft coral knit blouse, the way her hands hung relaxed by her side, just skimming her hips. He had memorized the expression on her face and wished, for the first time in his life, that he could paint. "Woman on the Threshold," he would title what would surely be a masterpiece.

"Nothing looks disturbed."

Dillon suspected that the only thing disturbed in the room was him. "I suspect my little trick with the wiring kept our friend out of here, but I shouldn't like to take any chances."

"Our *friend* was too busy shooting at me to figure out how to break into your dugout again." Kelsey admonished herself for using the doorjamb to prop herself upright. Without asking for permission, her knees were unsteady. And she couldn't delude herself into believing it was a delayed reaction to the stress of being shot at.

Dillon knelt beside the bed and lifted the spread. "Everything looks fine. Someday soon I've got to use the carpet sweeper under here."

"Don't worry about it. I don't plan to spend any time there."

Dillon realized he was finished. The room was safe, and it was time for him to leave. He got to his feet and faced Kelsey. She was in the same position, and the expression on her face hadn't changed. "You'll be all right tonight."

"Will I?" Kelsey forced herself to stop relying on the doorjamb. She stood straight, blocking the doorway. "And you, will you be all right?"

He nodded, because he couldn't trust himself to answer that one verbally. "Can I do anything for you before I go?"

She suspected he had just won the award for loaded question of the year. She stared at him.

"Sunset?"

"Do you know that no one has ever given me a nickname before?" She moved a step toward him. "I always wanted one."

He told himself to move past her and out the doorway, joking as he did. Instead he stood perfectly still. "Sunset's the only time of day when I know I'm a believer."

"And what do you believe in?"

He believed in her, but the moment he told her, he knew there would be no turning back. "Triumph, I suppose. Glory."

She stepped closer. "Then I should be proud."

"Proud because someone's seen who you are? You're the same woman you've always been. It's just that you don't give enough of yourself to others to let them see you."

"But I've given enough to you?"

Not enough. Never enough. Dillon knew that if he lived with her for the rest of his life, he would never have enough of her, because his need for what she had to give was insatiable. "I know you," he said simply. "It's only been days, but I know you."

She nodded again, moving closer. "And I know you, now that I've let myself."

"If you come any closer, you're going to know me much better."

She paused, considering his words. "I've never been sure I could give myself to a man."

"And now?"

"This man won't hurt me."

He prayed she was right, because this man no longer seemed to have a choice. He moved toward her until they were face to face and lifted his hands to her hair. "Stop me now," he said, his voice thick with unleashed desire. "Because there won't be any stopping in a moment."

The warning didn't frighten her. His desire didn't frighten her. She moved into the shelter of his arms. "I don't want you to stop. I want you to start."

He cupped her head, hungrily trailing kisses from her forehead to her cheek before he brought her mouth to his. Starting was simple, the most natural thing he had ever done in his life.

Kelsey curved against him, parting her lips for the ritual dance of his tongue with hers. Her hands rested on his shoulders, then stroked upward along the strong column of his neck to his hair. When his lips left hers, she rubbed her cheek against the rougher texture of his as she curved closer against him.

Dillon parted her hair and traced the delicate perfection of her ear with his lips and tongue. He could feel Kelsey's hands tighten in his hair and her body bend to his. She arched as he warmed her sensitive earlobe with his breath, then took it between his teeth and lips. She moaned in satisfaction.

He found her lips again, already parted and moist, and he played with them, nipping, kissing, soothing, until she had moved so close that their bodies were almost one. He could feel her breasts against his chest, her hips against his, her body safely cradling the part of him that yearned to have her completely.

As he kissed her, Kelsey explored Dillon with her fingertips, the smooth texture of his skin, the vibrant, clinging silk of his hair. Strangely, the more she had of him, the more she wanted. Where was the voice that should be warning her of the consequences of this? Instead the only sound she heard was the beat of her heart. She grew hungrier for new sensations, the feel of his chest against her naked breasts, the weight of his body covering hers, their legs intertwined, their hearts beating together.

As if he knew, Dillon shrugged out of his blazer, dropping it on the floor at their feet. Kelsey stroked her hands from his shoulders to the wedge of skin exposed by the open collar of his shirt. She hesitated only a second before she unbuttoned the first button, then bent to kiss the skin she'd exposed.

Dillon's hands rested at her hips. He felt the next button give way, followed by the smooth glide of her lips against his chest. He lost count in the ecstasy of her innocent exploration until his chest was bare and her hair was a fragrant veil over him.

"You haven't done this before?" he asked, groaning.

"No, I haven't." Kelsey trailed kisses along the vee of hair that ended at his throat. "You can't tell?"

"No."

"Good." She lifted his shirt away from his shoulders and slid it down his arms to the floor. Then she met his gaze. "That may not last."

"Don't stop, Sunset. I'll take my chances."

The warmth she saw reflected in his green eyes gave her the courage to continue. She stepped away and crossed her arms in front of her, lifting the hem of her blouse. For just a moment she faltered, unsure of what she would be offering him.

Dillon saw her hesitation. "The sight of you lives in my dreams," he said softly. "I've never seen a woman as perfect."

She lifted her eyes and let her lips curve into a smile. Then, with one swift movement, she tugged the blouse over her head, dropping it to the floor. Dillon smoothed his hands up her back and looped his fingers under the clasp of her bra. In a moment it was only a scrap of lace between them, and then it was on the floor, too. He held her away, drinking in the sight of her small breasts lifted toward him; then his hands left her shoulders to take possession.

Kelsey felt her knees tremble. She swayed, and his arms came around her, lifting her so that her breasts flattened against his chest. She was suffused with sensations that built as he rocked against her. When she felt the button of her skirt give way under his fingers, she pressed harder against him. When she felt the skirt drop to the floor, she felt gratitude.

Dillon reminded himself to go slowly, but it did no good. His desire for Kelsey had nothing to do with a long abstinence and everything to do with the woman she was. He stood back to drink in the sight of her again, glorying in the way she reached out for him.

Her outstretched arms were the last thing he saw.

The lights were extinguished at the same moment that a volley of gunshots shattered the windows of the sun porch. On the heels of the gunshots came the roar of an explosion.

Dillon grabbed Kelsey and swept her to the floor, covering her with his body for protection. There was a fierce rumbling from the walls around them, and the floor shook with the blast's intensity.

"Bloody hell." Dillon held Kelsey beneath him even though she tried to free herself.

Dazed, Kelsey stopped struggling and lay still. The rumbling stopped after a few seconds. "Bloody hell," she repeated, after everything had become deathly quiet. Dillon didn't move, and she lifted her hands to his face. "Are you all right?"

He wasn't sure he would ever be all right again, but he wasn't going to tell her that. Every nerve in his system was twanging from denial and shock. "I've heard of a woman making the earth move, but this is a bit absurd," he said, levering himself off her.

"You Aussies can joke about anything, can't you?" she said, anger flaring. "You're a weird bunch, you know that?"

But Dillon was on his feet, reaching for her. In a moment she was on hers beside him. "Find your clothes," he said, deadly serious now. "And get dressed. Then stay here until I tell you it's all right to leave the room."

"I'm coming with you."

"No you're not. Not until I see what happened."

"Don't waste your breath wishing out loud." Kelsey bent down and felt for her clothing. The room was now as dark as the cave it was, and there wasn't even the glimmer of starlight to lighten it. Still searching, she heard the door open, then shut, and she softly cursed every inch of carpet until she found her skirt and blouse.

In seconds she was out in the hall, feeling her way by pressing tightly against the wall until she came to the living room.

"Dillon?" she called softly.

There was no answer. She repeated his name as she edged toward the door.

Dillon was on the porch, talking to a thin, blond stranger. Dillon held a limp parcel of fur in his arms.

"Jumbuck!" Kelsey started toward him.

"Watch where you step," he cautioned.

Only then did she notice the condition of the porch. The floor was covered with shattered glass. Every window had been broken, and plants lay in disarray. Furniture was splintered, and the front door she had walked through was nothing more than a gaping hole.

"This is Kelsey Donovan," Dillon said, introducing her to the man beside him. "Kelsey, this is my closest neighbor, Alf Sweeney."

Kelsey nodded as Alf murmured something.

"Alf saw a ute speeding away after the explosion."

"*Ja*. A red one, the color of a bad tomato."

Dillon stroked the cat's fur, as if somehow he could bring Jumbuck back to life. "Somebody shot out the windows and set off the explosives in the process. If I'd used a bigger charge, it might have taken part of the dugout down."

"That's why you didn't use a bigger charge," Kelsey said, shutting her eyes and taking a deep breath. Reaction to both their aborted lovemaking and the explosion was just beginning to set in.

"I've got some things to do in town," Dillon said.

Kelsey looked up to see the two men exchange knowing glances. "What things?" she demanded.

"Some things to check out."

"I'm going with you." Kelsey reached for Jumbuck. She couldn't bear to watch Dillon stroke him any longer.

"I want you to come," he said. He looked down at the cat. "I've got a torch in my ute I can get for you. Then you can put Jumbuck on my bed and tuck a blanket around him."

"Dillon, he's—"

"Unconscious," Dillon finished for her. "Most likely his head was knocked during the explosion. He may come to, and he may not. But he'll be suffering from shock either way. He'll need to be kept warm."

Amazingly he was right. Kelsey could feel the slightest movement of Jumbuck's rib cage as he clung tenaciously to life. "I'll take care of him," she said.

He started toward the ute. "Get some clothes, too. You may not be sleeping here tonight."

She nodded, since that made perfect sense. "Have you thought about the dugout? Anyone can get in now."

"I'll be guarding it, Miss," Alf told her. "Me and my oldest boy. With shotguns."

"It's come to that?"

Dillon turned, his face grim in the moonlight. "It's come to that. And more."

They were halfway into town before Dillon spoke again. Kelsey hadn't questioned him; because she knew he would tell her where they were going when he was ready.

"I'm taking you to Melly's." Dillon continued to look straight ahead. "She doesn't work tonight, and you'll be safe there."

For a moment she didn't understand. "I thought we were going to try to find out who was behind all this."

"I'm going to find out. You're going to Melly's."

She felt betrayed. "No I'm not."

"I won't take no for an answer, Sunset. You're going."

"What makes you think you can order me around?" Kelsey faced him, although he was still staring straight out the windshield. He didn't say a word. "Answer me!" she said. "Do you think I'm your servant now? Is that what happens when two people make love?"

"We didn't make love," he pointed out. "And it's a bloody good thing we didn't, because if we had, you'd probably bring it up every time you didn't like something about me."

"Nothing that happened back there gives you the right to tell me what to do."

"We couldn't agree more." He wrenched the wheel to the left and pulled the ute to a stop at the roadside, then turned to her. "I'll tell you what gives me the right!" He grabbed her, hauling her across his lap and pinning her arms to her sides. Then he kissed her, forcing her back against the steering wheel. Before she could think to struggle, he pushed her back to her seat. Then he started the engine again and pulled out into the road.

"Caveman tactics!" Kelsey said.

"Too right."

"And you think that I'll go quietly now?"

"That would be too much to hope for. But you'll go, if I have to drag you kicking and screaming."

"My kicks and screams might be beyond your handling."

"We may have to put that to the test." He pounded the steering wheel in frustration. "Damn it, woman, don't you see that I can't let you put your life in danger? I care about you. If you come with me, I'll be worrying, no matter how able you are to take care of yourself. I need to move fast, and I need to go alone."

He cared for her. His feelings had been perfectly obvious, but he'd never told her so quite this way. Kelsey clamped her jaw shut. What did you say to someone who cared about you? "I just want to be there to help," she said finally, her voice softer.

"Believe me, you'll help more if you're not there. And if I need you, I'll know where to find you. Can you trust me to know what's best just this once?"

She didn't understand the warm glow suffusing her. She should still be furious. He was no different from every other man in the world. He'd been born believing he was superior, that women were there to serve his needs. But even as she tried to convince herself that she was right, she knew she wasn't. Dillon was different. And when she was with him, *she* was different. The Kelsey Donovan who was about to agree to what he wanted was a woman she was only just beginning to know.

"Just this once," she said stiffly. "And if I don't hear from you by midnight, I'll come looking for you."

He sighed. "I'll count on it."

Melly and Gary's dugout was just on the edge of town. The dugout was an egalitarian architectural form. From the roadside it was difficult to tell if the dweller hadn't earned back the price of his mining permit or if he had hit a vein of opal worthy of becoming the next crown jewels.

When Dillon stopped his ute, however, Kelsey realized there were exceptions. This was one.

"Gary does well in Coober Pedy, I assume." She looked out over the elaborate marble patio shaded by thriving trees and decorated with white willow furniture and flowering shrubs in pink brick planters. One side of the patio was bordered by a fan-shaped trellis covered with brightly blooming bougainvillea.

"He does well. Gary always has his finger in this pie or that." Dillon got down and came around to help Kelsey. She could tell he was in a hurry to go, because he was at her door before she could step down. "I had Alf ring Melly for me. She's expecting you."

"I still don't like this."

"I know." Dillon took Kelsey's arm and guided her along the walkway to the patio. Melanie opened the door before he could knock.

"Come in," she said, with no trace of her usual buoyant good spirits. "You poor thing," she said, giving Kelsey a sympathetic hug. "Alf told me what happened."

"I'm fine," Kelsey assured her. "And so is Dillon."

"You big oaf," Melanie said, poking Dillon in the ribs. "How could you put Kelsey into danger like that?"

Kelsey saw that Melanie was only half kidding. "It's not Dillon's fault someone's after us."

"Kelsey shouldn't be in Coober Pedy, then," Melanie said, still addressing her words to Dillon. "Why are you keeping her here?"

"Try getting her to leave and see if you come away with your fingers." Dillon dismissed Melanie's criticism and turned to Kelsey. "Don't worry about me, Sunset. I'm going to be careful." He clamped his hands on her shoulders and pulled her toward him for a kiss, ignoring Melly. "And don't you try to come after me."

"Yes, master," she said, venom mysteriously missing from her voice. "Don't take any chances."

He kissed her again, then turned and strode toward the door.

"Something new in Coober Pedy," Melanie said, watching him go. "You've been doing something besides getting shot at."

"Almost."

"Almost doesn't sound like fun."

Kelsey smiled absently, already worrying about Dillon. "This is lovely. Will you show me around?"

"I'd love to. Gary's gone for the night. He's off in Melbourne wheeling and dealing, so we have the place to ourselves." Melanie linked arms with Kelsey. "Now you can stare at his exhibits undisturbed."

"Exhibits?"

"Gary's a collector. This dugout is his own private museum."

Kelsey remembered that Melanie had told her that before. "What does that make you, then?"

"Oh, I'm part of his collection. Luckily he only collects his women one at a time, so I don't have any competition now, but who knows if that will last."

Kelsey couldn't let the breezy observation pass unnoticed. "You're not happy with Gary, are you?"

"Not happy with him, but even unhappier without him. Gary's one of a kind, like everything he collects. There's no chance of replacing him. And I keep hoping. . . ."

"Hoping what?"

Melanie laughed. "Hoping that one morning he'll wake up and realize what he's got in me. He doesn't have to search any further, because I'm the best he could possibly have."

"If he doesn't realize that already, he's hopeless."

"All men are hopeless. And all women are hopeful anyway."

The hallway was wide, and arched with the painstaking precision of a cathedral. The smooth freshly limed claystone walls were lined with works of art. Melanie stopped under the first group of paintings. "We have been passing through the hall of South Australian masterpieces," she intoned in a nasal voice. "As you can see, each of these paintings depicts a scene of Australian life. Notice the intensity of the light, the use of color, and the sensitivity of each artist as he captures his subject. Although none of these artists is well known, we have it on good authority that each will be famous one day." She dropped the tour-guide accent for a moment in an aside. "Gary's authority."

Kelsey admired Gary's eye for talent. "He's probably right."

Melanie resumed the tour. "And here, on this wall, we have paintings by the famous Aborigine family, the Namatjiras. The members of this illustrious family capture the outback in a manner that cannot be equaled."

"These are exquisite." Kelsey moved closer. "Melanie, these must be worth a fortune."

"Nothing's too good for Gary. In fact, nothing's ever good enough."

"Well, the man does have taste."

Melanie pushed her tousled hair over one eye coquettishly. "Doesn't he though?"

They wandered the rest of the hallway, examining Gary's collection. As Melanie ushered her into the living room, Kelsey stopped to stare at the life-size portrait on the far wall. Done in oils with a Rembrandtlike clarity of detail and contrast of light and shadow, the portrait was of a young woman wearing a scoop-necked, gathered blouse covered partially with a simple gray shawl. Most of her hair was hidden by a white mob-cap, but one long black lock fell over her shoulder, coming to rest provocatively at the peak of one breast. Her body was at an angle, her head turned over one shoulder as if to petition the artist with her pleading eyes. Directly in front of her was a line of ragged people in chains waiting to board a sailing ship.

The portrait would have been riveting under any circumstances. The fact that Melanie had been the model for it made it more so. "That's incredible," Kelsey said.

"Do you like it?"

"I more than like it."

"She looks like me, doesn't she?"

Kelsey faced her friend. "It's not you?"

"The painting's very old. She was a convict who sailed on one of the first prison ships to leave England for Australia. Her lover painted the portrait. He was supposed to sell it to make enough money to earn her passage back to England when her sentence ended."

"Did he?"

"The story is that he sold the portrait, then gambled away the money. She died here."

"It could be you, it's so like you."

"The resemblance was what attracted Gary to me, I suppose. He's had the portrait longer than he's had me. When we met my hair was long, like hers. And I used to have that same air of naiveté. My, how I've changed."

"Did Gary want to keep you like the portrait?"

"Oh sure. He flew into a rage when I cut my hair, and he hates the way I dress. But at least when he looks at me now, he notices me."

Kelsey was surprised that Melanie understood her own motivation so well. The zany clothes and the outrageous hairstyles were just ways of forcing Gary to see her for the individual she was.

She wondered if all men were like Gary. Who did Dillon see when he looked at her? The real Kelsey Donovan, or a woman he could mold into some image he admired? The flicker of doubt was fanned into flames by Melanie's next words.

"Take my advice, Kelsey, sleep with a man and enjoy him, but don't ever let him get to you. Because if you do, you'll find out that he owns you, body and soul, and you'll spend the rest of your life doing the craziest things just to make him love you."

The remainder of the tour took another hour. Gary's collections weren't limited to art. They included early settlers' furniture, Aborigine artifacts, ancient maps, rare books about Australia and an extensive accumulation of photographs. Melanie informed her that Gary had other collectibles at the Opal Showcase under lock and key, humorously complaining that she had never been kept under lock and key herself.

After the tour the two women sat in the den, watching a videotape. Like everything else he owned, Gary's video equipment was the best, and their choice had been extensive. Kelsey paid little attention, however. Her thoughts were filled with Dillon, and her gaze wandered to the clock as the time crept closer to midnight. She was just about to ask Melanie for a ride into town when someone pounded on the front door.

Kelsey sprang to her feet, but Melanie beat her to the den door. "You'd better let me get that. We don't know who it is," she pointed out. "It could be your friend with the gun."

"In which case I'd be better prepared to take him on."

"But it's not me he wants," Melanie said firmly. "So I'm as safe as can be."

Kelsey let Melanie precede her, but only by a few feet. By the time they reached the door Kelsey was anxious enough to rip it off its hinges.

Melanie put her ear to the carved wood. "Who's there?"

"Dillon," came the answering shout.

Melanie unlocked it, opening it wide. Dillon stood on the doorstep, one eyelid suspiciously swollen. "Kelsey?"

She was so relieved to see him that she could hardly speak. When she did, though, it wasn't relief she voiced. "You've been fighting!"

"Can I at least come in before you start giving my ears a bashing?"

"It looks like more than your ears have been bashed." Kelsey stepped aside, following Melanie's lead, and let Dillon enter. She restrained herself from hugging him. She wasn't sure he'd remain standing if she did.

Melanie rose on tiptoe to examine Dillon's face. "Let's get you into the den where we can have a look at that eye."

"Thanks, Melly, but I just want to go home. With Kelsey," he added, the expression in his one good eye as warm as a Coober Pedy summer.

"Is that safe?" Melanie asked.

"I doubt we'll be bothered again."

Kelsey wondered how he could be so matter-of-fact. "Are you going to do an 'aw shucks, ma'am, it was nothin',' on us, or are you going to tell us what happened?"

Dillon swayed, and she was instantly contrite. In a split second she had her arms around him for support. "Forget I said anything." She hugged him harder than was necessary.

"Serge has left town. In his tomato-red truck." Dillon rested some of his weight against Kelsey. She had never felt quite so soft, quite so warm. He wanted to stand this way forever.

"Serge?"

"It was Serge who shot out the windows. But he won't be around to shoot at anything again. He got my message."

She turned amazed eyes to Dillon's. "All this because I used a little karate on him at the pub? None of this had to do with Jake's accident?"

"It had to do with Jake's accident, all right, although I don't have the proof yet. But it seems that our friend Serge has been on opal for some time. He came across a small seam at the border of his mine and ours, and he got greedy. Tomorrow we'll start a new drive and see if there's enough opal in the Rainbow Fire to kill a man for."

Chapter 13

"You really think there's opal on our side of the boundary?"

Dillon lay back and let Kelsey handle the ute. They had said a quick good-night to Melanie, then started for home. The first minutes of the drive had passed in silence, and now he had to rally himself to answer her. "Serge thinks so."

"Then he tried to murder my father so he could move past the boundary into the Rainbow Fire and rat the opal?"

"He denies it, of course, but there's no denying he blew out the windows on the sun porch. His rifle was still in his ute."

"Are you going to tell Sergeant Newberry your suspicions?"

"I've already taken care of my suspicions."

Kelsey's temper had been on slow simmer since she had seen Dillon standing at the door. Now it boiled over, her soft tone no match for her words. "With no help from anyone, of course. But then, a big, strong Aussie man can do anything with one hand tied behind his back. He doesn't need anyone, not the police, not a woman with a black belt, not his friends. I'm just surprised you chased Serge out of town instead of lynching him. That's a much more effective do-it-yourself approach."

There was no answer from the seat beside her, which angered her more. "I know you, Dillon. There are men like you all over the world. You're so busy proving how big and strong you are that you don't even realize you need someone else occasionally."

When he still didn't answer, she turned on him in frustration. "Well?"

His eyes were shut, and his face was drained of color. Blood was seeping slowly from the cut over his eye, and the skin over one cheekbone was already turning black and blue. As she gazed at him, she saw the deep but uneven rise and fall of his chest.

She swung back around to stare out the windshield. Tears stung her eyes, and, angrily, she blinked them away. "Fool," she whispered, but she wasn't sure whom she was labeling. "Just what am I going to do with you?"

Alf was standing guard in front of the dugout when she arrived. His son, a boy of about eighteen, was nailing boards over the windows. A door of sorts was already back in place.

The glow from Alf's cigarette warmed the clean, honest contours of his face, which was just barely discernible in the light of a three-quarter moon. Kelsey got down and went around to help Dillon out.

He awoke slowly, groggy at first, until he finally realized where he was. "I fell asleep."

She couldn't repeat her lecture. For a moment he looked like a little boy, curls falling over his eyebrows, face flushed with sleep. She reminded herself that he was far from being a child, that he was a man like all the others she had known. He settled his scores with violence, and he prided himself on needing no one. Somehow she couldn't work herself back into anger, though. For that moment anyway, he needed her.

"Come on, you big bully. Let's get you inside."

He grinned a decidedly lopsided grin. "Should I remind you that Serge was the bully? I don't shoot at helpless women." He held up his hands in apology as her brows drew together. "God help me, I'm sorry. I forgot. There's nothing helpless about you, Sunset." Dillon pushed himself out of the seat and stepped down.

Alf strode toward them. "You've been hurt?" he asked in his lilting accent.

"Nothing serious," Dillon assured him. He put one arm around Kelsey's shoulders and leaned on her. "A few cuts and bruises."

"You found who did this?"

"I found him, yes. It was Serge Traovich."

"He's still here?"

"Let's just say he's remembered pressing engagements elsewhere."

Alf nodded. "I'll tell the other miners. He won't come back. No, not without your knowing."

Kelsey silently added Alf to the growing list of townspeople she was glad to know.

"Alf, thank you for everything. I don't think there'll be any more trouble tonight," Dillon said, extending his hand.

"Tonight?" Kelsey asked. She would have felt better if Dillon hadn't added that. "Are you expecting trouble tomorrow?"

"I'm just taking this one step at a time."

Alf nodded solemnly again. "*Ja*, that's the way to do it here. One step at a time, one day at a time." He was still nodding and muttering to himself when he beckoned his son and walked away.

Dillon watched them go. "Alf's a good sort."

"And you're a dead on your feet sort. Lean on me, big boy, and let's get you into bed."

"That's where we left off, wasn't it?"

She stopped, flustered. Those moments of intimacy with Dillon seemed as if they had happened a century before. She gathered her composure and started back down the path. "And that's where we'll leave off indefinitely."

Dillon couldn't blame her. Blood and bruises weren't the best aphrodisiacs. His head was spinning; every joint felt like a rusty tin woodman's. He suspected that if Kelsey undressed him again it would be horror not desire he saw in her eyes. "I can't blame you," he mumbled. "But you're sleeping with me tonight anyway."

"Now just a minute."

He started to tell her the truth. He felt certain Serge was gone, but Dillon wasn't taking any chances. As tired as he was, as much as he ached from the beating he had endured, he would be alert enough to hear any intruder tonight. He wanted Kel-

sey by his side to protect her. Luckily he realized just what she
would say if he told her that.

"It's not what you think," he said instead. "I need you to be
my ears tonight. Once I go to sleep, I won't wake up unless you
get me up. I really don't think we'll have any trouble, but just
in case...."

"Why don't you just say that you'd like someone warm and
soft in bed next to you to help take away your aches and
pains?"

He examined her words and realized just how true they were.
"Will you sleep with me, Sunset?"

He was both a big bully and an unrepentant little boy, just
like every man she had ever known. And, somehow, he was so
much more.

"On my side of the bed," she warned.

"No worries. I'm too whacked to do anything, anyway."

Despite herself, she felt a tug of sympathy. "You know, if
you hadn't gone and tried to act like a hero, you wouldn't be so
whacked."

"I won't have your life in danger," he said, pulling her closer.
"What would I do if anything happened to you?"

Something gushed through her, a warm spring that washed
away the barriers she had been trying to build against him.
"What am I going to do with you?" she asked softly, lifting her
face to his.

"Sleep with me. Dream with me. Mine with me tomorrow."

And though she looked for the resources to say no to the
second, she found that they had washed away, too.

Jumbuck lay in the warm cradle of Dillon's lap. He had
opened his eyes when Kelsey and Dillon came into the bedroom, then closed them again after a good look. His only other
response had been a faint purr when Dillon picked him up.

"I'll wager he's got one splitting headache." Dillon carefully stroked the cat's fur.

"And you know how that feels." Kelsey lifted one of Dillon's feet and slipped off his boot. The sock came off next, and
then she massaged the bottom of his foot, paying special attention to each toe.

He groaned with pleasure as she repeated her ministrations
on the other foot.

"Are you ever going to tell me what happened tonight?"

He heard the nip of sarcasm behind her words. "I'm not keeping anything from you. I'm just not sure my brain's relaying messages to my mouth. It got pretty bashed up tonight."

"Your brain or your mouth."

"Both."

"Someone should teach you some fighting skills," she said sweetly. "If I had time, I'd take you on."

He laughed a little, and the effort made him pale. "I have a few skills. It was just that the other three men had a few, too."

"Three?" She dropped his foot to the ground. "Three?"

Even Jumbuck stirred at the question.

"Three. Of course, one of them was out of commission almost immediately, so I suppose you could really say just two—"

"Why didn't you take on the U.S. Marine Corps while you were at it?" She slapped her hands on her hips and glared at him.

"They hadn't landed at that point."

"Were you trying to get yourself killed?"

Dillon stood, laying Jumbuck gently on the bed. "I had some trouble finding Serge. He must have known he'd been spotted racing away."

"Then you knew it was Serge by the description of his truck?"

"I was fairly certain, yes."

"And you didn't tell me?"

Dillon started to take off his shirt, but he paused at the first button. "Shall I go on? Or are you going to yabber at me some more?"

Kelsey had learned how little good yabbering did. "Go on."

He undid the buttons one by one. "He was at a mate's house. At least, the chap was his mate before I got there. He wasn't right fond of Serge by the time Serge finished talking."

"Why not?"

"Because he's Serge's mining partner. And Serge had neglected to tell him about the vein of opal he'd found."

"That sounds like the Serge we've grown to love." Kelsey watched Dillon spread his shirt wide. The room was partially illuminated by the fading glow of a flashlight and the flickers of a fat red Christmas candle she'd found in a drawer, but even in the dim light, she could see his battle scars. "Look at you!"

His chest was a rainbow of colors and guaranteed to turn black and blue. "Do you need ice packs?"

"Just sleep." Dillon stripped off his shirt and let it fall to the floor. "The other chap was Serge's cousin, a fairly decent sort, actually, but attached to his family. He gave me a good apology, though, when he found out what Serge had been doing. Family or not."

"Go on."

"I got there, and Serge had been filling their ears with wild tales. They didn't give me time to explain my side. I had to make time," he said, the dimple deepening in his cheek.

"Which you did at a certain expense to your own comfort."

"Worth every blow."

"And so all this—my father's accident, the attempt on your life, the dead kangaroo at the mine, and the shot fired at me—all this was because Serge thought that Rainbow Fire might have opal on the other side of the boundary?"

"Don't forget the shots tonight and the destruction of the sun porch."

By now Kelsey knew Dillon too well not to pick up on the fact that he hadn't really answered her question. "And you think all those things were Serge's fault?"

There was the briefest hesitation before Dillon answered. "It makes sense. It's the only thing so far that does."

"But you don't buy it?"

"I'm too groggy to think straight right now."

Kelsey instantly regretted the third degree she'd put him through. "We'll finish this tomorrow. Take off your pants while I get a washrag to clean you up."

"Pardon me?"

She tried not to smile. He seemed embarrassed. She liked the idea. "Your pants," she said in a no-nonsense voice. "Take them off. I'll be back." She took the flashlight and left the room, unleashing the smile as soon as she was in the hall.

She returned minutes later with a basin of warm water, soap and washcloths. She had also found bandages and disinfectant. Dillon was seated in the chair nearest his bed, and his eyes were shut tight. She paused in the doorway, struck once again by what a vital, appealing man he was. Even now, exhausted and aching, he was a man to fill a woman's fantasies.

"You're not going to hurt me, are you?" Dillon asked, opening his eyes just a crack.

"You big baby."

"I thought I was a big bully."

"That, too." Kelsey was strangely reluctant to cross the room and begin. She needed time to reflect on the night and everything that had occurred. She was afraid that if she began to touch him, there would be no time for reflection until morning.

"I meant what I said about being too whacked to do anything," he said with a grin, his eyes wide open now. "You look like you're not sure I was serious."

"Ridiculous." Kelsey crossed the room in record time. "Where do you hurt the most?"

"Why? Are you going to see if you can make it worse?"

She couldn't suppress a laugh. "I'll be gentle with you."

"That was supposed to be my line tonight."

"Funny how little things like explosions and rifle blasts can get in the way of a romantic evening." Kelsey smoothed the palm of her hand over his eyes so he would shut them. "I'm going to start with this cut over your forehead. I'll tell you when I'm finished."

She worked slowly, and she could feel Dillon relax under her careful ministrations. He had some nasty cuts and bruises, but nothing seemed serious enough to warrant a doctor. He needed a good going-over and a soft body to warm his bed through the night, and she was ridiculously pleased to provide both.

She was also ridiculously pleased to be running her hands over his body.

"You *can* be gentle." Dillon sighed, as if he had been holding his breath waiting for her to hurt him.

She marveled at the width of his shoulders and the firmly roped muscles in his arms. "Did you really doubt it?"

"I wasn't certain you'd let yourself be."

"I've been bruised after a fight myself."

"Karate competitions?"

"I don't like to compete. But I've had to, a time or two."

"And you've won every time."

He seemed so sure that she hated to disappoint him. "No, I'm afraid not. I don't have the killer instinct. I studied strictly so I could defend myself. There's this rule my *sensei* liked to repeat at every class. If you're attacked, run. Only fight if you have no choice. I took that to heart, and it ruined me for competition."

He shook his head. "And you wanted to go tonight."

"Somebody had to defend you."

He laughed ruefully. "Are you almost finished?"

"You've got a cut on this thigh." Kelsey tried not to concentrate on Dillon's bulging briefs only inches from her hands.

"Lord, Sunset. Let that one go."

"I'm afraid not." Kelsey ran her fingertips around the cut, probing gently for further injury. Then she wrung out the washcloth and began to carefully wash it.

"Ouch."

"You're awfully tense all of a sudden."

"Would you finish up down there so I can get some sleep?"

Kelsey couldn't help but notice that a fair share of him didn't seem sleepy at all. She finished quickly. "Done."

Dillon stood at the same moment that she straightened, brushing against her. He reached out to steady her. "Thank you."

Kelsey noticed the constricted sound of his voice. She cleared her own throat. "You're welcome."

He pushed her away. "I've got to get to bed."

She suspected that what he had to do was pull the covers up to his chin. "I'm going to my room to get some clothes. Then I'll probably take a shower," she said.

"I'll probably be asleep when you come back."

Except that he wasn't, although he didn't say a word when she reentered the room dressed in a knee-length T-shirt. The candlelight still flickered, and in the semi-darkness she couldn't see clearly. But she could see enough to know that Dillon's tightly squeezed lids didn't belong to a sleeping man. And, as if the bed had been surveyed and divided, he lay absolutely still, not so much as a fingernail on her side.

Kelsey set the flashlight beside the bed, then crossed the room to blow out the candle. She wondered what Dillon would say if she confronted him, but she immediately thought better of that. There was little she could say. Both of them knew now that aches and exhaustion couldn't extinguish the potent spark between them. Nothing could.

And she knew something more. This day was ending, and with it a chance to become Dillon's woman was ending, too. A part of her was grateful. It was a step she needed to think more seriously about.

But a part of her knew better.

* * *

Kelsey awoke slowly the next morning. She hadn't slept so soundly, so comfortably, in all her memory. She had felt completely safe, despite the events of the previous day and evening. And as she awoke and became more aware of her surroundings, she understood why.

Dillon's arms were encircling her, and her head was resting against his shoulder. Their legs were intertwined, and her T-shirt was twisted around her waist.

She wasn't nearly as safe as she had thought.

Kelsey wondered how to extricate herself without waking Dillon. She could feel the warm, even brush of his breath against her forehead, and she knew that he was still sleeping. If she escaped now, he wouldn't know how intimately they had held each other through the night.

She began with one leg, inching it slowly from its warm home between his. She tried to ignore the feeling of his hair-roughened flesh against the smoothness of her skin. But ignoring it was impossible. The difference in textures fascinated her. She wanted to slide her leg back and forth, memorizing the feeling.

Instead she continued to slip her leg from between his until finally she was free. In his sleep Dillon compensated by pulling her closer against his chest.

Kelsey's other leg was anchored securely at the ankle by the weight of Dillon's. She flexed her foot, searching for an escape route. She found one and began the slow process of withdrawal. Dillon murmured something in his sleep and smoothed his hand along her side to rest on her bare thigh.

Her legs were free, but the rest of her was far from it. And not the least of her problems was that she liked the way he was holding her. The motivation to continue separating herself from him was fast disappearing.

Kelsey lay still against Dillon and thought about the events of the day before. She'd had lots of time to think as she had huddled between dust-besieged rocks, her continued existence no more certain than the whine of another bullet. She had wondered what she had accomplished in her twenty-four years and who would miss her if she died in the middle of an outback tempest.

Her greatest regret had been that no one would. Her father didn't know her, and her other relatives wished they didn't.

There had been no time for friendships in her life, not at work, not at school, not even at the *dojo*.

And then, as she had fought not to move, not to give away her presence, she had realized one stunning, incredible thing. She was wrong. Someone would miss her. Dillon would. Despite a relationship that could be described only as brief and rocky, Dillon would miss her.

She had let Dillon know her in a way that no one else ever had. He was the only one in the world who had seen the whole Kelsey Donovan, the good, the bad, the proud, the stubborn parts and the vulnerable, emotional parts. He knew her, and he cared.

And he would miss her.

At that moment she had felt a stronger connection to him than anything she had ever felt before. And since that moment the connection had only grown stronger. But was she confusing gratitude for something else? And was she confusing their undeniable sexual attraction for something more important? If she succumbed to his lovemaking, would she leave Australia a happier woman? What had Melanie said the night before?

The words came back with absolute clarity. "Take my advice, Kelsey, sleep with a man and enjoy him, but don't ever let him get to you. Because if you do, you'll find out that he owns you, body and soul, and you'll spend the rest of your life doing the craziest things just to make him love you."

Kelsey realized she had already let Dillon get to her, and they hadn't even slept together—at least, not in the way Melanie had meant. She was only a step away from spending the rest of her life doing crazy things just to make him love her.

Because she was almost in love herself.

Dillon's hand drifted down her thigh to cup her bottom. She could feel each individual finger scorch her soft flesh. She hadn't believed a man could feel so good against her. She hadn't believed she could feel so good, period.

Dillon stirred, pulling her even closer. "Are you awake, Sunset?"

There was no use pretending otherwise. She forced herself to sound stern. "What are you doing on my side of the bed?"

"I think the question needs reversing."

"Well, if I'm on your side of the bed, it's because you pulled me over here."

"A smart man, even in my sleep."

"A smart aleck."

"You're strong enough to get away if you want."

Kelsey knew he was right. And she also knew that her own ambivalence had kept her from moving away faster. She wasn't about to tell Dillon that, however. "I didn't want to wake you up. You needed your sleep."

He chuckled against her curls.

Kelsey slid her hands up to his chest and pushed, but she didn't move an inch, because his arms tightened. "Time for the fun and games to end," she warned.

"Have they started?"

"That's just an expression. American slang."

"I don't understand it. Demonstrate."

"You're not going to like what I demonstrate, Aussie."

"Karate in bed?" He chuckled again, nuzzling his face into her curls. He kissed her head. "You always smell like lavender. My mother grew lavender, big glorious clumps of it in front of our house."

"I've always wanted to smell like someone's mother."

"You don't feel like someone's mother."

Kelsey didn't point out that if she stayed in bed much longer, she might *become* someone's mother. "It's time to let go of me."

Dillon didn't want to let go of her. Nothing had ever felt so right. The sensation of waking with Kelsey in his arms was dizzying. He had thought that by not asking a woman to share his life he was only denying himself the comfortable pleasures of a woman's body, a woman's softening presence. He hadn't realized he was denying himself completion.

"Yesterday," he said, "we almost made love. Was that gratitude because I found you in the storm? Did you need someone to cling to until you found your balance again?"

"Yesterday was yesterday."

"And today?"

She couldn't lie, and she couldn't be honest. Instead she chose a path halfway in between. "Today I don't even know my own name. I just know this isn't right. Not now." Not until she understood her feelings. Not until she was absolutely sure she could control what was happening between them. She would not fall in love. She would not spend the rest of her life trying to make Dillon love her.

Kelsey in his arms felt right to Dillon. More than right. Perfect. But as he forced himself to let her go, he knew how imperfect their relationship was. Kelsey would go back to the States. She would not remain in Coober Pedy, because there was nothing for her here except dust and drought and unbearable heat. They could offer each other nothing lasting. And even if Kelsey didn't yet understand that part of herself, she was a woman who needed love, who needed permanence.

He could give her one, but not the other. If he became someone else for her, a man tied to a desk chair in Sydney or New York, she would only be getting half of him, for the other part would be back in Coober Pedy, digging opals in his dreams.

Kelsey slid to the far side of the bed, then sat, pulling her shirt over her hips. "I'm sure you want a shower, too. Would you like to go first?"

"No, you go ahead."

She wanted to leave; she wanted to stay. She wished for the time only days ago when she wouldn't have had a decision to make. But even as she made the wish, Kelsey knew she didn't want it to come true. Because then she wouldn't know Dillon, and, despite her struggles, knowing Dillon was worth it all.

She forced herself to stand. "Shall I dress for the mine?"

"Dress for a long, hard day."

She risked a look at him. He was sitting up, and his head was in his hands. "Are you all right?" she asked softly, reaching out to touch his shoulder.

He moved out of her range, subtly but unmistakably. "I'm fine. Go have that shower so we can get going."

"Maybe you should take it easy today."

He couldn't imagine sitting around with Kelsey waiting on him, touching him, questioning him in that worried tone. Whatever aches he had were nothing in comparison. "Go take that shower."

Kelsey hesitated, but she knew her attention wasn't welcome. As she left the bedroom, she thought she heard Dillon sigh.

Chapter 14

Kelsey started the power winch that would bring Dillon up from the bowels of the earth. As she waited she removed her green slouch hat and waved the wide brim to stir a light breeze and scare away the small, persistent flies that were an outback fact of life. The breeze cooled her perspiration-slick forehead and cheeks, but did nothing about the flies. In fact, she suspected they were probably grateful to her for the breeze.

"I'm nothing but a blasted resort for insects," she mumbled, bending to wipe her face on the hem of her khaki shirt.

"Taken to talking to ourselves, have we?" Dillon peered over the top of the mine shaft that had taken them days of work to sink.

Kelsey glared. "It's the only game in town."

"No one ever said this would be fun."

Kelsey shoved her hat back on her head and forced herself to count to ten. None of what was bothering her was Dillon's fault, although most of it had to do with him.

"I'm sorry," she said, her voice as taut as her nerves. "It must be a hundred and twenty degrees out here, the flies are as thick as the dust, and the only opal I've seen in four days of hard work is hanging around your neck. Maybe I wasn't cut out for opal mining."

"No, you're a sane, intelligent woman."

"I'm not quitting, though." Kelsey's chin jutted at an angle that was all too familiar to Dillon. "So don't even ask."

"I wasn't going to ask." He looked at the dust- and sweat-covered creature before him and felt his admiration grow. Soon there would be no more room for admiration or any of the other emotions she stirred. He was dangerously close to exploding. He hoisted himself over the side of the shaft and unhooked the harness that had slung him from the winch. "When was the last time you got something to drink?"

Kelsey wiped her watch against her shirt and peered at it. "Too long."

"Let's take a break."

"I can keep going."

"*I* can't." Dillon was careful not to brush Kelsey as he passed her. He headed for the small screen tent that he had set up beside the space where he parked his ute. The tent was the talk of the pub and had almost usurped Serge's deceit as a conversation topic. The general consensus was that Dillon was in love. Why else would he be wasting his time making Kelsey comfortable when there was opal to be found? Dillon suspected that only rarely in Coober Pedy's history had so many of its citizens been in agreement.

Kelsey trailed behind him. She eyed the small tent with gratitude. Inside its mesh walls was freedom from flies and the worst of the sun. She watched Dillon stop beside the door. They had established a ritual. Before he entered he brushed away any flies on his shirt and pants; then he did the same for her.

For the last four days it had been the only time each day they touched each other.

Kelsey stopped closer to Dillon and methodically dusted his shoulders, chest and back with her hands, trying not to think about what she was doing. He did the same for her, brushing his hands lightly across her shoulders and breasts before she turned so he could swipe her back. Then he unzipped the tent flap and stepped inside, quickly making room for her to do the same. Kelsey zipped the screen behind her. "Did we get them all?" she asked, trying not to show how much his touch had affected her.

He muttered something without looking at her.

Kelsey shrugged, then turned to continue the ritual by running some water from the big plastic cooler into a metal basin.

She washed her hands, emptied the water into a pail, then washed her face and neck. She could feel her skin grow cooler by several degrees, although the water was almost as hot as the air. She emptied the basin again and filled it for Dillon.

As he washed, she filled two glasses from the second cooler. This one was colder, because she had packed it with ice that morning at the dugout. When Dillon was finished washing she handed him a glass and gratefully took her seat on one of the two deck chairs.

In the last four days Kelsey had worked side by side with Dillon, following his orders. She had hauled and bent and scooped as Dillon drilled the new shaft on the edge of the Rainbow Fire closest to Serge's mine. Although she and Dillon had worked side by side, they might as well have been hemispheres apart. He conscientiously taught her what she needed to know, but what conversations they had centered on mining alone. They were careful to steer clear of anything more intimate, and they worked such long hours that there wasn't time for anything more intimate, anyway.

Which was just as well, Kelsey reminded herself one hundred times a day.

Now, between sips of water, she searched for a carefully neutral topic other than mining. "Do you think we're close to opal?" she asked finally, defeated.

Dillon pulled his chair out several inches so he could stretch his legs in front of him without running into Kelsey. "I've no way of knowing."

"I'm beginning to think an engineering degree isn't much help out here."

"You're beginning to think like an opal miner." Dillon swirled his glass in his hands. "Do you know how your father and I picked this spot in the first place?"

"Surveyed it?"

"Two years ago Jake went looking for a place to start a new mine. About sundown he got a flat tire, just where our main shaft is sunk. His spare was flat, too, so he spent the night out under the stars and dreamed he found opal. I found him the next morning, and he already had the place pegged out."

Kelsey finished her water in silence. Her father and Dillon were crazy, but, worse yet, the story had given *her* goose bumps.

Dillon hadn't expected a response. What could anyone say about two men who had built their lives around a dream? "What did the doctor say about Jake this morning?"

"The same." Kelsey set her glass down and closed her eyes. "He's holding his own, communicating more each day. They've asked him about the accident, but he says he doesn't remember. They haven't told him about me, yet, but they're going to soon." She grimaced unconsciously, giving Dillon all the information he needed about her feelings. "But they've been saying that for the last four days."

"And you're tired of waiting."

Kelsey knew she was too confused to answer that honestly. She was glad her father was better. She wanted to see Jake— after all, that was why she had come to Australia. But when she left Coober Pedy, she knew she would never see Dillon again. And despite the stiffness and formality of their relationship now, she wasn't ready for that. "I can wait," she said carefully. "Especially now that no one has shot at me for a while."

"Little things mean a lot." Dillon stood, stretching. His restraint had its limits, and sitting across from Kelsey tested them sorely. "I'm going back down."

Sighing, she opened her eyes. "I'll get back to work, too."

Kelsey knew that Dillon was probably right. After four long days of drilling and examining every bucket of mullock that was brought to the surface, they had finally bottomed on an opal level—which Kelsey had learned meant nothing more than the type of dirt—opal dirt, or kopi, as some called it—where opal was usually found. They hadn't been lucky. There had been no opal chips or even slices of potch to guide them, only a narrow flint-hard band, then a peculiar pinkish claystone, a product of the gradual drying up of the inland sea that had once separated Australia from north to south.

The opal dirt was so unspectacular that Kelsey would have dismissed it immediately. Dillon had known better, although he had been disappointed that the opal dirt showed no signs of the gem itself. There was always the hope that a random shaft would bottom on a seam of opal and take away the necessity of searching. Now he was left with the task of deciding where to start his first drive.

"Then you're going to go back down and decide for sure where to tunnel?"

"I'll drive in the direction of Serge's mine. I'm just not certain what angle to take. Missing it by an inch is as bad as missing it by a mile."

Kelsey wished that they had been able to come to terms with Serge's mining partner. The young man had agreed to let them come into the Rainbow Fire from Serge's drive, but he had demanded a huge percentage of whatever they found. Instead Dillon had decided to sink his own shaft. They hadn't seen the young man since.

"We're doing a lot of work on the basis of what one wretched representative of the human race told you under physical threat."

"I've heard of stranger reasons for a hit."

"Like flat tires and opal dreams?"

He hunched his shoulders, dismissing her question. "I'm going to go down and pick at the face for a while. I'll decide where to start tunneling when we come back next week."

Kelsey had avoided looking at him. Most of their conversations for the last four days had been held without their eyes meeting. Now hers flashed to his. "What do you mean, next week?"

"It's almost Christmas, Sunset."

She was as surprised at the nickname as she was at the sentiment behind his words. He hadn't used his pet name for her since the morning when they'd awakened in bed together. "So?"

His eyes didn't flicker. "We're taking a holiday."

"I don't want to take a holiday."

"No?"

"Christmas doesn't mean anything to me."

"It means something to me. It means we don't work."

"Fine. Don't work. I'll come out here by myself."

"And do what?"

"Shovel the damn tunnel alone if I have to."

"No you won't."

Kelsey knew it was childish to pretend otherwise. "Why are you doing this? There might be thousands of dollars worth of opals down there just waiting for you to dig them out tomorrow."

"If they're there, they've been there millions of years. They can wait another day or two. Christmas doesn't wait."

"How long do you intend to stop mining, then?"

"Tomorrow's Christmas Eve. I usually take a week or two." He went on when he saw the disbelief on her face. "But we'll come back the day after Christmas, since it obviously means so much to you not to spend the holiday with me."

"This doesn't have anything to do with—"

He waved off her protest. "Anna and Gero always have a Christmas Eve party at their dugout. Father Christmas comes for the children. We're both invited."

Kelsey knew about the party. Anna had mentioned it the last time she had seen her. "I told her we'd be working up until dark tomorrow."

"And I told her we'd be at the party. We will be."

Kelsey watched him unzip the door and step outside. As if they'd known he was about to leave, a dozen flies swooped in.

Christmas Eve. Christmas with heat and flies and dust instead of snow and holly. Christmas in a strange country as far from home as she could possibly be and still be on the same planet.

Christmas with Dillon.

Kelsey washed their glasses, then emptied the pail of wash water. Despite the fact it was summer here, she had known Christmas was coming. The inevitable signs had been there. The decorations in the stores in town, Christmas carols on Anna's tape recorder, the jingle bells that decorated Melanie's red taffeta petticoat when she tended bar at the pub. There had been a certain Christmas spirit in evidence, too. Extra-wide smiles, an influx of backslaps, handshakes and party invitations.

Christmas with Dillon.

Christmas had never been a good time for Kelsey. It was a time for family love and shared memories. As a child she had watched Christmas from her place outside that warm circle and wondered why people who didn't really want her felt so obligated to pretend they did on this one day of the year. She had always received the regulation doll, the new dress, the orange and the chocolate Santa in her Christmas stocking, but she never received the love that went with them.

As an adult she had never tried to find that love for herself. Christmas was an inconvenience, a time when the *dojo* was closed, her students were on vacation, and she had twenty-four hours to kill.

Christmas with Dillon. As Kelsey listened to the power winch drop him back down the shaft she tried not to dwell on the ways this Christmas might be different. She would get through it, one hour at a time, just as she had gotten through all the others. Perhaps, if she were lucky, Dillon would do the same.

But then she had learned one thing in four straight back-breaking days of opal mining. Luck was a very relative thing.

She awoke on Christmas Eve morning with the sensation that something was wrong. The sensation was one she had learned to trust. So many things had gone wrong in Coober Pedy that her survival instincts were now honed to perfection. It was true that in the days since Serge had been aggressively escorted out of town there had been no more gunshots, no death adders, no explosions. Life had settled down to the rhythm of mining and avoiding intimacy with Dillon.

Now something felt strangely different. Her bed vibrated.

"Jumbuck." Kelsey sat up and sleepily stretched out her arms. Jumbuck climbed onto her lap, purring nonstop as he did. "To what do I owe this honor?"

"He missed you." Dillon stood in the doorway and forced himself not to add more. He had missed Kelsey, too. He'd been awake for hours, and he couldn't remember a time in his life when he had felt lonelier.

Kelsey pushed her hair off her face. "He's turning into an indoor cat. Next thing you know he'll start sleeping on your bed."

"I could adjust."

"What time is it?"

"Ten."

She couldn't believe she had slept so late. "You should have gotten me up sooner."

"Why? You've got the day off."

She yawned and stretched, trying to clear her head and re-erect her defenses. "Then you still intend to ignore the fact that we're almost on opal?"

"Don't be optimistic, Sunset. Even if Serge were telling the truth, the opal could have stopped at his boundary. We may find no more than a chip or two."

Kelsey could see that Dillon's mind was made up. "Then what are we supposed to do today if we're not going to work?"

None of the things he really wanted to do, that was for certain. Kelsey wanted none of the intimacy that Dillon craved, and he couldn't blame her. Not for the first time, he wished he could be a different man for her, one who could offer her the roots, the stability, the life, that she needed. He could only offer the love. And love wouldn't be enough.

"Would you like to spend the day with me?" he asked, continuing before she could refuse. "I know what you're afraid of, Sunset. But we were friends before we almost became lovers. Can't we be friends again?"

How could she refuse without giving away her deepest fear? She didn't know if she had the control to remain friends. She was perilously close to asking him for more. No, she was perilously close to *begging* him for more. She was fast sinking into the state Melanie had warned her about.

She swallowed and cursed her sleep-numbed brain. If there was an answer other than yes, she couldn't think of it without at least one cup of coffee and a shower. She did the best she could. "We're already friends. I don't know what you mean." She buried her face in Jumbuck's fur, muffling the last words.

In a moment she felt a tentative hand on her hair. She met Dillon's eyes. "We've both been working until we dropped. We're avoiding the truth. We're afraid to be close, to even have a real conversation, because we're afraid it's going to lead to more. Can we put that behind us today? Can we give each other a real Christmas?"

Everything inside Kelsey seemed to melt and run together. Four days of ignoring her feelings, four days of trying to ignore him, seemed to disappear. Her fingers were linked in his before she even knew she had moved. "You'll have to show me how."

Dillon had watched the change in her. For that moment she was as vulnerable, as open to him, as she had ever been. He blessed her slow-to-gear-up metabolism and lifted her hand to his lips before he reluctantly dropped it. "I'll have breakfast ready by the time you're done with your shower. Then I have some last-minute shopping to do. Would you like to come?"

Kelsey nodded and knew her feelings were in her dreamy, sleep-filled eyes.

Breakfast was steak and eggs and crumpets; Kelsey realized she would never want cold cereal again. She and Dillon talked without the barriers that had been between them, with Dillon telling tales of childhood holidays in Melbourne, and Kelsey telling about the year she had eaten hot dogs for Christmas dinner because she had secretly helped the Christmas goose to escape his pen in her uncle's backyard.

They cleaned up together, still careful not to touch, but no longer careful not to laugh together. The drive into town seemed shorter than usual, because Dillon told her stories about each landmark they passed. Coober Pedy itself had taken on a festival air, with decorated artificial trees in newly washed shop and restaurant windows, and Christmas carols blaring from cassette players.

Surprisingly, Dillon's shopping was all for local children. Kelsey found that he had a regular route he traveled on Christmas day to the homes of friends with sons and daughters who waited anxiously for him to appear. He bought candy and small toys to add to a sizeable stash he admitted to already having collected, and he bought paper and bright-colored ribbon to wrap them all.

They lunched on Greek food and exchanged greetings with everyone who came through the door. Kelsey had known Dillon was well-liked, but the smiles and hearty Christmas cheer directed toward her were a gratifying surprise. People still inquired politely about Jake's progress, but there was even more interest in what she was doing.

"You've become a local heroine," Dillon told her after one old man congratulated her on cleaning up the town.

"But I didn't do a thing. You're the one who got rid of Serge."

He leaned back in his chair and grinned. "They know that, but the consensus is that Serge left because he couldn't fight both of us."

She smiled, but his joking had triggered a question that had been bothering her. Now that they were talking easily again, she knew the time was right to ask it. "Do you really think the trouble is over?"

"Nothing else has happened."

Kelsey knew Dillon lied poorly but was good at evading questions. Almost anyone would think he'd just answered her. She knew he hadn't.

"I've noticed you don't let me out of your sight." She picked up her iced coffee and swirled it to mix the cream.

"What man would?"

"Nice try, but I'm not blind. I've seen the way you scout for trouble, the way you check the equipment and the mine for sabotage."

"Old habits die hard."

"You think he's coming back, don't you?"

"No." Dillon was glad to have a question he could answer easily. He was equally as glad that she hadn't asked again if he thought the trouble was over.

"Then you think the trouble is over?"

His head snapped up. "Serge is gone, and I doubt he'll be back."

"You're giving me the runaround."

"I can't see into the future."

"What are you still worried about?"

He gave an honest answer. "I don't know."

"Why are you trying to protect me?"

Because he had realized, much to his sorrow, that he was in love with her? Because if anything happened to her there would be little point in going on? He couldn't tell her either of those things. "Serge's confession explained a lot," he said finally, realizing he couldn't stall any longer. "But it didn't explain everything. Not by half."

"Like what?"

"The other two murders."

"They could have been accidents, or totally unrelated."

"There's still the comb I found in the mine with strands of blond hair tangled in it."

Kelsey frowned. "What comb?"

"The first day I took you down, the day the lights gave us trouble. I found a comb. It wasn't mine or Jake's."

"Weren't there others down there searching for my father? Couldn't someone from the rescue party have dropped it?"

"I thought of that. I've asked everyone who went down that day."

"Then the comb might have been Serge's. He had a reason to be in the mine."

"Serge isn't blond."

"Then maybe he took someone with him."

Dillon nodded. "And maybe they're still in Coober Pedy."

Kelsey finished her iced coffee slowly, examining Dillon's concerns as she did. Finally she thrust them away. "I think you need to stop worrying."

"Oh?"

"Serge had the motive to put you and my father out of commission. He wanted to take the opal from your side of the boundary. He couldn't risk doing that if either of you were around, because he knew you'd realize what he was doing. That's simple and straightforward, and believable. When I appeared on the scene he had to worry about me discovering him, too, so he tried to keep us both so busy we wouldn't know what was going on. Everything fits, Dillon."

"Everything except two murders, a comb and a hand-cast bullet."

Kelsey opened her mouth to tell him to put the whole thing behind him, but his last words stopped her. "What does the bullet have to do with it?"

"Serge's rifle was a semi-automatic. It used standard cartridges. The gun that killed the kangaroo and almost killed me was a different weapon altogether, a single-shot rifle, probably an old one." He didn't add that the bullet he had dug out of the mulga tree after the dust storm had also been plain-based lead. Kelsey didn't need to be reminded that she had almost died.

"Then maybe he owned two guns."

"Maybe. But no one knew about the other one if he did."

"You've been doing a fair amount of snooping."

He brought his fist down on the table. "Do you think I want you in any more danger?"

Kelsey stared at him. She had never heard a more open declaration of love. They were sitting in a hole-in-the-wall Greek restaurant in the middle of a one-of-a-kind town. People were coming and going, laughing and calling Happy Christmas to each other. One of the fluorescent bulbs over their heads was blinking on and off with the irregular rhythm of a junior high percussion student, and the only air-conditioning vent in the room was blowing ice-cold air at their ears and noses. And in the midst of this crazy place and this Christmas madness, Dillon was telling her that he loved her, even though he wasn't saying the words.

"Do you?" he repeated, leaning back and folding his arms over his chest. "Do you think I would let anything threaten you?"

Kelsey wondered if she were crazy, too. Was she hearing words he would never say? Didn't it make sense that he would want to protect her? Wasn't that just part of who he was? She knew she should brush off his question and forget she had ever believed, even for a moment, that what he felt was anything more than concern for a friend, for the daughter of a "mate." But, somehow, she couldn't.

She couldn't look at him anymore. She focused on a spidery crack in the table's surface. "Why does that matter so much to you? I've given you nothing but headaches. You've certainly paid your debt to my father by now."

Dillon knew he should evade the real heart of her question, just as he had evaded others she had asked. But, somehow, he couldn't. "Don't you know?" he asked softly, making no move to touch her.

She forced herself to look at him. "I guess I'm not sure."

He smiled unevenly. "If anything happened to you, Sunset, I couldn't live with it."

Love couldn't be that easy. She had yearned for it all her life, then fought it when she had found herself falling in love with him. And yet, here it was. Easy, uncomplicated, and so sweet she wanted to cry.

"I'm not used to people caring that much."

"Loving," he corrected.

His green eyes were so warm, so fiercely luminous, that she could hardly make herself look into them. "Do you fall in love easily?" she asked, and knew how insecure she sounded.

"You're asking how special you are?" He leaned forward and reached for her hand. "Completely special."

Kelsey looked down at their hands. She wanted to make a joke. She wanted to sing. Instead she cleared her throat. "Is this my Christmas present?"

"It's a gift. No strings attached. I guess you needed to be told."

"I guess I did." She met his eyes again. "This doesn't happen every day. I'm not sure what I'm supposed to say."

His eyes burned into hers. "How about thank you?"

She smiled and knew her smile was a little wobbly. "Thank you."

"My pleasure." He squeezed her hand, then let it go. "I think we should go back now," he said gruffly. "I've got packages to wrap before we go to Anna's party." He swung gracefully out of the booth, then reached for Kelsey to assist her. For just a moment she leaned against him, letting herself feel all the things she had been denied for a lifetime. Then she pulled away, confused, afraid.

She was sure of only one thing. She needed time alone. "I'm going to stay in town. Dimitri said my father's ute would be fixed again by today. I'll walk over and get it when I'm ready to come home."

Dillon felt Kelsey separate herself from him. He cursed himself for frightening her by telling her a truth she wasn't ready to hear. But he knew she might never be ready to hear it. She had been denied love for so long that it might always frighten her. He forced himself to speak calmly. "You don't really need to be afraid to come home. Nothing has changed."

"I have some shopping to do."

He made himself step away from her. Nothing would improve if he pressured her. "Then I'll see you after a bit."

"I'll be back in time to get ready for the party." She watched him walk to the counter to pay their bill. Then she headed for the door.

Chapter 15

Anna's dugout was an underground palace. Gero, her husband, was one of the fortunate few who had hit a large seam of crystal opal early in his mining career. A relaxed, easygoing man, Gero had decided on the spot that after he cashed in on his good luck, he was gong to retire from the endless drilling and tunneling, picking and shoveling that made up a miner's life. He would take his tidy fortune and invest it back in the town that had been so good to him. Easygoing Gero—who had the business instincts of a Wall Street trader—had seen that tourism would soon replace mining as Coober Pedy's reason for being, and he wanted to cash in on that, too.

The Pizza Palace was just one of Gero's ventures. He owned a small fleet of tour buses and a demonstration mine in addition to a shop that specialized in the gimmicky merchandise that appealed to the tourists he served. His home reflected his imagination and his wealth.

"I'm not dreaming this, am I?" Kelsey asked Dillon as she stared at the sparkling green pool that stretched away from her to end against sunlit windows.

"Quite a few dugouts have pools, actually. I plan to put one in mine someday."

Kelsey could picture a pool off Dillon's comfortable lounge. She could also picture Dillon slicing through the water with quick, sure strokes. Alone. When she tried to picture him swimming with a woman—a wife, perhaps—her stomach turned over.

And yet that was what would surely happen someday. Dillon wasn't a man to live his life in seclusion. He needed the love, the warmth, of a family. He was a man who would give unqualified, unlimited love in return.

He loved her.

She had spent most of the afternoon wandering the Coober Pedy streets trying to absorb it. She hardly knew what love was, but Dillon loved her. And she was so filled with emotion that she was afraid to speak, afraid her own feelings might come pouring out against her will.

"Did you bring your bathers?"

"I didn't know I was supposed to."

"I should have warned you. You Yanks don't do much swimming at Christmastime, I suppose."

"In Florida, maybe." Kelsey glanced at him, then looked away.

"Anna's oldest daughter, Gina, probably has something you can borrow, or I can take you back home to get a suit. But you'll have to go in the water. Everyone does." Without waiting for an answer, he strode off to find Gina, leaving Kelsey to continue gazing at the pool.

Kelsey knew Dillon regretted telling her his feelings. He had treated her with nothing except exceptional politeness since. She knew it would be up to her to break the strained silence between them. She just didn't know how, or what to say.

"Enjoying a real Aussie Christmas?"

Kelsey looked up to find Melanie standing beside her. For once she was simply attired in white shorts and a yellow blouse. Her arm was wrapped around Gary's in a stranglehold. Gary looked distinctly uncomfortable.

"It's different, but then I've never been a big fan of mistletoe and holly."

"I get nostalgic this time of year. I want to see all the annual specials on television. I want to buy everything in sight."

Gary extracted himself, with a pat on the arm for Melanie and a nod to Kelsey. "I'm going to see what Gero is up to, love." He took off like a man released from prison.

"Doesn't he love to be with me?" Melanie cooed.

"Maybe you should try ignoring him. Play hard to get."

Melanie dropped all pretenses. "I am going to play hard to get. The hardest. I've decided I'm going home after Christmas, and I don't intend to come back."

Kelsey was stunned. "I thought you were going to stay here forever."

Melanie's shrug didn't quite come off. "So did I. But I've got a remnant of sense left, even if you can't tell to look at me. While I do, I'm going to get away from Gary while I still have some pride left to take with me."

Kelsey tentatively slipped her arm around Melanie's waist. "Does he know?"

Melanie shook her head. "He won't care. He'll start looking for another woman for his collection. And his choice will be as vast as this damned desert we live in. He's so full of icy charm, women will line up to take my place."

"No one could take your place." Kelsey didn't know what to think about Melanie's declaration. She had seen little of Gary, but she knew from her few observations and Melanie's remarks that the relationship was a dead end. "I guess I'm glad for you," she said at last. "You deserve more than you're getting."

"I hope so." Melanie's face looked strained, as if the decision she'd made had been hard won. "Maybe we'll see each other back in the good old U.S. of A."

"Sure. North Carolina and Nebraska are practically next door to each other."

Melanie gave her a wan smile right before Gary signaled her to come to his side in the doorway. "Excuse me, won't you, Kelsey? The lord and master wants me, and that's so unusual, I'd better take advantage of it while I can."

Saddened, Kelsey watched her go. She didn't even hear Dillon come up behind her. "Gina sends you this." He handed her a royal blue racing suit that looked as if it would fit a teenager who hadn't yet earned her share of wolf whistles.

Kelsey pushed the conversation with Melanie out of her mind. "And you're going to swim?" she asked, stretching the taut fabric doubtfully.

"Couldn't keep me out of the water if you tried."

Kelsey went to find a place to change, running into Anna on the way. By the time she reappeared in Gina's suit, she had been introduced to everyone at the party, whether she already knew them or not. She had a drink in one hand, a plate of food that Anna had forced on her in the other, and Gero's fatherly arm around her shoulders.

Dillon was glad he was waist-deep in the water. The blue suit fit Kelsey like a second skin, emphasizing every curve of her body and the sleek length of her legs. She had tied her shining butterscotch curls in a riotous fall that bounced wildly each time she moved her head. Shorter, loose curls brushed her cheeks and neck. Her skin glowed with good health and natural vitality, and her eyes shone. He had never wanted her more, and he had never been more sure he wouldn't have her.

He hadn't meant to tell her that he loved her. Perhaps it had been an unconscious gamble. He was a gambler. Every time he went down into the Rainbow Fire he was courting Lady Luck. He had the credentials, the training to make a comfortable living as an engineer. Instead he wrestled with dirt and rock, putting his own sweat on the line for the chance to make a fortune.

He had put his heart on the line today with Kelsey. And, like the Rainbow Fire, it hadn't paid off. He had cursed himself for a fool the moment she walked out the restaurant door. He had known there was no chance that she would want him, would want to stay in Coober Pedy with him and face the conditions here. When a man gambled, he gambled alone.

And still, he hadn't been able to stop himself. Because some part of him had hoped that maybe she loved him, too.

He watched her search the room as she chatted with Gero. He lay back in the water and waited until her gaze came to rest on him. Her smile was tentative, but it bloomed for him alone. When Gero walked off to greet more guests, she set down her dishes and stepped into the water without taking her eyes off him.

She swam with the same grace that characterized all her movements, reaching him in seconds. He knew he must be a worse dreamer than he had thought, because he found himself hoping once more.

"The water's colder than I thought it would be," she said, stopping just short of swimming into his arms. She stood and brushed wet curls off her cheeks. "It feels spectacular."

Dillon tried not to concentrate on the way the suit pushed her firm breasts higher and outlined her nipples, which were taut from the shock of the water. He tried not to remember what they had felt like in his hands, not to yearn for the taste of them against his tongue. He looked away. "It stays cool because we're still underground, even though those windows lead to the other side of the hill."

She didn't want to talk about the water temperature and dugout architecture. She wanted to talk about love and relationships, but she didn't know what to say. "This is the right way to celebrate Christmas."

"You don't miss snow?"

"We only get a little of that where I'm from. But then, they didn't get a lot in Bethlehem that first Christmas, either."

He smiled, reaching for one curl that she had missed. He stroked her cheek with his thumb as he took his time pushing the curl into place. "So Christmas down under's not too bad?"

She drew a quick breath as the casual caress went through her like a bolt of lightning. "Not bad at all."

"Wait until you see the tucker Anna's prepared."

"She's already loaded up my plate."

"That was only a bit of a snack."

Kelsey knew she had run out of small talk as surely as if someone had reached into her brain and pulled a plug. She laid a hand on his bare shoulder, fingers just grazing the gold chain at his neck. She wished a touch could somehow take the morass of feelings inside her and solidify them, clarify them until the words she had to speak came fluently. "Dillon, I—"

The pool suddenly seemed to change dimension and become a living thing. The water heaved as if it had turned into a rushing river. Startled, Kelsey looked up to see Gero pushing his guests one by one into the pool.

Dillon's laughter was a deep baritone that warmed the empty places inside her. "Happy Christmas, Coober Pedy-style," he said, pulling Kelsey to rest against him away from the splashing and cursing of half-drowned guests. His arms crept around her waist and crossed against her abdomen, resting lightly on her hip bones. She settled against one rock-hard thigh, and her head fell back against his shoulder, tickling his neck with her wet curls. Lightly, slowly, his fingers smoothed spirals along the bare skin of her thighs.

Kelsey shuddered against him and shifted restlessly. She wished they were anywhere other than in the midst of a group of merrymakers. She wished she could turn to him and smother her doubts, her fears, in the warmth of his embrace and the heat of his kisses. Instead she rubbed her head against his cheek, letting him know that he was turning her body into something she didn't know or understand.

When the pool was too crowded and the splashing too tumultuous to ignore, Dillon's hands crept back to her hips and he turned her, then met her soft, lush lips with his own.

The kiss lasted only seconds, but it told Kelsey everything she needed to know about the control he'd exercised over the last four days and how quickly it was slipping. He pushed her away, then began to swim the length of the pool with swift, determined strokes. Kelsey swam to the side and watched him cut through the water, back and forth, until she knew he swam to exorcise the desire that had almost overwhelmed them both.

When she could watch no longer, she climbed out to find her clothes and change.

The rest of the party passed in a blur of Christmas cheer. Father Christmas came, looking amazingly like Gero with a white beard, huge red T-shirt and surfer shorts over a natural potbelly. Children squealed over toys and games that were a prelude to their family celebrations tomorrow, and adults exchanged smiles and good wishes.

They sang carols to the accompaniment of an accordion. Some Kelsey had never heard, with cattle drovers replacing wise men, and kangaroos and wallabies replacing the traditional ox and ass. Others were more familiar, and she found herself singing "Silent Night" with something akin to tears in her eyes.

She had never spent a Christmas Eve this way. These people weren't her family; indeed, they weren't even countrymen. But she felt a kinship to all of them that transcended bonds of blood or nation. She let her gaze wander through the crowd. Surrounded by their children, Anna and Gero sang in lusty, accent-laden English that only made the songs seem holier. Alf Sweeney, his two sons and the wife Kelsey had just met sat beside them, the accent different, the sentiment the same. Kelsey noted Dimitri, a tiny baby against one shoulder, his wife's head against the other. Even Gary and Melanie were holding hands, forgetting for a few precious moments the differences that separated them.

They were good people, kind people, people with dreams and heartaches and enough love to reach out to the stranger in their midst and make her feel that she was at home.

At home for the first time since she was a child of five.

Kelsey looked up to see that Dillon was watching her. Sh
wanted to tell him what she was feeling. This land of his, thi
town, was a special place. She had come to find her father, anc
instead she had found friendship.

And love. She drank in the now dearly familiar lines of hi
smile, the nose that wasn't quite at the center of a face that wa
more thoroughly masculine because of it. The green eyes tha
could burn with anger or glow with humor. The strong, wid
shoulders, the sturdy-fingered, callused hands.

One of Anna's children, a girl of four, was perched on hi
knee. He cradled her head against his shoulder as naturally a
if she were his own. Her expression was adoring, and as Kelse
watched the child put her thumb in her mouth and shut he
eyes.

Kelsey had found love. She had found a man worth a thou
sand others, and she had found him in the middle of the Aus
tralian outback in a town like no other in the world. Sh
wouldn't have to spend her life making him love her. He ha
given her that gift already. She would never have to fear him
never have to wonder if he would use his superior strengt]
against her. He was strong, but his greatest strength was hi
gentleness.

She didn't even know what the future would bring for them
She didn't even know if they had a future together. But sh
knew that they had this night.

The last carol was sung, the last bit of fruitcake eaten, the las
glass of wine drunk. When Dillon stood, cradling Anna'
daughter in his arms, Kelsey stood, too. The child was hande
back to her mother, and goodbyes were said. It was perfect]
natural for Dillon to take Kelsey's arm and hold her close a
they walked back to the ute, perfectly natural for her to mov
close to him on the front seat so that her hip rested against his
and her breast pressed against his side.

They drove the short distance in silence. Dillon parked th
ute by the light of a full opal moon that shot the warm out
back night with beams of silvered light. The star-dusted can
opy of sky met the stark, undulating ridge of hills and turne
it into a masterpiece of form and line.

They stood together in perfect understanding, watching th
magical transformation of desolate countryside into fairy-tal
splendor. Only when Kelsey shivered did Dillon touch her, an
then only to guide her to the porch.

She stood back as he withdrew his keys. Windows had been replaced and an intimidating dead bolt installed on the new door. Jumbuck crept out of the shadows and followed them when the door swung open, as if he had lived indoors all his life. He brushed back and forth against Kelsey's ankles, bestowing his own feline Christmas gift before he trotted off to enjoy the bowl of milk that now always waited for him in the kitchen.

"A knock on the head seems to have done the old fellow some good."

Kelsey smiled. "Sometimes all of us need a knock on the head."

Dillon turned to her, stepping far enough away to give her room if she needed it. "Has it been a good Christmas Eve, Sunset?"

"It has."

"Even if we didn't find opal?"

She wanted to tell him that she had found something more precious, but she was afraid to say the words. "Even then." She met his gaze without blinking, until nothing more could be said with her eyes. Tentatively she stretched out her hand. "Is it over yet, Dillon?"

His breath caught in his chest. His fingers touched hers. "Not if you don't want it to be."

"I don't."

His hand closed around hers. "Come with me."

She hadn't been absolutely sure where he would lead her, but she hadn't thought it would be to the lounge room. And she hadn't known there would be a Christmas tree.

Unknowingly she squeezed his hand. "When did you put it up?"

"This afternoon. While you were in town."

"I walked right by the doorway, but I didn't even notice it when I came back."

"You had other things on your mind."

He was right. *He* had been on her mind. Now she walked toward the tree, stretching her hand out to touch the tinsel-trimmed artificial branches. She had never liked artificial trees, but then, she had never been a real fan of Christmas trees, period. Now this one, slightly lopsided and sparsely trimmed, touched her deeply.

"It's beautiful," she said in a husky voice.

"It's not a flash tree. I couldn't seem to get it just right. The branches bend when you put them on, and you can still see where the—"

"It's beautiful." She turned and held out her arms to him. "You're beautiful."

"That I'm not." He circled her waist with his arms, his hands resting lightly on her bottom.

Kelsey turned her face up to his. She had the peculiar feeling that time was standing still, that the night would last forever, and that the world would never intrude again. "Kiss me, Dillon."

He smiled, and even when he spoke she knew he was smiling still. "I have something to give you first."

Puzzled, she started to tell him that she didn't want anything except him for that night, but he bent his head and kissed away her words. Then he reached around his neck and pulled the gold chain with the Rainbow Fire opal over his head. "I want you to have this, Sunset." Before she could protest, he lowered it over her hair, lifting it to slide the chain into place around her neck. "There's so little I can give you," he said quietly. "But I want you to have this."

Kelsey's hands came up to grasp the large stone that nestled in the valley between her breasts. There was nothing she could say. She knew what the opal meant to him. He never removed it, not even when he slept or showered. It was the symbol of all his years of hard work, all the dreams and sweat that had gone into the mine. It was hope that someday his dreams would pay off.

And now it was hers. She blinked back a sudden onslaught of tears.

"You'll wear it for me?"

She nodded. Then she dropped the opal and felt its weight sink against the cool cotton of her blouse. Her hands rested lightly on his shoulders, then stroked up the sides of his neck to rest against his cheeks. "I believe I'll kiss you," she said huskily. "And I don't think I'll stop."

"I don't know if I'll be able to stop, either," he warned.

"Good." Kelsey lifted herself on tiptoe and slid her hands into Dillon's hair. His hands met at her waist, and his sigh was a warm exhalation just before she kissed him. "Oh, Dillon," she murmured against his lips, "I was never sure this moment would come. Thank you."

He wasn't sure what she had thanked him for, the opal, the lovemaking that was about to occur, or simply the fact that he loved her. He only knew that her words made him sad.

"You never have to thank me, Sunset. I'm the one who's grateful." He felt her brush her lips sweetly across his, and he moaned at the gentleness, the innocence, of her caress. He wondered where he would find the patience to move slowly, to teach her the arts of love with the tenderness, the care, that she deserved.

He had never wanted a woman so badly; he had never, in all their days together, wanted Kelsey more.

She touched his lips with her tongue, just a quick flicker, then a more assertive movement that made him clamp his hands tighter to pull her closer. Their tongues met, his moving to the guidance of hers until there was no leader, no follower, only two people enchanted with the nuances of this slow, perfect mating.

Kelsey felt the kiss in every cell of her body. She had never understood that lovemaking was more than a simple act of pleasure. She hadn't known that it would be a merger, a joining together, that would blur boundaries and veil differences. He moved against her, and she wondered if his body was answering the unspoken call of hers, understanding more about her needs, perhaps, than she did herself.

He freed her blouse from the waistband of her skirt, and it wasn't until she felt the cool glide of air over her back that she realized how fevered her skin was. She lifted her arms, and he pulled the blouse over her head, tucking the opal against her breasts as he did. She wanted to know if his skin was as hot as hers; she wanted to feel that heat against her breasts. Her hands found the top button of his shirt, then the next and the next, until his chest was bare. He unclasped her bra and slid it down over her arms until there was nothing between them except the opal, and heat, and the unbearable pleasure of skin against skin.

She was a superbly conditioned athlete, yet her skin was as soft as velvet. She moved against him with the languid, coordinated grace of a cheetah, velvet on the outside, power, control and strength just beneath the surface.

She excited Dillon as no woman ever had. He hadn't known that he'd needed strength to match his own. He hadn't known he needed a woman who could match him in every way.

Now he knew. He shrugged out of his shirt and felt her nails
rake shallow furrows in his back. Her breasts flattened as she
arched against him, and he took her mouth again, hunger and
heat burning away the patience that had been in too short a
supply anyway.

It was Kelsey, though, whose patience ended first. Kelsey
who moaned for more and delved deeper in their kisses. Kelsey whose twisting, yearning body made demands he could only
say yes to.

Dillon lifted her in his arms and strode from the room. His
bedroom was dark and cool, and Kelsey felt the softness of his
comforter against her back as he laid her on the bed, following
her down to cover her body with his own.

Desire had built all day, had built for a week, and yet the
building had been nothing like this. It had been smoke and
spark. This was a conflagration of the senses, burning away any
doubts or fears or shyness, until she was flaming out of control.

She wasn't sure when Dillon removed the last of their clothing; she only knew when it was gone, because she felt such
gratitude. His body was lean and hard, muscle, bone and sinew
that left indelible impressions against her skin, a branding that
proclaimed that only he had the right to know her this way.

His mouth found one rose-crested nipple, tenderly at first,
but abandoning tenderness as she offered more to him, arching, twisting, pleading. Her passion took what control he'd had
left and turned it into raw, throbbing need. His lips grazed the
opal that lay between her breasts, and he thrust it to one side to
drop beside her.

"Nothing between us. There should be nothing between us."

Kelsey heard his muttered words and felt a joy as old as
woman. He wanted her totally. He wanted possession. And she
knew in that moment that he would have what he wanted.

"Nothing," she murmured, her head turning from side to
side against the pillow.

He buried his face where the opal had been, breathing in the
fragrance of lavender and aroused woman. The heady scent
twisted through him, strangling all the voices that told him to
go slowly. His hands locked beneath her, lifting her to his
mouth as he explored each sleek, perfect part of her.

Imprisoned, she could find no release for the unbearable
tension he was creating inside her. She couldn't move; she could

only submit to the fire of his caresses. She could only whimper or more.

Dillon knew there should be more time for adjustment, more time to let her open slowly to him. But he had no more time. Kissing and caressing Kelsey was more provocative than making love to any other woman, and he had stepped over the edge.

He had only enough control to assure himself that she was ready for him, as well. He raised his mouth to hers once more as his fingers slipped inside her. She gasped, closing her legs round his hand.

His reassurances were as old as man. Kelsey listened to the words flow over her, but she heard nothing of what he said, only the sound of his voice, the love that enchanted her until she was opening herself for him, inviting him to make her his in the only way he hadn't.

Dillon felt her whispered "yes" in every cell. He levered himself over her, and every sensitized inch of his body screamed out for release. His body was hot with fever and cold with sweat. His muscles tightened to steel clamps as he fought to control his desire.

Kelsey felt his struggle. The strength of his passion was the final element that set her free. Her body flowed against his, heat to heat, slick, smooth skin to slick, smooth skin. She grasped him with her legs, twining them around him until he was the prisoner.

"No more waiting," she said, arching closer. "No more."

He groaned and entered her, so caught up in the feel of her that he knew nothing of patience or holding back.

Kelsey felt his first thrust twist deep inside her like red-hot fire. The pain was nothing, the merging everything. She cried out and tried to bring him closer.

Dillon controlled his movements, sliding slowly, deeply inside her, his body still a stiffened caricature of the living man. She accepted him, and he moved faster, surer.

He opened eyes that had been squeezed shut as he denied himself the full pleasures of her body. She was looking at him, her eyes luminescent, clouded with both the joy and pain of becoming his woman. Restraint melted into love. Cast iron became human flesh as he no longer fought himself.

He rocked slowly back and forth, watching her pleasure build. His own pleasure was explosive, a transcendence that he

had never considered possible, a giving and a taking that wa
so total he knew no differences.

Kelsey stared into the green eyes that pulled her into his sou.
She went willingly, joyously, not caring that she would retur
a different person. Wave after wave of ecstasy washed over he
as she met him there at last.

Chapter 16

The flies weren't so bad. Not really. Three days after Christmas they still seemed to hum carols as they swarmed around Kelsey's ears. She had fine-tuned the Australian salute—a lazy sweep of her hand—until she had learned to keep the worst of them away.

But then nothing seemed bad about being in Coober Pedy. Not the flies or the heat, not the drought that had burned away everything except the sparsest vegetation. Nothing seemed bad, and everything seemed . . . possible.

Kelsey rose from a squatting position and stretched her arms over her head to smooth the kinks from her body. Leaning forward, she called down the shaft. "Is it going okay?"

A long string of generator-muffled curses was her answer.

She shrugged. "I guess not."

There was a clatter from below as the ladder they'd installed rattled against the sides of the shaft. Her heart did a now-familiar jig as Dillon stepped over the mullock rimming the opening. She wondered if she would ever see him again without thinking first of the pleasure he gave her when they made love.

She doubted it, because the pleasure was too explosive, the feelings he elicited too deep. She wondered if he could see those feelings in her face, read them in the way she was learning to move her body under his. She wondered if her dreams merged with his at night when they awoke ready to find pleasure again.

He held out his arms, and she slipped into them. Naturally. Gracefully. He was covered with dirt, and he smelled like the depths of Mother Earth, but she didn't mind. She looked and smelled just the same.

"No luck?"

Dillon hesitated, his arms tightening around her. Since Christmas Eve they had lived in a sensual haze. They had made love, slept, mined, eaten and begun the cycle again, paying no attention to clocks other than the natural rhythms of their own bodies. There had been nights when they had been down in the Rainbow Fire until midnight, days when they had mined the gem of their own passions with no regard for sunlight or moonglow.

He knew her body now as thoroughly as his own. He had watched her cry with satisfaction and laugh with the sheer joy of being with him. He had seen her grow calmer, surer, happier.

And he had watched the same things happen to himself. His arms tightened until he knew she was locked in them. For that moment, at least, she was his.

"I've got something to show you," he said at last.

Kelsey caught a breath. Something was different, but as well as she knew him, she didn't know what it was. "Opal? You've hit opal?"

He cursed himself for not realizing she would think as much. "No, Sunset. I'm afraid not."

She heard the desolation then and knew what he would tell her. "There won't be opal, will there? The drive's a duffer."

"Come see." He released her reluctantly, in no hurry to show her what he must.

She didn't ask any more questions, because she didn't want any more answers, at least not any sooner than she had to have them. She climbed over the shaft rim without another word. The ladder was slick under her feet and hands, but she was used to the feel of it. She wasn't as fast as Dillon, but she was fast enough to reach the bottom in less than a minute. Once there, she flattened herself against the side of the shaft and waited for him to join her.

For four days they had tunneled, using machines and jack-hammers, and then, finally, the old-fashioned time-consuming method of gouging by hand.

Dillon hadn't wanted to take the chance of destroying even one opal when they had drawn nearer to the Rainbow Fire boundary. They had decided to waste precious time rather than precious gem, and they had finally resorted to pick and shovel. Kneeling, they had taken turns driving in slowly under the roof of their tunnel, letting the opal dirt fall on the newly created floor to be sifted through with lights for telltale signs of opal.

Even though there had been no signs of opal, they had treated the dirt as if it were precious, "re-lousing" it once more to be certain they had missed nothing before they discarded it. Kelsey had learned to shovel like a real miner, sitting back on her heels as she pushed the shovel blade forward over the floor toward the mine face and under the fallen mullock. She had learned how to twist her wrist and wriggle the shovel handle to fill the blade, then how to lift it as she swayed back on her heels again to give a final thrusting jerk to throw the dirt neatly over her shoulder into a pile.

She had gotten so good that she rarely overshot and hit the roof, although at first she had earned more than one earful of dirt. What she hadn't learned was how to gouge out opals, because there had been none to practice on.

Now she waited for Dillon to join her before she began the stoop and crawl that would take her to the mine face. He took the last rungs three at a time, and they stood face to face. "I'm sorry," he said, touching her cheek for just a moment. "I wish this could have been different."

She wanted to tell him that compared to what he had already given her, finding opal seemed unimportant, but she knew it wasn't, not to him. "There are other drives."

"She's already a rabbit warren."

"Don't let her hear you're losing heart."

His smile signaled nothing except his disappointment. "Let's get this over with." He pulled the cord on the portable light until all the kinks were gone; then he handed it to Kelsey.

The first section of the drive had been tunneled by machine, and, stooping, she was able to walk unimpeded. The second part had been dug by hand, and she resorted to crawling. She followed Dillon, who somehow managed to compress his body so that he could do a crablike shuffle through the drive.

Their journey was short. It took several moments for Kelsey's eyes to adjust, and then several more moments for her mind. The neat, calculated drive that they had constructed inch by inch had been replaced by a gaping, ragged hole. "I don't understand," she said finally, clutching at explanations. "Did you use explosives after all? Did you just do this?"

Dillon didn't want to explain. He was too heartsick and too furious to have to tell anyone, especially Kelsey. "I didn't, Sunset. Serge or his partner was here. One or both of them took the opals they could find on their own side of the boundary, then took what belonged to the Rainbow Fire, too. He blew a hole a good meter or two into our side and gouged out what he could as fast as he could. The proof is right here."

He pulled a jackknife from his pocket and flipped the main blade. With a resignation she had never expected to see, he scraped across the ceiling of the drive until there was an audible ping. Then, with skill and delicacy he worked the jackknife into the rock and pried out a small stone. "Here's something he missed." Dillon handed the dirt-encrusted stone to Kelsey. It was the size of a peanut kernel. "There'll be more where that one came from. We might still pull as much as five hundred dollars worth out of here if we're careful. I'd say Serge or his buddy may have pulled thousands. Probably shattered another fortune in opals besides that, too, in his hurry. There are chips on the floor at your feet. Lower the lamp and watch them dance in the light."

Kelsey couldn't bear to. "There's nothing you can do?"

"How can I prove it? And how could I prove Serge or anyone else was responsible? Unless I'd caught them red-handed...."

Kelsey was almost glad he hadn't. Even in the dim light she could see murder in Dillon's eyes. "Let's go home." She watched him survey the drive, as if by examining it closely he could will himself to believe that the mine was still opal rich. Kelsey put her hand on his arm. "Dillon, let's go home. Please?"

His survey reached her. "I wanted to hit opal. For you." He gave a derisive laugh. "I wanted to hit enough that I never needed to hit it again."

"I know, but you'll make a big hit someday. I'm sure of it."

She didn't understand, and he knew it was just as well. In the last days, even with the promise of opal just ahead in the drive, he had still thought of little other than Kelsey. He had begun to believe that he could leave this place, could take the opal they would find together and build a new life for them somewhere lush and verdant, somewhere where a fly or two was only an addendum to lazy summer days under towering gum trees.

There would be no gum trees now, no lazy summer days. He wasn't fool enough to think he could leave Coober Pedy without opal in his pockets—if he could leave it even then. It wasn't that opal meant more to him than Kelsey, it was only that he knew part of him would always be here in the Rainbow Fire, even if he and Kelsey were together somewhere else. He could not give her less than all of him.

She would not want less, and she would not want this.

"Dillon?" Kelsey stroked her hand up his arm. There seemed to be nothing to say. "Let's go home."

"Someone should have told you not to give any of yourself to an opal miner, Sunset."

She forced a smile. "The obvious person to tell me that would have been my father. I suppose he did, in his own way."

She was right. That was one thing Jake had done for her. But she hadn't listened. Dillon took her hand and brought it to his lips for a kiss. "Let's go home."

On the drive back to the dugout there was no bantering, no innuendo-laden conversation guaranteed to have them in bed the minute they crossed the threshold. They sat in silence, possessed by their separate thoughts.

Kelsey wanted to comfort Dillon, but she didn't know how. She needed comfort, too.

She showered first. Dillon was sitting in the bed when she came into his room to dress. Her clothes hung there now, and her toiletries were scattered across his dresser. For the first time since Christmas Eve, however, she felt as if she didn't belong. She was a visitor, a visitor due to leave any day. And he was the man who was going to let her.

He rose without a word or a look to take his shower. She watched him go, and she realized she was blinking back tears.

Dillon stood under the pounding water and let it wash away the dirt of the Rainbow Fire. But nothing could wash away his misery, his fury, his self-hatred. Nothing could change him into the man Kelsey needed.

He had dried himself and dressed before he realized that he didn't know where Kelsey had gone. She was nowhere in the dugout; it was as quiet as a tomb. In the last few days she had begun singing to herself as she worked. She had a clear, sweet soprano that was a humorous contrast to the words of "Tie Me Kangaroo Down," her favorite selection. He would never hear the song again without an ache in his gut.

Her things were haphazardly strewn about the bedroom, and he thought about that change in her. The obsession with neatness had been replaced by a more carefree attitude. She was still neat—when she got around to it. But the change reflected her comfort with him and with herself. In subtle ways, his home had become hers.

Now, however, the untidy bedroom was a reflection of one more thing: her haste to leave it. Dillon strode from room to room looking for her, even though he knew she wasn't inside. He was almost to the sun porch when he heard a fierce shout.

He took the remaining distance in a leap, throwing open the door. Then he came to a dead halt.

Kelsey stood in the space in front of his patio, wearing a white *gi* and a rising-sun bandanna tied around her forehead. Her body stance was defiant. Then, as he watched, she relaxed and gracefully pulled her body to attention.

She hadn't seen him. Dillon pulled back into the shadows of the sun porch to watch. In a moment she shouted words he recognized as Japanese and began to move in a time-honored series of choreographed steps, the karate *kata*. She twirled, kicked, punched and defended herself with the twist of a wrist, the slash of a forearm.

She was everything beautiful in motion. She was liquid fire and unadulterated passion. She was elemental movement and absolute stillness. Each kick reached higher than the last until he could hardly believe she could balance. Her bare feet dug into the ground, then split the air so cleanly that he could almost hear molecules collide. She toyed with her imaginary opponent, bending low on knees that seemed elastic before she leaped at him, fists raised. She circled, and this time her stance was different, her hands open to slice through the air like sabers. Two shouts rang through the air and chilled Dillon's heart.

She relaxed and straightened again. Dillon could see that she was breathing hard. The sun was almost on the horizon but still sending blistering rays to burn the outback landscape. The dugout cast its own shade, but she was barely touched by it. And, somehow, he knew she didn't even notice.

She began again, this time executing jumps that looked more like ballet than karate. The dance was a deadly one, a warrior's dance. Inadvertently, Dillon shuddered, but not from repulsion.

Desire. He had thought he knew all its faces. Now he knew he never would. Desire would always be Kelsey, every facet of her, every twist of her body, movement of her hands, smile on her face. Desire would always be Kelsey, and it would never be assuaged.

Kelsey turned when she finished the *kata* and saw Dillon in the shadows. She hadn't heard his approach, hadn't thought of him once since she had begun. She knew that forever after it would take this kind of single-minded concentration, this fierce denial of her feelings, to forget him. And then only for minutes.

He stepped off the porch and came toward her. She was still breathing hard, and her body gleamed with sweat. As he approached she dragged the bandanna over her curls and began to wipe her face and neck.

He reached her and stopped her hand. Then he lowered his head to taste the salt-tinged flavor of her skin. She leaned into him, eyes closed, mind blissfully numbed. His hands spread over her shoulders into the open neck of her *gi*. He wanted to tear it from her, to take her there, the warrior, the woman. His woman.

She was his. In all the ways that counted she would always be his. And he had given himself so completely to her that there was nothing left to withhold.

He found her breast with his fingers and felt her shudder. He spread the fabric farther, trailing his lips down her neck and lifting her until his lips closed around one turgid nipple. She tasted of salt, sweat and woman, and he wanted to plead for more.

He lifted her, warrior, woman, soul mate, and carried her inside. He had no patience to strip away her clothes. He untied the black belt that bound her *gi* and tugged down the white elastic pants. Her skin was unbearably hot, her heartbeat so rapid he couldn't feel an individual pulse. She lifted to shrug her arms out of the *gi*, then reached for him, sliding her hands under his polo shirt to strip it away. She fumbled with his belt, her hands unsteady, until he impatiently pushed her away and took care of it himself.

She was more than ready when he came to her. She lifted to meet him, turning and twisting until she had taken him deeply inside her. She arched and withdrew and begged for more. He gave until nothing drove him except the fever of her body and the ache in his own. He gave until she was neither warrior nor woman. She was a part of him.

But afterward they slept without touching.

Kelsey got out of bed, showered again and dressed, leaving Dillon asleep. She had no desire to wake him. Reality could be faced later. For now he seemed at peace. Perhaps he had found opal in his dreams.

She was hungry, although she didn't know what time it was, but it was dark outside. They had missed dinner, letting other needs take precedence, but now her stomach was rebelling, reminding her that she had eaten nothing since lunch.

She was in the middle of grilling a cheese sandwich when the telephone rang. She balanced the receiver between her neck and shoulder, a spatula in one hand, frying pan in the other.

"Miss Kelsey Donovan?"

She frowned, recognizing the voice, but not able to place it. "This is Miss Donovan."

"Dr. Munvelt here."

She set the spatula on the stove and eased the receiver to a more comfortable position. "Yes, Dr. Munvelt."

"I have some bad news, Miss Donovan." There was a pause, and with peculiar objectivity, Kelsey could almost imagine the shy physician looking away from the telephone as if to avoid her eyes. "Your father left the hospital this morning."

"I don't understand."

"His physician in Adelaide just rang me. It seems your father took what few things he had there and walked out of the hospital about noon. No one saw him go. No one knows where he went."

Stunned, Kelsey couldn't think of a response. As if he understood, Dr. Munvelt went on. "I'm sorry."

"Sorry?" Kelsey leaned against the stove and closed her eyes. "He's well enough to walk out of the hospital, but he wasn't well enough to be told that his own daughter wanted to see him?''

There was another pause. And then, "He was told, Miss Donovan. This morning, right before teatime.''

Kelsey let the truth sink in. She understood why he hadn't told her that first. But there was no way the blow could have been softened. Jake had left the hospital rather than face her.

"I see," she said finally. "Do they think he'll be all right without care?''

"He's a long way from well, but he is thinking clearly, walking, talking. His physician there is cautiously optimistic.''

She focused on Dillon's calendar. Two more days before December ended. As many more before school began again and she was expected to be back in a North Carolina classroom. She had pushed going back from her mind, even thought of requesting another leave of absence. Now she knew she had no choice. "Will you give the physician there a message for me?''

Dr. Munvelt coughed in embarrassment. "Whatever you'd like, my dear.''

She noted the endearment and knew it hadn't come easily. "If my father comes back, I'd like him to be told that I've left Australia. I won't be back, but I wish him well.''

He coughed again. "I'll see that his physician is informed.''

Kelsey gently replaced the receiver.

"When do you leave?''

She looked up and saw Dillon standing in the kitchen doorway. He showed no emotion. "How much did you hear?''

"Only one end, obviously.''

"My father walked out of the hospital today. They don't know where he is. But he left after he found out about me, which was obviously not a coincidence." She didn't even try to smile. "I guess we could say I put him on the road to recovery, huh?''

"I should have left him in the bottom of the mine," he said fiercely. "He didn't deserve rescuing.''

She shook her head. "No, I should never have come." When he stepped closer she held up her hands to ward him off. "Wasn't the message clear enough without my having to hear it in stereo? He didn't want me. I must have been one hell of a kid.''

Dillon couldn't let her blame herself. "There's never been anything wrong with you.''

She knew he didn't understand. No one had ever wanted her after her mother's death. Not really. Her father, her relatives. Even Dillon didn't want her, not the real Kelsey Donovan, anyhow. He wanted her body, and he even believed he loved her. But he didn't want her. Not forever. No one had ever wanted her forever.

"I'll be going back just as soon as I can get a flight."

Dillon heard himself calmly reason with her even though he was in turmoil. "That may be difficult with the holidays."

"Then I'll swim." She lifted her chin.

"Kelsey—"

"There's nothing more to say, Dillon. I came here to see my father. That's impossible now. There's not anything else I can do in the mine. What other reason is there to stay?"

He wanted to shake her, to make her spill the emotions so obviously choking her. But what would he do if it all came spilling out? What could he say? Could he ask her to stay with him forever and share a life of hardship and drudgery? Could he ask her to nourish his dream?

"I'd hoped we would have some time..." he said lamely.

"Our time is up."

"You make it sound like a prison sentence."

"Never that," she said, realizing she was close to tears. She willed them away. "An education. For both of us."

She had never told him that she loved him, and now her words stabbed through him. "Is that what it's been, then? A lesson in sex? There's been nothing of love in it?"

"And what's love? Finding out that you can be forgotten like that?" She snapped her fingers. "I know that kind of love. Maybe it's the only kind there is. God knows it's the only kind I've ever seen."

She stepped back as he moved closer. "And you think I'll forget you?" he asked.

She snapped her fingers again, taunting him.

"You think I'll go down into the mine every day and not think of you, dream about you?"

"You'll dream of opal."

"And what will you dream of, Sunset, now that you know love's a sham?" he asked bitterly.

"I'll dream about the day I don't care anymore!" She swallowed, and her eyes filled. She retreated another step until the countertop bit into the small of her back. Then she dodged the arm that reached for her and turned to run.

Chapter 17

Once outside, Kelsey didn't know where to go. She knew it would take Dillon precious seconds to pull on enough clothes to follow her, but she knew that it might be all the head start she had. Jake's ute was parked near the road beside Dillon's, and without further thought she headed there. For once the ancient motor purred at the first twist of the key that hung in the ignition. She ground the gears in her haste to back away, but she made it out to the road and around the first turn with no sign of Dillon following.

She didn't know where to go. She didn't want to talk. She knew if she went to Melanie's or Anna's they would want to know why she was there. She had brought nothing with her, no money, no change of clothes, but she knew the motel was her best alternative. She could get a room for the night, then go back tomorrow for her things after Dillon had gone to the mine. She could make airline reservations from the motel, too.

She took the back roads, hoping Dillon wouldn't catch up with her. Tears spilled down her cheeks, and she wiped them against her shoulder. She had never felt so alone, even though she had been alone most of her life.

She was a dreamer, just as much as the man she had given her heart to. She had dreamed all her life of finding love, just as

Dillon had dreamed of opal. In the last days love had beckoned her just as opal beckoned him. Now there was no promise, not for either of them. His mine was empty. Her heart was empty. Both had gambled; both had lost.

She was on a short, deserted stretch just before she reached the edge of the town proper when the steering wheel spun out of her hands. At the same moment she heard the unmistakable sound of a tire exploding. She knew which one it would be, even as she fought to keep the ute from running off the road. Dimitri had repaired the front tire that had collided with the hill during the dust storm, but he had warned her that it was only patched, and almost worn through at that.

She pumped the brake and wrestled with the wheel until finally the ute hobbled to a stop. She got out to survey the damage by the light of the full moon. The tire was in shreds; that much was obvious.

Her choices were few. She could walk into town, or she could replace the tire with the spare that she knew was lying in the back. She was tempted to leave it, to make the hike and ask Dimitri to come back for the ute tomorrow. But she also remembered what Dillon had told her about vehicles being stripped and burned. If someone came along and destroyed Jake's ute, she would be responsible.

There was nothing she could do except change the tire. Her father might not want to see her, but she had no wish to leave him with worse feelings about her if he came back to Coober Pedy. She had been using his ute. It was up to her to take care of it.

Kelsey dried the remnants of her tears with the back of her hand. She would change the damn tire and be on her way. And would toughen up. She would never be this vulnerable, never let herself fall in love, again. Because she knew now that she had done just that. Jake's newest rejection was an ache inside her, but Dillon's refusal to ask her to share his life was more than an ache. She had been hollowed out, emptied of everything good. And only love, aborted love, had that kind of power.

She moved slowly around the back of the ute and released the newly repaired tailgate. It screeched in protest, flopping against the bumper until it was finally silent. She climbed into the back and lifted the tread-bare spare on its side to roll it out the end. Then she began to search for a jack.

There was no jack in her father's toolbox, although she found everything else she needed. Nor was there one under the front seat. The flashlight she had discovered lent an eerie urgency to her mission. Dillon would find her if she didn't hurry, and if she confronted him, she wanted it to be at the motel, where they were surrounded by people and his natural reticence would keep him from creating a scene.

There was nothing he could say to her that she wanted to hear. She wanted none of his compassion. She wanted no words of love unless they were laced with words of commitment. And those were words he would never say. He was an opal miner. Like her father, he wanted nothing lasting except the gem he mined.

She climbed into the back once more, fruitlessly searching the toolbox for something she could use to crank up the truck to change the tire. In a fit of anguished frustration she slammed the top down and, standing with one lithe movement, kicked the side of the box.

It twisted, sliding an inch to reveal a thinly etched line on the floor.

At first Kelsey wasn't sure what she was looking at. She stooped and trained the wavering beam of the flashlight on it. The connecting metal seams were so finely abutted that she had to narrow her eyes and move closer. She tried to shove the toolbox farther, but it was fastened tightly into the floor. She opened the top and emptied the box, then rummaged through the tools scattered on the floor to select a wrench to make quick work of the two large bolts holding it in place.

This time when she pushed it, it skidded to the side of the truck. There was a small, beautifully designed compartment where the toolbox had rested. It was hinged in two places. Kelsey fingered the hinges, then paused.

She had no right to look in this compartment. Its contents belonged to her father. He had obviously designed it for total secrecy. This was the man who had taught Dillon to wire explosives to locks. He would be a man who didn't trust banks, who didn't trust anything but his own wits. He would be a man who would feel sullied by another person breaching his privacy.

But she was no ordinary person. She was his flesh and blood, and somehow she knew she had to see what was there.

Carefully she lifted the top with the aid of a screwdriver. It creaked with the same grinding of metal as the tailgate, then swung to rest against the floor. She trained the flashlight into the hole, a hole that seemed much larger than the perimeters of the door. Her eyes took seconds to focus, then riveted on a small, metal box. She reached down to claim it, bringing it slowly through the door.

There was no lock. It opened easily to reveal a collection of old, yellowing letters. On the very top was a well-worn photograph of a child.

The child was her, the photograph a copy of the one she treasured.

Kelsey touched it with trembling fingers, then moved it to one side. She picked up the first letter and recognized her mother's script.

She couldn't read the letter, nor could she read the dozens of others, preserved for over two decades by the man who had forgotten her. Except that he never had. He had tucked her away, tucked her mother away, in this safe, private place that no one knew about. She wondered how often he had moved the toolbox, how often he had fingered the photograph, read the letters.

She wondered how often he had thought of her, and she knew the answer.

Often enough to make her heart ache for him.

The tears she had forced back streamed down her face again. They were healing tears. She closed the box and held it against her chest for a moment. Then, with something close to reverence, she bent to replace it. Jake would never know she had seen it. He would never know the gift he had given her. But she knew somehow that the gift would change her.

She was just slipping the box back into place when her hand brushed against a piece of canvas. At first she paid no attention, too wrapped up in her thoughts of her father. Then she realized that the box wasn't the only object in the hole. There was something else, something that extended far back into the corner of the hollow space. Something enclosed in canvas and padded heavily.

Kelsey removed the box once more, cautiously setting it against the toolbox. Then she lay flat and reached both hands as far as she could underneath the floor, carefully moving the canvas toward her. The parcel wasn't heavy, but it was bulky,

and she had to maneuver carefully to find the right position to
lift it through the trapdoor.

When the parcel finally lay across her knees, Kelsey examined it. She had no idea what it contained, but it was about
three and a half feet long and a foot in width, although she
suspected much of the width was padding. It was tied with
coarse brown string, and there was nothing about the size,
shape or wrapping to suggest what might be inside.

Kelsey hesitated only a moment. With the flashlight propped
to provide the light she needed, she picked at the knot until it
was untied. Then she unwound the string, taking care not to
tangle it, until it was a soft, round ball beside the parcel. Slowly,
carefully, she unfolded the thickness of canvas, then the padding, which seemed to be something similar to quilt batting.
When she finished, she could do nothing but stare.

A perfect skeleton lay on her lap. An opal skeleton of a giant
lizard with nothing missing except a skull. Even its flippers were
webbed with precious opal that flashed fire in the weak beam
of the light.

She heard a click then, a click that had sounded once before
as she had stood in the center of an outback dust storm and
hoped for rescue.

But the sound had portended something far more deadly.

Kelsey's head swung up, and she spun to look behind her.
Silver hair shone in the moonlight, and moonlight reflected off
the barrel of an old-fashioned rifle.

"So you found it before I did."

"Gary?"

He moved a little closer. "Were you expecting someone else,
Kelsey?"

She shook her head slowly, but it wouldn't clear. She was
caught in a slide show, and it was moving too fast for her to
catch any image and hold on to it. "Why do you have a gun
pointed at me?"

"Because you have something I want."

The slides flew at top speed, then began to make sense. Light-
colored hair caught between the teeth of a comb. Not blond
hair, as Dillon had thought, but silver. Hand-cast bullets that
would come only from the gun of a collector, a chillingly
beautiful antique like the one pointed at her now. A jeweler
with the nimble-fingered skills and the tools to pick any lock;
a man who was so obsessed with the things he collected that he

had lost all traces of human warmth and caring and replaced them with deadly charm.

She wondered why she hadn't seen it before. She wondered why Dillon hadn't. But then, the key to the puzzle was lying in her lap.

"What is it?" she asked, making sure there was no fear in her voice.

"A plesiosaurus. You're holding one of the finest specimens I've ever seen," Gary said, motioning to her with the muzzle of the gun. "It would be priceless even if it weren't opalized. Now it's more than priceless." The corners of his mouth turned up. "It's mine."

"I don't think so. I believe it belongs to my father."

"Brave words."

"Oh, more than words." She lifted the skeleton until it was a shield in front of her. "Try to take it from me, Gary. Or, better yet, shoot me and see if your bullet can miss every one of these precious, fragile bones. But then, maybe it wouldn't bother you to shatter it."

"I've killed before, Kelsey," he said, his voice an obscene caress.

She thought of the two men Dillon had told her about. "What did they have that you wanted?" she asked, buying time as her mind raced for a way out.

He seemed to relish talking about it, like a museum curator discussing his collections. "One had a picture stone. Do you know what that is?"

"No."

"The man who found it was an old prospector. He found it in an open cut mine, just a large field that a bulldozer had cut through looking for opal. The mine owner and his spotters had overlooked the stone, but the old man didn't."

Kelsey knew he was talking about Fizzle Fred. "Why did you want it?"

"It's a small stone, but the colors make a picture of a bird. I like to think it's an emu. Bit of a shame I won't be able to show it to you."

Her stomach twisted into knots. Gary was enjoying himself. "And the other?"

"Just a rock. A piece of blue ground with strands of opal running all through it. It wasn't worth anything much, but I liked it."

She shuddered. He had liked it, and that had been enough reason to take it, even if he had to kill. He was insane. "Why did you kill them? You have money. Couldn't you have made a deal with them?"

"They wanted to keep their little prizes. They wouldn't give me what I wanted, Kelsey."

Kelsey knew that even if she gave Gary what he wanted he would surely kill her now. She knew too much to go free. She clutched the skeleton tighter and tried to buy time for herself. "And my father?"

"Now there's a story." He lowered the rifle a little, but he kept it ready. He looked like a man reminiscing about the good old days. "Jake came to me with the skeleton. He got it out of the Rainbow Fire, but he didn't want Dillon to know about it. He was afraid Dillon would want to donate it to a museum, and Jake wanted cash. The skeleton was his ticket out of Coober Pedy. He was whining about getting old and having nothing to show for it. He'd had his heart set on making a big profit on some stones he'd sent to Sydney, but he'd found out that they'd sold for a lot less than he'd hoped. Jake knew I would be interested in the skeleton, and he didn't have the money to take it anywhere else."

"And then you pushed him down the mine shaft?"

"Not quite like that. I made Jake an offer, a good offer. He wanted some time to think about it. I was very generous and agreed, although I'll have to admit I lost patience with him once and took a few shots at him." He shrugged. "Funny thing, it turned out to be Dillon. He was driving Jake's ute."

Kelsey was beyond the point of being shocked by anything he could say. "You shot at Dillon, thinking it was my father?"

"I was going to sympathize with Jake, point out that maybe somebody else had found out about the skeleton, somebody he'd told when he was plonked. It was an ace in the hole for me, a way to force him to sell it quicker."

"Too bad your eyesight was so poor, huh?"

He shrugged again, almost as if he believed she was serious. "When Jake came back the afternoon of his accident, he didn't have the skeleton with him. I knew then that he was going to refuse. He told me that he had changed his mind, that his conscience had gotten the better of him." Gary said the word "conscience" as if he were discussing the plague. "He had decided to tell Dillon and let him decide what to do with the skeleton.''

"Dillon would have turned you down flat."

Gary nodded. "Jake's a crafty old bloke, but not crafty enough. I told him that if he didn't take my offer, I'd tell Dillon about the skeleton before he could. I'd tell Dillon that I'd found out Jake was trying to cheat him, and I just couldn't stand by and watch it happen. They'd been fighting recently. Dillon was getting tired of your father's drinking, his endless yarns. Dillon was pulling the whole load of the Rainbow Fire for them both. Dillon would have believed my story, and Jake knew it."

Kelsey clutched the skeleton tighter. She tried to gauge how long it would take to jump the side of the ute and dodge behind it. But there weren't even hills to hide behind here. The area was flat, desolate. The only thing on the horizon was Gary's car, parked so far down the road that he had been able to stalk her, lights off, without being seen.

She continued to try to buy time. "And so he agreed to sell it to you?"

"As I said, he was a crafty old bloke. He told me the skeleton was safely tucked away in a shaft that had duffered out. I told him he wouldn't get any money unless I was holding the skeleton in my hands. He said he'd go back and get it, but I knew he was lying. He was going to find Dillon and talk to him before I could tell him my story. So I told Jake I'd take him to the mine myself to get it."

"And that's when you pushed him down the shaft?"

"He lied to me. He lied about where the skeleton was hidden. I didn't realize it. I thought I could have the skeleton and the money I would have paid for it, too. So I pushed him down an old shaft when his back was turned."

Fury overcame fear. "Brave man. But he didn't die, did he?"

"There was no ladder in the shaft, so I couldn't check. And I had no time, because I knew Dillon was going to be at the Showcase at five-thirty. So I left him there. I hadn't counted on Dillon looking for him. But it didn't matter much when he was found. I knew that even if he lived, Jake would be too ashamed to tell anyone about the skeleton. And I was right."

"You're a real bastard."

He smiled. "Despite all that, old Jake almost had the last laugh, didn't he? The skeleton wasn't where he said it would be.

I'll wager he told me that because he was going to go down into the mine to get it and just not come back up. He knew if I came down to find him, he could elude me, maybe knock me out long enough to get back to town and talk to Dillon before I could. Underground, he'd be the boss, because he knew the mine. After I'd pushed him down the old shaft, I went down to look for the skeleton, but it wasn't there.''

"And you've been looking for it ever since?''

"Looking and looking and looking.'' He smiled his vacant, deadly smile again and raised the rifle to his shoulder. "But I don't have to look any further, do I, Kelsey?''

Dillon stepped out of the shower and toweled his hair dry. He had scrubbed until his skin was raw, but he could still smell Kelsey on his skin, still feel her body moving under his. And the pounding of the water hadn't drowned out her final words to him, either. "I'll dream about the day I don't care anymore,'' she had shouted at him.

What had he done? In the minutes since she had run from him, her words had rung in his head until they were all he could hear. He had fallen in love with her, but he hadn't trusted her to make her own decision about their future. He had made it for her. He had decided that he had nothing to offer, that his life, his town, had nothing to offer. And so he had offered nothing except his love alone.

It had been a cheap gift.

He had given her no choices. He had made choices for both of them. Now he faced the reason why. He was afraid she wouldn't choose him. Bloody hell, why should she? Look at him, at his prospects, his life. Why would she want him? Was she a fool? Or was she a woman in love?

He knew it was the last that he had to find out. And the only way was to ask her to stay with him, ask her to marry him. He had to give her that choice.

He had to, because there was a one-in-a-million chance she would say yes. And wasn't he a gambler?

He was almost dressed to begin looking for her when the telephone rang. He almost wrenched it off the wall, hoping it was Kelsey.

"Dillon, Melly here.''

Dillon knew she was crying. He had no time for another woman's tears, but he couldn't hang up on her. "What is it, Melly? I'm in a bit of a hurry."

"Is Kelsey there?"

"No." He decided it would be pointless to lie. The truth would be quicker. "We had a fight. I'm going to look for her."

He heard an unmistakable gasp before Melly spoke. "You've got to find her fast."

He grunted. "I can find her faster if I get off the telephone."

Her next words were choked out between sobs. "She's in danger. Oh, Dillon, Gary's after her. She's got something he wants, or at least he thinks so. You've got to find her before he does."

Her words made no sense. "Gary?"

"He killed old Fizzle Fred, Dillon. I was there when Fizzle Fred showed Gary an opal he'd found. A picture stone." She was sobbing so hard the words were slow to come out. "I found the opal tonight, locked in a case I'd never looked in before. I stole Gary's keys because I suspected...I suspected...." She broke down into more sobs.

"Suspected what?" he demanded.

"Suspected he was behind Jake's fall."

Dillon slammed his fist against the wall. "Why didn't you tell somebody this before?"

"I didn't want to believe it. I didn't have any proof, nothing except little pieces of conversation, things I could have misunderstood. And I loved Gary. I couldn't believe—"

"What changed your mind?"

"I found out this afternoon that Gary hired Serge to harass you and Kelsey. Serge called the shop from Perth, demanding money to keep quiet. I picked up the other phone by accident and overheard the whole thing. Then, tonight, I found the picture stone." She sobbed again. "You've got to find Kelsey. I don't know what else Gary's after, but he's after her."

The receiver swung side to side where Dillon had dropped it. Melanie's final words echoed into an empty room.

Chapter 18

The trunk of Gary's car was stifling. Kelsey could hardly draw a breath. She had explored every inch of the surface for a way to pop the lock from the inside, but there was no way. She was moving somewhere toward what would surely be her death. The only reason she wasn't dead yet was because she still held the plesiosaurus in her arms. Gary had forced her to his car with the rifle, but she had refused to relinquish the skeleton, knowing that holding it was her last hope. Gary did not want to take the chance of damaging it by shooting her. In his mania, he wanted it to be perfect, so that when it was finally his, he could lock it away in his collection of one-of-a-kind perfect things.

She knew he wouldn't let her suffocate in the trunk, because she had warned him that if she started to lose consciousness, she would crush the bones to dust in her bare hands first. She knew he believed her. He knew she could do it.

She wanted to crush *his* bones to dust. He was insane, but she felt no sympathy, not when he held her life in his hands. He had stalked her, and stalked Dillon. He had threatened their lives, hoping to keep them so busy that they wouldn't find the skeleton before he did. Then, when his own search had been futile, he had kept them under surveillance, hoping one of them would find it for him.

And she had.

She didn't know where Serge fit in, except that she suspected he must have been working with Gary. He'd been the perfect accomplice. He had wanted revenge on her for making a fool of him in the pub, and it had certainly been to his advantage to keep Dillon busy elsewhere while he blasted away the Rainbow Fire opal. Serge and Gary had fit together like two halves of a whole. Two halves of a wretched, stinking, rotten hole.

Her head began to swim. She was weakening from the heat and the fetid air. Each breath was painful. Just as she began to contemplate the destruction of the skeleton, she felt the car slow, then stop.

Warm night air rushed into the sweltering cavity as Gary threw the trunk open. Kelsey's first sight was the muzzle of his gun. "How are you feeling, Kelsey? Are you up to taking a walk?"

She imagined that he would like that. She would walk ahead of him, and he would shoot her in the back. If he were lucky she wouldn't even damage the skeleton when she fell. She gauged her chances of kicking the gun out of his hands as she climbed out. They were abysmal. She would make a last stand, but it wouldn't be here. She bought more time. "I'm not enough of a fool to walk in front of you. I'll walk beside you, just like I did to get to the car."

His laugh was like his smile. "Too bad you don't trust me."

"I trusted the death adder you left Dillon more."

"A nice touch, that, if I do say so."

"I'm not getting out until you stand back."

"My pleasure."

She sat up, then slid her legs over the bumper, holding the skeleton in front of her as she did. She knew he was only waiting for the chance to get a clean shot. She was out with a twist of her agile body, the skeleton still shielding her. She didn't take her eyes off him, but she knew immediately where he'd driven and what he planned for her.

"Isn't this getting old?" she asked nonchalantly. "How many people can you push down the Rainbow Fire without someone getting wise? Even Sergeant Newberry can't ignore this one."

"He won't ignore it," Gary agreed. "He'll just think Dillon did it. He thinks Dillon's behind everything that's happened. Newberry takes the easiest way out."

"I'll take the skeleton with me down that shaft."

"That would be a pity. It should be preserved for posterity."

"I'm a get-even kind of girl, Gary."

He motioned her towards the main shaft. "I don't think you know all the details, though." Kelsey saw she had no choice other than to move, and she began to back in that direction as he continued. "If you don't give me the skeleton, I'm going to make your death a nasty, nasty thing. If I have the skeleton, then I'll make it quick. One step backward, Kelsey. One quick step and it will all be over."

She pretended to mull over his words. "A nasty, nasty thing?"

"Bits and pieces of you gone, like that." He snapped his fingers. "These old guns are treasures. And I can reload in less time than it takes to kill you."

"And what will Sergeant Newberry say when he finds bits and pieces of me gone?"

"He'll think Dillon's a violent man. A lovers' quarrel. A feud over opal. Who knows what he'll think? But he won't think of me."

Kelsey bumped into something, a piece of equipment, she guessed. She scrambled to figure out exactly where she was as she cursed the moonlight that worked so well to Gary's advantage.

"If you turn around, you can see where you're going," he pointed out.

"If I turned around, you'll shoot me." She inched around the equipment as he closed in on her. She was beginning to get her bearings. The machine at her back was the tunneling machine they had used to begin the drive. To her left somewhere would be the Calweld drill. And then left of that the main shaft. "You know the main shaft has padlocks?"

"Locks don't worry me."

She was worried enough for both of them. Escape seemed unlikely, and even a black belt was no match for a gun. She continued to inch her way, taking care not to give him an opening to shoot her. The skeleton was clutched against her chest like armor.

They played the deadly game of cat and mouse until she brushed against the mullock heap to the side of the main shaft. She saw one chance and one chance only of taking him by surprise. When he stooped to pick the lock, he would be vulnerable. He knew about her self-defense skills, but she prayed he was like most men, a chauvinist who didn't believe he had anything to fear from a woman. She decided to reinforce that impression.

"Gary, you don't really want to kill me." She put just the right note of fear in her voice.

"You're right. I don't. You've a special, rare sort of beauty." Gary motioned her backward. "But I must."

"But I don't want to die."

"Can't blame you for that."

"Can't we strike a bargain? What if I give you the skeleton and promise not to tell anyone?"

"You're smarter than that, Kelsey."

She let a sob shudder in the air between them. It wasn't hard to conjure. "There must be something I can do."

"Yes. Be a good girl and hand me the skeleton. I'll make this easy for you." He leaned over to grasp the padlock, but with a sinking heart she saw that he hadn't lost one bit of his concentration. The gun was still trained squarely at her heart. She had found a man who didn't underestimate her. It was too bad he was also the one who wanted to kill her.

He stooped, balancing the gun across his knees, still aimed precisely at her chest. The speed with which he picked the lock was breathtaking. There was no time for her attack before he was standing to flip over the iron cover so that it flopped across the other padlock.

The night became deathly still. There had been nightbirds singing, Kelsey realized. Now there was nothing, not even the moan of the outback wind. "What will it be, Kelsey?" he asked, motioning her toward the shaft. "Quickly, or piece by piece?"

She moved slowly as he closed the distance between them. Her options were so limited that the decision wasn't hard. She watched him stop six feet in front of her.

"The skeleton's yours, Gary," she said, her voice trembling.

She watched him nod, then stretch out one hand. "A wise choice."

"Yours," she repeated. "But you're going to have to catch it first." With her last words she heaved the skeleton straight up in the air. Then, in the split second it took him to leap toward it, she spun and jumped into the shaft.

Jake's ute lay abandoned by the side of the road. Dillon braked to a halt behind it, shouting Kelsey's name. There was no answer. Not even the wind.

He was out his door in double time, searching the ute and area around it for clues. He saw the flat tire immediately, then the open trapdoor in the back. He gave the metal box beside the toolbox a cursory investigation. He felt sure Kelsey had seen it, touched it, perhaps wept over it. But he knew it had nothing to do with her disappearance.

Except that if she had gone voluntarily, the box would have been back inside the hole, the trapdoor would have been closed and the toolbox replaced to safeguard what was inside.

Gary had her. Dillon knew it as surely as he knew his own name. He didn't understand why, and he didn't understand how, but he knew that she was in trouble. The worst kind.

He dropped to the ground, training the high-intensity beam of his torch along the roadside. He hadn't lived in the bush all these years without absorbing the skills of those around him. He had sat at campfires with Aborigine men so proficient as trackers that they could tell the last week's history of any piece of earth just by giving it one glance. They had taught him some of their skills in exchange for noodling for opal in his mullock. Everyone had come out ahead. Now he was gut-wrenchingly grateful.

There had been no struggle, but Kelsey's footprints were unmistakable. He recognized the tread of her sneakers and the way her shoes gripped the ground. There were other prints, too. A man wearing boots with new leather soles.

The tracks weren't hard to follow in the soft dirt. They took him down the road, past his own ute to a place where an automobile had been pulled off the road. The footsteps ended where new tire tracks began. The tires had spun on the soft shoulder before they had pulled back onto the dirt road. They headed away from town.

Dillon got back into his ute and followed them. The right rear tire had a worn tread on its left side. If the ground remained soft enough and the traffic light enough, he knew he would be able to distinguish it just by stopping at each intersecting road to see if the auto had turned off.

He did just that until it was clear where the automobile had been headed. He didn't know why, but Kelsey was willingly or unwillingly going to the mine field where the Rainbow Fire was located. Without wasting any more precious time checking tracks, he floored the accelerator and headed there himself.

The aluminum ladder burned Kelsey's hands as she fell. She had managed to grab one side, but the metal was so slick that it didn't stop her. Flailing wildly, she kicked against a rung and felt it give. Her foot fell against the next, then the next, before she found purchase.

She clung to the ladder momentarily, until the shaft was suddenly lit with the glare of the generator-powered light. Gary wasn't wasting any time. In seconds he would be shooting at her, and his aim would be true. She jerked the electric cord that dangled beside the ladder, once, twice, before the shaft was dark again. Then she scrambled into total darkness. She heard a curse above her, and a shot ricocheted against the shaft walls, missing her by feet. Her fear changed to exultation. She was escaping, and she had destroyed his best means of finding her. They were equal partners now. He had the gun, but what good would it do him if he couldn't see her?

She reached bottom just as the ladder rattled above her. He was coming down. She had expected no less, but her momentary elation was quenched as she began to picture the mine and where she would go.

It was blacker than midnight, a depthless void in the center of the earth. She had spent so little time here that, try as she might, she couldn't remember any of its twists and turns. She paused, wondering if her best defense was just to stand at the base of the ladder and attack when he neared the bottom. But she knew he had the gun with him, and one sound would alert him to her presence. He could shoot her in the dark.

She would be safer if she hid. The mine was a rabbit warren of tunnels. If he found her, backed her into a corner, she could fight then. As always, the best defense now was to escape.

She began to feel her way along the wall as swiftly as she could. If possible, the mine got darker the farther she got from

the shaft. The total, unrelenting darkness was as terrifying as
knowing that Gary was coming after her, but she pushed on
anyway, because she had no choice.

She listened to the sounds of his descent. There was a gun-
shot, and she thanked God that she hadn't waited at the bottom of the ladder. He was guessing that she had and acting
accordingly. "Kelsey," he shouted, "it's no use. Give up."

She knew he hoped she would answer, that she would give
him some clue to her whereabouts. There were four chambers
going off the shaft, because Dillon and her father hadn't
wanted to take the chance of missing opal in any direction.
Gary wanted to know which chamber she had entered.

She pushed on, taking care to move silently. She was going
too slowly, but she couldn't go faster without giving herself
away. She came to a side chamber and paused. If it was a dead
end, she could end up pinned against the wall, waiting for Gary
to find her. If it was a tunnel connecting this chamber and the
next....

She passed it by, afraid to turn off. She heard the sound of
something clattering to the floor, followed by cursing somewhere behind her. Then she heard Gary's shout.

"I've been in this mine before. I know every bloody nook
and cranny. You can't hide. I know it better than you do."

Kelsey knew he had been in the Rainbow Fire searching for
the skeleton. Then she knew something even more frightening. He had a light. She saw the tiniest pinprick reflected on the
walls of the chamber. It came from the darkness somewhere
behind her. It flamed, then disappeared.

Matches. She pushed on farther, wondering how long a book
of matches would last. Would it be long enough to help him
find her? Was he still in the main shaft, or had he chosen the
correct chamber? Was he even now closing in on her?

She heard no footsteps behind her. Praying he had chosen
another tunnel, she moved on, stooping as the ceiling got lower
and began to curve. She came to another intersection and debated whether to turn into the new tunnel. It seemed narrower, lower, and she passed it by.

Minutes passed as she felt her way along the tunnel, minutes
when she heard nothing from Gary.

And then, in a voice that was frighteningly close, she heard,
"I've got a candle, Kelsey. You'd forgotten about the candles,

hadn't you? But I've been here enough to know where they're kept, and I've got several now. I'll find you.''

She realized he was in a nearby chamber, probably only yards away, even if they were yards of rock and dirt. She moved faster. He said he had candles now, and she had no reason to doubt him. When he entered her chamber, she would be in clear sight.

She heard a scraping sound in the narrow tunnel she had bypassed, and she hurried on, knowing that he was cutting through. Dim flickers of light preceded him. She knew because even though she didn't turn, the tunnel was growing lighter. The absolute darkness had been breached.

Kelsey flattened herself against the wall, praying that the candlelight wouldn't expose her. She was only yards away, but there was still a chance he wouldn't see her if he turned and followed the passage back to the shaft.

He didn't. She saw the candlelight first, then the candle. Last, she saw Gary.

Surprisingly he was no longer carrying the rifle. She felt a thrill of hope. In a fair fight she could beat him. He outweighed her by a good seventy pounds, but weight meant nothing. It would be difficult to maneuver between the narrow shaft walls, difficult to hit and kick, but she could do it. She had trained for such a moment.

He turned unerringly and held the candle out in front of him so that its rays just touched her. Then, in his other hand, he held up what looked like another candle. Kelsey knew better. It was gelignite, the form of dynamite used to blast through rock in a drive. Dillon kept it in the supply room, too.

"A candle in one hand," he said holding out the candle. "Death in the other."

His insanity had never been clearer. She knew that reasoning with him was impossible, but she tried, anyway. "If you light that, you'll blow us both to kingdom come."

He shook his head. "Just you. Move, Kelsey."

She knew what he planned. The tunnel must end soon. He was going to back her up against the face and light the explosive. Then, from a safe distance, he was going to listen to the walls come down around her.

She didn't intend to cooperate. "Go ahead and light it," she said, starting toward him. "But I'm going to take you down with me, Gary."

He laughed and waved the candle near the fuse. "Do you know your way out of here, Kelsey?" He laughed again. "I hope so. *I* do, you know." He waved the candle again, and this time it contacted with the fuse. There was a hiss as he tossed it toward her. The gelignite landed three yards in front of Kelsey's feet. Then he blew out the candle.

The sudden darkness took her by surprise. Now there was only the tiny spark from the fuse. Part of her noted that the gelignite hadn't exploded on contact. She hadn't been able to tell just how long the fuse was, but she knew she might only have seconds to get clear. She ran directly at the spark, remembering exactly where it was in relation to the walls at her sides. She expected to be blown to bits any moment, but the gelignite didn't explode until she was well on the other side of it.

She had chosen a straight path, using the glowing fuse as her marker. Gary had expected her to feel her way along the walls, but by running instead she covered enough distance to be out of the worst danger when the walls began to crumble around her. She had also stuffed her fingers in her ears, but even after the explosion no longer rang through the tunnel, she could still hear it resounding inside her head.

She ran into a wall. Arms flat against it, she felt her way, trying to put as much distance between herself and the instability of the explosion site as she could. She could hear rock falling behind her, and she knew the tremors could trigger more.

Gary was waiting in the chamber under the main shaft, holding a lighted candle and another stick of gelignite. "You found your way out," he said, congratulating her. "I'm surprised."

She looked down at his feet. The gun lay in front of him.

"Don't make me pick it up," he cautioned her. "If I do, I'll have to put the candle and the gelly in the same hand. Who knows what could happen?" He motioned her toward the tunnel she had just left. "One more should do it, Kelsey."

"You're really crazy," she said, beginning to back into the tunnel. She could feel the tremors of the first explosion. Rocks were still falling.

Gary kicked the gun ahead of him as he followed her. Finally he stood in the entrance. She stood as close as she dared, prepared to rush him the moment the candle touched the fuse.

She never got her chance. Arms locked around Gary's neck from behind, cutting off his air supply, and he dropped both the candle and the gelignite. He grabbed the arms, trying to wrench them loose, but they squeezed and squeezed. With supreme effort he twisted, bringing his elbows against a hard, male abdomen. The man holding him didn't even flinch before he slammed a sledgehammer fist to Gary's face.

"Dillon!" Kelsey threw herself on the gun at the men's feet and grabbed the candle, which, miraculously, was still burning. By then they had taken the fight out into the main chamber, to the floor. They rolled over and over until, in the near darkness, she wasn't sure who was who. She set the candle against a rock so that she could grip the rifle with both hands. "Stop. I've got the gun. Gary, I'll shoot you without a thought," she screamed.

The men ignored her, something more primal than guns on their mind. She heard a banging against the floor and grunts of pain. She moved closer, until she was sure the head had been Gary's.

Dillon was winning, the stronger and more courageous fighter of the two. Kelsey trained the rifle on Gary, but there was no clear shot. They rolled over again, then again. Dillon was on top, his hands at Gary's throat when Gary's fingers closed around a rock. Before Dillon could react, Gary smashed it against the side of Dillon's head.

The shock was just enough to stun Dillon so that he lost his grip. Gary twisted from underneath him and followed the rock's blow with his fist. Dillon grunted, and Gary freed himself to reach for the rock again.

Kelsey reacted without thinking. The gun hit the floor, and she leaped forward. Her foot rose in a swift, vicious kick. Gary screamed as his arm fell uselessly to his side. He turned to her, his expression disbelieving. Then he fainted.

When Dillon staggered to his feet, she threw herself into his arms.

"Watch that hug. This is the good guy, remember?" Dillon felt Kelsey tremble against him, and he buried his face in her curls.

"How did you know where I was?" she asked.

Dillon heard welling tears in her voice, and he held her tighter. He was never going to let her go. "Melly warned me about Gary. I tracked you here."

"Melly knew?"

"She's suspected something was wrong for a while. She found out for certain tonight and rang me."

"And you fought for me."

He laughed shakily. "How'd I do before you rescued me?"

"You could use a few pointers." Then she began to cry.

Dillon held her until his shirt was soaked. Gary groaned at their feet. "Come on, we'll go up and lock him in. Even he won't be able to get out."

Kelsey didn't want to let Dillon go. "He can pick any lock."

"Yes, but I'm going to take about twenty feet of ladder with me. He won't get up the sides with that arm. He can stay here until morning, when Sergeant Newberry can dispose of him."

There was a clatter on the ladder behind them, and a male voice. "That won't be necessary, thanks. I'll take him now."

They turned. The police sergeant made the last rungs in one well-coordinated leap. "I say, Ward," he said, with a grin, "you beat me to this one."

"Barely. What brings you here? Planning to rat some opal?"

The sergeant flashed a badge and another grin. Dillon squinted to read it; then the two men exchanged knowing looks.

"Then you've been after him all along?" Dillon marveled.

"All along. The South Australian police took me on temporarily. I had to have a reason to be snooping around town." The sergeant-who-wasn't slipped the badge back in his pocket. "So sorry about focusing all the suspicion on you. For a while I really did think you might have been working with our friend here. After that, it was just part of my cover."

"You've been after Gary all along?" Kelsey didn't know what to make of their conversation.

"I was here to investigate two murders. I suspected him almost immediately." Sergeant Newberry paused. "You do know about those?"

"He admitted them to me," Kelsey said.

The sergeant gave her a triumphant grin, teeth flashing in the candlelight. There was no trace of the slimy witchety grub now. "Good job. We'll look forward to a statement from you."

"And he pushed my father down the shaft."

"You can put that in your statement, too."

Dillon was still in the dark about Gary's motivation. "What did he want from Kelsey?"

"I can answer that." Kelsey proceeded to tell them about the plesiosaurus, just the way that Gary had told the story to her. "I imagine it's safely up top somewhere, probably in the trunk of his car."

"So Jake tried to cheat me," Dillon said.

Kelsey thought of the letters and the picture in the lockbox in Jake's ute. "He changed his mind, though, and it almost cost him his life. Can you forgive him?"

"If he ever gives me the chance."

"I hope he will. Right now I think he's probably too ashamed to face me or you."

Dillon hugged her harder. "Why did it take you so bloody long to get Gary?" he asked Newberry.

"It took so bloody long because he's bloody good at what he does. He's a real psychopath. No feelings, no trail to follow. We're lucky we got him at all."

Kelsey shuddered, and Dillon held her close. "There'll be no statements tonight," he told Newberry. "Kelsey's right whacked. We'll be in first thing in the morning." He tried to move Kelsey toward the ladder.

She stood, feet firmly rooted. "There's gelignite in the tunnel. You should put it someplace safe."

"It will keep."

She shook her head. "There were more tremors. It could cause an explosion and take down the rest of this mine."

Dillon knew hysteria when he saw it—in all its forms. Kelsey was exhausted, frayed to the very edges. There was no point in arguing. Without a match to the fuse, the gelignite was relatively harmless. Miners had been known to carry it around Coober Pedy in their pockets, sheepishly disposing of it when they were reminded by a store proprietor. But he wasn't about to give Kelsey a lecture. He just wanted to get her home. "I'll be right back," he told her. He stepped around the sergeant, who was handcuffing Gary's arms behind him. He was sitting on Gary's back, whistling as he worked.

Dillon started into the tunnel. The candlelight barely lit it, and he was just about to give up on the gelignite when red flames leaped from the walls where the last rocks had fallen. He moved to the wall, running his hand over it in wonder. A noise alerted him to Kelsey's presence. He turned to see her come into the tunnel. "Bring the candle."

"You found the gelignite?"

"Forget the gelly. Bring the candle."

She did as she was told. Sergeant Newberry had set up a high-powered flashlight and wouldn't be left in darkness. He was still whistling.

She walked into the tunnel, the candle just in front of her. The flame leaped for her, too. She turned, wide-eyed. Dillon was watching.

"Rainbow fire?" she asked softly.

He caressed the wall once more, then left it behind as he walked toward her to fold her in his arms. "Rainbow fire," he acknowledged. "Enough to warm us for the rest of our days."

He finally had something to offer Kelsey, yet the words wouldn't come. Dillon lay beside her the next morning and watched a frown cross her face as she slept. She had slept restlessly through the night, often reaching to him for the comfort he had willingly given. They hadn't made love. He had known that this time the words had to come first.

But the words weren't there.

How did you tell a woman you wanted her forever? Telling her that he loved her had been simple in comparison. His love had been freely given, demanding nothing in return. But if he asked her to stay with him, and she refused....

Now there was nothing she could blame her refusal on. He could leave Coober Pedy. Once the opal had been taken from the mine, he could leave—at least, he thought he could. He could offer Kelsey more than heat and drought and flies. He could offer her paradise.

And she could refuse it. She had never told him that she loved him. The closest she had come was to tell him that she hoped that someday she didn't care so much.

Lying in bed watching her sleep-soft face, those words didn't seem much to go on. She was a woman any man would die for. She had the courage of ten, courage that had saved her life and his last night, and trapped a murderer. She had beauty, with intelligence and, under the pride and the temper, sensitivity. What would she want with him? He had the opal he had sought for so many years, but what was it worth without her?

Kelsey awoke and knew that something was wrong. She lay quietly, without opening her eyes, and remembered the events of the previous day. Her eyes opened slowly. She was confused about where she was. She remembered falling asleep in the lounge room.

Wrapped in Dillon's arms.

She turned her head and found him staring at her. She was obviously in his bed.

"I fell asleep in the other room."

"I know you did."

"You brought me in here."

He smiled and brushed her cheek with the back of his fingers. "We were talking about rainbow fire. You fell asleep in the middle of your first glass of champagne."

She remembered now. The plesiosaurus had stood in perfect opalized symmetry on the table at their feet. "You'd had that champagne for years. It was pretty potent."

"I'd been waiting all those years for yesterday."

She reached up and touched his face. "Was it worth the wait?"

He didn't know what to say. He had wanted, dreamed, worked for opal. Now he had it, and he could hardly think of it. There was something he wanted more, and finding it was going to be the hardest thing he had ever done.

"I'd give it all away if you would stay with me," he said, reaching for her hand. "Not here," he hurried on. "I couldn't ask you to do that. We'll go somewhere else. Wherever you want to go. But I need you, Sunset. I need you in my life. You're the only kind of fire I can't live without."

She stared at him through sleep-fogged eyes that were rapidly clearing. "You want me?"

"I do. I have from the beginning. But I couldn't offer you anything. I had nothing I could give you except hardship. Now I can."

She narrowed her eyes. "You wanted me, but you weren't going to let me decide if I should stay?"

He knew he had let himself in for trouble. One dimple dented his cheek. He laced his fingers through hers and held her hand away from him. There was no telling what that hand might do. "I was going to come after you last night anyway and ask, before we found the opal. Pretend we didn't find it. Love me. Marry me. Live with me forever."

"Here in Coober Pedy?"

"Bloody hell, Sunset. Do you *want* to live in Coober Pedy?"

Her lips were turning up, just like his. She couldn't stop the process. "Bloody hell, I bloody well do, mate. There's no place like it in the world. And where else would I mine for opal? Mining's in me blood."

Through the put-on accent he could see she was serious. "You would really live here? After everything that's happened?"

"I love this town, I love the people, but I'd live anywhere with you. I'd go to the ends of the earth."

"This *is* the end of the earth."

She shook her head, and her hair swirled provocatively across the pillow. "Oh no, my love," she said, reaching up to pull his lips slowly to hers. "This is the land of rainbow fire. The land where I'll raise my children. This is the earth's beginning."

Epilogue

f the wedding's half as nice as the party last night, it will be
erfect." Kelsey reached up to straighten Dillon's tie. He had
ever looked so handsome as he did at that moment, nor as
ncomfortable. "We should let you get married in your hard
at," she teased him. "You'd like it better."

"I should think it'd be more fitting for a church with a winch
nd a bucket for an altar."

"More fitting, but more shocking to your American
riends." She reached up and kissed his cheek, then leaned
gainst him as his arms came around her. "We're going to be
appy."

Dillon still couldn't believe that Kelsey wanted to share his
fe. They had spent the last week taking thousands of dollars
orth of opal out of the Rainbow Fire. Now it was Kelsey who
as planning where they should look for the next big hit. He
ad come to realize that if he ever wanted to leave Coober Pedy
or good, he would have to bind, gag and throw her over his
houlder.

And that wouldn't be easy.

"Do your friends approve of me?" she asked, her warm
reath tickling his neck.

"The town's in love with you."

She knew it was true. She had more friends here than she ha
ever believed she would make in a lifetime. Even Melanie ha
chosen to stay on after Gary's arrest, trying to pull together
life and a spirit that he had almost shattered. She would be
the wedding.

"I didn't mean the local population. I meant Julianna a
Gray. And Paige."

He laughed. "They more than approve. Paige tells me t
two of you are going to start an opal exporting business to Ne
Zealand."

"She's got the business sense, I've got the opals."

"They couldn't not love you, Sunset."

It was important to Kelsey to be loved. She knew it no
And, best of all, she had all the love she could ever hold rig
here in front of her.

"I want to be your wife," she said, rubbing her cheek again
his shoulder.

"Then you'd better get dressed."

"Not with you here. We've got to have a few secrets."

He kissed her, and the kiss held the promise of the lon
pleasure-filled night ahead. "I'll wait on the sun porch wi
Jumbuck."

She untangled herself from his arms reluctantly and watch
him close the bedroom door behind him. Then, giving herse
a mental shake, she went to the closet to begin dressing.

Her wedding dress was street-length, oyster-colored si
trimmed with elegant Belgian lace. Anna, who was to be h
matron of honor, had made it for her after a trip to Adelai
to find the fabric. Anna sewed as well as she cooked, and K
sey knew she would never look this beautiful again.

She was almost ready when she heard the doorbell ring.
was either another of the steady stream of well-wishers or o
of the local children who came frequently to gaze at the plesi
saurus skeleton. Their rapt expressions were yet another re
son Dillon wanted to donate the skeleton to the Natio
History Museum of South Australia. Everyone deserved to s
it. In the meantime he kept it under lock and key unless t
children were viewing it, waiting to find out if the donati
would be legal without Jake's permission.

Jake himself had never resurfaced.

There was a knock on the bedroom door. "I'm just ab
ready," she called.

"You've got another visitor."

Kelsey gave her hair one more fluff before she pulled on the circlet of flowers that had been flown in from Adelaide as a present from Julianna and Gray. Gray was going to be Dillon's best man, and a radiantly pregnant Julianna was going to serve at the reception. Kelsey looked forward to knowing them better in the years ahead.

Kelsey took a deep breath and opened the door, then walked down the hall slowly. At the door of the lounge room she stopped, posing. Dillon turned, blocking her view of their visitor. His expression told her everything about his love for her, and his pride.

Then he stepped aside to reveal an old man, grizzled beard neatly trimmed and hat twisting in his hands.

Kelsey swallowed, unable for a moment to move. Then she started across the floor to stop just in front of him.

His faded brown eyes watered, and he blinked as he examined her from head to toe. Then he awkwardly stuck out his hand. She could see that he was trembling.

"You look like your mother, girl," he said, swallowing hard.

Her eyes dropped to the hand that was still extended. Then she took it and clasped it between hers. "Maybe you can tell me about her, Jake," she said softly.

"There'll be time for talking."

Kelsey felt Dillon's arm around her shoulder, and she relaxed against his warmth. "I'll look forward to that," she told her father. "More than you know."

* * * * *